THE FALCON'S RISE

NATALIA RICHARDS

A NOVEL OF ANNE BOLEYN

The Falcon's Rise

A Novel of Anne Boleyn: Book 1

Copyright © 2019 Natalia Richards
ISBN-13: 978-84-946498-8-2

M

MadeGlobal Publishing

For more information on
MadeGlobal Publishing, visit
our website
www.madeglobal.com

Dedication:
For my mother, who shares my passion for history

Geoffrey Boleyn of Salle – Alice, daughter of Sir John Bracton

Sir Geoffrey Boleyn – Anne, daughter of Lord Hoo
c. 1406–63

Thomas   Sir William – Margaret Butler   Elizabeth – Henry Heydon
d. 1471   1451–1505

Thomas Boleyn – Elizabeth Howard   John   Anthony   William   James – Elizabeth
1477–1539   d. 1538   d. 1552   1493–1561

Mary   Anne – Henry VIII   George – Jane
c. 1498–1543   c. 1500–36   1491–47   c. 1504–36
m 1. William Carey
m 2. William Stafford

Elizabeth I
1533 – 1603

Alice Isabel – Sir John Cheyney Cecily Simon
– John Fortescue   of Kent   d. young   d. young

Edward   Anne   Jane – Philip Calthorpe   Alice – Robert Clere
– Anne   – John Shelton   1487–1536

John Clere – Anne, daughter of Sir Thomas Terrells of Gipping
d. 1527

Edward Clere – Frances, daughter of Sir Richard Fulmerston

Edward Clere d. 1606,
m. 1. Margaret, daughter of William Yaxley of Suffolk
2. Agnes, widow of Sir Cristopher Heyton

Sir Henry Clere, d. 1622

Boleyn
Family
Tree

Prologue

The women moved silently in the fading light. Outside, rain pattered against the windowpanes while the wind blew the dying blossom off the cherry trees. Fluttering down, it caught the attention of one of the ladies. She walked over to the window. 'Such a beautiful day has ended in nature's tears,' she murmured.

Her companion glanced up and continued to place what few items there were on the table. A loud knock on the door startled them both, and a man entered. He threw his black cloak carelessly onto the chair and opened a ledger, his face betraying the distaste he felt for his task. 'May we proceed, please, ladies?'

The two women stared at the items. 'There is very little, sir, but we have gathered what there is.'

'Begin,' said the man.

The older woman spoke: 'Item: One rosary carved from the wood of the Holy Cross – to be given to the Lady Elizabeth Boleyn. Item: Two gowns of black taffeta, two pairs of black sleeves, one hood and one pair of silk shoes, to be given to the Lady Mary Stafford. Item: One Flemish ivory comb inlaid with gold, to be given to Master Henry Carey.'

As he reached for the ink with his quill, he noted the traces of long, auburn hair. God, he felt tired. Perhaps he should go and stay with his sister in Essex and leave the stink of London.

The woman continued: 'Item: A diamond, ruby and pearl ring for the Lady Elizabeth.'

'Let me see,' said the man. He studied the ring, holding it at arm's length, for his eyesight was poor. The gold work was fine, very fine indeed. He undid the catch and peered at the tiny portrait of a lady inside. The other side, designed to hold another picture or perhaps a lock of hair, was empty. He snapped it shut for he did not wish to look at the image. 'Nothing else?'

The woman shook her head.

'I will see she gets this,' he added, and placed it on the wooden tray along with the rosary. 'Continue.'

'Item: One book, badly worn, entitled *'The Golden Legend'* with silk marker.'

The man picked up the book with its torn pages and broken spine and with a cursory glance, threw it on the bed. 'Burn it. His Grace wants nothing left of her.'

The woman nodded. 'As His Grace wishes.'

Silence followed as the items were gathered up and the gowns piled onto the man's outstretched arm. He moved towards the door.

'Sir,' said the woman, touching his shoulder, 'you will see that these few possessions reach the people for whom they are intended?'

The man gave a cursory nod, his gaze lowered. He stopped, turned around, and narrowed his eyes. 'Do you swear there is nothing else?'

'We swear, sir. The poor lady had only what you see.'

The man grunted. 'Well – well as you say. But take nothing from this chamber. Nothing. His Grace has ordered the bedding, coverlet, hangings, everything destroyed.' He paused for a moment, as if remembering something.

'Well, I wish you goodnight,' he said, the tone of his voice a little kinder.

'Goodnight, Master Kingston,' the older women replied softly, closing the heavy door. She sighed with relief.

'Now we shall perish in Hell for forswearing an oath,' whispered the younger.

The elder took her cold hand and held it tightly. 'Not so, my love, God knows we were unable to help the lady in her trials, but we can help her after her death by telling her daughter the truth. We know that they will twist and tear her memory apart, making her witch and monster in one breath. But Elizabeth – her daughter – will know the truth. She is too young now, but with God's will that I live long enough, it will come to pass. Elizabeth will know her mother from the moment of her gracious birth to...'

They held each other for a moment before the elder sank to her knees on the hard, wooden boards and groped beneath the bed, disturbing the rushes. Her searching fingers paused. 'I have it. Now let us leave,' she said, bringing out a ribbon-tied package and hiding it beneath her cloak. With hoods pulled closely about their faces, the two women left the chamber and, with the last of the torches extinguished, left the Lieutenant's lodging in darkness. Past the scaffold they hurried, unable to look towards the pitiful sight.

'Come, hurry dearest,' whispered the elder. 'We have what we came for.'

The Tower of London,
18th May 1536

*'Tomorrow I shall be myself, with
yesterday's ten thousand years…'*

All my hope is gone. I am trying to show courage, but
what is courage? Only fear that has said its prayers, and I
am done with praying. I am to die tomorrow morning –
Ascension Day – and there will be the end of it. I am almost
thirty-six years old, and I have lost everything. I am tired,
and yet I want to live! I care nothing for myself, but for my
baby, my own, my sweet Elizabeth. How does a mother leave
a child in this way? How will she understand why she can no
longer feel the warmth of my embrace? In this sad chamber,
I have rambled about my childhood and the carefree days I
spent at the court of Margaret of Savoy. She has been dead
these six years past, but I trust I shall soon enjoy eternal bliss
with her in Paradise, for I have done much good in my life.

My gaoler's wife has picked a sprig of cornflowers for me
– the flowers of Heaven – and as I gaze into their blue petals,
a thousand memories flood my mind. My hours on this earth
are short, and so I take my precious secret from underneath
my bolster and open it. So many papers, for over the years I
have recorded everything my memory serves me, or was told
to me by my nurse and my mother. Now, because we must
part, I offer this labour to you, my darling Elizabeth. You
alone shall know the truth, for many lies and false reports
will circulate after my death. This, and my precious ring, is
all I have to give to you. As my fingers trace the pages, full of
promises and plans, I close my eyes and think back. Where
am I? I am far away – back in a time when all time was mine.
When Hell was just a word to frighten little girls, and the
gillyflowers were blooming…

Hever Manor, Summer 1505

'Nan Bullen! You wicked, wicked child. Look at your gown. Marry, I should have you whipped at a cart's tail!'

My ear rang from the hard slap. I started to cry and dropping the clods of earth, turned to look at the figure towering above me, obliterating the bright sun. I flinched as the dark shape roughly shook my shoulders.

'For – for you, mama,' I began, but my words were lost as I was dragged, feet off the ground, down the gravel path, past the old sundial and back to the manor. Stumbling and struggling to keep up with my mother's furious pace, I twisted round to spy the dismantled rose beds and heaps of earth. I had no idea what I had done wrong. I had assumed that the new garden arrangement would delight her. It had not.

'Mary? Mary Orcharde! Take this child out of my sight and teach her more useful pastimes than digging the earth like a – a pig in muck. Go to!'

With a thud, I fell at my nurse's knee.

'Mother of God,' said my mother, 'what do I do with her? She looks like a wild Gypsy child, all eyes and straggling hair.'

My appearance must, indeed, have been frightful and my large, dark eyes, brimmed with tears.

Striding over, my mother bent down and pulled off my coif, tearing the ribbon.

'Ow!'

'So unlike your sister, Mary,' she muttered, 'so fair and winsome, not a demon tearing around like a farm boy. How can two Bullen children differ so in both looks and temperament? For shame!'

My bottom lip began to quiver. She was right. Where my older sister Mary appeared timid, I was full of nervous energy and could never sit still. Always the first to explore a new path, I would run ahead, tearing my gown or losing a shoe in the mud, daring the children on the estate to follow.

My mother forced my dirty fingers up to my face with an exasperated cry. 'You might have inherited your Howard eyes from me, but by the living God, your manners spring from an Irish bog! Look at these hands. I said look at them!'

She shook me hard and then turned and stormed out of the chamber with a swish of her heavy gown.

I began to sob as Mrs Orcharde sat me on her knee and pushed back my straggling hair. 'Cheerily now, Nan, take no notice of such a pother. She is out of sorts because your father is away on business, and today is her name day. Can you imagine, my pet? Twenty-six and still with the bloom of a rose.' She brushed the hair out of my eyes and, spitting onto her kerchief, used it to dab the dirt off my tear-stained face. 'Now, now, no more tears, let me make you look comely for your father's return.'

Sorrel, our wolfhound, pushed his damp nose onto my lap, weakly wagging his tail, glad that the shouting had stopped.

I slipped down from Mrs Orcharde's knee and, holding on to his metal collar, followed her up the oak staircase to the chamber I shared with my sister. As I sat on my wooden stool, the nurse started brushing out my long, thick hair.

'Am *I* pretty, Mary?' I asked, swinging my feet before me.

'God's death what a question,' chuckled my nurse. 'Your sister might be fairer of hair, but you have the eyes. Lord, bless me they are so big and dark.'

'How dark?' I asked.

My nurse ignored my question and continued her brushing. 'Mary, my little chick, might be the golden sun in this family, but you are the silver moon. When your father was a little boy I used to tell him that we called the moon the Blessed Virgin's lamp, for does she not hold the moon in her hands so that the stars can twinkle by its light? No, Mary might be the sunny day, but you, my little one, are the dark night – cool and mysterious.'

'What is Thomas?' I asked again, curious to hear of my older brother.

She put her brush down and tickled me until I squealed.

'He,' she laughed, 'is Jack Sauce.'

I wriggled around to face her, glad that she lived with my family.

'Mary,' I said, stepping into a clean shift, 'when do I get replaced? My sister says that one day I get replaced and live with another lady. Why does mama want to replace me? Does she not like me anymore because I run about?'

My nurse fastened up the loose ties of my shift, turned me about, and placed her hands on my tiny shoulders. 'Good Lord above, what foolish ideas have been put into your young mind now? You will be *placed*, little one, not *replaced*. It is a different word. Your mother cannot teach you everything you need to know to be a great lady, so, God willing, you will go to a grand household to learn these things. One day, your father is hoping you will follow in your mother's footsteps and become a lady-in-waiting at court – when you are a little older, my chick, and have learnt to be a useful and a pleasant companion to the next queen, whoever she might be. It is your future.' She shook her head. 'Replaced! Marry, whatever next?'

My eyes opened wide as I stepped into a simple grey gown. 'But *why?*'

'Why? Why, to learn, of course. At court you must be able to play music, sing, recite poems, compose your own delights on the lute, harp and virginals, and be able to entertain important company. To play the lute well signifies to the world that you have an educated mind. You will learn courtly dances, and be such a little lady that you might even catch the eye of some fine, noble gentleman.' She chuckled. 'Oh, Nan, you will make your parents very proud – but mind now, not before your sister. She, as the eldest shall have the first opportunity, but there is no need to dwell on this for a very long time. There,' she added, straightening my gown, 'snug as a pig in pease-straw. Now, I must go and see if your apron is in the garden. Dear, dear, such a storm we have had today, but now everything is mended.'

She clapped her weather-worn hands to her knees and, with a sigh, rose stiffly from her stool.

I skipped over to the window and climbed up onto the oak chest. Standing on tiptoe, I watched the ducks bobbing in the moat below and, some moments later, spied Mrs Orcharde talking to my mother. I loved my nurse, for she would always take my part and spoil me. She had nursed my father when he was a boy, and looked as old as time with her thin, grey hair coiled in a long plait beneath her white coif, and her ruddy, broken-veined cheeks. She would sit and tell me of the things that father had done, and how she had adored him. She said he was her little tomcat, for his mother, Dame Margot, cared little for him as a child, and Mrs Orcharde quickly took her place in his affections. I loved her, too, for she told me that I was a bright child and to give no thought to the strange little finger on my right hand, which divided into two tiny fingernails. She would kiss it and say 'why, my pet, it is just the same as Dame Margot's.'

Chapter One

'All time is mine.'

Blickling, Rochford and Hever, 1497-1509

The spiteful say that 'Nan Bullen came from no-where.' That is untrue. My Bullen family were originally of French extraction, and a John Boleyn had settled in Salle, Norfolk, many years ago. As Lord Mayor of London, my great-grandfather, Sir Geoffrey Bullen, enjoyed life as a successful merchant. He married a wealthy heiress, Anne Hoo, and bought Blickling Manor in Norfolk, and Hever Manor in Kent. His son, William, my grandfather, also married an heiress, Margaret or Dame Margot, as we knew her, the strong-willed Irish daughter of Thomas Butler, 7th Earl of Ormond, one of the richest men in England, having made his fortune from wool. She had been born at Kilkenny Castle, in Ireland, the seat of the Butler family. A magnificent castle, it overlooked the River Nore, the great park and six acres of green land. Two families ruled in Ireland – the Butlers and the Fitzgeralds – and since the first hated the second, the Butlers supported the English in the Pale against them. As a descendant of the first King Edward, Dame Margot never let anyone forget her noble blood. Her father married a second time, but having no male heir, her eldest son – my father – was destined, one day, to inherit the baronies of Hoo and Rochford, and the Earldoms of Wiltshire, Ormond and Carrick.

My father grew up in the company of three younger brothers: Uncle William became a rector in Norfolk, Uncle James ran the estate at Blickling, and Uncle Edward tended his lands in Norfolk. His four sisters were my aunts Anne, Alice, Jane and Margaret.

My mother told me how Father, as a young man, aimed to marry well, obtain a respectable position at court and seek advancement through the rich earldom of Ormond. In this first part, he looked to the Howard family – a family connected to the most powerful landowners in East Anglia. However, when King Richard was killed at Bosworth Field, Thomas Howard found himself having to prove his loyalty to the new king, Henry Tudor. The king was suspicious of his nobles from the start, and my Howard grandfather, desperate to recover the title of Duke of Norfolk, found himself thrown into the Tower prison, where he languished in disgrace. Eventually, on his release, the king appointed him Lieutenant of the North to prove his loyalty. In April 1497, four months after the death of my grandmother, Elizabeth Tilney, he married her cousin, Agnes Tilney, a rich heiress from a Lincolnshire family. Allowed to return to court, his climb back to favour began.

＊　＊

In the meantime, my father watched as a captivating, brown-eyed beauty danced among the queen's ladies. As the daughter of Thomas Howard and Elizabeth Tilney, my mother, Elizabeth, had been born and raised at Ashwell Thorpe, in Norfolk. She enjoyed a happy childhood with her many brothers, protected from the turbulent times in which she lived. As a child, she was unaware of the business of kings, or the fact that the family supported the Yorkist cause. Mrs Orcharde described how, at eighteen years old, she was one of the loveliest girls at court, slender and lithe, her golden brown hair growing thick as far as her waist. Even the court poet, Master John Skelton, described how she was *'lusty to look upon'* in his poem *'The Garland of Laurel'*.

She, in turn, had watched young Master Bullen carrying out his father's business. He was a man of good standing riding out to Blackheath to suppress the Cornish rebels in their uprising against the king's taxes. A competent jouster, he enjoyed making his horse leap and cavort in front of the ladies to gain their admiration, particularly my mother's. Father was determined to make his move and win her, and win her he did. Now, the Bullens were brought into the sphere of the Howards and with it came the hope of greater favour yet.

But what of the Howards, what were their thoughts? Considering Father's family connections, the proud Howard brothers should have been delighted, but secretly they scoffed. They felt that Thomas Bullen aimed too high in courting their Howard sister, for had not my mother's brother, Thomas, married Anne Plantagenet, the daughter of the fourth King Edward, thus connecting the Howards to royalty? They failed to mention the fact that the fortunes of the Howards were still at a low ebb indeed. Thomas Howard, Earl of Surrey, was not a duke, for the title was still under attainder, and the premier duke in England was the proud and troublesome Duke of Buckingham. Father only smiled to himself and stood his ground. On balance, it was a fair match for the Howards, for my father reminded them of the great wealth *he* would inherit one day, through the rich earldom of Ormond. Ever a gambling man, he had played his hand well.

I asked my mother to describe the day she had married

my father, and she said how, on a warm, June day, she had stood inside the cool church at Salle, in Norfolk, in her new green gown, her beautiful hair loose about her shoulders. Bunches of lavender decorated the church, filling the air with a heady scent, and as dusty beams of sunlight illuminated the Bullen coat of arms, my mother knew it was a good omen. My father, waiting beneath the stained glass windows of the church, a short step from the chapel of St Thomas, had smiled at the gathering of family and friends. It had been a happy day, and after the marriage ceremony, she told me that they had decided to live at Blickling Manor, in Norfolk. This land, prosperous from the wool trade, was the home of my Howard relatives and scattered with their many properties, along with the great manors of our neighbours, the Morleys and Sheltons.

Life, she said, was good in Norfolk and to her delight, she quickly found she was with child.

In February 1498, a child was born and christened Thomas, after my father. Dark-haired and lusty, he was everything my parents had hoped. Then, barely recovered, my mother fell pregnant again, certain in the knowledge that she would have another son before Twelfth Night. But it was not to be. A fair little daughter arrived and was named Mary, after the Blessed Virgin.

● ●

By 1500, King Henry Tudor had, despite constant plots, managed to hold onto his throne for fifteen years. His heir, the young Prince Arthur, soon to be at his own court in the Welsh Marches, awaited the arrival of his bride, Princess Katherine of Aragon from Spain. It was tragic that Edmund, his baby brother, had died but his younger brother, nine-year-old Henry, Duke of York, appeared as hearty as ever. He was with his beloved mother, Queen Elizabeth of York, at Eltham Palace, no doubt teasing and taunting his two sisters, Mary and Margaret, in his boisterous, demanding way. Mother said he wished it was he marrying, rather than Arthur, but he still looked forward with great excitement to the coming wedding. With his good looks, he knew that he would steal everyone's admiration compared to his pale brother. However, Mother said that Prince Arthur was tall and would make a handsome groom to match his Spanish bride, who was said to be very comely, with blue-grey eyes and long golden hair.

I, too, was on my way, for that cold winter my mother was yet again expecting a child. She busied herself with the other ladies-in-waiting, sewing gifts for the Spanish ladies when they finally arrived – for there had been a setback in the arrival of Princess Katherine – and choosing fabrics and jewels for their own gowns. Everything had to be perfect, for the foreign ladies, they were told, were beautiful and exotic and so the English ladies must make every effort to outshine them.

The queen's chambers rang with laughter as merchants filed into the royal chambers carrying the most beautiful cloth – grosgrain, sarcenet, taffeta and velvet. But joy proved fleeting. Immediately after Candlemas, my mother's favourite brother, Henry, died aged twenty-one. Deeply distressed, she told me how she had become troubled with a swelling of her legs, and after the funeral at Norfolk, was advised to return to the quiet of Blickling Manor. There, her female relatives tended to her in the coming months, although they knew she would be desperate to return to the excitement of the court. To make matters worse, my dear Aunt Jane died, and Father became depressed and withdrawn.

As the spring unfolded, my mother lay open-laced and bored, at Blickling. When the shutters were finally closed, blocking out the view of the pink May blossom, she lay hidden away from the outside world and waited. Waited for her pains to begin…

I never tired of hearing of that day in late May. Mrs Orcharde would repeat the story to me again and again until

I had every detail fixed in my head. It was a Friday, late in the afternoon, and as the storm passed and a heavy shower of rain ceased to fall, Hannah pulled the drapes closer and stoked up the fire. No chill must be allowed to creep into the stifling air. My mother had given a final cry and fallen back against the bolster in exhaustion.

'Why, Elizabeth, you have a beautiful baby girl! Thanks be to God.' My Aunt Margaret, leant forward to kiss my mother's flushed cheek.

'Is she well-formed?' asked Mother, as Dame Margot unfolded a clean coverlet.

'Marry, Elizabeth, she is,' said Aunt Margaret, 'and Lord, what a healthy pair of pipes! We shall visit the shrine of St Walstan, to give thanks as soon as you are recovered, for the babe has arrived on his holy day. Why, his church is the fairest church in Norfolk, and this little mite will be the fairest in all Norfolk, too.'

As my mother closed her eyes, sweat glistening on her brow, my aunt took her hand. 'Come, come, Eliza, do not fret, you will have another son in time. You are highly fertile – all Howard women are. Besides, she will make a fine playmate for your little Mary.'

Mother told me how, although small, I had squalled loudly and let it be known that I was most unhappy to enter this strange world. The midwife handed me to my mother, and as she gazed down at my head, covered in dark, downy hair, my mother placed a comforting fingertip into my tiny mouth.

'Anne. We will call her Anne.'

My crying had ceased, and as I gazed at her with my wide eyes my aunt leaned close.

'Hello, my precious,' she whispered, moving back the linen cloth. 'What a tiny wretch you are.'

Sitting on the bed, she laughed and said I reminded her of my mother when she was out of sorts, red-faced and ill-tempered.

My Howard grandmother, Agnes, entered the chamber.

'Tell Thomas would you, Agnes?' asked Mother, as Dame Margot held a glass of reviving, spiced wine to her parched lips. 'Tell him we have a daughter.'

Agnes had smiled and left the chamber, as the midwife began to sort out the swaddling bands.

The next to enter was my nurse, Mrs Orcharde, holding the hand of my sister. Little Mary toddled forward, thumb in mouth, peeped at me, and promptly screwed up her face. 'Ugh.'

Mrs Orcharde picked her up and held her against her stout hip. 'Fie! Give the poor mite a chance,' she said, 'why, in a short time she will have the bonny look of all the Howard babes – you see if I am not right.'

My aunt, plumping up the bolster, then signalled to the wet nurse, Mrs Everton, ruddy-cheeked and plump as a butterball, to step forward.

'You have nothing to fear, Madame,' said the wet nurse, lifting me. 'All my babies suckle right well, and this little mite will be no different. She will soon fatten up,' she said. 'Now, we must get her swaddled.'

Outside in the gallery, my father took Agnes hurriedly to one side. 'Agnes, is Elizabeth well? And – and the child?'

My grandmother told him matters were as they should be, with no complications, thanks to God and his good saints. He had a fine, healthy girl to be named Anne, in honour of her great-grandmother.

'Thanks be to God. It is, indeed, a fitting name,' he had said, slumping into a chair.

My young aunts, Anne and Alice, hugged each other, but it was Alice who later told me of the flicker of disappointment in my father's eyes.

'Will the babe thrive?' he asked. Agnes nodded and squeezed his hand reassuringly.

'She is very small, Thomas, but the signs are good, and Mrs Everton is heavy-breasted with milk. We will baptise her quickly though, and Elizabeth will stay in her chamber until she is churched.'

My father nodded and took out from his tunic a small, ivory box. He opened it to reveal an exquisite pearl brooch, in the centre of which sat an emerald, as green as the Irish grass.

'Give this to Elizabeth, will you please, Agnes? It was my grandmother's. Tell her she can wear it at the marriage of Prince Arthur and Princess Katherine. I know she is looking forward to the celebrations and it will please her.'

Agnes took the beautiful piece and held it up to the light from the window. 'Why, Thomas, the emerald brings good luck to those born in May, and Elizabeth can pass this to the child when she is older. It will bring the mite good fortune and a long, happy life.'

My father had made as if to speak, but paused. 'Tell me – the child. It is…'

Agnes nodded. 'I know, my dear, I know. The child is well-formed, and you now have two lovely little daughters. Elizabeth was born to bear babes, and you are both young. More boys will follow; you mark my words. As to this one – why, she is a Norfolk child. She *will* survive.

●　●

He was dead. The king's beloved heir to the throne, so recently married to his lovely princess, lay cold on his bier and the court lay silent in shock. Four months before, the handsome fifteen-year-old boy and his new wife, along with my mother and the court, had joyfully celebrated the be-trothal of his sister, the thirteen-year-old Princess Margaret, to James of Scotland. My father had jousted in front of the king, court and the Scottish ambassadors and it had been a spectacular show to impress all present. Prince Arthur's brother, Henry, had cavorted on his new horse, enjoying the admiring glances. Now, he pondered his change of status, for he was no longer just the second son destined for a position in the Church, and he quickly became aware that people were now pandering to his every whim.

At Blickling, my mother told me how she had placed her hand on her unusually large belly, and knew from the lusty kicking that she carried a precious boy. But her thoughts were with the queen. To lose one's son was grief indeed, but to lose a prince?

'The king is distraught,' she had said, as my Aunt Alice placed a woollen shawl around her shoulders. 'I hear he locked himself away in the bowels of Richmond and would not eat.'

'Aye, Elizabeth, and the poor queen herself still lies weak with grief. It is a sad, sad time and a hard time, for all about the country, families are overburdened with debt and financial worry.'

'Don't talk of money, Alice, Thomas becomes most irritated if I spend anything these days. I had no idea he was so miserly when we first met, but I soon learnt.'

'Well, he and His Grace are as one,' said my aunt. 'I tell you, this king is like a great spider at the middle of a web, drawing men like flies to pay him what he thinks they owe him.'

It was true. Londoners, merchants, tradesmen and ordinary folk – all were required to fill his coffers with gold. Nobles were punished with crippling fines over the least offence and had no choice but to pay if they were to avoid death or imprisonment.

'And who,' my aunt continued, 'does the odious deeds for him? Edmund Dudley, royal councillor and thief. It is through him and Richard Empson that the king keeps control. Of course, they plead that they are only carrying out the King's orders, but they are perverting justice for their own ends, and one day they will pay the price.'

'I hear,' said Mother, pulling her shawl tight against the draught, 'that young Thomas More is speaking out against the king again.'

'Yet he is still allowed to visit the queen at court,' replied my aunt, 'regardless of him proclaiming that Londoners are being choked to death to pay the king his money.

'And are you surprised, Alice? The king may have united the Yorkist and Lancastrian cause with his marriage, but he has been haunted for years with continual plots from pretenders wishing to take his throne. Year after year he has no peace and lives in terror of the country returning to a civil war.'

'I agree; there is much misery.'

'Indeed,' said Mother, 'and now we have lost our prince. Such a gentle boy and so well-mannered – just like his lovely mother. Oh, he was precocious, but he had such a love of books and learning. Did you hear it is whispered that he died from too lusty a laying with his young wife?'

My aunt raised her eyes, never one to forgo an opportunity to listen to gossip.

'The physician said he suffered a pain in his groin at Easter-tide and within the week lay dead at Ludlow. The princess is now at her palace in Croydon, seeking comfort from that frightful Spanish woman, Donna Elvira. She never lets the princess out of her sight and controls her household in all things. None of us cares for her, and all wish she had been packed off with the rest of those ugly women in Katherine's train. What a lie to say they were beautiful – they had *moustaches*! As to those hideous gowns and headdresses, why, they looked like Turks. If that is Spanish fashion, you can keep it. Well, now the king has just one precious son left, Henry, Duke of York. The future rests with this one boy. What will that future be?'

'But he is considered a strong child,' said my aunt, 'and physically everything his brother was not.'

'Well, I cannot but worry about bringing a child myself into such uncertain times,' my mother replied. 'As to the safety of the realm resting on one prince, it is folly. Should anything –'

'Hush, now, Elizabeth, do not say such things, the king

might have more sons yet. Besides, Prince Henry is a fine boy who is well on the way to youth and manhood. I admit he is aware of his change of status and that his sense of importance knows no bounds. But he will be a glorious king, beloved by every man, and will, if we are favoured, bring rewards to this family. You wait and see – these are a pregnant woman's fancies.'

However, after grief came joy, for, in June, my mother gave birth to twin boys, christened Robert and William. My father celebrated with a great family gathering, something he had not done when Mary and I were born. Sadly, neither of the babes would suckle at the breast, and within a matter of weeks, both were dead and buried.

Again, my parents were heartbroken, but my mother insisted on returning to her duties at court, where the gentle queen left her to sew quietly and recover from her loss. My mother loved the queen, who tried to cheer her with her fool, Patch, and when Mother could not smile, she would lay her hand on her shoulder, sharing a mutual grief.

A good queen, beloved for her charitable works, she was the perfect foil to her husband's difficult nature. Placid and calm, Mother said she adored her children and spent hours teaching them to read and write herself. She was particularly close to young Henry.

My mother was young and strong, and quickly rallied from her loss. Not so the queen. She listlessly fingered the black velvet cloth brought before her and sighed. She confided her fears to my mother, for at the age of thirty-six, she knew she was too old to bear more children. The king dismissed such fears and set to the making of an heir as soon as decently possible. Alice Massey, her midwife, became anxious for she knew any pregnancy at the queen's time of life was fraught with danger. She was right, too. Elizabeth fell with child, but by the following February, on the day that she had been born, she was dead, along with the baby daughter she had christened Kate.

The bells of St Paul's tolled in the foggy, dark days of winter and London mourned the passing of this lovely, gentle woman. The king fell near to death with grief and remorse, locking himself away and refusing business for weeks. Having truly loved his queen, he was utterly lost without her. However, the worse affected was Prince Henry, who refused to come out of his chambers, or eat any food. Utterly distraught, he grew sullen, difficult and withdrawn, and even his fool, John Goose, could not cheer him. The king, unused to this behaviour, was at a loss what to do and left him to cry alone. Mother told me it was heartbreaking to see the boy, for he was just eleven years old. She, in the meantime, knelt at her *prie-dieu* to pray for him. In April, she prayed to God to still the anxious beating of her own heart, for yet another child was on its way.

※　※

In July 1503, as life at court continued apace, my father took his place in the great procession of Princess Margaret, as she took her leave for her new home in Scotland.

Even the frugal king made sure his dear daughter departed with great pomp, and the colourful cavalcade proceeded as far as Berwick, staying at Collyweston, the home of the king's beloved mother. My mother worried about how the princess would fare, with her mother so recently dead. She watched the young girl depart from Richmond Palace, my father riding among the gentlemen of the court, and told me how although magnificently attired on her white palfrey, she had appeared desperately homesick. Her new husband would be fifteen years older, and although she tried to look imperious, she must have been terrified of what lay ahead.

In November, to my parents' great joy and relief, my little brother Henry, or Hal, as he was named in honour of the future king, was safely born. A bonny baby, strong, fair and plump like the prince himself, my father could not have been more delighted when the good news reached him in Northumberland. Now, the Bullen family enjoyed the security of two boys, Thomas and little Henry. England rejoiced, too, for the lovely Princess Katherine was not to return to Spain a widow, but was to marry Prince Henry when he reached fifteen years of age. King Ferdinand and Queen Isabella, having no intention of losing the English alliance, had ordered Dr de Puebla to negotiate the terms with the English council. The days of uncertainty were over at last.

❋ ❋

Being of so tender an age, my early memories of life at Blicking Manor, the family home in Norfolk, are not clear but little has changed of the house. It still boasts a fine wooden drawbridge over the moat and a courtyard. The splendid staircase separates the main chamber and the chapel, and a long gallery gives a beautiful view across the water. The gardens stretch away into the distance as far as the woods, where once stood a large mill, but that is long gone. I do have pictures in my mind of grey skies, looming low and wide over flat fields dotted with windmills. I also recall that I was enchanted by this strange, flat, land, and often watched the wherries, their white sails flapping in the breeze, as they made their way languidly along the waterways. It was a silent place, and in the great clouds above, skylarks swooped and dived above the water where dragonflies hovered in the reeds. At that time, sheep grazed as far as the eye could see, and the great wool trade with the Netherlands paid for the many fine Norfolk houses, flint churches and priories. In fact, the manor boasted a very pretty church, and it was there that I was baptised.

At Baconsthorpe Castle, I was told that over three thousand sheep were kept on the Heydon's vast estates. But all was not sheep. At Kenninghall, my Grandfather Howard owned a moated property with apple orchards that produced excellent cider – up to three great casks a year. He began renovating the old timber building, using the excellent Norfolk clay for brick making, and we would occasionally stay as guests. Father enjoyed helping with the building's management and showed some considerable skill in organising the work.

In February, we visited Shelton Hall with its beautiful park, fishponds and dovehouse. It is a vast, moated brick house owned then by Sir Ralph Shelton, and my father's sister, Anne, had married his son, John Shelton, in 1503 when she was twenty years old. She was not a favourite sister, and never became a close aunt but, yet again, this clever match delighted the Bullens, for the rich Sheltons owned much land in Norfolk and Suffolk. Aunt Anne gave birth to a girl christened Margaret, or Madge, who became my first cousin and grew up to be an attractive child. We also visited our relatives, the Calthorpes and Cleres, and Mother spent the chilly, dark days gossiping by the fire and enjoying their hospitality.

However, her greatest delight was to attend the Friday market on the coast at Cromer. When we arrived there, the noise on the quayside was alarming, for people jostled and shouted as they picked up the squirming crabs and haggled over the price. Not even the bells from the tallest church tower in Norfolk could drown out the cries: 'Fresh mussels! Fresh whelks! Fresh lobster!'

The many sea birds overhead shrieked as if in competition as to who could make the most noise. Mother would flap the birds away with a curse as they swooped down onto the market tables to try and grab a morsel. No, the birds never deterred her from visiting Cromer, for she loved the lobster and said it was the best for miles around.

I stared in fascination at the fingers of the young children as they picked the fish from the barrels, and cut into them. 'But *why* are they so?' I asked.

'Because of the work they do,' came the reply. 'Their tiny fingers are raw and bleeding from cutting and slicing the catch, for their knives are keen. See, some even have their fingers cut off.'

I fixed my eyes on the bloody stumps and dirty cloths wrapped around the children's hands until I was pulled away to the next stall. Standing there under the striped canopy, cold in the blustery March wind, I was ready to return home. Besides visits and outings, there were also processions on holy days throughout the year, such as to the shrine at Walsingham. The most colourful, and rowdy, was the annual St George's Day celebration. Enthralled by the great wicker dragon, gilded and covered with painted canvas, I watched as ten stout men carried it through the streets of Norwich. Mary squealed when the dragon spat fire and ran to hide behind Mrs Orcharde. I only stood on tip-toe and tried to spy the actual arm of the saint as it lay in a gilded box studded with precious jewels, carried high on a bier by chanting priests. It was a sacred, mysterious sight to my young eyes and in the evening we enjoyed the bonfires, dancing and roasted pig. However, what made St George's Day so memorable that April Day in 1504, was that on returning home my mother announced that she was with child yet again. This time my father was less delighted. He felt his income was not high enough to pay for the upkeep of a larger family and, as a result, matters remained frosty for some time. Little did he know that his fortunes were about to change.

* *

The crash of a bucket on cobbles caused the mares to start with fright and whicker in their stalls. Pulling at its halter, one of them swung its quarters around and barely missed stepping onto the body of my grandfather, William Bullen, lying on the straw. He had been tending to his favourite mare when a servant, hearing the commotion, ran to his aid, and discovered that his master had died from apoplexy. His body was carried to the oak table in the Great Hall. Although deeply saddened, Mother told me that Father could not hide his relief at this turn of events, for he now inherited Calthorpe, Wykmore, Mickelbarton, and the fortified manor house of Hever in Kent.

'Thanks be to God,' he said, as we returned home on a damp October day after the burial at Norwich Cathedral. Fractious and bored, I had incurred Mrs Orcharde's displeasure during the dreary service, and had cried incessantly. I had even managed to lose my blue coif.

'That his pain is over,' he added, hastily. 'God is merciful – and – and we now have the inheritance.'

'Thomas, what a monstrous thing to say. The poor man fresh in his grave next to his dear mother and here you are talking thus. It is unworthy and unseemly. Your mother is distraught at losing her husband.'

Even though my grandfather was fifty-four years old, Mother said it was a shock for he was such a strong, vital man.

'That may be, but by God, Elizabeth, we require more money than we presently have. Fine clothes and entertaining have to be paid for, bills settled.'

'Thomas, we are hardly poor. We have family money, as you are well aware.'

'Yes, and I refuse to go cap in hand to your father or mother-in-law or to Ormond whenever we need the roof fixing.'

'You took money from your father quite happily,' my mother pointed out.

Father stood by the fireplace, resting his head wearily on his clenched fist, as she paced. Did she not understand? With three fine boys – Thomas, Hal and the latest babe, George – he must look to their future. Besides, he did not *take* anything. He accepted. God's blood, she made him sound like a thief. Of course, with five children, this inheritance could not be timelier, for we could now live off the manor's profits and move home. For some time, my father had wanted a house nearer to Richmond and the court, but until now did not have the money to purchase or repair one. He finally decided that the manor at Hever would be perfect, for it would be but a day's ride from the king, even less to the palace at Westminster. It was true the manor would have to be renovated to make it a suitable family home, but now, with his position as Squire of the Body *and* his inheritance, his project could begin.

*   *

I do remember quite clearly standing with my brother Thomas, watching my father as he bent over a large wooden table, studying several rolls of maps and drawings. The chamber appeared eerie as the torches flickered in their sconces, making the shadows of the men standing there dance on the white plaster walls. Father had great plans for Hever, and his experience at Kenninghall, in construction, was to stand him in good stead. He turned confidently to the gentlemen standing around the table.

'Hever is low lying here – and here,' he pointed. 'When was the last flood from the Eden?'

'Last winter, Sir, since the moat around the castle is joined to the river, resulting in the flooding of the courtyard.'

We peered around the corner of the door and one of the gentlemen in a fur-trimmed, green coat, smiled. I bobbed quickly behind the doorframe, but it was too late.

'God's death, Nan, Thomas, why are you not abed? You will freeze to death in your shifts.' Father's voice softened. 'Well, as you are here, come, come here and see the new manor.'

He lifted me to the table, and I stared down at the parchment covered in drawings, scribbles and annotations. My brother, leaning on one elbow, trailed his finger along the border of the scroll.

'See, here is the garden,' said Father, turning the plan around. The man standing next to him nodded.

'My wife wants plenty of gillyflowers, violets – and strawberry beds – here on this side. The flower roots will have to be gathered by the local women in large quantities. What is the going rate?'

'Approximately four pence a bushel,' came the reply.

Father grunted. 'Get it down to two.' He put me down, and I stood by the table as he continued.

'Here we will enlarge. We will keep the two wings, but the building requires developing. I have in mind a novelty – a long gallery running the entire width of the manor – one hundred feet long. What say you?'

One of the gentlemen stroked his chin. 'It can be done, Sir, if we put a ceiling over the Great Hall and the kitchen. As we cannot extend the stairs in the Great Hall, we can move the front of the manor forward – here – to form a staircase gallery. Since the timber frame is not load-bearing, I cannot see a problem.'

Father smiled. 'A staircase gallery you say? Why, *excellent*.' He leaned forward. 'We lead guests from the hall – here – up the main stairs, through our private apartments, along the staircase gallery and up the stairs to the Long Gallery above – here – thus placing the entrance to the gallery at the east end.'

'Exactly, Sir, for what is the use of having fine tapestries, paintings and pewter if not to show them off by means of a longer route up to the main walkway? Plus, it gives the impression, if I might make so bold, of a far more impressive residence.'

The men murmured in agreement.

'Good,' said Father, rolling out the plan further, 'at the same time as we build the gallery, I want several tiers of oriel windows projecting out from the walls, with new coloured glass to house the Bullen heraldry. It will give a feeling of space and light, less austere, and away from the old style and fashion. I want this to be in the new mode.'

'We can get good stone from the quarries at Allington and Maidstone,' offered one of the gentlemen, rolling up another plan, 'and source timber from Eaton Bridge.'

'Can it be done within the year?' asked Father. 'And at what cost?'

The man put on his cloak, fastened the clasp and shrugged.

'You are not stopping the night, Geoffrey?'

The man shook his head.

'Thank you, Thomas, but I must return home to Eaton. No, with enough labour and a dry summer I would say the house could be habitable by Christ-tide. Besides, they can labour by torchlight if necessary. Inner plastering could take a while to dry, but the main structure would be in place. Plasterers are insisting on sixpence a day.'

'Make it fourpence,' said Father. 'And the gallery?'

'A conservative guess of seven pounds in total. Would you be able to oversee the work?'

Father shook his head. 'Not from here, but my mother has suggested we stay at Rochford Manor, in Essex, one of her family properties belonging to Old Ormond. It is convenient for, with only a few miles ride to Westcliff, I can pick up a barge and go straight down the Thames to the court at Richmond.'

'Most convenient,' agreed one of the younger men. 'But tell me, the old earl, how is it with the gentleman? I hear he is having trouble moving with his sticks.'

Father grimaced. 'Hardly a surprise when he is crippled with rheumatism. He is too old to be on the Privy Council and knows it, but he cannot be told. He is typical of the Butlers – proud and quarrelsome. If Elizabeth even gently suggests retirement, he lets out a stream of oaths and ends up in a coughing fit, fighting for breath. Well, I hope to God I live as long as he has done, and still retain my wits and spleen!'

I gave a stifled yawn as Thomas took a rolled up plan in both hands, and poked me hard with it. I gave a loud whine.

'Children,' said Father, 'go to, get to your beds before I call Mrs Orcharde, and take Sorrel with you. Now, may God's blessing be upon you.' He placed his hand upon our heads and, handing me a flickering candle in its pewter holder, we scuttled off down the dark passageway and back to the warmth of our beds.

*   *

Sorrel bounded back and forth impatient to be off. The carthorses, on the other hand, stood patiently in the biting wind, blowing warm air from their nostrils and shifting their weight with a disgruntled sigh as their girths were tugged and made tighter still. Furniture, pictures, hangings and personal belongings were loaded onto the carts, and all made ready for the journey to Rochford, in Essex. Tied to the back of the carts stood the sumpter-horses, laden with grain and fodder, and behind them several mounted servants.

'Did you have to strip the place?' Father fastened down the heavy canvas cover. 'Rochford is moderately stocked with furnishings,' he continued, tugging hard on the leather strap. 'There, that should do it. This wind is really taking a hold. For the love of God, will someone stop that cursed dog barking?'

His bonnet blew off in the gusty wind.

'Do not fuss, Thomas,' said Mother, holding on to her blue bonnet and veil. 'It was you who insisted I did not waste money on buying new cupboards. Since that is the case, I want our finest things with us, and the rest can stay. I do not want the people of Essex or Kent to think we are beneath them – I am a Howard, am I not, James?' she said, catching her breath, and turning her horse around to the mounting steps.

As my young uncle smiled, the look on Father's face made it clear that he did not wish to be constantly remind-ed. My uncle picked up the horse's hoof to inspect it, and slapped it on the rump.

'At least at Hever we shall be closer to the court,' said Mother, as she eased herself into the saddle.

Her horse tossed its head and pawed the ground im-patiently as I was lifted up behind and strapped into the wooden seat.

'Mrs Orcharde, take Hal, George and Thomas in the cart, and Hannah get mounted. Quickly girl!'

She turned our horse towards my father. 'Talking of the court I wonder how our new Archbishop of Canterbury, will fare?' she asked.

'Warham has not been Lord Chancellor five minutes,' said Father with a grunt, 'and is not a young man. But His Grace has faith in him. More to the point, let us see how Suffolk and George Neville fare now that there is a new law against keeping retainers. His Grace is paranoid about such nobles, always has been.'

My mother frowned. 'Well,' she said, 'all of Europe is desperate for him to remarry. It is all we ladies talk about. There is even a rumour that he might marry Princess Katherine himself, but I gather her mother is too horrified to consider the proposal seriously. I hear Margaret, the Regent of Savoy is also to be considered.'

'Aye,' said Father, 'and King Louis has offered him his cousin, Margaret of Angoulême, and promises that if he will take her, he will send His Grace the leg of St George.'

'Why,' said my mother, 'the body of the poor saint must be scattered across half of Europe! Anyway, is there anything of interest at Rochford I should know of?'

''Tis a small place,' he said, 'with a weekly market on Thursdays, a fair on Easter Tuesday and four tavern houses, one I think is an inn. There are manor houses and, of course, the great Priory of St Mary's, at Prittlewell. No, what is really of interest is the royal park with its two thousand acres of superb boar and stag hunting.'

'And?'

'And the fact that where there is hunting, there is His Grace and his court. Furthermore, should the king decide not to ride back to his palace at Richmond, he can rest with us and enjoy our hospitality. You know how tired he gets these days.'

'Oh, but he will bring the young Prince of Wales with him,' said Mother, her eyes lighting up.

'Maybe, and there again, maybe not. Since Prince Arthur's death, he lives in morbid fear of any ill befalling his precious son. He will not let him hunt, joust or do any manly thing that a lusty thirteen-year-old boy desires to do. He cannot even leave his chamber without walking through his father's first.'

'Well, since the queen's death, Thomas, His Grace has become morbid. She could soothe him when others cannot. Still, did you hear, Mary? The king himself in our home.'

My sister smiled, and adjusted her hood, as the groom led her horse forward.

'Mother's home,' corrected Father, 'for the present. Anyway, as your father keeps reminding me, we must never forget this family's fortunes are hitched to the king and his court, like an ox to the yoke. We must put our faith in him, and when the time comes – as come it must – we must put our trust in his successor.'

'Well, Thomas, this king might be morose and tight-fisted, but father tells me the others are worse. Why, the Emperor Maximillian gambles away his money, King Louis is unchaste, King Ferdinand is a thief, and King James of Scotland perfidious.'

'Then we must thank God for our good fortune,' said Father, mounting his mare and leaning down to clasp his young brother's arm.

'Good day, James, be a good lad,' he said, 'I will contact you on our arrival.'

Sorrel bounded ahead barking, as the cart creaked and lurched out across the cobbles.

While we rode, my mother explained to Mrs Orcharde how the manor of Rochford had once been owned by the fifth King Henry, and later the Woodvilles. It had passed down through the Butler family and the Earls of Ormond, and my great-grandfather, Thomas Butler – known as Sir

Thomas Ormond de Rochford – managed the Rochford estates restored to him by King Henry VII. He did much to add to the manor over the years although it was still unfinished in parts. Now he was too old to take a great interest in the property and complained about how the mildew and mists did nothing for his creaking joints. Even now, he was at court, in Greenwich, nursing a heavy cold. The manor then came to our family through Dame Margot and her sister, Anne. Dame Margot showed no interest in it whatsoever and would have been happier staying in Norfolk or returning to Kilkenny. Even Mother was not certain of the move.

'Are you sure Rochford is suitable?' she asked, trotting up beside my father. 'I mean, should His Grace visit,' she said, clicking our horse on, 'would not the other Ormond properties such as Hawkswell Hall, or New Hall be more comfortable? And what of company? You know I cannot abide being alone and the Morleys at Great Hallingbury will be two days' ride away.'

Father turned back to glance at his mother, some way behind in the cart, wrapped in her wool cloak. 'Do not fret, Elizabeth. Since the manor and parish church are the centre of the community, you will find yourself constantly occupied with charitable works and housewives' complaints.'

'Thomas, I mean people of quality – my own kind – not fishwives and suchlike complaining of the cost of whelks.'

'I am jesting,' he said, resting his hands on the front of his saddle. 'There will be feasts enough as I will be expected to entertain the local landowners from the Rochford Hundred.

'Oh?'

'It is an area of administration covering roughly thirty parishes, the same as the Sheriff's court, but quarrelsome and not easy to manage. Old Ormond had their measure, but he had more patience than I.' He sighed. 'No doubt I shall spend my time sitting in the Great Hall, listening to the locals' demands and preventing them from spitting each other with their fine swords.'

My mother frowned.

'No, Elizabeth, Rochford will serve our purpose for the time being and, besides, you will have the Scropes nearby at Hockley Hall. The Staffords have Southorp and Northorp manors, and they will visit when hunting or fishing – trust Buckingham to have access to the finest oysters in Essex. He has them sent to his manor at Penshurst. Mayhap one day he'll eat a bad one.'

I tightened my grip as our horse stumbled on the muddy track.

'Did I tell you I have a proposition to make to my mother?' he continued, glancing back again, and laying his hand on our horse's bridle to slow its pace.

'I have said nothing as yet, but one day I intend to own her Ormond properties with their farms and revenues. I am willing to grant her an annual income, and she can live comfortably with us if she chooses. When Old Ormond dies of course,' he added.

'And if His Grace allows it,' corrected Mother. 'But I agree, it would be better if she lives with us permanently, rather than in Kilkenny. You know how forgetful she is becoming and strange in her ways.'

'Better or not, *I* have no intention of living on the measly sum of fifty pounds a year. I mean for this family to rise. Remember my words, Elizabeth, remember.'

❖ ❖

The journey towards the south of England proved tedious, as we made our way with our convoy of loaded carts through the countryside. I nestled down into my red woollen cloak and stared up at the grey sky. A bird, which Father explained was a harrier, hovered above, curious as to what we were about, and a harsh wind blew across from the coast making the arms of the windmills spin around. On the flat, desolate land sheep grazed, dotting the horizon like dandelion puffs, and young shepherd boys, raw-faced from the cold wind, ran to meet us as we jolted along the sodden track. They grinned toothless grins accompanied by rude gestures. Mother became most indignant when, with a loud thud, a large clod of earth hit the side of one of our carts.

'Did you see, Ralph? Did you *see*?' she twisted around in her saddle.

Our servant wheeled his horse back towards the young boys who laughed as they ran away.

'Let them be, Elizabeth,' said Father, 'let boys be boys. We must press on and reach Taverham before nightfall and curfew are upon us. Ralph! Let them be.'

As our horses lumbered through the heavy mud, the flat, open pastures of Norfolk receded and made way for the hilly lands and forests of Suffolk. Passing through Sudbury, we stayed in Lavenham, visiting the bustling cloth market in the square, while Father looked to some business at the Company Hall. Mother and my nurse, carrying Hal, bought fine trimmings and peacock feathers, while George, in Hannah's arms, wriggled and squirmed as she tried to stop Thomas running ahead.

We travelled on to Ipswich, where we lodged, and on to the ancient Roman town of Colchester, until we reached the open land of North Essex. Shoals, sands and numerous tiny islands studded the land. Shaggy-coated horses grazed on the salt marshes, raised their heads in curiosity as we passed, and continued to tug at the sparse clumps surrounding the muddy creeks.

As the hours passed, the vast sky turned to the colour of pewter, with no hint of the sun and, circling above, the black and white oystercatchers hovered on the wind. We stopped and rested at the Hey Bridge, and Sorrel, nose to the sky, watched as overhead a great number of wildfowl noisily flew across from Northey Island. Father shielded his eyes.

'See,' he said, pointing, 'excellent fowl are plentiful in Essex, and men travel from London to shoot. It is far better than Plumstead Marshes.'

'Well, I hear they return full of ague,' said Dame Margot, sliding down from her horse to stretch her legs. 'Just as they do at Rochford, with its bad drainage.' Her boots squelched into the mud. 'And what of the land? Not as good as Ireland, I'll warrant, or Norfolk. Which reminds me, when will my horses be sent down?'

'Mother, dear, why not pick some sea lavender for your clothes chests?' said Father, noticing the clouds of blue flowers growing in misty abundance. 'Eliza tells me it is excellent at preventing moth.' He gave my mother a look of despair. 'Come, there is a fog coming in off the water,' he said, 'we should not tarry long.'

※　※

The final part of our journey took us past winding creeks, flooded ground and treacherous paths to Malden, Purleygh, and across an old wooden bridge to Hawkswell. Tired, Father wiped his brow and pointed out a church tower in the distance. We then continued through ancient parkland and woods, and finally arrived at a gatehouse on the south side. The gateman jumped up from the ground, took off his cap and opened the wooden gate wide to let us pass through. I peered through sleepy eyes at the smoke curling up into the air from the red brick chimneys, feeling tired and hungry.

'Welcome, sir, the manor is made ready, if it please you. The fires are lit, and the beds are warmed.'

Father glanced across to the cart where his mother nestled in her furs, sound asleep, her mouth lolled open. He nodded. 'Aye, and the horses are weary. See to them, Ralph,' he ordered, kicking his mare forward.

※　※

Rochford Manor, made of red brick from its own kiln, still stands in several acres of fine land. A pretty moat surrounds the manor on three sides, and there are high, octagonal towers with arrow slits around a large inner courtyard.

Inside, we discovered the Great Hall, a beautiful chapel, a spacious beamed kitchen, and plenty of comfortable chambers strewn with dried meadow grass. They were not lavishly decorated, and the furniture was sparse, so it was as well that Mother had insisted on bringing her hangings and turkey carpets. Spiral staircases of oak wound round to the top of the towers, and the delightful brick arches gave a feeling of space. From the tiny casement windows in the towers, one could see far across the meadows, and although it was not a grand house, Father intended to continue the renovations started by Old Ormond. A short walk across from the manor stood the church of St Andrew, its high red brick tower visible from miles around. The Ormond coat of arms, carved in stone above the west doorway, left no doubt, then or now, as to who built this fine landmark. We children thought it was wonderful, yet within a matter of days, Dame Margot complained that the bells disturbed her rest, and in a fit of pique threatened to have three of them taken down and sold. Such an act would not have endeared her to the good people of Rochford.

Spring at Rochford proved glorious, for the parkland lay covered with a profusion of bluebells, and the trees shimmered with cherry blossom. By summer, snapdragons, cowslips, primroses and violets tumbled across its ancient pathways and, once free from our lessons, it became a paradise in which to run and play. Butterflies and bees filled the arbours, and I would follow Mary as we ran through the grassy meadows until I was tired. Tumbling down on to the grass I would rest my chin on my hands, and watch while Mary plucked the blossom from the trees and made a garland for her hair. It was the perfect adornment for her pink cheeks and golden hair

In the warm evenings as the red brick of the house glowed pink in the setting sun, we would watch as the men working in the fields returned to their homes. At dusk, the bats swooped around the old eaves of the manor, and Mrs

Orcharde, wiping her hands on her apron, would hobble out to the churchyard and call to us to come into our beds. The more impatient she became, the more Mary laughed, and I did too, happy to follow my sister in the game. We would hide in the grass and stifle our laughter or crouch behind one of the gravestones. If we were unlucky, John Thorley, the rector of St Andrew's, would stride out of the church at that very moment, and our game would be up.

● ●

To everyone's relief, Dame Margot settled into the manor, and her fine horses were sent down from Blickling. As long as she was able to canter out across the daisy-strewn meadows, she was content as she could ever be. Mother was also content, and when home from court would walk the short distance to the market square to buy ribbons and feathers from the travelling merchants. Although it was far from the excitement of court, she enjoyed the novelty of having her fashionable clothes admired. In fact, she delighted in telling the women which colours the queen's ladies were wearing at court and which trimmings to buy.

● ●

Father was away a great deal, either at court or over-seeing the work at Hever. He had employed a great many people to work on the building, mostly from the surrounding villages, and thankfully due to a dry summer, the work was proceeding well. When he did return home, he would busy himself repairing the old wood mill, and we would sit nearby on the steps of the stone well and watch as he held the nails between his teeth. He planned to export wood up to London and start a small business via the River Roach. I can see him now, sweat on his brow, as he hammered away. He liked physical work for he said it took his mind off his financial concerns and gave him an outlet for his nervous energy. He would have been ill-tempered to know that Mary, Thomas, and I had been playing on the roof of the mill, but he never caught us.

With his duties at court, it seems he was forever running between the three places, but he had a tremendous amount of stamina, needing little sleep. He told us how the king was most interested in his project at Hever, and had graciously agreed to visit when next hunting in the Weald. This made Mother excited, and she consulted the king's own gardener at Windsor Castle, Master Chapman, for advice on the best place to site her strawberry beds, orchards and arbours.

In the late autumn, my mother returned to court only to find a great sickness raging again in London, and Princess Katherine in bed with a fever and stomach pains at Durham House. She dismissed all but her closest ladies. Was it the plague? Mother said the king did not wait to find out. As the hunting season was underway, he and his courtiers fled. Travelling from lodge to lodge, he escaped to the open spaces of the countryside far away from the foul air of London. We heard how he kept the prince close to him, allowing him to ride, but not hunt. While out, he was informed of urgent business requiring his attention on the Isle of Sheppey, and he quickly took a barge up the Thames. Staying a few days at Sheppey, he decided not to return to the palace at Greenwich but instead, crossed the water to Sheerness. The king and his courtiers were coming to Essex!

● ●

'You might have warned me – we are not prepared.'

My father threw his bonnet onto the table, as I gazed down from behind the wooden rails of the upper gallery.

'And how, Mother, was I supposed to know? Can I divine the weather?'

Dame Margot peered out of the window at the boisterous crowd in the courtyard and muttered. Torrential rain poured down like spears from Heaven as she rubbed frantically at the steamed up glass.

'His Grace is passing through,' continued my father, 'and ended up caught in this foul storm. He wants rest for his horses, wine and a piss-pot. Nothing more. Nan, Mary, stay where you are out of the way and do not come down.'

He glanced across as my mother rushed in through the side door. Her cloak, heavy with rain, clung to her, and wet grass soiled her boots.

'Dear Lord above, I am drenched,' she laughed, removing her green cap and tidying up her damp, straying hair. 'Fresh bread has not long been baked over in the bakery, and I have told Mrs Cleary to lay cold meats, fish, and cheese out immediately on the long table in the Great Hall. There is wine, good wine, in the cellar. Hannah! Quickly, girl, take my cloak. And light the sconces, it is gloomy in here.'

As she spoke, the iron-studded door flew open with a cold blast of wind and rain, and a crowd of laughing men and barking dogs tumbled into the hall, accompanied by the smell of sweat and horseflesh. I sat on the staircase peeping through the wooden rail and stared down at the richly dressed courtiers assembled below. Feathers on bonnets dripped and drooped onto thick fur collars spiked with rain. My mother and Dame Margot swept to the ground, as my father bowed low.

A tall, sparse man stepped forward. 'I am more grateful than I can say, Lady Bullen,' he said.

My mother kissed the proffered ring and Mary grabbed my arm.

'*Look*, it is the King,' she whispered. 'See the rich sables around his shoulders.'

I stared at the man as he smiled. What teeth he showed were black, and, under his now ruined velvet bonnet, his face appeared long and hollow-cheeked. However, although his wet hair fell grey and sparse, with his mouth pursed he was not an uncomely man. Once he might have been well-favoured. Could this be the ogre whom Mrs Orcharde said ate wicked children who refused to go to their beds? The ogre glanced around and shook the rain from his furs like a bedraggled dog shaking its coat. A page moved forward and handed him a goblet of spiced wine. He drank a little from the cup and placed it back on the platter.

'A good day we had of it until now,' he said, wiping his hand across his mouth. His voice sounded mellow with a strange, unfamiliar accent.

'Aye, Your Grace,' said an elderly man, 'but I will be more at ease when you remove your wet cloak. It is not good for your chest to get damp.'

'Indeed, Dr Linacre,' said the king, unfastening the clasp from his heavy furs and placing them on the man's outstretched arms, 'indeed it is not.' He paused and looked up, his eyes narrowing.

'And who do we have there?'

I shrank back as every eye in the hall followed his gaze.

My mother stepped forward. 'My children, Your Grace – would it please you if they came before you?'

The king smiled. 'Why, Lady Bullen, you know I have a great fondness for little ones,' he said, as a chair was placed behind him. As he was sitting, the door opened letting in a great squall of rain, and a young boy, dressed in a grey coat of damask edged with lynx fur, blustered in. Behind him jostled a group of grinning young men, all vying to stand as close to him as possible. Courtiers stood aside and swept a bow to the boy as he strode forward, his wet face flushed red beneath his bonnet.

'Father! Father! I cannot find my best hound, Briar,' he wailed. 'Your man will have to go back for it. Will you order him now, Father, will you?'

The king raised a bony hand, and the boy snapped his small mouth shut. He stood appearing rather agitated and fit to burst. His father then beckoned towards Mary and me, and my mother gestured for us to come down the staircase. Neither of us was dressed in our best gowns, but plain Norfolk cloth of grey and blue. However, my hair, neatly braided in a long plait with a blue ribbon, was not in its usual state of disarray. We stepped forward until we reached the chair and curtsied. I raised my face to the cruel monster as it leant forward and placed a finger under Mary's chin.

'What an enchanting creature you have here, Elizabeth,' he said, turning to my mother.

She smiled proudly. 'Indeed, Your Grace, this is Mary, and the other child is Anne. We are also blessed with three fine boys –Thomas, George and Henry.'

'*Three* boys, you say? Ah, how fortunate you are,' came the wistful reply. 'You are indeed blessed. I miss my little Margaret now she is Queen of Scotland and gone from us. It is good to have the company of little ones, for they teach us to view the world through innocent eyes.'

My own eyes then met those of the King of England. They were dark blue, hooded and tired, and one seemed to bear a cast, but they were not unkind, for the skin around lay heavily wrinkled. His nose, large and arched like a hawk, accentuated his jutting chin, and he appeared very swarthy. His clothes were dark and elegant, with a brooch containing a portrait at the neck of his shirt. It glinted in the candlelight and was quite magnificent.

'Do you know who this is?' he asked, seeing me stare at the huge sapphires. I shook my head as, without warning, he reached out, picked me up and sat me on his bony knee. I could smell rancid breath and sweat as he tapped the brooch.

'This is my lady mother, the Countess of Richmond. She is the dearest person in the world to me, next to my son here. Will you come to my court, little one, to meet her?' He gently turned my cheek.

I stared up into his face and shook my head again.

'Does she not speak?'

A ripple of laughter filled the air.

'Ah, well, you have the darkest eyes I have ever seen,' he observed, 'like great pools of water. What mischief will you do with those, I wonder? What hearts will you break?'

Polite agreement filled the hall as the king put me down and stood, shaking his head in amusement. In an instant, his nobles surrounded him ready to do his bidding. I tugged his gown and, surprised, he bent down.

'I have a brooch, too,' I whispered.

He laid a hand on my head and smiled. 'Well, one day I would like to see it – one day when you come to my court. Come, Harry, we must eat. Mountjoy, Oxford – we will speak later. Lady Elizabeth, lead the way.' He turned to my grandfather Howard.

'Thomas,' he said, 'when you have recovered we must talk privately. I have a grave matter on my mind, and it will not give me peace. Night and day it disturbs me, and I must seek your advice.'

My grandfather bowed stiffly, gave a wince, and leaning heavily on a stick, followed the king through to the Great Hall.

• •

'Well, Father, what matter is on the king's mind?' asked my mother, placing a small dish of oranges on the table.

My grandfather glanced across to where I sat with Mrs Orcharde, Mary, Thomas and Hal. The logs crackled and spat in the fireplace as we played a clapping game.

'Oh, never mind old Mary, she is half deaf,' she said, little considering my curiosity or how my young ears strained to catch every word, even though I understood little.

'Tell me what was said, and for Heaven's sake sit down before you fall down. Look at you. Really, you are sixty years old and should not be jumping fallen trees on a spirited horse. You might have been killed. Now, what is this grave matter?'

My uncle entered the chamber and kissed my mother on the cheek. He picked out an orange from the silver bowl and began picking at the peel with his teeth. 'She is right, Father, you took a bad fall.' He spat a piece of peel down onto the rush mat.

My grandfather pulled out a chair and lowered himself into it, impatiently beckoning the serving boy to bring over a stool. With his foot up he gave a great sigh. 'The damned animal put its hoof in a rabbit hole, no more, no less,' he said, avoiding Mother's searching eyes.

'Anyway, Katherine is the grave matter.'

'The princess?'

He nodded and shifted position.

'As you are too well aware, the Princess Katherine's mother has died. Before she died, she did everything in her power to ensure the Princess would become the bride of Prince Henry. You could say she and King Ferdinand forced our own king's hand, although neither party wants the Anglo-Spanish treaty destroyed, for it is essential for trade and England must have Spanish protection.'

'So, this marriage to Henry and peace with Spain will be a good thing,' said Mother, brightly, moving closer. 'As you say, we must keep the friendship of Spain against the French, particularly if they ally themselves to Scotland.'

'Aye,' said my grandfather, 'for no man can harm England like King Ferdinand of Spain, and he knows it. Well, everything has its price, and if peace means King Ferdinand demands gold for the marriage settlement, so be it. I live in constant fear of another civil war, as does the king and council, and any unrest in the realm risks an uprising from the blasted Yorkists, Irish and Scots.'

'Thomas tells me,' said Mother, glancing at her brother, 'that on the council, Fox is very pro-Spain, and as such will carry the Staffords, Poles and Greys with him.'

'Indeed,' said my grandfather, 'but His Grace is deeply troubled. He fears in his conscience that Katherine should not marry her dead husband's brother. He says it is a sin in the eyes of God, which, of course, it is. It is written in Leviticus.'

'But is it not written in Deuteronomy that the wife of the deceased should not marry another, but his brother should take her up and continue his line?'

The company stared at my mother.

'My God, since when did you become a cleric?' asked her brother, with a laugh. 'I've never read scripture, nor ever will and by Christ's blood I'm not afraid to admit it.'

My mother turned to face him. 'Well, I have a good grounding in theology as you well know. Anyway, it is quite ridiculous. The princess swears on the Blessed Sacrament that she did not consummate her marriage with Prince Arthur. She is a maid, still. And besides, the pope has granted a dispensation allowing the marriage to go ahead. Since he speaks for God what is there to fear?'

'No – the pope speaks for himself, Elizabeth,' said my grandfather. 'By granting a dispensation, he is ensuring that any heir of the future English monarch will be a friend of the pope and support him in his wars, else be a self-professed bastard not entitled to the crown. Besides, God and the pope are not on the council, Archbishop Warham is, and he denies the power of the pope to grant a dispensation. Well, he and Fox are heading for a major quarrel, and it will not be breached. Fisher refuses to be drawn.'

'And what is one man?' asked my uncle, popping a piece of orange into his mouth.

'One man now, the rest of the country later,' said my grandfather. 'Warham has planted the seed in His Grace's mind and, as a scholar and a divine, His Grace respects him.'

'But the pope is above ordinary men, including such councillors,' said Mother, rising from her chair to plump up the bolster behind him. 'I still do not understand what there is to fear.'

My grandfather gave a wince of pain as he sat back. 'I have told you. The truth – and the fact that any future heir might be proved illegitimate.'

'Preposterous! Who would ever say such a thing?'

'My own interfering wife for one.'

'Lady Agnes?' asked my uncle, raising a brow. 'Why

surely not?'

'Very amusing, but you know too well how she refuses to keep quiet, being an intimate in Katherine's bedchamber. As the first lady of the household, she should know better than to gossip, and repeat to anyone who'll listen, how Katherine was Arthur's true wife. If this new marriage goes ahead, it will be seen, on a political level, how the Howards, at present at least, do not agree with this marriage and are ranked openly against the king, the Nevilles, Percys, Poles and Courtneys.'

My mother opened her mouth to speak.

'No, Elizabeth, I *know* what Katherine swore to the council, and I know what rumours my wife is spreading. Agnes thinks we have nothing to lose, Ferdinand everything. He wants his two hundred thousand scudos and England's friendship, and urges Katherine to be a dutiful daughter and marry quickly. God knows what lies he has made the princess swear to. But the king cannot afford for any shadow to fall over his son's future. I tell you this and mark it well. If Prince Henry marries Katherine, His Grace fears the whole matter will come back to haunt him like a phantom. And I agree with him. It is an unnatural act – and it is a mess.'

My mother placed her hand on my grandfather's sleeve. 'Come now, the king sees demons where there are none. These are an old man's fancies conjured up in the dead of night. Let the prince have his princess and the world rejoice, including us. What possible concern can it be of ours who he marries?'

'Do not play the fool, Elizabeth. You know very well it is of Howard concern,' said my grandfather, 'for, having the ear of the princess, the Staffords are placed even closer to the throne. Buckingham's kin is in the innermost royal circle, and since they hate the Howards, it will go badly for us.'

'So, agree to the marriage,' said my uncle, with a shrug. 'Do as Mother bids and keep your fears to yourself.'

'Father,' said Mother, 'the loyalty of the Howards is no longer in question, and you will get the dukedom back, regardless of any interference from the Staffords.'

My uncle laughed, still chewing the orange. 'By God, we will, I promise you. All we require is time, a new order – and patience.'

My grandfather rose stiffly, and as Mother passed him his stick, he paused and looked across to where we sat.

My uncle stopped chewing and followed his gaze.

'Well,' he said, his face thoughtful. 'every dog has its day. One day there will be a court full of ambitious young Bullens with Howard blood – this much I can also promise. And then we will see. Then we will see.'

∗ ∗

The April wind had dropped, and the climate turned mild as we travelled west to our new home. Mrs Orcharde sat in the cart with Hal, and Thomas trotted beside her on his favourite cob. Father explained that Hever Manor, once a fortified farmhouse bought by my great-grandfather, had been improved by my grandfather, who decided to keep the moat, the gatehouse keep and the curtain wall, giving the appearance of a castle. Unfortunately, making it more habitable proved difficult due to the plague, since any workmen returning from the infection in London were ordered to stay away, thus delaying the work. Now though, it was complete and once more we were on the road.

'Kent is rich in produce with good grain and barley,' said my mother as we rode. 'The fine fruit here is much sought after, and I expect the orchard I have planned will do very well in the warmer climate. Better than at Rochford with its damp mists. Do you not agree, Thomas?'

My father trotted up to her side with Mary behind, arms firmly around his waist. 'I do, Eliza and, God willing, we will have more than enough for our purposes.'

'I hear there is a goodly fair held on St Mark's day at Eaton Bridge, selling wool and other such stuffs,' said Mother, pulling our lazy horse up sharply as it stumbled on the rough track.

'Aye, quality cloth, Elizabeth,' said Father, turning to see Dame Margot trotting up behind. Her lips were pursed as her spirited grey mare, frustrated by the short rein, threw its head impatiently up and down.

'Well,' she said, bringing her stick down on her mare's flanks, 'I am told Kent wool is of an inferior quality to our Irish wool, and the cloth not cheap to buy. Still, I am sure cost will not be of the slightest concern,' she said with a sniff, glancing at my mother. 'I imagine Kent will be inferior in many ways to Ireland. I liked Ireland. Ireland suited me very well.'

'Well, Mother, it is better to be with family, and I am sure you will find something to your liking.'

'Will I?' came the icy reply.

We trotted on in silence, passing vineyards which, come September, would hang heavy with grapes, and I watched as the sunburnt women tied the curling vines to the wooden poles.

'We will carry on to Eaton Bridge,' said Father, 'and try and avoid the marsh at Parson's Hole. We are not far off now.'

Half an hour later, he kicked his horse forward and, turning in his saddle, took off his bonnet and wiped his brow. 'Well, Elizabeth – Mother,' he said proudly, throwing out his arm, 'there it is. There is our new home.'

We halted our horses and gazed into the distance.

Dame Margot narrowed her eyes. 'It is not what I would call a manor – more like a castle.'

There, nestling amidst great oak trees, woodlands and rolling grassland was indeed a small castle, with a portcullis and a moat. Painted in pale yellow ochre, it made for a warm, inviting appearance. However, here there were no great towers or old-fashioned wooden shutters, but a house boasting the finest glass-paned windows. To the right stood a pretty, grey stone church and a man, gazing in curiosity at our convoy, stopped his digging. As people began to hurry towards our party, I smiled at Mary. We had arrived at our new home.

'It pleases you, Elizabeth?' asked my father.

I stood holding my sister's hand, wrinkling up my nose at the smell of new timber, plaster and paint.

'Oh, Thomas, very much.'

He kissed her cheek as she continued.

'It is lovelier than I could ever have imagined. Do you not agree, children?'

Father gave a satisfied smile and glanced across to his mother as she flounced through the door.

She refused his offer of wine and instead ran her fingers along the window ledge.

'Brick dust,' she muttered under her breath, 'bad for the lungs but, I'll admit, the artisans have excelled themselves.'

She was right, for the Great Hall had been painted with the most beautiful, intricate patterns making a bright array of colour.

'Come, let us continue.'

We entered the dining hall, and I gazed up at the windows bearing the Bullen heraldry, at the great fireplace, and the large Dutch sideboard. Mother immediately began opening its doors, most anxious to put her silver and pewter plate on display as soon as possible.

On the upper floor, Mary and I entered a small chamber with a fireplace. Father walked over to the window and peered out.

'See – I did not forget, Elizabeth – your strawberry beds are down there to the left.'

My mother laid her hand on his arm. 'Oh, Thomas,' she said, 'so they are – and there are my fruit trees. We shall have a splendid crop.'

'Now,' said Father steering her out of the door, 'let me show you the Long Gallery. It is a marvel of space and light, fit for every manner of entertaining.'

'Oh, but where is Margot?' asked Mother turning round.

Father shrugged. 'Probably looking for Thomas. That or

gone to find fault with my design of the new stables.'

*   *

Hever Manor was the perfect place to raise children, for it was a comfortable family home, with a pretty stone bridge over the moat. It was built around an inner courtyard, and the heavy ivy tangled itself around the brickwork, and dark green moss embedded itself in the cobbled stones. Behind the manor, there was a rose garden, a herb garden, a medicinal garden, and a garden full of gooseberries, barberries, sweet wild strawberries, mulberries, and fruit trees. In the cool dairy, we made our soft, curd cheese and we had fine stables and a slaughterhouse. We also had a laundry, a buttery, a brewery and a stillroom, and from the bakehouse the smell of warm, fresh bread wafted each morning through the windows.

Our estate workers and servants, numbering about fifty, lived in their own dwellings and took care of all our needs. Ducks, geese and hens wandered freely over the stone bridge and into the courtyard, much to my mother's annoyance, as she hated their clucking and squawking. She was much in fear of birds, and only allowed Mary and me to have a linnet on condition it never left its cage. Mary felt sorry for the poor creature, but George thought its pitiful chirps and futile fluttering highly amusing. He would gurgle with delight and point in wonder whenever a feather floated down between the bars.

*   *

While Mother was away at court, Dame Margot was supposed to watch over us, but she was always lax, and usually irritable. I know she preferred Mary to me, allowing her to behave as she wanted, without a care. Perhaps she saw her own dark, Irish wildness in me and did not like it. Or perhaps it was because we both had the same disfigurement. I know not. Either way, she spoiled Mary with candied fruit and called her 'my perfect, honey maid' and other such endearments. Mary was her favourite, and knowing this I would sulk, and become difficult. Thus, Dame Margot liked me even less. She would not tolerate any noise or the sound of screeching, particularly in the afternoon when she took her rest. Since the death of grandfather William, we often heard her sobbing in her chamber, and I suppose she missed him.

For our lessons, Father employed a governess, Mrs Margaret Geddynge, to teach the basics in reading, writing and the Bible. She also taught the children of the Duke of Buckingham, a short ride away at Penshurst Manor, and we were fortunate to have her patience. I thought she was pretty for a governess, with her auburn red curls escaping from her coif and fine green eyes that twinkled when she laughed. I gather from estate gossip that the duke found her rather comely, too. Mrs Geddynge taught me that there could be no good governance without service to God first. I must also pray to the Holy Virgin, and read only of virtuous lives. In fact, the very first book she gave to me was called 'The Golden Legend' and I never tired of hearing about the lives of the saints. I have it with me still after all of these years.

When barely five years of age, I was expected to stand on a chair in front of her and recite faultlessly in Latin, the psalms, the Paternoster, the Gloria and the Nicene Creed, which I did with ease. I delighted in learning my Bible because a good knowledge of scripture, I was told, was central to my education. I practised my letters of the alphabet by writing them out on my hornbook, again and again, and repeated simple words in French. I quickly began to develop an ear for the language, for both my parents spoke fluent French to Thomas, Mary and me as often as possible. However, Mary proved lazy in using her mind, but she was far from a dullard. She would gaze out of the window, dreaming of brave knights, and curl the tendrils of her hair between her fingers as she watched the rabbits hop in the grass. The slightest thing would distract her from her books, but she cared not a jot.

• •

The following January, an unseasonably warm wind blew across the estate, and several workers fell sick. Mrs Orcharde, abed over the Twelfth Night revels with a fever and cough, began to recover, but Thomas and I soon took the same symptoms. A week later, one still grey afternoon, my little brother Hal fell ill too. A fever wracked his body, followed by chills, but no matter how much Mother wrapped him in red flannel and placed him by the kitchen fire, he lay listless and pale. She tried to make him swallow wild cherry and hyssop syrup to ease his chest, but Hal dribbled it out with a wail of misery. Mrs Orcharde then suggested catnip and vervain tea to ease his fever, but to no avail, and my mother could not quieten his cries. For four days and nights, she and Mrs Orcharde sat with him, trying herbs and linctus, but it was clear that even lungwort and thyme were failing. My mother, fearful from experience, bent over the little body and sobbed. Hal, listless, would not take the soothing honey water, and so on the fifth day, Dame Margot roused herself.

'The physician is on his way,' she said, putting on a clean apron. 'Hannah, take the girls out and Nan – cease your *infernal* coughing, you are shredding my nerves. Stay below until you are called.'

The girl hurriedly took my hand as we were shooed down the staircase.

In the inner hall, Mary, Thomas and I sat for what seemed like an age, until Mrs Orcharde joined us, wringing her worn hands, and still blowing into her kerchief. It must have been an hour later when the silence broke, and the main door flew open with a great gust of wind.

Sorrel burst into frantic barking as the physician, followed closely by the family chaplain, Richard Davy, entered, stamping their muddy boots on the rush mats. Our servants hurried forward to take off their cloaks, and one of them

kicked Sorrel, who growled and wandered over with a re-
signed whine. He sat on my foot with a heavy sigh, resting
his head on his paws. Blinking up at me with his huge brown
eyes and furrowed brow, he knew that something was amiss.

Finally, Mother called for us to come up to the chamber
and I dutifully followed behind Mary and Thomas. As she
opened the door I smelt the oppressive, stale air and, on
Mother's bed, saw Hal.

Grandmother moved forward, tears in her eyes and sank
to her knees by the bed. 'God forgive him. Oh, God forgive
him, he is not here,' she whispered. 'My son is not here.'

Hal appeared to be very still as Mother threw herself
onto his little body with a wail, her face crumpled in grief.
'Ah, my little lamb,' she moaned, smoothing his brow. 'Oh,
my darling boy, my little one, hush now, I am here.'

I stood silent, watching the confusing scene.

Eventually Mother, her face tear-stained and distraught,
rose up. 'Say goodbye to your brother, children,' she whispered, between choking sobs.

Mary moved first and leant towards the still bundle on
the bed. She kissed the smooth cheek, as Thomas stared
sullenly at his shoes.

'Anne, say goodbye to your little brother. He is no more,
but gone to God.'

I jumped at the voice. It was Dame Margot. I moved
forward and looked at Hal. What did she mean? He was still
lying on the bed. I could see him.

'Nan, do as you are told!' my grandmother snapped.

'No!' In a fit of temper, I ran out of the chamber and
down the stairs, snapping the strap of my shoe in my haste. I
stumbled into the walled garden, disturbing the black rooks
as they huddled waiting for scraps of food. Sliding my back
down the crumbling brick wall, I crouched on the path,
oblivious to the spiders in the ivy and soiled myself. No one
came to find me, and I sat alone.

Hal died in the fading winter light and was later buried

at Hever church with a posy of winter flowers. I was too young to understand why he was there, or to understand the finality of death, and it bothered me greatly. Was it not cold and lonely in the dark church? How long would he be in there?

Mary Orcharde sat in her chair inconsolable and cried out bitterly how God should have taken the old such as her, and not the innocent young. But the greatest grief was born by my father, who was at Eltham with the king. On his return, he railed at my mother asking why God had taken another boy, rather than Mary or me – useless girls. I was puzzled by his outburst and thought that Mary and I must have done something very bad. But I contented myself with the thought that when Hal came back, Father would no longer be cross and all would be well again.

Robert, William and now little Henry were all lost as infants. As a result, only Thomas and George remained to inherit the Hoo and Butler estates and were spoiled and cosseted according to their station.

● ●

The old king was near to death, first with a disease of the throat, and afterwards with a disease of the joints. It was April, and since London was rife with the plague, he returned by litter to his palace at Eltham, to be closer to his son. The world waited in suspense, but by June, to everyone's secret dismay, the king recovered and a great tournament was held at Greenwich to celebrate. The prince, not allowed to joust, waited impatiently for his time to come. But how long must he wait? King Ferdinand of Spain maintained a continuous stream of correspondence with him, and sent a message saying when the time was ripe he hoped the boy would ascend the throne, unopposed. Should it not be the case, Spain would come to his aid. Ferdinand promised he would even ride in person at the head of a vast army, for he said he loved the prince as a son.

Then, in December, great celebrations were held throughout England as the king's youngest daughter, Princess Mary, was married by proxy to Prince Charles of Ghent. Bonfires and beacons were lit at Eaton Bridge, Maidstone and Allington, and the processions continued for several weeks. We held our own celebrations, for my Aunt Alice married Sir Robert Clere, High Sheriff of Norfolk. The year finally ended on a note of great rejoicing.

Chapter Two

'My course is set.'

Hever and
Thornbury 1509-1512

The king was dead, as was my beautiful brother, Thomas. As the April wind blustered, shaking the daffodils and the spring buds, Prince Henry was carried in state, and my brother Thomas was carried to his grave. It was supposed to be a new start, full of promise, hope and life, for the soon-to-be-crowned king was not quite eighteen years old, and the most beautiful prince in Christendom. But for my family, it was a time of great grief as Thomas wasted away with a disease of the lungs. The light in my father's life, he withered away like a dry leaf, and my father was devastated. How could his boy be dead, his firstborn, the one he loved the most? Older now, I understood death, but it did not make the loss any easier, and a great sadness fell over the manor at Hever. As for my father, I caught his listless eyes staring out of the window, and he refused to go to the stables where Thomas's horse pined in its stall. The animal sought exercise, but was left instead to weave its head from left to right, bored and fractious. Father eventually had it destroyed. He could not even bear to have Thomas buried at Hever where his memorial would serve as a constant reminder of his loss, but instead had him interred at the church at Penshurst Manor. Now, only George could advance the family name, and he became my parents' darling.

It was a difficult time, and hard for my parents to be joyful. Not so the young king, for his father had left him unimaginable wealth, and he was at last free to do as he wished, especially with regard to Katherine. However, his guardian and grandmother, Lady Margaret, Countess of Richmond, ensured his council were more pro-French than Spanish, with more soldiers than clerics at the table. They would advise him with regard to his marriage, a matter he must not rush into. Although they were afraid of Ferdinand and his ships, they were still concerned about the legality of the prince marrying his brother's widow. However, King Ferdinand, through his letters, advised Prince Henry that he would be committing a far greater sin by abandoning his daughter, Katherine. Besides, the fear of displeasing God and being left childless was ridiculous! Why, the King of Portugal had married two sisters and enjoyed numerous offspring. Surely proof the argument was but a feeble one?

The headstrong young prince readily agreed, for he saw himself as a noble and pious knight, the rescuer of the abandoned widow treated so shabbily by his father. He wanted the Spanish princess, Katherine, for himself, and no man was going to advise him otherwise. Besides, his sister Mary adored Katherine and encouraged him even further.

* *

On the morning of the eleventh of June, as pink clouds scudded across the sky, the Prince married his princess in a secret ceremony at the Observant Friar's Chapel in Greenwich. It was the most private ceremony possible, with no officials present, and it left the terrified council no choice but to agree to a public ceremony. In the following furore, the prince boasted he was now his own master and cared not a jot what others thought. How could they complain when he had only obeyed his father's wishes? Besides, Katherine had sworn an oath that she and Arthur had not consummated their marriage. His grandmother, Lady Margaret, remained sceptical and severely reprimanded the friars for their involvement in the matter, fearful that some dreadful event might occur, dispensation or not.

After the marriage, my parents attended the coronation on a perfect summer's morning. As the great procession passed through London, cannon roared, and bells rang out. Mother told me how the crowds shouted and cheered for joy, jostling for any space they could squeeze into, and hanging low out of window embrasures. The girls, blushing in delight, threw down summer roses, blew kisses and chanted 'We want Harry!' as the new king passed, winning hearts with his dazzling smile. The city blazed in a riot of colour and the plaster initials 'H' and 'K', along with the symbols of Tudor roses and Spanish pomegranates, festooned the triumphal arches from Westminster to Charing.

As the Archbishop of Canterbury crowned this beautiful young man, it was like a new dawn. Unlike his thin, ailing old father, this lusty king shone like the sun, a breath of fresh air. Jousts and a coronation banquet followed, sparing no expense, but it was also a time of sadness, for within a week the new king's beloved grandmother lay dead. Some said she had died of shock at the secret wedding ceremony, but most agreed she had eaten too heartily of a cygnet and drunk a surfeit of Rhenish wine.

●   ●

Summer brought forth new hope for my own grieving family, for the new king wanted to be amused, and cast around for those pleasing to him. It was not long before my father attracted his attention. At the coronation, the king created him a Knight of the Bath and then Squire to the Body. The king also competed with him tirelessly in the tiltyard, for my father was a competent jouster as well as highly skilled at tennis, bowls and cards. A natural linguist, he spoke French and Latin better than anyone else at court and the king knew this able man might be of use. Appointed Keeper of the Exchange at Calais and the Foreign Exchange in England, at thirty-two years old, my father's star was rising. But he was not popular with some of the other courtiers, for his tongue and wit were cruel, and he did not have the natural dignity of such nobles as Worcester, Dorset or Suffolk. He was also easily swayed by stronger men such as my Uncle Howard. Easily bullied himself, I think that is what made him harsh on servants and those he thought of as lowly in station.

My mother, meantime, continued at court in attendance as lady-in-waiting to Queen Katherine. With her striking looks, she was where she most wanted to be, at the centre of one of the most exciting courts in Europe. Witty and full of vitality, everyone noticed her, including the king, who found her captivating. There were even some who hinted she enjoyed his company too much, but she cared not a fig for jealous gossip. She delighted in the attention and, wishing to be accommodating to the king, my father turned a blind eye to her flirtatious ways. Besides, it meant nothing for the king was deeply in love with his perfect new wife.

* *

Even though the fire blazed in the great fireplace, it felt chilly as we sat one April afternoon in the Long Gallery at Hever. I was eleven years old, and my parents were home from court. Mother deftly plied her needle, the silken thread dangling from her mouth, Mary sat reading, and George practised on the spinet. It was painful to listen to him as he repeated over and over the same tuneless piece, but Mother said he must not be discouraged. In fact, since the death of

Thomas he could do no wrong, and soon he would be going
to court as a pageboy and take part in the entertainments. I
wished I could go. I wanted to see new places and new people,
and I felt restless and bored. Kneeling on the window seat, I
gazed into the distance at the spire of St Peter's church. The
rain rattled noisily against the window pane and, combined
with the strident chords of George's playing, woke Dame
Margot from her nap. She walked into the gallery, a woollen
cloak draped across her shoulders, and sat by the fire.

'Thomas, the Queen is not recovering,' said my mother,
glancing at her. 'There is concern for her welfare. We ladies
at court are at a loss as to what to do.'

My father did not raise his eyes but continued reading.
'Well, the loss of Westminster Palace has hit us all badly,
especially the queen. Such fine tapestries and paintings
destroyed. I gather the fire broke out in the kitchens and
the Lord Steward threatened to hang himself if the culprit
was not found. Her Grace has lost personal letters, belongings, and –'

'Thomas, it is not the loss of the palace, but her baby
boy. It is losing her child that grieves her.'

He looked up. 'Do not forget I was a pallbearer at his
funeral. It was not easy for me, thinking of my own sons and
what might have been. But she is young, Eliza, and more
boys will follow.'

'You are right, of course.'

'Indeed I am. Why, this king is as strong and hearty a
prince as ever lived, scattering his seed throughout the realm
on girls who have barely reached maturity. No maid is safe.'
His voice dropped to a whisper. 'I gather Bessie Bryan is but
twelve and with child by him.'

'Thomas, please, the children are present, and besides,
such rumour is tittle-tattle. The king is much enamoured
of his queen, and I gather such boyish pranks are not to be
openly discussed.'

'Well, open or not, it is discussed among certain people

how this Bessie's mother is five hundred pounds better off for raising such a docile girl. A fortune for a moment's pleasure.'

'Fie,' said my mother. 'We try and keep such matters from the queen, for she is secretly unhappy with her husband's dalliances, particularly his prowling after the Duke of Buckingham's younger sister. You know what a storm that caused. The proud duke saw such attention as an insult, not an honour. The king flew into an indignant rage with the queen for believing everything she was told, and hotly denied the scandal. He was so furious he ordered all the ladies-in-waiting present to be turned out on to the street for scandalmongering.'

Dame Margot laughed out loud.

'Oh, for the love of Heaven,' said Father, 'the king does not like to be found out with his fingers in the pie. He was also angry with the damned duke for daring to interfere with his amorous adventures.' He paused.

'Is the queen sick in body?'

'No, Thomas, the sickness is in her heart and soul. She is constantly on her knees praying and barely eats. She drinks tansy infusions in the hope of conceiving, and prays at night to dream of juniper berries as a good omen. It is pitiful to watch.'

My father grunted. 'Tansy infusions, juniper berries, nothing but old women's fancies. And the woman is naïve. No, she knows her duty – she must stir herself from her apathy and raise her husband to lust.'

My brother continued to thump out the discordant notes, oblivious of the conversation. *Plink, plink,* tuneless *plink.*

Kneeling on a cushion on the window seat, I pressed my nose against the cold windowpane. '*L – u – s – t,*' I said slowly, spelling the letters out. My warm breath made the glass steam a little as I traced the letters with my finger.

'Marry, it is over a year ago, and this sort of grieving is unChristian,' said Father, putting down his papers. 'Your poor brother Charles has not long been in his grave, but you showed dignity and bearing. Why, when you lost my boys, you did not blow away like a dandelion puff, though God knows the pain was great. No, Howard women are strong and know their duty. Katherine's business is to give the king heirs – nothing else should concern her. Her son has died, barely two months old and yes, I am sorry, for England must have stability and a prince. God knows we cannot have a return to anarchy.'

'As in Scotland,' said my mother, folding her embroidery, 'why, look at Queen Margaret. The poor young girl has not had a single babe survive, one after the other dead – three less than a year old.' She began to sort her silks, for she and the queen's ladies were busy making badges for the coming French invasion.

'Well,' she continued, 'let us pray the babe she now carries survives. Mary, come and help me.'

My sister eagerly joined her for she loved to sort the different colours of thread, and showed a fair talent for needlework.

'His Grace is much preoccupied,' said my father, 'If it is not Spain causing him damned grief, it is France. Emperor Maximilian, King Louis, King Henry, the pope, King Ferdinand – all of them – formed the League of Cambrai against Venice and Milan to prevent them from expanding their territories. Now, King Louis wishes to expand *his* territories and has attacked Venice, committing terrible atrocities. The League of Cambrai has fallen apart, and it concerns the Holy Father greatly.'

'How?'

'How?' repeated Father. 'Because King Louis might conquer the pope's other territories in Italy. King Ferdinand of Spain does not want Louis stealing his own land in Italy; neither does Emperor Maximilian want France rummaging unchecked through Europe. As for old Louis, he has a lust for domination – he has his eye on Milan next.'

'But where does that leave our king?'

'Well, you might ask. King Henry is young and vain-glorious, and it has been easy for his father-in-law, along with Queen Katherine, to encourage him to join them in defending the pope in a new alliance – 'The Holy League.' He has written to the pope declaring, by force of arms, how England will teach Louis to hold his ambitions in check and drive the French from Italy. Pope Julius has taken the title of Most Christian King away from Louis, reconciled himself to Venice, and given his kingdom to our own king. France is now seen as England's enemy and the enemy of Christendom. Our king sees himself as the pope's defender and cannot refuse such a holy war. He is bent on glory, whatever the cost, and has nominated himself the pope's own champion.'

My mother wound the thread around Mary's out-stretched hands. 'But to attack the pope's authority is un-thinkable,' she said, shaking her head.

'Indeed, but the pope is grasping and licentious,' said my father. 'Queen Katherine and her father reminded our own king that he ought to reclaim his ancient title of "King of the French", and take back what he considers to be his French lands, proving himself another King Henry V. His Grace longs for another Agincourt and to be taken seriously as a power in Europe. We want it too, except for those fumbling old fossils he inherited from his father on his council.'

Mother smiled.

'No, the king is bent on spending his massive fortune on war, and who is to gainsay him? Which of his friends want to stand against him? Not I.' He shuffled his papers together.

'Well, it is natural for a young man to have such friends,' said Mother. 'Men such as my Howard brothers – particularly Edward, whom you know he favours the most – or Compton, Brandon, Carew, and Neville. They are reckless, daring young blades who hunt, compete at the lists, and are always at his side.'

'Your brother Edward is a man of soundness, but as for Edmund, I have never known a more embittered young man. But who is to blame the king? Kept a prisoner by his paranoid father, not able to go out but by his leave? No wonder he wants to break free of restraint and prove his might.'

Mother narrowed her eyes as she rethreaded her needle. 'What say you of this new man, Thomas Wolsey? I gather he has been appointed Prebendary at York Cathedral.'

'Indeed, Eliza, but he has his eye on far higher things yet.'

'He seems very active in the king's cause. I hear he takes on the work of a hundred men to give the king his wishes.'

My father laughed. 'Wolsey would piss for the king if he could, and has far advanced in favour since he began his career as the last king's chaplain. He seems to have a genius for administration. As royal almoner, he has been intent this past year on building ships at the new dockyards in Woolwich and Deptford to give the king more power for his war. And war will come, you'll see. No, Wolsey, now he is on the king's council, has pushed for this war, for he knows it is what the king wants, and he, like his master, is an adventurer.'

George, to everyone's blessed relief, finished playing and wandered over to Mother. She stroked his nut-brown, curling hair as he stood by her knee, and brushed it tenderly from his eyes.

'Your father, Elizabeth, hoped to become the king's chief advisor, but Wolsey has bullied him down, and Surrey accepts he has lost to him. Fox and Ruthal want an Anglo-French peace, but Wolsey will have none of it. He has pledged to raise over sixty thousand pounds himself for this war and has seduced the king into thinking it is better for him to handle the tedious details and mindless, petty bureaucracy while the king takes the glory.'

Father stared out at the blustery weather. 'Irresistible.'

'It is interesting,' said Mother, handing Mary more thread, 'how Wolsey is actually overtaking his mentor, Richard Fox, and yet Fox holds no grudge against him. A rare thing at court.'

'I can assure you there was nothing noble-spirited in that move. Fox by name and fox by nature, for no word is safe with him. He pushed for Wolsey to be on the council to support him against your father.'

'Well,' said Mother, 'as Lord Privy Seal, Fox might be the most important man on the council, but he is an old man in his sixties. His days of ambition are over, surely?'

'Possibly, but the king will still use his experience in the war against France and, more importantly, as his godfather, he trusts him. Fox will stir his creaking bones for one last blast of glory. But know this, Elizabeth. The king has the measure of Wolsey and his enormous capabilities, and it suits him to play when he wants and use where he will. Besides, Wolsey is convivial company. The king likes that, for they share a great love of architecture and art and he is very inventive. At present, he is working on some new entertainment from Italy – something called a masque. Councillors are bound to be jealous, but he never tires, never rests and is never anything but mild-mannered and affable. He is worth watching closely.'

Mother smiled at Mary as Father continued.

'Of course, men like Buckingham hate him for Wolsey is vain and his social inferior. The old king did not trust the duke and now he is richer than the Archbishop of Canterbury. But things are changing.' He leaned forward in his chair. 'In the future, Elizabeth, I am convinced that the king's council will not be dominated by only powerful nobles, but by clerics, lawyers and household men. This king respects ordinary, thinking men of talent, irrespective of title. Such men might rise to dignity and honour and fill the highest offices of state. In effect, leapfrog over hereditary rank and take the place of the nobility. Anything is possible, Elizabeth, and my way forward will be with hard work, reliability and some measure of talent.'

'Mother?' I turned around. The rain appeared to be

easing, and I yearned to go out and ride. I felt sick and tired of hearing of politics.

'Do not interrupt, Anne.'

I slumped down at my grandmother's voice, and picked up the book by my side, flicking distractedly through the pages.

'The king's great friend, Charles Brandon, admires Wolsey, and Wolsey admires him,' Mother continued.

'Of course he does. They are both base-born and shit sticks to shit,' came the reply.

My mother frowned and Father stared back.

'What?' he raised his eyebrows, 'the pride of the Howards – and you are wise to this being one of them – makes them hate Wolsey's base origins. Among the ambassadors, Wolsey is known as "the orb" and Brandon his "satellite".'

'Since when is he base?' asked Mother. 'His father managed lands and tenements aplenty and was a successful merchant. He could certainly afford to send his son to Oxford.'

'Well, I dislike him, and he dislikes me for my Howard connections.'

My mother appeared unconvinced.

'No, it is true, Elizabeth. Wolsey's support will further my aims so I will be civil to him and hide what I truly think. I do not intend making enemies. Watch him. The king is not weak, he is inexperienced, and Wolsey is the older man by eighteen years. Well, one day the young lion will outgrow the older dog – wait and see if he does not. But not yet, eh? No, if the almoner thinks to keep the king from meddling where he shouldn't meddle, what harm? Besides, your father is no innocent in this either.'

'Oh?'

'He has ingratiated himself with the young king and engaged him in such a course of play and idleness as to have rendered him quite negligent of affairs. As a result, he is willing to entrust the affairs of the state entirely to his ministers. Well, let the king have his grubby little distractions and leave business to them – to us.'

My mother glanced over. 'Anne, you will damage the spine of that book, bending the pages so. Sit still, it is unseemly to fidget in that manner.'

I did as she said with a frown.

'I must say, Thomas, I am glad you will be in the Low Countries on the king's business.'

'Well, let us hope for a better crossing than last time. I detest the narrow sea, and he knows it. It amuses him to hear of my green, retching face.'

'At least he pays you, my love.'

Father picked up his papers with a grunt. 'Not enough, for the new Spanish ambassador, Luis Caroz, receives five gold ducats a day from his master. Five gold ducats, I tell you. Anyway, I shall be leaving tomorrow evening. Please ensure Mrs Cleary has packed several of her special preserves for gifts.'

As he arose, he turned – the great sheath of papers under his arm – and ruffled George's hair.

'Anne, go out if you must, but Mary, attend to your lessons – I hear your French and Italian are not as good as they should be.'

Thus it was that my father, along with Dr Young, Dr Wingfield and Sir Edward Poynings, left home to proceed on his mission as ambassador of the king in the Low Countries.

● ●

Throughout the towns and villages of England, all talk was of the coming war, as men in every alehouse and bear pit discussed the thrashing of the French. Meanwhile, life at Hever continued quietly throughout those hot, lazy days and into the misty autumn. I rode out on my mare, Ciara, with Mary and George, cantering through the golden leaves that swirled around the manor gate, determined to find a new path or a secret way.

Although Ciara proved fast and wilful, I could handle

her with ease and had no fear of falling as I jumped the
crumbling stone walls. It felt good to feel the sharp air on
my cheeks as I galloped ahead, and try as she might, Mary
could never catch me. Although the eldest, she would end
up in tears, saying I was spiteful to leave her so. George was
not in the least bit bothered, and trotted behind, his legs
flying on his little brown mare. Sitting by the great weeping
willow, I would tease Mary for being a baby and skim stones
across the pond, ignoring her tears. If it was too wet to ride,
we stayed indoors, and Mary and I would set up the indoor
butts, shooting our bows the full length of the gallery. The
following year, George was deemed old enough by the law
to own his own bow and arrows, and I can still see the excitement in his eyes as my Uncle Edmund presented them to
him. Grinning in delight, George ran his fingers along the
supple wood of the bow and ran off to show the gardener.

● ●

It was early in July 1512 when a horse clattered into the
courtyard. One of our grooms steadied the skittish animal as
the messenger dismounted, and strode into the main hall. He
removed his velvet cap and revealed a head of thick, auburn
hair as he bowed low.

Mary pushed past me, in haste, on the staircase, and I
saw Mother receiving several letters. My sister smiled sweetly
at the messenger, as he bowed again and left the hall, and
moved to the window to watch him remount his horse.

Mother studied the seal on the first letter, opened it and
read the contents.

'Oh, it is from your father, in the Low Countries,'
she said. 'He tells me he has utterly charmed the Dowager
Duchess of Savoy and is having great success at her court,
in Mechelen. I see.' Her smile faded for a moment, for she
knew that my father could be utterly charming when he
chose to be. Perhaps she remembered when he used to be
charming to her.

'The king is so pleased with Thomas's handling of affairs that he has magnanimously granted him five manor houses as a reward.' Her eyes opened wide. 'Oh! But there is more,' she cried, turning to Mary. 'Your father has persuaded the Regent to have you placed at her court and join her young *demoiselles*! We are honoured, do you hear, Mary, honoured! What a magnificent opportunity this is for our family. Oh, wait till I tell Lady Wyatt.'

'But – but when is this to be, Mother? When am I to go?' Mary turned quite pale.

My mother appeared lost in thought. 'New gowns, you will have to have a wardrobe of new gowns – the best we can afford,' she said, perusing the letter again. 'Oh, this is such a stroke of good fortune!'

'But *when* will I have to go?'

Mother glanced at her in irritation. 'What? Well, I do not know, the details have not been finalised. It is up to your father.' She carried on reading. 'Oh, see, your father says the court is brimming with Burgundian princes, as well as the finest poets and artists in Europe. Did you hear, Mary? Princes.'

I listened as Mary remained silent and walked over to the stairs where she sat down on one of the steps.

Mother put the letter onto the table and opened the second.

'Well, what could be more exciting than that? Let us see.' There was a pause as she started to read. 'Ah, I thought as much. The moment Hannah brought in the honeysuckle I knew there would be a wedding. Why, George, there you are.' She turned as my brother walked in, a small piece of wood in his hands.

'Whose wedding, Mother?' I asked.

'Let me see first,' said George, pushing me out of the way. Mother held the letter above her head, laughing. 'It is my dear brother's wedding, your Uncle Thomas, and since you know his wife died recently – God rest her soul – he seeks another bride. He must have an heir and his new wife is to be Elizabeth, the Duke of Buckingham's eldest daughter.'

George groaned at the dull women's talk and, taking out a small knife from his pocket, began to whittle at the wood.

Mother walked over to the window. 'I heard talk but this is very sudden. Well, well – the Howards and the Staffords united – I wonder what your father will say of such a coupling? Edward Stafford holds a grudge against the crown for old debts, and as Constable of England, he is the highest noble in the land. Yet he takes on the air of a prince, and cares not a toss if he offends anyone.'

She opened the third letter and laughed with delight. 'Oh, how splendid. Your dear aunt, Lady Anne, has been safely delivered of a girl – Mary. The name suits very nicely and I am sure she is as adorable as your little cousin Madge. By the saints, we have indeed been blessed with good news this day.'

She looked up, her face thoughtful. 'Now, what on earth shall I wear for this wedding? It will have to be new… I shall have something made specially. As to the Court of Savoy! Such fortune! I cannot believe my daughter has a place there; I feel quite overcome.'

She handed the letters to me and hurried up the staircase, beside herself with excitement.

I stood alone, ignoring Mary.

'Will the Duke's house at Penshurst have sweet things to eat?' George yawned.

'I do not know. I expect so,' I said. 'It will be terribly important – and you are not to fidget at the ceremony.'

He pulled an indignant face. 'I will not!' he cried, 'I am nine years old, not a baby.'

He tugged my long plait, making me squeal.

Without warning, Mary burst into tears and ran from the hall, colliding with our governess.

'Stop this arguing this minute!' cried Mrs Geddynge, staring around in surprise as Mary flew past. She caught

George roughly by the sleeve of his shirt.

'Stop it! Really, what children you are. Nan, I am ashamed of you. What is this?' she muttered, snatching the letters. She read the first one, and I gave George an ineffectual push. He stuck his tongue out in response.

'Ah, now this will be a grand affair, and most interesting for this family,' said our governess, sitting down on the long bench, 'but I gather it will not be at Penshurst or Greenwich, for the duke has quarrelled with the king again. It will be at Thornbury, the duke's grand residence in Gloucestershire. As for young Elizabeth, *mes enfants,* I know a secret…' and with this, she tapped the side of her nose.

'What? Tell me now,' I demanded, glaring at George.

'Well,' she whispered, carefully looking around, 'I know in good faith that Elizabeth loves another, the duke's ward, young Ralph Neville. She cried so bitterly to her father that he tried to stop the match, but your Uncle Howard would have none of it, for Elizabeth comes with a grand dowry of two thousand marks. Well, the duke offered his other daughters, Catherine or Mary, but he would only have Elizabeth. She tried pleading but it was useless, and the duke gave way to pressure from your grandfather. Marry, Lord Thomas Howard is thirty-five years old and she, but fifteen.'

She turned to me. 'Poor child. She will go to her marriage loving another.'

Mistress Geddynge then rose and clapped her hands together. 'Well, let us leave this love prattle, she is to be wed, and there the matter ends.'

My mother returned and chided my governess for filling our young heads with scandal and gossip.

I turned to George as he proudly held up his piece of wood.

'Look,' he said, 'it's a bird – well, it will be when it's finished.'

I stared at the wood, screwing up my nose, thinking it looked more like a boat. Where were its wings?

'George, will you marry one day?'

He did not look up but grimaced, his curls falling over his eyes. 'No, I do not like girls – except you, of course. I would not mind marrying someone like you as you like to ride fast and can fight like a boy. As long as I can still have my mare I care not. Look, it's good, isn't it?'

I nodded as he held out the wooden shape as if it were flying and then ran off to the kitchen where he was sure of a treat from our cook, Mrs Cleary.

● ●

The wedding at Thornbury, in the West Country, was the first grand occasion that I attended. The journey took over a week, for the dirt tracks were appalling. Through Guildford, Newbury, West Swindon and the beautiful Kingswood forest we travelled with our escort, staying at religious houses in great comfort, for the good nuns provided us with ale, a warm bed and meat. I noticed that Mary appeared flushed and I wondered if she was ailing. She had been withdrawn and quiet after she had left the hall in tears, but had refused to say what the matter was.

When we arrived at the duke's gateway, I turned and stared in wonder at the tall windows set within three high storeys of crenellated brick. Surely this was a great castle? We clattered through the gatehouse, into the inner court-yard with its portcullis and shield of the Stafford family, and across the cobbles. Outside, the duke's men in their black and red livery ran up and took our horses' bridles, leading them to the stone steps. My mother, stiff from riding and in no mood for niceties, struggled with her long grey gown as she dismounted.

'By the mass,' she grumbled, 'the duke outshines the king himself. This is no home – it has become a fortress.'

She appeared genuinely shocked as she dismounted, and one of our escorts lifted me down, trying to avoid the deep puddles.

'Elizabeth!'

A tall, thin young woman came rushing down the steps, arms outstretched. It was Alianore, Duchess of Buckingham, and she was wearing the most beautiful blue gown I had ever seen. Its square neck, encrusted with blue stones, matched the blue lappets of her velvet hood and she smiled as we curtsied.

'Ah, how Mary has grown! Such a charming young lady.'

My sister smiled as I stood ignored and I wished George had been allowed to come instead of her, but he had stayed behind with a summer cold. As they chatted, I stared about in curiosity.

'I am sorry, Elizabeth, if your journey was tiresome and your head hurts, but we have experienced such unusual rain for late summer.'

The duchess laid a sympathetic hand on my mother's sleeve as we walked inside.

In my haste, I tripped on the step.

'How is Dame Margot? My husband says the old Earl of Ormond has retired from court as the queen's Chamberlain and Sir William Blount has accepted the post.'

Mother nodded. 'Indeed he has. Old Ormond can hardly move, and the queen has insisted he return home and enjoys his properties.'

The Duchess smiled. 'It is a great shame that my husband refuses to attend the court, at present,' she continued, 'but as you know, there has been yet another bitter disagreement. The king fears he is allying himself with the Howards through this marriage for some mischief, and broods over the power of the nobles, just as his father did. Ned feels slighted, saying we are as good as any Howard, or Tudor, and his hot temper will not let matters rest. Things between them are not cordial, hence we are celebrating the wedding here, rather than at court,' she added. 'He has still not forgiven the king for putting his younger brother in the Tower these three years past.'

My mother interrupted, excitedly. 'Oh, it will blow over,

my dear, do not fret, but listen, I have such news, Alianore, such wonderful news. Mary, our lovely girl Mary, has been granted a place with Her Imperial and Royal Highness, the Dowager Duchess of Savoy, at her court in Mechelen. She is to attend her as one of her *demoiselles* and live at the palace amidst nobles and princes. It is such an honour!'

'Oh, Eliza, did Thomas arrange this? Come, you must tell me every detail.'

* *

The long sleeves of my cream brocade gown were uncomfortably tight. As I fidgeted, I was also aware that the small, cream cap perched precariously on the back of my head might fall at any moment. With my long hair unadorned, I knew I appeared childish. Mary, on the other hand, a vision of elegance in a pale blue and silver gown, pearls woven into her fashionably crimped hair, looked divine. I felt jealous, for as usual, she was the centre of attention with everyone smiling upon her. I turned away and instead studied the colours in the paintings, the statues, and the beautiful tapestries not only on the walls but on the floor, the actual floor where people walked. Such extravagance! The magnificent flowers in front of the altar had even been fashioned into the shape of the Stafford shield and depicted the Stafford knot, the swan, the blue ermined mantle and the spotted antelope.

I glanced around and spied the Duke of Buckingham dressed in dark red velvet, embroidered with silver roses, talking to my Howard relatives. He was taller than the other men about him, florid of face and rather plump, but he smiled good-naturedly. The sound of a fanfare caused him to turn round, and six young boys with bunches of rosemary tied to their green sleeves entered the chapel. As they processed, they threw rose petals onto the turkey carpeted floor. A few moments later they were followed by a young man carrying a golden bridal cup. He faltered a little, smiled, and caught Mary's melting brown eyes. She smirked back at him from under her long lashes, and it was the nearest thing to a smile I had seen from her since leaving home. After the young man, came the musicians, playing their tabors and pipes, decked in wondrous shades of gold from rose to copper, and after them a host of young maids carrying bridal cakes and garlands of gilded wheat.

The preacher, Dr Manderville, walked down the aisle himself, and at the door of the chapel greeted the bride and groom. The young bride wore the most beautiful robe of grey tissue with a long, floating train, and I could smell her amber perfume wafting as gently as a blessing as she passed. She wore a silver circlet upon her flowing hair, which fell to her knees, but there appeared no smile on her trembling lips. I then looked at her groom dressed in russet brocade, his cap brimming with black feathers. A short, spare man with brown hair and a long, arched nose, his face remained, as always, inscrutable.

My mother nudged me. 'What say you, Nan? Is not my brother, our new Lord Treasurer, handsome?'

I said nothing for, in truth, I had always thought Uncle Thomas resembled the rats I had spied on the estate, sharp-faced and beady-eyed. He stared at me, his eyes as cold as a dead cockroach.

After the wedding, came the banquet, and I was quite overwhelmed by the sheer variety of the dishes, each produced on a solid silver platter. There were pastries with pine nuts and sugar, partridges, gilded calf heads, capons, pigeons, turtle doves, peacocks, and chicken soaked in rosewater. For something sweeter, pages served golden lemon and dandelion cream with apple wedges. To drink, I sipped 'Lamb's Wool'. Made of stewed apples, the heavily whipped cream floating on the surface gave it a woolly appearance, hence its name. With its spicy nutmeg and cinnamon flavour, I thought how much George would have loved it.

After everyone had eaten, the musicians struck up a chord, and the guests moved aside to watch my sister dance.

Although not smiling, she danced gracefully around the Great Hall with her partner, accompanied by the sound of viol, lute and rebec.

'Is she not delightful?' crowed Mother loudly, to anyone within earshot. 'She is going to the court at Mechelen. The regent has asked specifically for her since my Thomas is a *very* close and trusted friend.'

She must have said it twenty times, and I began to seethe even more with jealousy.

As the hours passed, I sat forgotten on a stool, plucking at the leaves of my herb posy, itching from my uncomfortable gown. As to Mechelen, wherever it was, it was unfair that Mary should be honoured so, even though she was the eldest. I was far more suited to such a position, for I was studious and my French more fluent. I pulled off my cap and sulkily watched the performing bear dance to the beat of a tabor. Not even its ridiculous yellow coat and jaunty red feathers made me smile.

At the end of the evening, amidst much lewd merrymaking, the bride and groom were led away to the bedchamber. However, as I pushed through the great tangle of revellers, I noticed that the bride appeared to be in tears.

'Why are you sad?' I touched her sleeve.

She leaned forward to kiss me amidst the urgent press of people, and I felt her wet cheek.

'Pray for me,' she whispered.

I was then pushed rudely aside as her new groom, laughing and jeering with his drunken friends, slammed the heavy oak door in my face.

❦ ❦

Back in our chamber, I found it hard to sleep. My thoughts jumped from jealousy over my sister one moment, and concern over Elizabeth's tears the next. The constant tossing and turning disturbed Mary, and she padded over to me. 'Why are you restless?'

'Because of Elizabeth,' I replied, only half truthful.

'What of her? I am the one who is to be sent away. It is *so* unfair.'

I turned to face her. 'Is it right that she should she be so unhappy on her wedding night?'

Mary shrugged. 'No, she should not be unhappy, for she is going to have knowledge of her husband, and he of her, and they are going to make a child. What is sad about that?'

'But she does not want him,' I half sat up.

'Oh, come now, Nan, he is not that hideous. He might have a bad temper, but he is fluent in French, is skilful at cards and gambling and has a very large –'

'Nose.'

'Manor,' she added. 'He is ambitious and, no doubt, will soon be rich which bodes well for us. As you understand quite well, the point of such a grand union is for the woman to produce sons. If she is really unhappy, she can always find her pleasures elsewhere.'

I frowned.

'What have I said?' asked Mary. 'As long as people are discreet it is of no matter. Once they have sons, Uncle Thomas will be at court and she will remain in the country. Her part of the arrangement is that she will have grand manors, gowns, jewels, fine things and children to take care of. That is the bargain brokered. You know that it is the way when noble families and princes marry.'

I thought for a moment. 'Are we noble?'

'Mother thinks so. You know a woman of such standing has no choice when it comes to marriage. It is far too important a matter. Her father decides, and there is an end to it.'

'Mary, our parents would not do such a thing, would they? I mean, Mother would not wish to see any of us unhappy, would she?'

'Unhappy, Nan? Unhappy? She appears to care nothing for my feelings thus far, sending me away to God knows where.'

I stared at her face and thought she might start to cry.

'Anyway, Nan – I do not intend to be married off against my wishes. Besides, Aunt Muriel married Thomas Knyvett without the king's permission. Mother married where she chose, too.'

She glanced at me from under her lashes, waiting for me to say something. 'Oh, Anne, I want to love the man I marry and have his children. To give my love and know that I am truly loved back, like in the tales of the troubadours. It is in my nature to be kind and generous. Besides, I already know that to have someone say they love you and feel the weight of their naked body upon you, is quite the most intox –'

I sat up, all thoughts of Elizabeth quite forgotten. 'What do you mean?' I whispered.

Mary, her brown eyes shining, hopped into bed beside me. We snuggled up together under the coverlet.

'If I tell you a secret you must *promise* to say nothing. Ever. Do you promise?'

I nodded.

'If you tell anyone, I will get one of the wise women at the Eaton Bridge fair to put a curse on you – do you understand?'

She turned her face close to mine. 'Do you recall Master Gilley? The tall, red-haired messenger, on the grey horse?'

I nodded, not sure if I did or not, for there were many different messengers that came to the manor.

'He and I have shared a tryst.' She looked at me expectantly, eyes shining. 'Well – what do you think?'

She waited for my response.

'Say something, Nan,' she said poking me. 'We have lain together as a man with his wife and made a union of our bodies, hearts and souls.'

I pulled back, staring incredulously at her. 'But, Mary,' I gasped, the full impact of her words dawning on me. 'Are you betrothed?'

There was a pause.

'Betrothed? *Betrothed?* Why, you silly goose, how could I be betrothed? He is married already.'

'Married?' I repeated, in horror.

'Yes, but he does not love his wife one jot. She is a complete shrew who refuses to bed with him, and he says he is going to leave her. He said he will tell her soon, when the time is right, and she will be packed off to relatives. He will then marry me. Oh, Nan, I am mad with love for him, and that is why I burst into tears when Mother said I was going to the regent's court. I cannot go. I cannot be apart from him. We have been meeting in secret these six months past, and I will not give him up.'

I stared at her as she fell back against the bolster and blustered on.

'He – he said such wonderful things to me, and in the end, I could not resist lying with him. He is so tender and warm, but I was afraid that if I said no to him, I would lose him. He said he would leave the court and never see me again if I did not prove my love.'

She gave a faint smile.

'But, Mary,' I said, pulling the coverlet up further. 'I do not understand. What of his wife? She cannot be put away.'

'Yes, she can,' she argued, 'since she is not a wife to him, not in the proper sense. She has broken her sacred vows by not proving buxom and bonny in bed. By law, she can be put aside.'

She turned her face to me. 'Oh, Nan, you can see for yourself how handsome he is, so tall and strong, with that wonderful copper-coloured hair I find so adorable. And he has taught me things I did not know could be done between a man and a woman; delightful things, *secret* things.'

She could see that I was not convinced and, leaning up on one elbow, appeared uneasy. 'Look, it is a secret, and no one must know, certainly not our parents or, God forbid, Dame Margot.'

'But are you not afraid of getting with child?'

'No, for Edwin – that is his name – showed me how to prevent the man's seed taking root. Besides, if the worse should happen, I can always undo the thing with a tincture of marigold and ivy.'

'Oh, sweet Jesu,' I whispered, staring at her now eager face. 'You will have to tell our confessor, or you will go to Hell and burn forever and ever. As to Father, if he knew he would have the man thrown down a well. You know what rages he gets into. Soon he will be searching around for a suitable husband for you, someone of good birth. That *is* why he is sending you to the regent, is it not?'

'Well, it will be too late. We will be married. Look, I would much rather stay at home,' she said, 'but what else can I do?'

'Mary, for the love of God, how can you possibly want to stay at Hever? It is so dull! At court, there will be dancing, hunting parties, and new clothes to wear.'

'Well, you go then,' she said, irritated.

'Listen, Mary,' I said, taking hold of her arm. 'Father means this family to do well and he is looking to us, and George, to achieve this through marriage. He will not want to have a daughter who is known as a – a…'

I floundered, not knowing the right word.

She pulled back from me.

'Go on, say it, say the word – a harlot. You are heartless, Nan, and you have a sharp tongue just like Father and Grandmother. How on earth would you know anything of love and such things – a silly, awkward girl.'

Behind her bravado, she sounded thoroughly unsettled. 'I am not going to tell anyone, Nan, and certainly not our confessor at St Peter's. The secret oath of the confessional means nothing to him. No, you are my sister, and I have shared my greatest secret with you, but it must stay a secret – for the moment. Now, swear an oath on your life and stand to it.'

I mumbled I would tell no one and she seemed

more at ease.

'You are wrong,' she flopped back onto the bolster. 'Father is a realist. He would swear that I was the Virgin Mary herself if there was any chance of advancement, although I bet Uncle Thomas is behind my having to go away. I hate the way he stares at me, as if ruminating on some murky thought.'

'Why did you not tell me sooner?' I lay back.

Mary sighed. 'Because you would disapprove and your childish outburst has just proved I was right to keep quiet.'

I stared at her. 'I am not a child.'

Her hand fumbled beneath my bolster. 'Then what is that?'

'She is mine, leave her alone,' I said, wrestling my doll from her.

Mary flopped back with a sigh, but I was unable to stem my curiosity.

I turned my head. 'Mary?'

'What now?'

'Was it – is it pleasant doing what you did?'

'Oh, Nan, it is bliss, I told you. Each fibre in your body tingles with delight as you wait in expectation of what is coming next. One day you will find out for yourself. Now, go to sleep,' she said, rising and kissing my forehead, 'and dream of your husband-to-be. Oh, we shall have a nursery of fine boys between us, I promise. You wait and see, it will all work out.'

She put her finger to my lips as she hopped out of my bed and returned to her own. Before long I could hear her steady breathing, but I could not settle. It felt strange sleeping in a bed by myself, but the duke could obviously afford every luxury for his guests, even children. I also felt angry that Mary was going to leave me behind. As to her behaviour, outside of marriage, it was the gravest of sins for a woman to lie with a man. And yet, did not everyone think she was pure and innocent, particularly Dame Margot? Mary, I grumbled to myself, was never truly chastised, for she always charmed everyone and had them wrapped around her little finger. She always did what she wanted, without a care, or a reprimand, and now she would have a whole new, fashionable wardrobe and be the centre of attention at court. Why should such bad behaviour be rewarded? Turning onto my back, I lay staring upward towards the rafters. In the moonlight, I could see the blue plaster painted with silver stars, and a large cobweb stretched across the beams. For over an hour I tossed and turned, wondering what I should do. Finally, I slipped out of bed and padded barefoot to where Mary lay sleeping. I shook her gently.

'Mary,' I whispered. '*Mary*.'

I shook her again, and she moaned. 'Oh, for the love of God, what?'

'Mary, I want a suitor too.'

She sat sleepily up. 'What? Were you not a moment passed prattling of Hell and damnation, and being of good account. Why the sudden change?'

'I want to prove to you that I am not a child.'

'No – no, absolutely not,' she said. 'It would not be right. Besides, men like a woman with a woman's shape.'

I crossed my arms over my flat chest as I stood in my thin linen shift. 'Mary, I am nearly thirteen,' I urged. 'Oh, Mary, *please*.'

She glanced at my crestfallen face. 'Is it what you really want?' she pushed her hair from her eyes.

I nodded and she yawned.

'Honestly, Nan, you change like the wind. Well, if you insist. I will ask Edwin to bring one of his friends with him next week when he comes to Hever – but it has to be our secret. And do not dare back out or I will look a fool. One of the estate cottages is empty at present, and no one goes there.'

I gazed at her face.

'You do understand what will be expected? Are you sure it is what you want?'

I said I did, and smiled. It was exactly what I wanted. As I slipped back into my bed and listened to the sound of a dog barking in the courtyard below, I turned my face into the bolster and threw my doll down onto the rush mat.

*   *

'She has done *what?*' bellowed Father, throwing his papers onto the chair. A few fell to the floor and scattered as Sorrel barked in agitation. 'Here? Here on the estate?'

'Thomas, for the love of Christ calm yourself,' said my mother, glancing nervously towards the door. 'No one must know of this.'

They did not know that I stood quaking behind the great tapestry in the library, desperate to escape my father's wrath.

'By God, she'll know of this,' raged my father, raising his fist as if to strike her.

My hand flew to my mouth in fright.

'Thomas, stop, the servants will see you,' said Mother, lowering his arm.

He shook it from her in disgust.

'How could she do this to us?' he asked, close to Mother's face. 'Now – at the very time when, God knows, I am making my way at court, and trying to better this family. This is *your* doing.' As he jabbed his finger at her the garnet stone on his ring flashed in a dusty beam of sunlight.

'Do not dare blame me,' said Mother.

'Fah! Women's business, and where were you? Where was my mother? What was she doing? Too busy looking the other way, or dozing, I'll warrant, and this is the result. Poor Mrs Orcharde is too old and half blind – I told you to retire her years ago. But no, you never listen to me, Elizabeth, by God, you never do. That – that – oh! I cannot even bring myself to say the bitch's name. By Christ I'll break her neck when I find her!'

'Thomas, for the love of Heaven, you are too hot,' said Mother. 'Keep your voice down.'

Father stopped his pacing and turned on her. 'You and that woman lazing upstairs have failed. Failed on every count, I tell you. God's blood what am I to do?' His face had turned puce with rage.

'Stop blaspheming,' came the angry reply. 'You are over loud, and people can hear in the courtyard. We must think clearly on this. No one must know, not even my brother, do you hear?'

Father paced frantically around the library, biting his nail, deep in thought.

'I cannot have it, Elizabeth. I tell you I cannot have it known that any such – such knave is associated with our name – it would ruin my prospects. Who can we marry her to after this? Who on God's earth will want her?'

I stood back from behind the tapestry, trembling with fear, terrified Sorrel would sniff me out from my hiding place.

'They shall not know, Thomas, not even the Wyatts, who, I might remind you, are arriving here from Allington in the next few weeks. No one shall know the details, not even your mother. But we must think – think calmly what to do next. And pray.'

'Jesu,' said Father, 'what of the chaplain? There can be no gossip.'

'Be calm,' said Mother, 'nothing will be said. The chaplain will say nothing for the sake of the family he serves. He is our creature. Leave it to me.'

'Leave it to you? Leave it to you? Look what happens when I do!'

As I peeped out, he turned around, and I jumped back.

'And what of this base bastard, will he talk? Has he talked already?'

Mother shook her head. 'No, I have spoken to him and offered him the opportunity of taking up a new posting in Ireland if –'

'You have done *what?*' exploded Father.

'If you approve,' she said, boldly standing her ground.

'The decision rests with you.'

'By the Mass it does,' said Father, turning away. He paused. 'What opportunity?'

'On the Ormond estates. It keeps things in the family, so to speak. He seems satisfied with the promotion and the pay, as I knew he would be. I have said I have recommended him, and if you authorise the decision he will leave immediately. He will not be returning, why should he? He has been warned that it is not in his best interests to do so.'

'God's blood, woman, you had better be right.'

'Well, thank you for your faith in me, Thomas.'

My father picked his gloves up off the desk, still not appeased. 'Fine clothes, flirting, and flummery, you women are interested in nothing else,' he muttered, as he made to leave. 'By God, she's her mother's daughter. She gets her ways from you,' he pushed aside the heavy drape.

'Oh, yes, throw that old argument at me again!' cried Mother. 'It suited you well enough to look the other way as I recall. Well, she is your daughter too, Thomas, so go to Hell! In fact, go back to your gambling and wagering in Mechelen and do not bother coming back!'

I heard her storm out of the library as Sorrel clattered after her, whining in confusion.

Certain that she had left, I tiptoed up the stairs and pushed open the creaking door to the bedchamber I shared with Mary. She was sitting on the bed resting in Mrs Orcharde's arms, her dishevelled hair covering her face. In only her linen shift, her arms limp around my nurse's neck, she gave a shiver with cold and distress.

'Oh, Mary,' I whispered, horrified by the sight before my eyes. Mrs Orcharde glanced up, bidding me come in and close the door. As I saw my sister's face I began to tremble with shock, for her eyes were swollen from crying, her nose and cheeks were blotchy, and a large red lump throbbed on her cheek.

'Has she gone?' asked Mary.

'They both have,' I said in a small voice, glancing at my nurse who appeared somewhat confused.

'What is it, my lamb,' asked Mrs Orcharde, 'you must tell me. What has merited this terrible beating?'

My sister looked at me. 'You heard what happened, Nan?' she asked, sniffing.

I nodded.

'Please, please, tell me, sweetheart,' urged the old nurse again.

'Oh, Edwin,' murmured Mary, wiping her eyes with her hand.

'Who is this Edwin, my pet?'

'Did Mother do this to you?' I asked as I sat next to her on the bed.

She nodded.

'I saw her, Nan,' said my nurse, rising. 'Your mama's sleeves were rolled up and she carried a birch cane in her hand. She was standing by the main door, waiting, watching for my young lady's return, her face white with anger. As I hobbled in, she told me to go to my chamber and stay there, and I knew something frightful was coming. Well, I sat on my bed and waited for the storm to break, and oh, sweet Jesu, it was as if the hounds from Hell had broken loose.'

Mary grimaced with pain as she moved. ''Tis true, Nan. No sooner had I walked through the door than Mother grabbed me by the hair, dragged me up here and threw me onto the bed. That is when the beating began. With each thrash of the cane, she called me a whore, and I fell, knocking my cheek on the side of the bed. Does it look dreadful? It feels so hot and sore.'

I shook my head, unable to speak.

'Oh, I heard her,' said Mrs Orcharde, 'such lewd language. Sorrel barked, and there was such a din that I was beside myself, wringing my hands not knowing what to do.'

'Do – do you know how she found out?' asked Mary.

I walked over to the fireplace, my back turned. I did

not want to look at her broken face. 'From the chaplain, Master Davy,' I mumbled, 'but I do not know why he would be going to visit Mrs Addiscombe when he knew she was not there.'

'Our chaplain?' Mrs Orcharde's eyes widened.

Mary nodded. 'He came into her cottage – and found us both together on the pallet.'

I felt my cheeks burn.

'What? Talking alone? Unchaperoned?' Mrs Orcharde was alarmed.

I turned around and saw Mary's wet cheeks turn a deep pink.

'Not exactly.'

There was a moment's silence.

'Well, what then, my chick?'

'We were caught lying together. As man and wife.'

Mrs Orcharde appeared bewildered.

'Naked,' added Mary in a small voice, her cheeks colouring even deeper.

Mrs Orcharde let out a shriek and threw her arms into the air. 'Holy Mother of God!' she cried, crossing herself piously.

Mary and I stared at her.

'Oh, Holy Mother of God!' she cried again, before sobbing hysterically.

Mary rose slowly off the bed, wincing with pain, and hobbled over to her put her arms around her. Mrs Orcharde appeared to crumple and held both rough hands up to her face.

'Oh, dear God in Heaven! How have I brought my young lady up to behave in such a manner?' she shook her head. 'How could you do such a thing? A Christian young lady brought up to fear God. Oh, this is my doing, my fault. How could you do this to your family, to your good name? Oh, I shall be sent away, I shall be held responsible and sent from this house. Where will I find another position? Oh, my heart will break with sorrow!'

'But – but you are not to blame!' I cried out, in alarm.

My sister tried to soothe her, but it was no use. Our nurse sat inconsolable on the stool, rocking backwards and forwards, weeping and wailing. I started to panic. Mrs Orcharde must not be made to go away!

'Mary, do something,' I urged.

George poked his head around the door. 'What is going on? Where is everybody and why are you crying? I have been fishing and caught a carp. Mary why are you still in your shift, and why is there a lump on your face?'

My sister limped painfully towards him. 'It is nothing, George. Please go away. Mrs Orcharde is not well.'

He stood staring at her. 'Well, why are *you* hobbling then? What is the matter?' he persisted.

'Please, George,' my sister steered him firmly back out of the door. 'Later. I will come to you later, I promise.'

'Well, I don't want to hear,' he said in a sulk, turning to go.

Back in the chamber, our nurse held her apron over her face as she mumbled incoherently. I led Mary over to the window, stepping carefully over a broken bowl of flowers, some open books, and a candlestick.

'Father was in a terrible rage,' I said. 'I was hiding behind the tapestry and thought he was going to strike Mother. Was it really worth it?'

'Yes,' she said, dabbing her eyes with a linen square and inspecting the eyelash caught in it.

'But, Mary,' I whispered, glancing back at Mrs Orcharde, 'why did you do this?'

She leaned forward close to my ear. 'Well, you can talk. *You* were very keen to have your own lover but a week passed. Good job he was sick, or you too would have been caught. No, you were quite prepared to be pleasured by his friend, and that makes you just as bad. Don't be such a little prig!'

'I was not, I agreed to no such disgraceful thing,' I whispered.

'Liar, you did!'

I glanced back as our nurse gave another wail.

'You are in this as much as I am! Anyway, we are to marry.'

'Mary – Father is sending Edwin away. He is going to Kilkenny.' I watched as she sank to her knees and began to cry again. I sat down beside her on the wooden floor, and smelt the lavender in the rushes.

'No! That is not true,' she said miserably, her eyes red and tearful. I told her exactly what I knew. Well, I thought, my heart unmoved, this is what you get for being a fool.

'Mary, I heard Mother say how he would be glad to go to Ireland. He had no intention of marrying you, and was only amusing himself.'

She turned to me, horrified. 'Why are you being so cruel, Nan?'

'I swear to you on my life, it is true. Ask Mother.'

Mary sat with her head on her knees in despair. 'Oh, I am heartbroken!'

We sat awhile in silence, but then, on hearing the sound of footsteps outside in the passageway, Mary instinctively rose and moved behind Mrs Orcharde. As I turned, Mother burst through the door. She appeared more composed than before, but her face was as white as a church candle. She glanced at Mrs Orcharde. 'Leave us, Mary,' she commanded, with a flick of her head.

The old nurse raised herself and left the chamber in great sorrow. As she closed the door, Mother walked up to my sister and slapped her hard across the cheek. I flinched as Mary squealed and sat down upon the bed, crying afresh, her cheek glowing even more crimson.

'What in the name of God and his holy angels have I been teaching you all these years? You give yourself in marriage to the man your father chooses, without a qualm, or protestation. He alone decides for this family's honour, grace, and benefit. How could you waste yourself on such a knave!

What gift do you now bring to your husband in marriage? Where is your maidenhead? In the mud!' She threw her arms open in despair. 'Your father is beside himself, and I cannot blame him. But it is done and we cannot undo it.'

'But, Mama,' wailed Mary.

Mother refused to soften and glanced at me. 'No one will ever know of this, do you hear, Nan?'

'Of course not, Mother, you have my full obedience.'

'He will be sent to Ireland. Your father would have him butchered right now and out of the way permanently if he could. It was only my intervention that has saved the wretch's life.'

I watched my sister blow her nose. It appeared she now had a nose bleed.

'Now – we will have to rethink the situation with the regent,' Mother walked over to the window, 'for by God and his holy angels, we cannot lose this chance.'

There was a long silence as she stood gazing down, her outline dark and ominous against the light. Outside I could hear the geese landing noisily on the water and somewhere the whinnying of horses. I stared at Mary again, dabbing her nose with her now bloodied sleeve, then looked down as my mother turned and spoke.

'I wonder,' she mused. Ignoring Mary, she walked over and pushed the stray strands of hair neatly back over my shoulder. Her fingers traced my cheek. 'Yes, I think we might still do very well out of this. Very well indeed – but we must act quickly.'

● ●

It was an unusually warm day when my parent's closest friends, Sir Henry and Lady Anne Wyatt, came to visit from Allington, in Kent.

As we sat in the new rose garden at Hever, Mother talked to Lady Anne of the latest news at court. My parents had soon made up their quarrel with the result that my mother was with child yet again. She smiled at Lady Anne's children: Henry aged twelve, Thomas, aged nine, and Margaret, aged three. I thought Thomas quite wonderful – almost the brother I had lost – and we quickly became friends, for we both loved dogs. He owned a greyhound called Rufus, and I still recall his wide, green leather collar with bells that tinkled when he shook his great head.

As they gossiped together, we children clustered around Sir Henry, for George and Thomas never tired of hearing of his daring deeds as a young man. George pestered Sir Henry, hoping he would tell his heroic tale for the hundredth time. 'Tell us again, Sir Henry. Tell us again, *please*,' he begged, and Sir Henry laughed and started his story, his young audience scattered at his feet.

'Well, when the pretender, Richard of York, came to power, I would have none of it. I stood fast against him for he was false to take the throne and I did not hold with his ideas and administration. My loyalty was to Henry Tudor and, for this loyalty, King Richard threw me into prison. I was held down by four men and forced, in the king's own company, to have –'

'Mustard!' cried George, jumping up, making Lady Anne and Mother turn round in alarm.

'Yes, indeed, mustard and vinegar were poured down my throat. Can you imagine? I was then left to starve to death in my dungeon. But do you know what saved me, Nan?' I smiled politely, for Sir Henry still spoke to me like a child.

'I know, I know,' said Thomas, his hand waving in the air.

'You shush,' said George, giving the boy a push. Rufus glanced up from gnawing on his bone and growled. He was protective of the boy.

'It was a cat,' stated Mary with a sigh, spoiling the suspense. Everyone groaned at her outburst for Mary was far too old for this game. Mother narrowed her eyes as she stared, for she was still angry with her.

Sir Henry smiled indulgently. 'Yes, Mary, by day a black

and white cat would creep to my prison bars and drop a
dead pigeon next to the grating.' He winked at my mother.
'Month after month I ate those pigeons. I detest pigeon now,
but I have a soft spot for cats and will always have them at
Allington.

'What happened next?' asked George.

Sir Henry sipped his lemon cordial and wiped his lips.
'Well, I did very well when the first Tudor king – our true
king – ascended the throne, and I became a guardian for his
son, our young King Henry. I am now on the Privy Council,
I am a Knight of the Bath and, with your father, joint constable of Norwich Castle. We have both done rather well for
ourselves.'

Lady Anne smiled as Sir Henry finished the dregs of
his drink. I rolled my eyes and squeezed up beside Thomas
Wyatt. He was such a charming boy, quiet and refined, with
dark blue eyes, and brown, tousled hair. He sat, cross-legged,
scribbling on a piece of paper and when I asked him what he
was doing, he told me he was writing a poem.

'Does it tell of a cat?' I asked, but he shook his head
shyly and would not let me see.

George wandered over with Margaret, bored with
the adults.

'What is this?' he grabbed the paper, causing it to tear.
There was a scuffle as George and Thomas rolled on the
grass, and George won. George then sat up, breathless, and
started to read out loud, but Thomas was angry.

'Stop it! It is not finished!' he cried, sweeping back his
tumbling hair.

George sloped off in a sulk, brushing the grass from his
hose, as Thomas sat with me again, beckoning to his dog.

'One day, I'll read this to you,' he said, straightening
out the torn, crumpled piece. 'I like writing poems, but as
yet they are not very good. I want to write, but I'm not sure
about what yet. In two years' time I hope to go to Cambridge
and learn to write poems in Latin, Greek and French. Master

Erasmus is professor of Greek there, and I want him to teach me.'

'Erasmus?' I asked. 'Why do you think he has such a peculiar name?'

'Erasmus is not his real name. His real name is Master Gerrit Gerritzoon. It is the fashion among certain scholars to take Greek names.'

I thought Thomas clever and held out my hand to his. 'Will you write me a poem?' I asked.

He smiled and promised he would. I noticed his fine, white teeth and thought he was the boy I liked most in the whole world.

As we sat, our parents spoke of the young king and Mother seemed very enamoured of him. 'He is twenty-one, young and bonny,' she smiled, as Hannah refilled her cup.

Lady Anne nodded. 'It is good to have young blood again. What say you, Henry?'

Her husband settled back on the bench and stretched out his legs. 'He is an extraordinary prince of immense worth. Well versed in half a dozen languages, plays many musical instruments, sings, dances and composes music. He understands astronomy, mathematics, is ever at the latest book – are you listening, Mary?'

Mary glanced up from the daisy chain she was making and offered it to Sir Henry.

'Charming, she is absolutely charming,' he said, taking the outstretched flowers. 'Such a lovely girl.'

Mother spoke up. 'Talking of lovely girls, I see the king is inordinately fond of his sister Mary Rose, and has his new ship bearing her name. Soon, God willing, she will be Princess of Castile, for she has been set to marry the young prince Charles these past five years. It is a pity she is so moonish and mettlesome. You should see how she rules her brother with tears and tantrums and then, on getting her own way, is all smiles and sunshine. She will run riot around her betrothed, since the boy is barely twelve and she sixteen.'

'Well, age is of no import,' said Lady Anne. 'The king has Queen Katherine and is much delighted with her. I gather she rules with him as a true daughter of Spain and he relies on her wise counsel.'

Sir Henry grunted. 'He would do better to listen to his councillors rather than to woman's prattle. What does she know? She should be raising a nursery of boys. I prefer it when women see to their household rather than meddle in affairs of state.' He studied the icing on his honey cake, before taking a nibble.

Lady Anne raised her eyes.

'I disagree, Henry,' said Mother, 'the queen is a woman of unsurpassed learning and culture and is a match for any man. She has studied the Roman poets and orators, is passionate for literature, music, and the arts. She speaks French, Latin and yes, some English. I gather when the king does invade France with his armies, she will govern this realm. He trusts her to rule as regent in his absence for, I think – no, I know – she has the steadiness of temperament he lacks. Surely, a woman of some capability?'

Sir Henry smiled, for he knew how to needle her. 'If it does come to war I shall, of course, be going,' he said, avoiding his wife's eye.

'What? Oh, for the love of God, Henry, you are too old!' she protested.

'Not as old as Surrey,' he countered. 'Besides experience is needed in these matters and my presence will be expected.'

There was an awkward silence.

'When is Thomas coming home?' he asked brightly, trying to change the subject.

Mother bristled with annoyance, determined not to let the matter of intelligent women drop.

'He has recently returned to the court in Mechelen and will probably be away for some time to come. He appears to amuse the regent who, as a mere woman, is managing her affairs very well.'

Sir Henry laughed at her. 'I hear,' he said, trying to change the subject yet again, 'Antwerp is the loveliest city in the world. One day I might visit.'

Lady Anne looked up. 'Not unless you intend trading in wool or spices, my dear, although I would prefer it to taking up arms.'

As laughter followed, my mother appeared tense. 'There is something I have been meaning to discuss with you both,' she said. 'Mary, would you go and take the children to play somewhere else, they are too loud today.'

My sister tried to catch my mother's eye but she looked away.

George, Thomas, Henry, and Mary, with Margaret in her arms, walked off, glad for an excuse to be away from the dull conversation but I did not follow. Instead, I sat behind the tree with my book, unnoticed.

'You are ill with the child?' asked Lady Anne, leaning forward in concern.

My mother laid a hand on her arm. 'No, not all, my dear, although I am finding this pregnancy a little troublesome. It concerns Nan.'

My ears pricked up.

'The Dowager Duchess of Savoy has agreed to take Anne, as one of her *filles d'honneur* early next year.'

I gave a gasp, dropped my book and moved closer.

'Anne? Surely you mean Mary?' corrected Lady Anne, glancing at her husband. I watched as a pink flush appeared on my mother's neck.

'No – Anne,' she said, brightly.

The Wyatts stared at each other, astonished.

'But – but Anne is the younger, Elizabeth,' said Lady Anne. 'It is against convention to send the younger daughter. It is – forgive me my dear – an insult to Mary. People will ask questions, and you know how they like to gossip at court.'

My mother put her hand up to silence her. 'That may be, but Thomas wants Anne to go, and he does have the final word. Either way, this is an excellent chance for this family. She will return to Queen Katherine's court an accomplished young lady fit for a good marriage.'

'But why Anne?' asked Sir Henry. 'Mary is nearly fourteen, a young woman of an age to go. She should go. She will be bitterly disappointed. What will you tell her?'

My mother appeared flustered as I sat holding my breath. 'There is nothing to tell her. Her father wishes it, I wish it, and the Archduchess has agreed that Anne will go to her court to further her education.'

I squeezed my eyes tight shut in silent delight, for what could be more wonderful or exciting? What did I care what my sister might think or feel? She was a fool.

Lady Anne took a sip from her cup. 'I see,' she said.

'But why not Mary?' pressed Sir Henry.

His wife glared at him over the rim of the cup.

'Thomas knows – we both know,' continued my mother, 'that she will not do the best she can for this family and she requires – no, she must have – supervision.'

'What are you saying?' Sir Henry narrowed his eyes. 'She will be supervised in the most moral court in Europe. It is a magnificent chance for her, and she is the eldest girl. You cannot deny her this opportunity.'

An awkward silence followed.

'What I mean by supervision is in her lessons. Mary is not – is not one for study. She speaks some French and a little Spanish, but I fear it is not enough. She should be further advanced at her age and would not be able to converse very well. Oh, she is charming, dances with extraordinary grace and sings like an angel, and she is going to grow up into such a pretty young woman. But there is a lack of sense about her.'

Sir Henry laughed. 'A woman requires sense when she has beauty? You would hold her back because she is not *sensible*?'

'Do you really think Anne the better prize, Elizabeth?' asked Lady Anne.

I wanted to laugh but dared not. Of course I was better than my sister!

'No, dear, not physically for I can see that Anne will never have Mary's fresh complexion, although she has something else I cannot quite explain. A charm, not obvious at first perhaps, but combined with a lively temperament is somewhat unusual. I – we – both know Anne, although younger, is further advanced than Mary, and we must make a good impression.' She smiled, a little too gaily. 'Anne will go to the regent and in the meantime, I will keep Mary close by me at court for further tutoring. She demands far more help than Anne ever does with her languages and easily loses interest.'

No one looked convinced.

'Well, I think Mary is delightful,' said Sir Henry, not letting the matter drop. 'She is quite an accomplished musician and already writes pretty chansons. You should be proud of her.'

Mother ignored him and continued. 'Anne, under the regent's guidance will concentrate on her French. She will speak it each day, without respite, although even now she has a fair grasp of the tongue. She is at an age when language comes easily, and she has inherited a natural ability from her father.' She looked around at the silent faces and blustered on.

Anne must be able to fully understand and converse with the regent, for the lady speaks no English.'

Lady Anne placed her cream wool shawl around her shoulders, for with the sun down the air had turned chilly. 'Well,' she said, 'I am sure you will both do what is most advantageous for the family, and Anne is a willing girl. She is pleasing now she has grown out of her tantrums. Do you remember how she would squeal and squall with rage as an infant if she did not get her own way? Oh, and do you recall the time she threw her doll down from the top window into the moat at Allington? She is very like you!' Lady

Anne laughed at my mother's indignant face. 'Come now, Elizabeth, I agree Anne might not be the comelier of the two, but she could do well, and I envy you this opportunity.'

'Well,' said Mother, 'for all the preening and primping she does you would think she does think herself the fairest. She is forever fussing with her hair. But then so did I at her age.'

I frowned. It was true, I did spend hours in my chamber in front of the mirror, trying out different ways to dress my long hair, but how did she know? Besides, I was well aware that Mary always stole the attention, and so I had to try even harder to get noticed.

'Well, you have changed your tune,' said Sir Henry, putting his goblet down. 'When will you tell the girl, Elizabeth?'

'I have not decided, but perhaps in six or eight months' time. In the meantime, Anne will concentrate on her French. But come, let us go inside for I feel a storm is in the air.'

The three of them rose and walked down the path back to the manor.

As I sat behind the tree, I hugged my knees and squealed silently in delight. I was almost thirteen years old and did not need to be kept at home, under my grandmother's eye. I wanted to see the world for myself, experience new adventures and meet new people. I was tired of the children on the estate, the workers and the occasional visitor. Nobody of any worth even knew I existed. Besides, I told my conscience, what I had done was all done for Mary's sake. She had not wanted to go away, and so everything had worked out perfectly, as I planned. She would stay behind, and I, using my wits, would get exactly what I wanted. Mary would be none the wiser – and Master Richard Davy would never know who had left him the incriminating note.

◦   ◦

The cold and damp of hard winter months crept into young and old bones alike. As life continued, Mary was not allowed a moment alone, for Father insisted that Dame Margot must walk with her, read or watch while she plied her needle. She was not allowed to ride out and found it insufferable. Our governess continued to teach our lessons and every day I laboured at my French. When the snow fell thickly one morning, George rubbed the glass of the schoolroom window. 'We should be outside playing, not in here learning dull lessons,' he moaned.

When Mrs Geddynge appeared and saw that we were away from our books, I expected a whipping, but to my amazement, she too looked out of the window. 'It does look pretty,' she smiled, 'and I think you should get some fresh air. I will give you an hour's sport if you promise me two hours of work afterwards.'

We were delighted and ran to fetch our furs. Outside lay white and silent, and our steps were muffled as we crunched in the snow. George immediately started throwing snowballs and pelting the walls. Within seconds there was a loud, shrieking voice and I shielded my eyes as I looked up into the watery sunshine.

'Not in the courtyard! Not near the panes of glass!' The voice was that of Dame Margot, as she waved her stick out of the casement window. Mary, pulling a face, quickly disappeared. 'Out, out all of you, you are disturbing my rest! Go round the back in the fields if you must throw things. Really, George, look at the mess you are making.' I looked at George and then at the slush splattered brickwork, and thought for one horrible moment he might throw his missile at her. He did not, but threw his snowball at the door instead. He gave out a shout, and the chase was on, over the bridge and into the fields.

❖ ❖

That night the manor fires smelt of wintergreen and pine as they snapped and crackled in their hearths. I pushed the heavy door of the chamber open and stood quietly, half eyeing the fire and half watching my mother. She bent her head as she wrote by the light of several candles; her golden hair cascaded over the fox fur collar of her saffron velvet night robe. As I stood, I must have made the candles flicker with the draught for she turned her head.

'Come in, Nan, come in. Don't stand there and let in the cold.' Mother put down her quill. 'There. I have written to say how honoured and grateful we are for this opportunity.' She tapped the sander over the paper, blew gently and folded it carefully. 'The matter is settled and you, my young lady, will be going abroad.'

'Oh, Mother!' I exclaimed, noticing how thin and pale she appeared. She had lost the child she had been carrying, for it had come too early, and had spent the last month resting in bed, tired and listless. It would be the last child she carried, for she knew she was now too old to bear more.

She turned to face me. 'You are going to the court of the Dowager Duchess of Savoy, to advance your education and learn how to be a maid of honour.' She reached over for a large book, sighing at the effort, and opened it at the marked page. 'Her palace is here in Mechelen, in Flanders – can you see on the map? This is where your father works as an ambassador.'

I peered at the colourful map with its drawings of sea gods, a compass and ships. 'Will I see him?'

My mother closed the heavy book. 'Yes, I expect you will. Now, I would prefer you to go after your next birthday as thirteen is an acceptable age to start.' She put her writing materials away in the drawer of her desk and turned the little key. 'You will be going, Nan, to be educated, and mix with the finest people in Europe. I can teach you how to run a household, but your father knows that, in time, moving in the right circles will lead through marriage to advancement for this family. This is a great opportunity, come about only through your father's good grace and effort.'

I moved forward and kissed her hand. 'Mother, I will

not let you down.'

She smiled and stroked my cheek, her beautiful eyes catching the candlelight. I thought how dull they appeared. 'Hannah will accompany you as a lady's maid as far as Antwerp, and then she will travel on to visit her relatives. I will go part of the way with you.'

'Tell me of the Duchess,' I was curious.

'Well, she is the daughter of Maximilian, Emperor of the Holy Roman Empire, King of the Germans, and his first wife Mary of Burgundy. The duchess – or regent as she is known – is a great lady and you will learn much. When she lived in Spain, she taught our own dear queen, who was twelve at the time, how to speak French. Now, what do you know about the Holy Roman Empire?' She took my hands in hers.

'It is a collection of states in Europe, including Germany and Austria,' I replied.

'Indeed,' she nodded. 'Now, I will tell you a little of the lady's background. Through the emperor's marriage, the Low Countries came to the Habsburgs. When she was two years old, Margaret was betrothed to the Dauphin of France and she lived at the French court until she was nine. When the betrothal was annulled, her father married her to the heir apparent to the Spanish throne. He died, and she married another – Duke Philibert of Savoy. He was her husband for only four years, and the poor woman is now a widow again. Her brother – a beautiful young boy named Philip – married Juana, the sister of our own Queen Katherine. Do you recall he died some years ago?'

I did not.

'The States-General of the Netherlands agreed that the duchess should be Governess General of the Burgundian Netherlands and guardian of her royal nieces and her nephew, Charles. Her father, busy with his vast territories, was in no position to look after the children and so his daughter took his place.'

I nodded, intrigued, as she continued.

'The duchess entered Mechelen in triumph and now represents her father at the *Hof van Savoyen* palace, where you are going. She speaks fluent French, some Flemish, Spanish and Latin – but not English – and is a great collector of beautiful works of art.'

'No English at all?' I asked, somewhat perturbed at what I had already heard.

'None, therefore you must continue to study hard at your French.'

'What is the palace like, and the city of Mechelen?'

'Well, your father tells me that the regent prefers it to be a home rather than a cold palace. Imagine, a home in the capital of the Burgundian Netherlands. A city made rich from its trade in tapestries, linen and alabaster, and full of fine merchants' houses, and churches. Margaret used to live at the court in Brussels, but when she moved to Mechelen the court followed her, and great prosperity came to the city. People from different cultures are drawn to it, for it is a city of great tolerance and diversity, with openness to free thinking. There is much the regent's court can teach you, and when I see you on your return, I expect you to have grown into a very cultured young lady.' She kissed my forehead.

'Does she have a dog?' I glanced at Sorrel. As he lay asleep by the crackling log fire, he was obviously too hot for he was panting.

Mother laughed. 'I expect she has many and if you are pleasing to her, you might be allowed to look after them yourself.'

I stood pondering this thought.

'Now, return to your chamber, Nan, and give thanks to God in your prayers tonight for this great opportunity.'

Chapter Three

'Now thus, now thus, now thus.'

The Court of the Regent,
Mechelen, 1513

'Across the Narrow Seas my fate is set,
And leaving makes my heart full sore,
And yet I go with thoughts of God above
In faith that he alone directs my sail.
God grant a happy fate in serving my Lady,
And return with gladness in my heart
To hear again the sweet voice of the nightingale,
And marvel at its song upon the Kentish Bough.'
Anon.

January did not start well as we made the cold, hard journey to the priory at Greenwich for the funeral of my dear Aunt Muriel. Small in stature, kind and gentle, she was my Grandfather Howard's daughter by his first marriage and had been happily married to Sir Thomas Knyvett, a great favourite of the king. Tragically, he was killed in a sea attack against the French in August the previous year. Devastated, my aunt pined away, prophesying she would see her husband in Heaven before the winter snow melted.

She was true to her word, eating nothing, until, weak and frail, death claimed her too. She was twenty-six years old and left two daughters and four beautiful boys. The king, losing his friend, felt as devastated as my mother.

Her funeral was a grand Howard affair, held with great ceremony and honour, but the weeping and wailing saddened me as I stood in the bitter cold of the churchyard with the queen, my mother, and the queen's ladies. The ground lay sprinkled with snow, and I was glad to repair to the great dinner held at Lambeth, and feel the warmth of the blazing fire.

●   ●

In February, Mother's brother Henry died, but she insisted on attending the queen at Greenwich and continue to assist her with sewing the countless banners, pennants and tabards for the forthcoming war with France. The stitching continued late into the night. However, a feeling of fear and dread began to pervade the court, for a terrible plague raged in London claiming the lives of as many as four hundred people a day.

In March, news arrived from Thomas Spinelly, the English agent to the Netherlands, informing the court that Pope Julius II had died in January and a new pope had been duly elected – Pope Leo X – a Medici. He granted King Henry the title of 'Defender of the Faith', much to his joy and honour, for he wished to be considered a serious power in Europe. With his allies in the Holy League, Father said the king was now ready for conquest and relied on the boundless energy and optimism of his minister, Thomas Wolsey. Wolsey was well aware that before the king left the country for France, the Tudor throne must be made safe, with no risk of an uprising from the House of York. Under his influence, the king agreed to the execution of Edmund de la Pole, Earl of Suffolk, the leading Yorkist claimant to the throne. The white rose with its sharp thorns was, he hoped, hacked down for good.

Father also mentioned how other members of the council were jealous of Wolsey's closeness to the king, but that Wolsey only smiled. Night after night, his chamber flickering in the candlelight, he worked on, determined to turn the king's dream of martial glory into a reality.

In April, my mother lost yet another brother, my Uncle Edward. Appointed Lord Admiral of the Fleet, he had taken part in the English attack upon the French. Desperate to avenge Knyvett's death, he had sailed away totally unprepared and mad with rage. To avoid capture by the French, he had scrambled overboard into the sea, where he drowned from the weight of his armour. He was a popular commander with his men, with great charisma and courage, and the mourning was great. Although there were no children from the marriage, it did come to light that Uncle Ned had sired two bastards. It broke Aunt Alice's heart. As a great friend of Charles Brandon, he asked him in his will to take care of one of the boys. Mother had adored her brother Ned, and as his death came close on the heels of her losing both Henry and her stepsister Muriel, it proved a bitter blow.

❦ ❦

Supervising my new wardrobe that spring helped Mother to recover from her black humour, for it kept her mind busy. Although I tried to stand patiently in the Long Gallery as she chose the cloth for my new gowns, I only fidgeted. She cast a critical eye as the cloth was draped for effect and, fussing and tweaking, shook her head.

'Really, Mrs Davenport, it must fit well at the elbow, I do not want them thinking our Nan is ill-dressed. Everything must be in the Burgundian style,' she said to the seamstress. 'We do not want to appear provincial. What does it say again in the letter?'

Mrs Davenport took the paper from her sleeve and started reading: 'Sleeves full with deep revers, not split in two parts, in the Italian style. Bodice laced at the front, the waist dropped, not high, and cut separate from the skirt. A demi-ceint or chain, hanging from the waist is most fashionable.'

Mother nodded thoughtfully.

'The fabric must be rich in decoration,' continued the seamstress, 'particularly animals, birds, and flowers. They say English embroidery is the finest in Europe, but for tailoring one cannot beat Antwerp.'

'Well, I thank God you learnt your craft there,' agreed Mother, pulling out my kirtle to check the length. 'Now, there must be more fullness here – no skimping – at least six yards. And there must be no train behind, for that is not the Burgundian fashion. Hannah, fetch me the sample dolls Thomas sent over. Now, shall we try the rose gown next?'

Mrs Davenport, copper pins in her mouth, nodded and lifted the pink robe over my head.

Mother straightened down the front of the hem, and stood back to get a better view. She frowned, tilting her head to one side. 'No, it will not do,' she muttered, 'The neckline is too low for a young girl. The regent runs a sober court.'

The seamstress pleated, folded and draped the gown while I watched Sorrel limp past. He appeared very thin these days. As I breathed out, I felt a pin fall to the floor.

Mother paced up and down, casting her eyes over the list of items produced to date and read them out loud: 'Item: One robe of tawny brocade lined with cream taffeta and fox fur. Item: One robe of gozzling green brocade, embroidered with berries and leaves lined with cream taffeta in the Flemish style. Item: One robe of ladies' blush pink lined with ivory sarcenet…'

She lowered the list. 'Should we have sent to Bruges for caps? I hear they are the finest in the world. No, no, she can acquire them there. And what of yellow – what do they call it in Italy? *Biavo*? I hear it is a most popular choice for gowns.'

I felt terribly important and thoroughly enjoyed the great fuss around me. There were boxes of gloves scented with almond and civet, garters of satin ribbon, coifs in cotton, and flannel and knitted petticoats. In a large basket, there were sleeves lined with coney, squirrel and otter, all scented with lavender. I also have to admit that I thoroughly enjoyed the uncharacteristic jealousy displayed by Mary, but it was her own fault that I was going in her place. This was *my* chance. Needless to say, she was put out and sat in the recess of the window, blowing her nose into a linen cloth, and sighing. Eventually, Mother's patience, ever frail, snapped.

'Mary!' she cried, 'will you stop sniffling right now, or I shall have you whipped. We are in no doubt that you have a cold, but can you think of no one but yourself? Do I not have enough to bear at present? You can see how this tries me.'

I stood feeling amused as Mary sneezed again.

'It is not fair,' she croaked. 'Why do I have to make do with country fashions, when she has new styles to choose from? I am the eldest, I have a right to look fashionable, too!'

Mother threw the list in her hand to the floor and walked up to Mary.

'*Right?* You have a right?' She leaned close to my sister's disgruntled face. 'By the Mass, you gave away your rights but awhile back, my lady, and do not forget it. You are nothing without this family, nothing. Now, go to your chamber and stay there!'

Mary ran out in tears.

Mrs Davenport had dropped her box of pins, and I watched as they scattered across the floor. Sorrel jumped forward to root among them and jerked his head up as one pricked his nose. I smiled. Foolish dog, how I would miss him.

'And you can take that smirk off your face,' said Mother, turning towards me. 'You are getting your ears pierced later, so there will be plenty of tears then, I can assure you. Really, you and your sister will put me in my grave before the day is out.'

● ●

Father returned from the court at Mechelen a month later than he intended, for the Channel was far too dangerous for the English ambassadors to cross, due to French hostilities. He waited with them at Calais, along with the marshal, Sir Richard Wingfield, and discussed how many tents, carts, and horses were to be dispatched by Thomas Wolsey for the coming campaign. When Father did return, he thought it safer if I took ship to Antwerp and then proceed by barge, rather than travel inland across French territory.

My parents were to ride with me as far as Dover, along with a Master William Grey, Ralph, one of our most trusted servants, and Hannah. Father had wanted to ride to Harwich and let me sail from there as it was cheaper, but Mother insisted on visiting the shrine of St Thomas, at Canterbury. I heard the argument in the estate office and Mother shouting at Father's miserly ways, but she got her way. Once there, I, along with Hannah, would be handed over to Monsieur Bouton, Captain of the Guard to Charles, Prince of Castile, who would see us both safely to Antwerp. Hannah would visit her family for a few weeks and return later to Hever, while the Captain and I would continue to the court in Mechelen. Having already escorted a young Flemish girl from the regent's court to England to join the household of Princess Mary, he was now taking an English girl back.

The night before my great journey I could not sleep for excitement, for I felt the luckiest girl in Christendom. I had lain, wide awake, staring at the shadows on the walls and wondering about my great adventure. When the dawn chorus began on that June morning, I was already dressed.

'Good. Is there anything else?' Father checked his bag for my letter of introduction and licence to travel. Mother shook her head and adjusted her riding cloak. 'Well, let us depart,' he ordered, mounting his horse.

I stood, my hair whipping across my face, and

smiled at Mary.

Blithe as ever, she was now quite content to stay behind, all thoughts of Edwin forgotten. She held me tight in her arms. 'Oh, I shall miss you, Nan, and you must write to me. Promise?'

I felt a prick of conscience, but I brushed it from my mind as George placed a small amber cross in my hand. 'It will keep you safe at sea – from pirates.' He smiled as I tied the amber cross on its brown velvet ribbon around my neck.

'Thank you, brother,' I said, as he kissed me. I would miss him very much.

As the servants loaded up the horses, I was lifted onto my mare. She turned on the spot, swinging her quarters around in the courtyard, restless to be gone, and Mrs Geddynge pulled George away from the sliding and slipping hooves. Then, taking hold of the bridle as the horse jittered and pawed the cobbles, she leant towards me. 'Remember, Nan, you are there to learn. Be of good cheer, quiet and modest, and be a credit to the Bullen family. Your Father will want to hear of your progress, and so you must write when you are able. I shall expect you to return an accomplished young lady, do you hear?'

I smiled and nodded.

'Here, wait, don't forget Bethany!' Mrs Orcharde hobbled out into the courtyard waving my wooden doll. As she tucked her into the saddlebag, I felt foolish taking a doll, but did not have the heart to remonstrate.

'Oh, my little lady, my dear little lady,' she cried. 'God keep you well and safe, my precious.'

She turned away as Mrs Geddynge, shaking her head and dabbing her eyes, rushed forward holding a small book. 'Don't forget your psalter,' she said, 'and keep working hard at your French. Promise me?'

My father wheeled his horse out of the courtyard and, raising his hand, wished God's blessing on all present. 'To Dover, William,' he ordered and, kicking the horses on, we cantered out across the estate towards the East road.

＊　＊

The countryside lay green and fresh with dew as we rode, stopping for the occasional rest and refreshments at a village inn. However, everything from the spitting rain to the great ruts in the dirt track caused by the ironmasters' carts received a sour comment from Father. Now and then, Mother would point to something and ask me to repeat it in French, which made a fine game with which to pass the time. When we fell quiet, the only sounds were the horses' hooves,' the bleating of sheep as we cantered past, and the occasional pheasant, flapping unseen in the hedgerows.

We pressed on, making our detour towards Canterbury, down the Pilgrim's Way to the edge of the city.

'Keep close,' said Father. 'It will be crowded, and we must not be separated. Really, Elizabeth, a market day is not a good day to travel,' he added, as a herdsman pushed past, trying to keep his cattle in line.

'And how else do I acquire my silk threads?' Mother took a step to avoid a long line of beggars and chanting pilgrims.

I stared at their bare feet and ragged garb as we passed, and Mother put her gloved hand disdainfully to her face as we trotted on. The odour of sweat and grime was overwhelming.

We clattered over the drawbridge of the Westgate with its enormous round stone towers, and pushed through into the city. As we passed the hospital, an old, crippled man hobbled into our path and sprinkled Mother's horse with a brush dipped in water. The horse pulled up its head with a snort, forcing Father to halt.

'What in God's name does he want?' he asked, as the crowds jostled around. The man, bent with some deformity, produced a mouldy shoe with a note pinned to it and held it up to Mother. She bent down to take it, read the scribble on the note, kissed the shoe reverently, and gave the man a coin.

'Becket's shoe,' she gathered up the reins. 'A blessing

from such a holy relic is worth a penny.'

I stared, fascinated, as the man tucked the shoe back into his coat, ready to accost another pilgrim.

As we continued towards the Company Hall and the Cheker of Hope Inn, I gazed around entranced, for I had never seen such a great crowd of people packed into the narrow, crowded streets all advertising their wares. The fetid air curled around my nostrils as we turned slowly down Mercery Lane, where offal and animal remains lay piled high beside the stalls, and blood ran freely into the gutters. Pigs' heads dangled from hooks, along with rabbits, ducks, and geese, and they gave a sickening stench to the confined space. Mother told me that the produce was often tainted, and blood from the meat used to stain the fish to make it appear fresher. However, the food alley was so gloomy from the overhanging, timbered houses I could hardly see the state of the produce, fresh or not.

As we turned into the Butter Market we came to another standstill.

'God's death, curse these crowds!' cried Father, 'we can move neither forwards nor backwards. I knew this was a mistake.'

'Thomas, mind your tongue, we are in a holy city,' said Mother. 'Have a little patience.'

We pushed through to Christ Church Gate but were halted as two men grabbed our horses' bridles.

'No animals past this point, sir.' One of them held out his hand expectantly. 'But we can hold them here while you go in.'

I looked up at the great cathedral in front, part of it covered in scaffolding and watched the workmen dangling high up in the air. Strapped to a harness, they appeared to be mending one of the great stained glass windowpanes.

'Well, we can go no further, Elizabeth, but I am not leaving the horses and our belongings here. William, Ralph, Hannah and I will wait while you take Nan to the shrine. But do not tarry long, mind, for we are in the thick of it here.'

I wandered with Mother amidst the crowded stalls beneath the cathedral walls. Religious statues, wooden crucifixes, medallions, medals, miraculous phials holding the blood of Christ or the tears of Our Lady were all on sale to be bought by eager pilgrims. Mother bought me a silver medallion bearing the image of our Blessed Lady, Star of the Sea, and pinned it to my coat. There was such a din as people argued and haggled over prices that I could hardly hear her speak. Once inside the cathedral a great throng of pilgrims, some richly dressed and some ragged beggars, crowded the aisle. As we walked over to Trinity Chapel, I spied the elaborate tomb of St Thomas. Two hooded monks stood on guard on the stone steps, holding lighted tapers, and in each corner, great candles blazed.

'Such treasures,' I whispered. 'It is beautiful.'

My mother bent down close to my ear. 'The Archbishop was brutally murdered very close to here. But come now, we must pray. When we have finished, we will visit the mercers' stalls and buy new threads and a roll of fine cloth from the Walloons.'

*   *

The following day we continued on our way until we gazed down upon Dover.

'There ahead, Nan,' said my father, pointing, 'is what the local people call "Paradise," because the pier provides a safe harbour for the ships. What think you?'

I squinted across at the great castle, my hand shielding my eyes from the bright June sun.

We then made a steep descent down the winding hill into the bustling harbour where two large forts stood, their standards fluttering in the strong breeze.

'See here, Ralph?' said William, removing his cap and scratching his shaved head. 'Two hundred years ago, ten thousand French bastards burnt this place to the ground

– begging your pardon, my lady.'

I stared amazed, not at his words, but at the harbour full of ships, their sails fluttering and billowing in the wind.

'Well,' he said, 'they will get their sorry arses licked soon enough when we launch across the Narrow Seas and invade them from Calais. Three hundred of our finest warships will set sail from here, and then, by God, the French fuckers will find themselves roasting in the fires of Hell, will they not, Thomas?'

Father and Ralph laughed, but Mother turned her horse away.

'Pity *The Regent* sank last year,' he said. 'Still, His Grace is now building *The Great Harry*.

'Aye, William,' said Father, 'one thousand, five hundred tons this time, bigger and better than the cursed French ship. It will be the first two-decked warship we have ever built. Wait till they see that great bitch! His Grace has also commissioned and transported thirteen great guns from Germany and Mechelen to give the French a blast they will not forget.'

They laughed together, oblivious of Mother's disdainful stare.

'England is gripped with war fever, and it cannot come too soon,' said William. 'The royal forests fall daily, hacked to pieces to make gun carriages, cradles, and engines of war.'

Ignoring the talk of war, I took in the sights, smells, and noise of this fascinating place. Above, the seabirds cried and circled, swooping down to fight and squabble over the scraps of stale fish and rubbish, reminding me of Cromer.

We turned up a cobbled street, narrow and steep, and stopped outside The Bell Inn. A boy hurried out, took my horse's bridle and turned it around. I dismounted at the steps, and Father gave the lad a coin as Mother walked stiffly to the water trough and sat on the edge. She dabbed her kerchief in the dank pool and bathed her neck, stretching her stiff back. My father ignored her and slapped his horse's rump as the boy led it away. He was still in a bad humour with her for spending money in Canterbury and leaving him standing with the restless horses. For two hours he had waited, seething with impatience.

'Now, Nan,' said Mother, 'when we have rested and taken refreshments, we will go to the church of St Mary-the-Virgin and pray for a safe journey.'

• •

At eight o'clock the following morning, the sky some-what grey, we made our way down to the harbour. There was a great deal of noise and bustle as men dressed in strange attire dragged barrels of supplies and goods up the gangway, cursing and spitting as they worked. I could not help but stare at their grimy jackets of blue and white horizontal stripes, and scarlet hose.

Mother pulled me aside. 'Sailors, Nan, vile men. Come away.'

I gazed on, curious, as we walked down the wooden planks, greasy rats squealing and scurrying at my feet. At the bottom, a tall, well-dressed gentleman with a ruddy complexion came striding forth. He bowed to my parents, and he and father clasped arms. I thought he was exotic with his strange accent and feathered bonnet, but from here on Monsieur Bouton, Captain of the Guard, was to be my escort.

'There is your ship, Thomas, *The Gryphon*,' he announced, pointing to the distance.

I saw that the vessel waiting for me was not particularly large. In fact, it appeared quite long and narrow, and I wondered how it would float without toppling over, for there were many people waiting to board. Father checked the documents and handed them over to my escort.

'We will leave you here, Nan,' said my mother, 'and wish you God speed. Hannah will be with you, but may the Blessed Virgin go with you, too, my child. Oh, how I envy you!' She was tearful and held me close, kissing and stroking my hair. I clung to her tightly, one eye on my father as he stepped forward.

'Come, now, come, this is no way for you to begin,' he said impatiently, placing his hand on my shoulder. 'You will be home soon with much to tell the others. Now, run along with Hannah. Go to, quick, quick.'

I kissed my mother's cheek, as wet as the dockside stone, before she gently pushed me away. Taking hold of my hands, she bent down and looked into my face. 'Remember, Anne, your great-grandfather's motto – repeat it to me.'

I held my chin high. I had longed for this chance and I would not be afraid. 'Now thus, now thus, now thus,' I said.

Mother nodded, straightened her back, and quickly dusted the shoulder of my green, woollen cloak. 'Good. So be it. Now, thus, this is your chance,' she said, 'your chance to learn how to serve a great lady at a great court, your chance to learn all she can teach you. God bless and keep you, my child. Oh, blessed St Anthony and guide of pilgrims, direct Anne's steps in the straight path. Protect her from shipwrecks and all harm, and bring her safely home. Amen.' She pulled me close to her again. 'Wait! Here, take this.' She pressed a silver shilling into my palm, and I closed my fingers tight. 'For luck, Nan.'

●　●

I took my escort's hand and stepped down onto the waiting boat, ready for the boatman to row me to the ship. When we had alighted onboard, I was shown to a tiny wooden cabin, barely high enough for me to step into. As the captain slid the door to one side, a grey cat carrying something bloody in its jaws darted out. I stepped carefully in, not sure what else I might find. The cabin was dark, and as I placed my doll on the narrow bed, I heard the lapping water and smelt the musty dampness as the boat bobbed and tilted. I overheard the sailors say that poor weather was on its way and gave Hannah a brave smile, for she seemed anxious as she glanced about for somewhere to sit. Then, as the pilot called out, the ship's bell clanged, and the vessel began to drift away from the harbour. Sailors moved in every direction, and as I peered out of the little door, I saw they were toothless and grimy as they hoisted the sails. In the corner of the deck the cat sat, yellow eyes closed in contentment, licking its bloody paw. I stepped out and reached for the wooden rail of the boat, feeling exhilarated that now my great adventure would begin.

As the harbour and magnificent white cliffs began to recede, the captain told me to go back to my cabin with Hannah while he fetched something to eat. He returned with a wooden tray on which stood three pewter bowls of salted cod pottage, herrings with cheat loaf, cheese and three flagons of small beer. I drank the beer and shuddered, for it was as sour and bitter as a crab apple. I picked at the bread and cheese but pushed away the herrings.

'You do not like the fish?' asked the captain.

I shook my head. 'No, Monsieur, my mother tried to make me eat raw herrings once when we visited Cromer, and I was very sick.'

'But they taste good from that particular part of the coast,' he said, breaking off a chunk of bread. He smiled as I ate the cheese and we sat in silence.

Within the hour, the wind grew much stronger, and as the ship began to lurch, the smell of the fish made me feel ill. It lingered in the small cabin, and I begged leave to go onto the deck for some fresh air. My escort agreed and sat me down on a trunk out of the way of the busy sailors. Although I repeatedly swallowed, feeling cold and uncomfortable, I could not stop the rising bile, and I voided with such force it caught the broom of a passing sailor. He carried on sweeping the wooden boards clear of water, and now vomit, without a word. On his shoulder sat a small, chattering monkey and, without warning, it shrieked and jumped onto my back. I squealed in terror at the hideous creature and, throwing it off, heaved again. The monkey squealed too and leapt to a high rail baring its tiny, sharp teeth at me as if laughing.

'No matter, my lady,' said the captain, 'everyone spews forth sooner or later.'

I looked down at the vomit and with tearful eyes, shivered. This was no adventure, this was dreadful, for each time I looked up, the horizon rolled out of sight, and my stomach lurched along with the ship. My father was right to hate crossing the sea and my eyes brimmed over with tears.

'Pray, do not let the monkey return,' I wailed, swallowing the bile mixed with bread.

The captain put his arms around me and took me back to the cabin. There he laid me on the narrow pallet and covered me with a rough, red coverlet. I felt frozen. Hannah opened a small pouch and handed me a ginger lozenge as the monkey ran screeching in and leapt onto the table. It held something wet and slimy in its paws, and my escort shooed it out.

'Detestable wretch,' he muttered, dragging the sliding door shut. I decided I hated it too, for with its tiny, wizened face and long, thin limbs it looked like a devil.

'The ship,' I said, sucking the sugary comfit and snuggling down, 'how does it know where it is going? I have read books of exploration, but do not fully understand.'

The captain sat on the edge of the narrow bed and turned to face me.

'Well, as the pilot has the care of the ship, he must have instruments of diverse fashions. The most important tool of these is the ship's compass. From this, he can plot the course from port to port. He must be cunning and an expert on the movement of heavenly spheres, such as the moon, the stars and the sun. He must know the rains and the winds, the ebbing, flowing and even saltiness of the sea.'

'What of the sailors?' I asked. 'Where do they come from?'

'They come from the Southwark or Antwerp stews, and are mostly thieves,' he replied. 'This way they can at least be fed, for they eat better here than they might if they were just vagrants on land.

'And what of Antwerp?' I asked, now warm beneath my cover.

'Why, Antwerp is the loveliest city in the world, and one I know well, as you do, do you not, mistress?' He turned to Hannah, then continued. 'It rose to prosperity when Emperor Maximilian quashed the rebellion in Bruges and transferred the trade to it. It is a country of prosperity where goods from the New World, the East and our own world, exchange hands, particularly pepper. It is a city of diamonds, emeralds, and pearls and is linked inextricably to this great age of voyages and exploration. It is the vital centre of Europe and traders of every different nationality seemed to fill its flat, cobbled squares. The old citadel has twelve gates around the city, and the River *Dijle* provides the waterway to Mechelen. The whole city is a dense network of natural waterways, the like of which you will never have seen before. But come, you look pale, try and rest awhile.'

※　※

It was some hours later when I was woken by screaming from the deck and the clattering and sliding of furniture in the cabin. The ship, it appeared, was caught in a terrible summer storm and seemed beyond hope of ever reaching safety. The rain lashed down in torrents onto the deck and into the cabin, and outside I could hear the clamour and yells of the men as they slipped and fell. The monkey made no noise, and I hoped it had lost its grip and fallen into the sea. Thunder crashed, and I shut my eyes tight as the lightning lit up the cabin.

Hannah squealed 'St Elmo, protector of sailors! Come to our aid!'

Holding fast to George's little cross, I fixed my eyes on Mother's medallion and refused to be afraid.

When dawn finally broke, I was awakened by the noise of church bells ringing, and a hammering and clinking on the dockside. When I looked out, I saw great Dutch *fluyts* and carracks waiting to unload their cargo, which hung precariously from cranes and pulleys. We had reached the safety of Antwerp harbour. As we were rowed to the quayside, the harbour master directed our little boat to its mooring. The captain carried me onto dry land and set me carefully down, but my legs felt unsteady. To my utter dismay, the monkey ran ahead intent on eating whatever rubbish it could find. I watched as it picked up a piece of dirty apple peel, nibbled it, and tossed it away in disgust. But I was still fascinated by what I saw ahead. Amidst the bustle of activity, richly dressed merchants quarrelled and bartered with each other, and my escort pointed out the barrels rolling and bumping noisily down the wooden planks.

'Wool, tin, and cheese from England,' he said. 'Salt fish and dried fish from Norway, furs from Russia, wines from Bordeaux, Burgundy and the Rhine, and fruit from Spain. Over there, is sugar candy from Candia in Greece. Look – see how they break open the boxes to check the contents? The spice importers bring many rare and expensive wares, too, such as incense and ivory as well as senna, anise, cumin, and cloves.'

'What is that strange smell?' I asked, as we pushed through the great press of people.

'Saffron, my lady,' came the reply. 'It takes the briny taste out of salt meat, but the spice merchants from Egypt also sell saffron to the Flemish painters to make their yellow pigment. Do you know where the best saffron in the world is grown? You should.'

I could not think for my mind was tired and my ribs ached from retching.

He smiled. 'It is in the village of Walsingham, in Norfolk.'

'Have a care, my lady!' Hannah pulled my arm as a large woman, carrying a great basket of apples knocked into me, sending the apples rolling in every direction. The woman cursed in some guttural tongue as we quickly moved on.

'Ah, I have found you!' Hannah flew into a woman's embrace and then introduced her brother and sister. They talked briefly as I watched the scene on the quayside before she turned to me. 'I must leave you now, Mistress Anne,' she said, with a bob, 'but I wish you Godspeed and leave you in the capable hands of Claude.'

The little group then left and, taking the hand of my escort, I watched as they disappeared into the crowd.

We walked to the square, crowded with merchants, horsemen, carts and housewives, and then on to the waterside where we were to embark for Mechelen. There, the barge covered with canvas swayed on the canal as two boatmen attached the ropes to a horse's harness. The heavy animal stood patiently on the bank, feeding from its nosebag, oblivious to the pummelling and pulling as the men tied the rope knots. Once we boarded, a handbell rang, and the horse moved forward without any prompting. I imagine he had heard the bell many times and did not need to be told.

The barge gradually began to move as a boy steered the horse and the boatmen steered the barge, and we started our journey along the waterways of this strange land. Here the scene was very different from the rolling countryside of Kent, for it was flat and wide, making the dozens of church spires visible for miles. A great many windmills studded the meandering landscape, and within the space of an hour, the light had changed from yellow to pink, and from mauve to grey, illuminating the countless wet ditches. The tall buildings blended in perfectly with the natural colour of the land for they were the most beautiful colours of ochre, brown, russet and grey. As we glided past the narrow houses, I could see that their wooden facades were brightly painted and their deep-cut gables intricately stepped.

On we meandered, through the dense network of natural waterways, under narrow bridges and past crooked houses almost touching each other across the water. When we reached the open, flat countryside, tall, swaying reeds lined the banks of the river and I observed the long-legged birds high in the trees.

'Heron,' said the captain, opening his knapsack to reveal bread cakes, a green-coloured cheese, and some walnuts. I nodded, for I had seen such birds in Kent.

'Their lofty flight,' he continued, 'is due to their fear of storms, and so they fly above them. As nature's weather vane they tell the onset of rain.' I looked after them, shielding my eyes, as the birds slowly and gracefully launched into the air.

Gradually, we made our approach to Mechelen along the River *Dijle,* the sun sinking to a golden globe in the pink-streaked sky. In the distance, above the jumbled roofs of the houses, I pointed to a high tower.

'What is that, Monsieur?'

'Ah, St Rombout's church, and you will see that the tower is still being built. It will be higher yet when it is finished.'

'And the village?' I asked as we sailed past neat houses and churches. My questions were endless.

He looked patiently up. 'Not a village, but the *Groot Begijnhof* where good, Christian women live and do charitable works. On the right is the Convent of Bethany. Over thirty convents lie within and outside Mechelen, which is why you will see very little begging here. People work, or they receive care.'

I thought of the beggars standing by the gate at Hever and the bread we gave them as our Christian duty.

As we approached the mossy, grey, crenellated walls of the city, I observed how the river was now becoming quite congested with sailing boats, rowing boats, and barges, and we had to wait while a wooden bridge was raised to let our boat through. As the officials on the quay finally waved us along, we passed the great *Winketpoort* gate, and entered the city of Mechelen. We then came to a second bridge, with a tollhouse on the quayside and an enormous crane, and I saw a large crowd of people gathered about. There was a great deal of noise and activity as the boatmen pulled in their sails and started unloading huge barrels, presumably of beer and wine, from the barges. They shouted and called to each other in a strange language as ropes were hoisted and barrels steadied.

'All transport must stop here to unload,' said the captain, as one of the boatmen threw a rope to the men on the quayside. 'Ships carrying goods have to stay here for three days to sell their produce at the markets in Mechelen before moving on. It is a fair system. Some produce will be wool from Scotland,' he said, pointing to a large, wooden crate as it swung across the water from a merchant's boat. 'We have the best weavers here, but Scotland, for all its war-mongering, has the best wool,' he added.

As I stepped out of the boat up to the quayside, I felt quite sick again. 'Oh, Monsieur! What *is* that terrible smell?' I cried, covering my mouth, afraid I might retch.

'*Vismarkt!*' said an official, observing my pale face and making a swimming motion with the flat of his hand. He then checked our papers and nodded that all was in order.

'As he said, the fish market,' said the captain, with a laugh. 'You can smell it throughout the city, but you will get used to it. Madame Regent asked the townspeople to have it moved further from the palace, but they refused. They said if they have to tolerate the stink, then so must she.'

As I stood on the steps brushing down my cloak, a finely-dressed woman stepped forward from out of the crowd.

'Claude?' she enquired, lowering her hood to reveal the lappets of her crisp, white headdress.

'Lady Middlebourg,' he answered, kissing her outstretched hand. 'It is always such a pleasure to see you. How lovely you look – enchanting.' His eyes lingered appreciatively. 'This is our young lady from England, Anna Boullan.'

I made a slight bob, and she smiled in delight. 'Anna, welcome to our beautiful city. I am here to accompany you to the court.'

'How is your mother?' asked my escort, taking her arm.

'She is well, Claude, but her eyesight is failing. And you?

You must have experienced the dreadful storm we had here.
The child looks pale and tired.'

They talked together as I stood, nauseated by the smell
of fish, until we walked away from the quayside and on to
the slippery cobbles of the street.

'Now, my lady,' said the captain, turning to me, 'your
belongings have been sent on ahead, so as it is a beautiful
evening we will walk to ease the limbs, and see something
of this fair place. I shall be your guide, and when Madame
Regent speaks with you, she shall be amazed at your knowledge of her city.'

As we walked beside the small canal, or *vlietje*, young
boys with great buckets of water sluiced down the cobbles,
and girls carrying large, empty baskets stacked them up
ready for the following day. Stout, red-faced women with
raw, cracked hands dismantled the striped awnings of the
stalls and turned to me with toothless smiles. I jumped out
of the way as a scrawny, greasy dog snarled and snapped, and
a spitting cat leapt under a basket.

'Everything happens on this street,' said my guide above
the noise, 'for mutton, fish, grain and money are traded
here. Everything is for sale. Why, if the city dog catcher sees
that slavering dog there he will kill it and sell its pelt to the
Glovers Company.'

I looked back at the cowering dog and thought its
flea-bitten coat would make a poor pair of gloves.

'Yes, you have come to a wealthy city, my lady, and the
houses behind on the Salt Wharf are the finest in the city.'

I gazed in wonder at the strange buildings, all brightly
painted in pale pink, green or blue. Each front bore an image
in plaster, stone or wood of an animal or some other such
device. One was named *'The Golden Fish'*, another *'The
Mermaid'*, and yet another *'The Heron.'* England did not have
such odd lodgings as these, for they were very tall and narrow
– some five storeys high – with tiny paned windows, arches
and stepped roofs. I was told they were built upwards, rather

than sideways, due to the shortage of land and building space.

We continued on until we approached a castle-like building, crenelated with small turrets, and flags that fluttered in the breeze.

'That, mistress, is the *Schepenhuis,* or, as you might say, the Aldermen's House where the Great Council of Mechelen resides. Since justice is done there, it is a place of great importance.'

A little further we stopped at a large bustling square, crowded with striped covered stalls and booths where housewives and young boys were busy either buying or selling goods. I stared at the strange objects hanging from hooks and was told they were great fat sausages. I watched as one was chopped open and a housewife tasted it. She nodded her head enthusiastically as other women started to gather about her.

It was then that I was confronted with the sight of the church and its tower.

'Is it not magnificent?' asked my guide. 'St Rombout's contains the holy bones of the blessed saint himself. It is a wondrous church of immense height, and from the top, you can see Antwerp. It has numerous bells – one of them is named the '*Jhesu*' – and here in the Low Countries, we pride ourselves on our beautiful chiming bells. The church tower is not yet finished, as you can see from the scaffolding.'

I gazed up and wondered if any of the churches seen thus far on my travels would ever be finished.

Lady Middlebourg stepped forward. 'I'm afraid more money is required from the good people of Mechelen to continue building, but they will be happy to pay and thereby spend less time suffering the torments of purgatory. God loves a generous soul!' she said, smiling.

'This large square,' she continued, 'is the *Grôte Markt,* and it is a meeting place for traders, perhaps on their way from England to the Rhine, or pilgrims staying at the hostel of St Rombout. As you can see, it is busy and, no doubt, you will purchase goods here for my lady.'

We stood listening as the great bells of the church chimed the hour, and Monsieur Bouton closed his eyes in ecstasy. 'Sublime,' he murmured. 'I hear the bells and, although I was not born here, I know I am home.'

We continued past the crowded square with its fine houses, inns, and hostels, to the Town Hall, the Cloth Hall and the Belfry. On we walked down a narrow street to a small, open square called the *Veemarkt*. It was obvious from the numerous piles of dung – and the smell – that animals had been here, and I was told this was where beasts were bought and sold on market days. I then noticed, across from the *Veemarkt*, a magnificent turreted building of white Brabant stone, glowing pink from the setting sun.

'Is that the palace, Monsieur?'

'No, my lady, you are looking at the palace of Margaret of York – the *Keizershof* – or Imperial court. She has been missed these ten years past, God rest her soul. See the many windows? However, our destination is the regent's palace – *the Hof van Savoyen*. Come, ladies.'

We walked a little further until we reached a large church with an enclosed wooden bridge high above the cobbles, and I could see that it was linked to the side of a grand adjacent house.

'This is St Peter's church and on the other side of the palace is the chapel of St Julian,' explained Lady Middlebourg. 'The convent of the Black Sisters used to be here, but the regent shifted it six years ago as they cared for plague victims. She did not want to risk any contagion to the royal children.'

She shook her head at the thought as several richly dressed gentlemen on horseback trotted past. I felt uneasy. Move the fish market, move the holy sisters – what sort of a demanding woman was I about to serve? We continued on in silence until I saw it – the regent's palace – exactly as Father once described. As I stood there, gazing up at the great wooden gate, guarded on both sides, my heart began to race. Here I was in a strange land with people I did not know, did not fully understand and might not like. Having sinned against my sister by stealing this opportunity from her, I wondered if I would now be punished. What if the *mère des filles* in charge of the maids had a bad temper and beat me? What if the regent was cruel? What if the other girls were spiteful and made fun of my strange finger and sallow looks? What if … I did not have a single friend or member of my family with me at this moment, but I swept aside my fears. This is what I had wanted. I was not a child anymore. As I took a deep breath, I remembered that I was a Boleyn and a Howard and repeated to myself again 'Now thus, now thus, now thus…'

* *

The noise of the wooden shutters opening and the soft light pouring into the wood-panelled chamber caused me to stir. I squinted and watched as a chamberer, sleeves rolled up and apron on, dusted around the embrasure. Her untidy hair fell from a stiff linen coif, and she impatiently pushed the loose tendrils back. Two other maids swept the floor with brooms made of stout twigs, and in the beams of grey light they sent up a flurry of dust motes.

A young woman entered the chamber carrying pale blue flowers in a blue and white bowl, and bobbed to me before placing them on the oak table. 'It is six of the clock, my lady, and I am here to dress you ready for your audience with the regent.'

I gave a thin smile, for I was somewhat confused by her Brabant French tongue. I slid out of bed in my chemise and peered out of the paned window. Standing on tiptoe, I could see that my chamber was situated at the top of the palace above an enclosed, cobbled courtyard.

'Is she pleasant, the Lady Margaret?' I asked, turning.

To my surprise, the girl put her finger to her lips and lowered her eyes. 'I am here to dress you, my lady, not gossip.

Gossip is forbidden by Madame.'

I splashed the cold water from the proffered earthenware bowl over my face and dried it on the white napkin. The young woman placed my rose-coloured gown over my head and began to lace the sleeves. She then placed a cap of pearls on the back of my head. I turned to the steel mirror, and a small girl with dark eyes stared back. When I turned around, a cup of warm, frothy milk and a small manchet loaf with cold beef were laid out on the table.

'Now, eat,' said the young woman. 'Then I shall take you to Madame.'

• •

As we walked, it soon became apparent that this part of the palace was undergoing major reconstruction work, for masons, builders and carpenters were up and busy, eager to work in the cool of the day. They stepped to one side as we passed by. We continued down a grand staircase to the courtyard outside, where yet more workmen wheeled barrows of broken stone and brick. Dust flew, and I gave a great sneeze. The gentlemen-at-arms crossed the courtyard and opened the enormous wooden doors. They revealed, at the top of a staircase, two magnificent stained glass windows, and hanging from the ceiling, an enormous, wrought iron candelabra. I paused to look closely at the tapestry on the wall, for it portrayed a unicorn set amidst a background of *millefleurs* and was brilliant in its colours. The opposite wall, covered in burgundy-red damask and patterned with gold, gave the effect of great opulence.

'Come – *come*,' said the maid, 'do not tarry, for Madame does not like to be kept waiting.'

We walked briskly up the stone steps, passing a pretty open balcony with a private view of the courtyard below, and finally paused outside an arched doorway. Above it, stone gargoyles stared down, their twisted faces pressed to their books and, above them on a stone scroll, the chiselled words *'Fortune, Infortune, Fort une.'* I nervously smoothed down my gown.

The two guards withdrew their halberds as the maid, curtsying, announced my arrival. A moment later a muffled voice from within cried *'entre!'* I felt my heart quicken as I followed the maid into a chamber that appeared to be crowded with cabinets full of curios and housed a great aviary of twittering birds.

'Mademoiselle Anna Boullan,' announced the maid, before disappearing.

I was left alone, staring in abject horror at the sight before me. Perched on a large chair sat the most monstrous woman I could ever have imagined. Brown-skinned, short-armed and hunchbacked, her feet barely touched the floor as she sat fanning herself with a great painted fan. Her gaudy, orange-coloured garb – I could hardly describe it as a gown – was trimmed with red and yellow tinsel, and her hair lay hidden beneath a monstrous, yellow winged cap. Around her neck, she wore a great many chains – all tangled and heaped upon each other – and heavy pearls dangled from her drooping ear lobes. Her eyes were cast down, her lips badly painted and I noticed her short, fat fingers were heavily be-ringed. She reminded me of the monkey on the ship, brown and wizen-faced. Horrified at the ghastly sight before me I wanted to flee from the chamber in terror. The seated woman glanced up quickly with her bulbous, myopic eyes and grunted. I dropped to a deep curtsey onto the turkey rug, feeling my heart pounding beneath my bodice. What in the name of Heaven had I come to? Was God punishing me for my cruelty towards my sister? Then, as I raised my eyes, four little dogs flew into the chamber barking and bounding towards me.

'My dearest child, welcome, welcome to my court!' A red velvet drape swept aside, and a smiling, beautifully dressed woman entered. She was wearing a black silk gown with a girdle of white enamelled roses, and from it hung a gold filigree paternoster. A white cap covered her hair, along with a white widow's barb, and, on top, sat a coif of starched white linen. The ugly vision on the chair quickly scrabbled to its feet and hid behind the drape.

'Ah, shush now, little ones, get out from under my feet! Bella, you naughty little dog, stop that noise!' The woman walked towards me, her arms outstretched.

'Rise, rise, my dear, how delighted I am to see you. Now, we must speak in French for I speak no English. Come – come and kiss me, do not be afraid.'

Sweet Jesu, I thought, what a relief! As I kissed, her I smelt the sweet odour of rose water. I noticed she was taller than average, her forehead full and round above fair, sandy brows, and I caught a glimpse of golden, curled hair. I knew that at thirty-three she was, in reality, past her bloom, but she was still quite lovely. Her nose was broad, and her jaw jutted forward, but she had soft, hazel-brown eyes. Her full, sensuous lips gave way to large even teeth as she smiled and scrutinised my face.

'Now, let me look at you. Why, you appear to be as dear a creature as your father described. Mariska, please bring some cordial.'

A young girl hurried out of the chamber as I glanced nervously at the ugly little dwarf scuttling over to the window seat.

'Ah, Anna, you must not be afraid of my innocent child here – I do not like the term fool for she is no such thing. Her name is Neutken, and she amuses me greatly.' She turned to the woman who, instead of curtsying, hopped clumsily around and bowed like a man, left and right. Much relieved, I was now rather curious.

'Now, I have heard much from your father and gather you have a dog at home – do you like my dogs?'

I must have appeared puzzled for she smiled. 'I will speak slower my child for no doubt my accent is strange to you.' She picked up one of the little dogs for me to hold, and as

I nuzzled its silky fur, the creature twisted round to lick my face, making me giggle.

'His name is Beau, and he is a rude little fellow for he chews everything. His sisters are Bella, Bianca, Bisou, and Bonbon. The greyhound by the hearth is Balzac.' On hearing its name, the hound raised its head briefly, and then laid it back on his paws.

'Why, Madame, I love dogs very much,' I said, stroking little Beau.

She smiled as the ugly dwarf moved forward, balancing a parrot on her arm.

'Apart from Neutken, my parrot here is my constant companion. He is very old; his plumage is somewhat faded, but he understands French, do you not?' she stroked the parrot's head.

I put the puppy down, and the parrot stretched out one of its clawed feet as if reaching for me. I stepped back.

'Come now, Patou, do not frighten my young visitor. Be nice,' chided Margaret, feeding the parrot a piece of apple. It took the morsel gently in its claw before putting it up to its great, hooked beak.

'I love my birds, as you can see,' she said, pointing to the aviary behind. 'Now, let me show you something else.' She walked over to a cage in the corner of the chamber as I stood watching with curiosity.

'Come, come look,' she beckoned, smiling. 'I have many pets, including a marmoset – but this one you will find most amusing.' She then picked up a large ball of chestnut-coloured fur. The ball gave an indignant squeak as she placed it in my hands. 'This little man is called Coco, and he is a guinea pig from the New World. He cost me a great fortune. Have you ever seen such an odd creature before?'

I stared down at the peculiar thing, somewhat round and shapeless, its breath rapid as it peered out with small, beady eyes.

'Madame, he does not look like a pig,' I ventured.

Margaret laughed. 'No, indeed, he is not a pig at all. Come, let us put him back in his warm bed and talk of more serious matters.'

We moved to a double seat, and Margaret bade me sit down beside her, rather than on the floor cushion.

'Now,' she said, making herself comfortable, 'I am pleased to hear you have a godly love of learning. The education of women must be encouraged, as must their virtue. My court here is the centre of music, art, and poetry and you shall leave here a cultured young lady. I have promised your father as much. Do you like beautiful things, Anna?'

I nodded, although apart from the brooch given to me by my mother, and a shell decorated mirror from Mary, I did not own anything of value or beauty.

'Well, when I have more time, I will show you my wonderful collections of crystal, glass, enamel, and silver, and you will become quite a connoisseur.'

My eyes then moved to two wooden busts on a shelf. Painted in life-like colours, their eyes appeared to stare back at me.

'With respect, Madame, may I ask who these might be?'

Margaret turned round and rose. 'These? Why this one,' she said, picking up one of the busts, 'is my dear, deceased husband, Philibert. He was my life. Was he not handsome?' She put the statue back in its place and straightened it slightly. 'The other is of myself. I am lucky to have the talent of my sculptor Monsieur Conrat Meit.' She lifted my chin and scrutinised my face. 'Why, I shall enjoy your bright company for you exude curiosity and have no fear of speaking out. I like that. There will be much for you to learn here and many places for you to see. But, as usual, I have talked far too much. Soon you will meet my young wards, but for now, you must go to see the Countess of Hochstrate, la mère des filles, who will be responsible for your welfare. Welcome to my court.'

The woman stared at me intently and walked slowly around as I sat motionless on a stool. The grey damask of her gown swished as she moved, and her white Flemish cap showed a hint of fair hair beneath. Sharp of face, her green eyes narrowed.

'You are a bright girl, I hear,' she said, in excellent English, her hands folded neatly in front of her gown, 'but you are very small and under-developed for your age. I would say delicate. Do you have a good appetite? Do you walk in the fresh air?'

I said I did and looked up into her pale face.

She raised her brow. 'Why they have sent someone so young, Heaven alone knows. Well, since you cannot be a maid of honour, I shall have to think about where to put you. Now, tell me again, how old are you, nine?' I felt indignant.

'I am thirteen, my lady.'

'Oh, my goodness, my dear you appear so very slight. Well, I see we shall be placing you with the other *demoiselles* after all. Do you bleed?'

I was taken aback.

'Come now, do not be abashed. You know of these things? We have no secrets at court, and under my charge you will have no secrets from me. Well?'

'Why, not as yet my lady – but I –'

'You will. You will. Your body still thinks it is a child so you must grow strong and ready for your monthly courses.' She smiled, encouragingly. 'Ready for marriage. You must be agreeably fleshy for your husband-to-be, strong for future childbearing. With the grace of God, and with sound train-ing under my guidance in womanly and courtly arts, you will make a good marriage for your family and your time here will not be wasted.' She folded her hands. 'Now, it is as well you understand your duties.'

I was not at all sure what duties she meant, and it must

have shown on my face.

'Do not be concerned, for you are primarily here to be educated.'

As she opened the window a cool breeze floated in, and outside on the clipped grass a group of courtiers were enjoying a game of bowls. Their laughter, and the click of the wooden balls, drifted through the window.

'Firstly,' she said, turning around, 'the duty of a maid of honour is to attend the Regent Margaret – or Madame as she insists on being called. Now, let me tell you how she spends her day, for you will have to know where to be at any given time.' She cleared her throat and began. 'Madame rises at five in the morning and insists her dogs are taken outside, for she absolutely will not have them fouling her chambers. When they have returned, she feeds them herself and prepares for Mass in her private chapel in St Peter's church. A private covered walkway links it to her bedchamber. We attend Mass, and afterwards Madame will eat privately and not be disturbed. Having eaten, she makes her way to the Presence Chamber and sits listening to requests from any who wish to approach her. With vacant offices to fill, papers to sign, and disputes to settle there is much to attend to. Many people come to her, including ambassadors, noblemen or foreigners and she is very careful to note the names of every person presented, and pass any complaints on to the Master of Requests. You might be required to assist her, but usually, her closest confidantes are at hand. Do you understand?'

I said I did.

'At noon, she dines in private – sometimes in public – and you will be required to ensure there is nothing she needs. You must be pleasant and gay and take her mind off the heavy affairs of state. She likes to hear music while she eats, for it soothes her stomach and chases off the cares of the morning. Why, you may even be required to sing, if you can.'

I hid the thrill I felt inside, for I knew my voice was pleasant.

'But not yet, my dear, only when you have settled in. Madame would not want it to be an ordeal for you.'

I felt disappointed for although it was one thing to sing with Mary at home, and quite another to sing in front of such an illustrious person, I wanted to show off my talent.

'After she has dined, Madame might attend her council on appointed days, or return to her chamber to study her art collection. She is compiling a great inventory with Monsieur de Belges and finds it most absorbing. She might go for a walk with her dogs, or relax by reading or sewing with her ladies. She also likes to spend some time each day with the royal children for they give her great joy and solace. After Vespers, she spends her evenings reading state papers and dictating to her secretary. Retiring at nine o'clock promptly, the royal children are brought to her for a blessing.'

My eyes followed the lady as she paced about, twisting the amber ring on her finger.

'When not required, you will attend your lessons, and I will give you a timetable for your instruction. You will not have a moment to think of home. Now, the maids must learn to behave in a pleasing manner. Do you know what this manner might be, child?'

I hesitated. 'A maid must be virtuous and – and …'

'Yes, yes, go on – she must be virtuous,' prompted the Countess, 'for without virtue all else is but dust.'

'And – and peruse only books for moral instruction,' I added.

'Indeed, Anna, when she writes, she should not copy idle verse or frivolous ditties, but rather some sentiment from Holy Scriptures.'

I had evidently made a good start. 'A maid must have a modest demeanour, but not be dull, sad or pensive for she must be entertaining.' I gave her my best smile, and she appeared taken aback.

'Indeed – just so – and she should bear herself well and have a gentle, educated manner, but not be opinionated.

She must be industrious, obedient, trustworthy, loyal and discreet. But what of her duties?' she asked.

I remembered my mother's instructions. 'To always be helpful to one's elders.'

'That is correct, for a maid must be helpful at court functions and, ideally, be fluent in French, Latin or Spanish. Many important people such as ambassadors and dignitaries visit the court, and you will be encouraged to converse politely with them.' She narrowed her eyes. 'Do not become one of those vain people who insist on only talking to people of a certain rank. A lady must be polite. Madame's father, the Emperor,' she said, 'is a wonderful example of how to be charming with people of all classes, and Madame, thank God, has inherited his talent.'

She closed the shutters to block out the noise from the bowling green. 'When older, no doubt, you will become a lady-in-waiting like your mother, and it is of great importance you take heed of '*Les Triomphes des Dames.*'

She picked a book from her bureau and held up the bound, red leather cover. 'Here is your own copy. Do not mislay it, for no court lady can succeed without it. It will be as your Bible.' She opened the pages. 'Each poem in this book describes the virtues of a lady-in-waiting, and how they can succeed at court through impeccable behaviour and beautiful appearance. For example, when you dress in the morning, it describes in exquisite detail how to put each item on with the utmost care. Everything is described from your under linen to your stockings, petticoats, sleeves, kirtle, and jewellery. If a woman does not have a beautiful face she can still appear beautiful through her dress. Her taste must be exquisite, subtle and flawless. She should wear colours to suit her complexion, wear nothing gaudy or over decorative. A single strand of pearls is far finer than a multitude of gold chains, trinkets and gee-gaws.'

I immediately thought of the hideous Neutken.

She walked back to the shelves and selected another

small volume. 'This book is the *'Livre de La Cité des Dames'*, and recounts the deeds of one hundred and forty virtuous women, some mythological, some real. Madame loves this book and insists it is part of her maids' reading.'

I nodded, but in truth, I was beginning to feel bewildered.

'Do not look perturbed, for I am telling you a great many things and you cannot possibly remember them all. For the present, it is well to observe the other girls. Watch when they converse and when they fall silent, when they sit still and when they become animated. Do not fidget or gnaw at your nails, like the prince. It is shameful.'

I put my hands behind my back, but it was too late.

'I see,' she said. 'Come, let me see your fingers.'

I slowly put out my hands, trying to hide my little finger, but she straightened them out and turned them over. 'Well, at least you are not a nail biter. Bitten nails make one look neurotic, and we cannot allow such a thing. What is wrong with this finger?'

I pulled my hand away and hid it in the folds of my gown.

'Come, come, Anna, do not be foolish, each of us is born with some defect or other. You must learn to make the most of the gifts God gave you and be ingenious with those parts you may not have been blessed with. You will find a way to hide this, for such trials given by God show the world our sin.'

Since I had been born with my strange finger, I wondered what I could have done in the womb to offend God.

'You, too, will devise some method to make it less noticeable and concentrate on those features you were blest with – your beautiful bright eyes and pleasant expression.'

I relaxed my tense hands.

'Good. Now, I will leave you here awhile to think on what I have said and later you will swear an oath of fealty to the regent. You will also receive an embroidered badge of marguerites, as worn by all of Madame's ladies and young girls on their gowns.' She walked to the door and turned towards me. 'You know, I notice everything, my dear, and I can already see there is something quite intriguing in your manner. I cannot quite place it at present, but I am never wrong. I think you will do well here, very well indeed.'

* *

The host of ladies surrounding Madame Regent appeared very comely indeed. The Countess of Hochstrate introduced me to each one in turn. On the left stood Lady Reynenebourg, Lady Brederode, Lady Verneul, Lady Waldich, Lady d'Aultroy, Lady Hallewyn, Lady Rosimbos, and Lady Longueval. On the right stood the two Neufville sisters – Lady Saillant and Lady Middlebourg – the lady who had accompanied me to the palace – and finally in front, stood Lady Barbe, Lady Cerf, and Lady Lallemand. I desperately tried to memorise their names, as I stared at the silver badge of marguerites pinned to their gowns. The *demoiselles* came from the leading Flemish nobility such as the Ravensteins, the Van Cleves and the Gruuthuuses, and as I moved down the line, the smiling girls said their names: Greta, Gertrude, Giovanna, Ariella, Anika, Angelique, Gabriella, Veronique, Fleur, Edda, Maria, Arabella, Concetta, Isabelle, Beatrice, Christa, and Rosaline. I was to be the eighteenth. However, when I came upon this last girl, I was taken aback, for she was the most beautiful creature I had ever seen. Her hair, the colour of spun gold, flowed loose over her shoulders and on it she wore a netted cap. Her eyes were of the palest blue, her skin pink and flawless, and she was plump and full breasted. She wore a gown of rose-pink to match her name, and the colour looked astonishing on her. With my sallow skin, rose-pink did not suit me half as well.

When the introductions were over, the ladies and *demoiselles* dispersed, but the girl with the flame-red hair and high-coloured cheeks lingered behind. She smiled and put out her hand.

'I hope, Anna, you will be my closest friend,' she said, as the other maids went about their duties or to their lessons. I could not help but stare at the disfiguring freckles sprinkling her flat nose, but she did not seem to notice.

'My name is Beatrice van Broekaert, and I am fifteen years old,' she said, in English. 'Let us walk together.'

'Have you been here a long time?' I asked, as we made our way down the main stairs and into the courtyard.

'Three happy years,' she replied, as we moved out of the sun's glare into the shade of the red brick wall. 'Madame is kind and has a genuine affection for her girls.'

'I took the most awful fright when I was first summoned to meet her,' I said, stepping aside to avoid a boy carrying a large platter of bread loaves. 'I thought that ugly little woman she keeps was the regent, and feared I might faint with horror!'

'Neutken? You thought *Neutken* was Madame?' Beatrice gave a peal of laughter. 'Why, how very amusing!'

I looked at the gap in her front teeth and thought she was the least attractive of all the girls.

'Neutken was a favourite of Madame's husband, Philip, and has her confidence in all things. She is actually very sweet and, as you saw, is allowed to wear the most outrageous clothes and jewels. She flounces around the palace like a queen, but she is loving and loyal to Madame, with some influence, and it would be wise to keep on her good side.'

I was unconvinced. 'Who is that woman wearing a black eye patch?' I asked. 'She was staring at me when I first arrived.'

Beatrice leaned against the wall, and I noticed the patterned brickwork, so complex and decorative in style.

'You mean Signora Elvira Manuel? She is an embarrassing guest as nobody wants her here. She came from Spain to England as your Princess Katherine of England's *dueña*, and caused conflict with the old King Henry by promoting Burgundian interests. Elvira is no longer a friend of Queen

Katherine, and so it is rather awkward her being here.'

'Well, everyone here is very kind,' I said, forgetting the woman at once, 'but they do seem to talk a lot.'

'Madame does if you get her onto her favourite subject of the royal children and her treasures!' said Beatrice, with a laugh. 'It is just the way of the Flemish people, and you will not find nicer people anywhere in the world.'

'Do you have brothers and sisters?' I asked, my mind darting about, full of questions.

'I have three older brothers – Johan, Klass, and Cornelius. They have wives and children and live in Antwerp.'

'Why, I have a brother,' I said, turning to her. 'George. I have an older sister, too, called Mary.'

'Older? But why is she not here? Is she ugly and kept hidden away?'

'No! She is very pretty, with golden brown hair. However, her – her French is not good, and my parents thought it best to keep her at her studies.' I could not tell my new friend how I had betrayed my sister to take her place.

'I would love to have a sister,' said Beatrice, as we walked further along the path. 'My brothers behave like rough bullies.'

'Well, I prefer my brother to my sister,' I replied, standing well aside as a lady passed by with a small monkey on her arm. I stared in distaste at the chattering creature, its beady eyes darting beneath its jaunty yellow cap.

'Are your parents well-matched and content?' she asked.

'Content? Why, yes, I suppose they are,' I replied, somewhat surprised at her peculiar question. 'Father is the best French speaker at court, and you will have seen him here at the palace, for he is one of our king's ambassadors. It is through him that I came to be here.'

'Ah, yes, I have seen him for you have a similar appearance.'

'Really? Well, I have his pointed chin. However, I have my mother's eyes and my Irish grandmother's spirit – so I am

told. Is Madame like her father?' I asked as we stopped by the
fountain. 'Father says he is always short of money and cannot
be trusted. He says he's a great lia –'

'Shush, Anna,' said Beatrice, pulling me aside, 'you must
never repeat such things here at court where people might
overhear.'

I rubbed the sleeve of my new gown.

'Anyway, I have met the emperor many times and he
really is very devout and rather old-fashioned.'

'How do you mean, Beatrice?'

'Well, he sees himself as a great knight of old, obsessed
with tournaments and chivalry. He has written a story of a
knight called '*Precious Thanks*', and it tells of how he sets off
on a perilous journey to claim his beloved. Having won her,
he goes on crusade and saves Christendom. It is a true love
story, for it tells how the emperor wooed his own bride, his
beautiful Mary of Burgundy – the mother of Madame. It is
very romantic.' She placed a hand on her heart and sighed,
making me laugh.

'Where does he live?' I asked, thinking I would like this
great man.

'They say in the saddle for he is forever restless, wander-
ing over his lands, but his favourite palace is in Innsbruck,
where he hunts the chamois in the mountains. When you do
meet him, I think you will be surprised for even though he
is the Emperor, he is an approachable man. He likes people,
but –' she added in a whisper, 'he flies into frightful rages and
breaks tables and chairs.'

The thought of my father and his temper must have
shown on my face.

'Oh, do not look so worried.' She leant close to whisper.
'He only rages when he has no money, for he seems to be
forever in debt. Your father is right. Money is a constant
embarrassment to the emperor.'

'What of your family?' I asked.

Her face clouded. 'My father met my English mother

at court when she was a lady-in-waiting and they married, hence my excellent English. They manage to tolerate each other by seldom being in each other's company. Since Father owns a great deal of land, the rents allow him to live like a nobleman – forever out hawking and hunting. Nothing else concerns him, except money.'

How familiar that sounded.

'And your parents have placed you here, like me?' I asked.

Beatrice brushed her unruly, copper-coloured hair from her eyes. 'Yes – for the time being.' Her voice sounded strained.

'Have you been promised to anyone yet?' I pressed.

'Should I be?'

I was taken aback by her sharp tone and fell silent. But my silence did not last long for I was bursting with curiosity.

'Why does Madame keep such an old parrot? It must be ancient. And all those birds twittering and flying indoors. My mother would hate it, for she cannot abide birds.'

Beatrice smiled. 'Patou is very dear, for he gave Madame much consolation when she was a lonely girl. He is practically blind now, due to his great age. As to the other birds, Madame's father is a great bird lover, and he used to carry cages of songbirds around with him, even to council meetings. The prince, too, has many rare birds and the Countess of Hochstrate's husband – Count Antoine Lalaing – cares for them. His gown is often covered at the back in bird shit, but we do not tell him!'

I put my hand to my mouth to stifle a giggle.

'Hush, Anna, Count Lalaing is *very* important for he is Madame's closest friend and advisor.'

'What of the prince?' I asked.

Beatrice shrugged. 'We have little to do with him. He suffered a poor start in life, losing his father, Philip, when he was seven. When Philip died, his mother Juana went mad with grief, keeping his corpse with her for weeks and even opening up the coffin to see if he had come back to life.'

'Ugh,' I replied, 'how disgusting! Fancy having a lunatic for a mother.'

Beatrice's eyes darted around. '*Stop it*, you really must be more discreet in what you say. You cannot just say whatever you think.'

'Why? Why may I not speak my mind?'

'Because you are at court now, and any false word is reported.' She moved closer to my ear and whispered. 'The prince is not actually stupid, but he is a little – odd. The poor boy has suffered much ill-health and has been unhappy of late. It is strange for he eats like a glutton, yet he never seems to put on weight. You can smell vomit on his clothes, too.'

I thought he sounded as mad as his mother, but this time said nothing.

'You must never repeat this,' continued Beatrice, 'but he yearns for independence from Madame, even though he loves her deeply. He has his own court and everything from his own choir to councillors, artists and musicians, but she still rules him. The Sieur de Chiévres, Lord High Chamberlain, is behind his dissatisfaction and is pushing the boy to cut loose the ties. Some say Chiévres is a foolish old man and there is no love lost between him and Madame, for she did not want him appointed to the post. Since he is for everything French, and Madame is so anti-French, you can imagine the chill between them.'

We stopped by the dovecote and watched as the doves preened themselves in the sunshine.

'I have been told Madame's court is large,' I mused, my finger brushing one of the gentle birds. It bobbed on the wooden perch and fanned out its tail feathers.

'It is, for it consists of masters of the household, gentlemen of the chamber, advisors, secretaries, guards, a confessor, chaplains, almoner, and servants. The royal children have a staff of eighty, just for themselves. I expect the English court is far larger.'

'Perhaps. Oh, I long to go, for Mother says King Henry

is full of bonhomie and amusement, although the queen is sometimes sad. She is desperate to give the king a prince.'

As we started to wander slowly, arm in arm, back towards the gallery, I stopped to admire, yet again, the beautiful Flemish tapestries and Beatrice made me laugh with her tales of the court. I was truly delighted to have found such a pleasant friend, and all thoughts of home vanished in the excitement of this new and intriguing place.

* *

The following morning at nine o'clock, I left the *petit cabinet,* or private closet, with the regent and her four la-dies-in-waiting, including Lady Middlebourg. As we contin-ued on, past a smaller chamber or *cabinet le jardin,* Margaret chatted freely.

'In there,' she said, 'lie my finest treasures. Monsieur Contault, assisted by a *valet de chambre*, takes care of my collection, for it is the finest in Europe.'

I listened, intent on remembering all I could.

'I have clocks, pomanders, sculptures, board games, and counters. From my mother-in-law, Isabel of Castile, I have the most exquisite rose made out of gold and enamel. At the centre, sits a great ruby and seven pearls.' She gave a tinkling laugh. 'Why, I am like a magpie with a great desire to collect beautiful things!'

We walked back towards the main staircase and halted outside the large double doors.

'Here, my dear, we dine in a large public chamber or *sallett* – thus.' She flung the grand doors open wide, and the gentlemen sitting turned, scrambled to their feet, and bowed low.

'Breakfast is at seven, dinner at noon, supper at six and we dine by the rules of the strictest etiquette and protocol. I, of course, do not dine here for I have my own private dining chambers. The Countess of Hochstrate has, I am sure, in-structed you on where to take your meals and in what order of precedence.'

I nodded, but was not sure if I would be able to remember.

'As *mère des filles* in charge of the young maids and ladies of the household, you must take heed of her, or she becomes most agitated,' she whispered, her face in a mock frown.

We walked back down the main staircase and Margaret stopped. 'This is the grand entrance to my palace, Anna, and you were brought here when you first arrived. When the sun shines,' she said, pointing, 'light from the stained glass window floods these marble steps with red, gold, blue and violet rays. There is, of course, meaning and purpose in this – red stands for charity, gold for faith and strength, azure for justice and purple for authority. You see, we must never miss an opportunity to convey a royal message. You can also see how the windows depict my family's noble crests. It never fails to impress my visitors when they first arrive at these steps, do you not agree, ladies?'

We descended into the courtyard.

'You must forgive my artisans,' said Margaret, nodding to the workmen as they took off their caps and bowed. 'We are forever building, improving, and renovating – I have a mind to have an open gallery here – a covered walkway where I may take the air in inclement weather. Please continue, gentlemen,' she said, as we stooped beneath the scaffolding.

On the first floor, we paused outside another large door, and Margaret reached for a key on her girdle. There were several locks to open, but finally, we entered the chamber, and I could see that this was a magnificent library, bright and light, for it boasted several fine windows. On the many shelves, the books were bound in velvet or gold brocade with golden clasps.

'Since I wish to share my books,' said Margaret, 'this library is open to visitors. Here you may read Aristotle, Livy, the letters of Seneca or old romances such as *'The Round Table', 'The Story of Jason'* and *'Merlin'*. I do love romances!

Here we also find the writings of Boccaccio, Phebus, and Artemidorus.'

I stared around in utter delight, for there were far more books here than in the library at Hever.

'My librarian used to be Monsieur Jean Lemaire de Belges, but he left to work at the French court, some two years ago now. He always teased me about how one day he would leave and now that he is gone, I miss him.' There was a sad pause. 'Well, as you can see,' she continued, 'I have over twenty royal portraits on the chimney breast, all related to me by blood or marriage. See, here is your own king's noble family.'

I stood in front of a portrait of old Henry Tudor, painted on wood. I admit it did bear some resemblance to the man I vaguely recalled meeting at Rochford Manor.

'He wears the Order of the Golden Fleece – a great honour. Do you know, I was once considered as a bride for this king?'

'Madame, how does the artist manage to make the colours appear so bright?' I asked, peering closer.

Margaret gave a pretty, tinkling laugh. 'Why, Anna, to achieve such work a painter must be an alchemist.'

I opened my eyes wide. 'A *magician*,' I said, and her eyebrows arched in surprise.

'Why, yes, I suppose he is. Come, come over here and look at this beautiful panel. It is the Mystic Marriage of St Catherine and her features are those of my own dear mother.'

I told her I knew the story from *'The Golden Legend'*.

'Mixing paint is a very skilled job,' continued Margaret. 'For the finest black, you must use carbonised ivory ground with vinegar and water mixed with soot, and stored in a pig's bladder. For a clear white, you must use white lead. For yellow, take grains of Avignon, powdered alum and water –'

'Or saffron, Madame,' I said brightly. 'Monsieur Bouton told me how merchants sell saffron in Antwerp.'

'Indeed, Anna, and for gold take real gold, for blue – ah,

blue – take lapis lazuli from Arabia or Persia ground to a fine paste with resin, wax and linseed oil.'

I was totally enthralled by her knowledge and said as much.

'When I was a young girl – your age, at Amboise, in France – Monsieur Perreal, the French painter and engineer, tutored me. Do you paint?' she enquired.

'I sometimes draw, Madame,' I replied.

'My court painter here is Monsieur Bernard van Orley, a painter of immense talent. I, too, love to paint and two years ago I was given a book bound in violet velvet with silver clasps. However, when I opened the cover, the book contained a set of oil paints with silver shells to mix them in. Remind me to show you. But now, come, I would like you to see this.' She pulled away a silk cloth from a small painting. 'This is the most amazing counterfeit, a wonderful work of art.'

I stared at the image of a young girl and Margaret stared at me in expectation. 'Well – what do you think?'

I looked again.

Margaret saw my confusion and spoke. 'It is a painting of myself as a girl of eleven years old,' she said. 'Can you imagine? To see myself as once I was. Extraordinary!"

I stared at the young girl before me, dressed in velvet the colour of ruby wine, a great red jewel at her neck, and then back at Margaret.

'I know, I know,' she sighed, blushing, 'we must all grow older, but once I was very fair.'

'But Madame, by your gracious leave, I think you are still very comely,' I said, and she laughed at my boldness.

After some time, we walked back into the courtyard and passed the vines, which I could not help but admire.

'We have them tied against this wall as the brick heats up in the sun, and encourages their fruit,' explained Margaret, pushing back a stray branch. 'It is magnificent, is it not? To the left are the Festive Hall and the Reception Hall where I

receive important guests, or hold banquets and entertainments. I must say, having the kitchens below is the most
ingenious design, for the rising heat warms my apartments
above! But now, let us proceed out of the back gate, for
the prince enjoys his own household at the palace where
Margaret of York once lived.'

'Madame, is it true that the duchess caused much mischief?' I asked.

Margaret stopped walking. 'And what – mischief – have
you heard, my child?'

'Why, I heard she supported Peter Warbeck against our
king's father, believing he was the Yorkist Prince escaped
from the great Tower in London.'

She smiled. 'Well, I shall tell you a secret, my dear. We
all did. We all thought he was the beautiful boy known as
the 'White Rose' – especially my father who showed him
great honour. He was the darling of the court here, and I
know Margaret loved him much. She wanted to think he
still survived, unlike his poor brother, and had been spirited
away to Portugal. When he came here, he was treated like the
prince we thought he was.'

'But he later confessed to being a puppet, Madame, and
a liar,' I said, repeating the gossip I had heard spoken on the
estate at Hever.

'Perhaps. Perhaps his mind was addled with fear, and
he thought that he could save his life by telling his torturers
whatever they wanted to hear. He did not deserve to be
hanged like a dog to die.'

'Oh, but –'

Madame put her hand up. 'Enough, Anna, let us not
speak of such things again.'

We walked out through the great guarded gate and
entered the palace opposite, its white stone bright in the
morning light. Courtiers, dressed in the most exquisite
clothes, swept low as Margaret passed the public gallery, the
kitchen with its great chimney and the small courtyard. She

finally halted.

'This we call the gatehouse, and I have turned this part of the palace into a nursery. I want my young charges to play freely here in the fresh air and to study with the utmost joy. I myself enjoy the pretty, enclosed rose garden where one might sit and read, and there is a large park should one wish to walk farther.'

•   •

Inside the palace, a small, rather plump woman in a burgundy red gown and a black hood with long lappets, approached. Margaret turned and placed her finger to her lips.

'Good day, Lady Beaumont,' she whispered, as her ladies fluttered behind. 'Let me see what my young people are learning today.'

She drew the drape aside and brought me forward. There, heads bent over their books, sat a boy and three girls chanting Spanish in unison. An old gentleman paced between the desks tapping his palm with a short, silver stick. On the walls hung charts and maps, and a great wooden globe took pride of place at the front of the chamber. Sunlight streamed through a window showing the exquisite blue, white and yellow tiles on the floor, and a small dog lay beneath one of the desks. After listening for some minutes, Margaret walked forward from behind the drape. Immediately the children stood, the boy giving a grave bow and the girls a low obeisance. The tutor, startled, turned around.

'Good morning, children,' said Madame, 'I can hear your Spanish is improving. You must speak a little each day until it becomes like your own tongue, natural to you and pleasing to the ear. Now, I have brought with me a little companion – Mistress Anna Boullan, from England, the daughter of my dear friend Sir Thomas, the English ambassador who amuses us so with his tales.'

I curtsied low.

Margaret pointed to the children. 'Prince Charles,

Count of Flanders, is thirteen years old, betrothed to your beautiful Princess Mary of England. Then we have Eleanora at fifteen years old, Isabeau, at twelve and little Marie at eight. Katherine and Frederick live at the court in Spain.'

As I rose, the girls smiled, but the fair boy only cast me a languid, uninterested look. His overlong face appeared pale, and his jaw fell lax. I thought he looked nothing like a prince for he was thin and frail and his expression appeared rather vacant. Eleanora looked most like her brother, for she was tall and thin with a jutting lower lip and a long, sallow face. Isabeau and Marie were the most attractive of them all by far.

Margaret turned to me. 'Lady Beaumont here, our Grand Mistress, is in charge of the royal children, and their Spanish tutor is Signor de Vaca. Madame de Poitiers teaches French and under her guidance is Madame Simone Symonnet. Come, come forward.'

A slender, dark-haired, young woman, dressed in a grey gown, stepped forward from behind the table and curtsied. Margaret placed her hands on my thin shoulders and smiled at the woman. It was not returned.

'Anna speaks and understands French, do you not? Now, I shall put you under the tutelage of this lady and see how you progress. Your French will improve to such an extent that when next I see your father, I will inform him that you are to be my only interpreter.'

I stared at the sullen woman and was not sure if I would like her one bit.

'Now, I have a mind to play. Do you like music?' she asked, walking over to the spinet. 'Monsieur Bredemers is a fine organist and teaches my wards to play and compose. I keep only the best composers in Europe here at court.'

She sat on the burgundy silk stool and began to play, her fingers lightly tripping over the keyboard. 'Music has been my passion since childhood due to the care of my father, for he has a great love of music. It was he who first taught me how to sing the praises of God. Our young prince here also has a great love of music.' She glanced at the boy, and he proffered a faint smile.

'I, too, have some small skill in composing,' she continued, modestly. Too modestly, for I had once overheard my father praise her extraordinary ability to compose chanson. She began a familiar round and waved her hand, encouraging us all to join in. While the prince sang the alto, we girls sang the descant, and Margaret closed her eyes as if she were far away in another place.

'Never cease to sing, children,' she said loudly, above the pitch of our voices. 'Never, for it is a jewel beyond price and measure, more than any princely thing on earth.' When the song ended, she closed the lid of the spinet, and her eyes appeared moist.

'Now,' she said, her reverie over, 'I have much to do.'

With a swish of her gown, she left the chamber, followed by her four ladies, while I remained with Lady Beaumont, Madame Symonnet and the royal children.

⁕   ⁕

Early one morning after Mass I was instructed to go to the prince's palace, where my new French tutor awaited my arrival. Beatrice accompanied me to her quarters, off the nursery wing, and we chatted all the way excitedly. Arriving at a door, I knocked, and when the door opened, Beatrice left me to return to the palace.

'Mistress Anna Boullan,' a lady announced.

The woman who rose from her chair gave a shy smile, and I responded, likewise. Madame Symonnet was prettier than I remembered when I first met her in the royal schoolroom. Over her dark hair, she wore the now familiar Flemish white cap covered with gauze, and her plain grey gown appeared neat and untrimmed.

'Anna,' she said, 'come in, come in.'

I moved forward and curtsied.

'Please do not mistake my shyness for indifference, for

I do not mean to be so. It is my way until I get to know people. Here, please.' She pointed to a stool, and I sat before her. 'May I call you Anna or would you prefer Anne?'

I said that at home I was always called Nan, and she nodded. 'Nan, I understand very well how everything is most strange to you, so I will speak in English. I came here myself, from Calais, only a year ago, with my husband who teaches at the court of our young prince.'

I began to feel more at ease.

'Well, Nan, I am here firstly as your teacher, a task I will share with my husband, but I also wish to be your friend.' She bent down. 'I wish to be gentle for here we do not believe that a child can learn in an atmosphere of fear, for it destroys the mettle of the spirit. Our method of teaching,' she continued, 'follows a pattern insisted upon by Madame, using kindness but firmness. Here we do not use the English way of beating knowledge into a child.' A frown clouded her face. 'But come, let me tell you why Madame insists on this unusual way of teaching. When she was but an infant, the good lady was blessed with a wonderful governess called Madame de Segré. There were no beatings or whipping boys, and this gave her the confidence to make mistakes without fear of punishment. This gentle lady watched over little Margaret with infinite kindness and care, moulding her young nature until she became the extraordinary person she is today. Now tell me, Nan, do you, too, wish to be ordinary or extraordinary?'

I leapt in with my answer. 'Oh, extraordinary, Madame.'

'Good, very good, for I can already see that you have a natural grace. However,' she said, her face serious, 'do not ever presume to waste my time, for it would prove a great ingratitude to Madame and a vexation to your family.'

I replied I did not intend incurring the displeasure of either.

'Our promise to you is that we shall do our best to teach you with kindness and fairness. In return, you must promise to work to your utmost ability. Can you work hard?'

I nodded, for in my heart I could not wait to try.

'I wish our young prince was as eager,' she sighed. 'Monsieur Adrian, professor of theology, undertakes the education of the prince and tries to be patient, but the boy would try the patience of a saint, for he vacillates from apathy,' and here she lowered her voice – 'to the most violent outbursts of temper.'

I recalled the languid, uninterested gaze the boy deigned to give me in the schoolroom.

'It is hoped our own enlightened Erasmus will, one day, teach him the works of Plutarch, Cicero, and Aristotle, and make him a great philosopher. He is, at present at Cambridge, in your own country, teaching Greek. He sometimes comes here with his friend Thomas More, to visit the beautiful home of Monsieur Busleyden, who is one of the councillors in the Great Council.'

I remembered how Tom Wyatt had once spoken of this interesting Master More. 'Madame, they say Erasmus wishes to leave England and never return, for he complains the English beer has given him stones in the kidney and he feels perpetually unwell. He is very delicate.'

'No doubt he is upset by the fish smell from the market here in Mechelen,' laughed my tutor. 'Well, I am glad we are in accord in our aim to work hard. We shall read from the chronicles of Froissart, Virgil, Chaucer, and French fables. Oh, there is much for a young mind to explore. Now, I wish to hear how well you read French.' She took a book from a small desk, opened a page, and handed it to me. 'Please stand and recite this short passage.'

Chapter Four

'Who dares to say the sun
speaks false?'

La Vure, Lille, and
Château d'Antoing
Summer and Autumn 1513

n the second day of July, we left the oppressive heat of Mechelen, and journeyed to Margaret's summer residence at La Vure, on the outskirts of Brussels. Built of cream-coloured stone, its numerous banners fluttered from its grey turrets, and roses entwined themselves around the balustrade of the terrace. We were to reside here for the summer months, for each year Margaret enjoyed riding in the cool, shady woods or walking beside the great lake. Here she could hunt and hawk to her heart's content, her gown plain and her hair as loose and free as a maid's.

Although she, of all people, was overburdened with work and needed to rest, Margaret had insisted on taking two large, iron-bound trunks containing all the papers that related to the financial arrangements of her household with her, for she left nothing unattended. The emperor had insisted that it was good for the health of the young Prince Charles and his sisters to come too, and besides, Margaret could not bear to leave them behind. Her dogs and guinea pig were also included, although her parrot stayed behind for he was old and stiff and it was thought best not to move him.

One particularly hot, sultry afternoon, the ladies, gentlemen, and maids descended onto the terrace, where a black and white striped canopy had been erected to provide shade. Even the dazzling blue dragonflies could barely bother to beat their wings and rested in the shade of the tumbling walls. Now and then, the aroma from the roses wafted across as I helped the *demoiselles* unfold the stools, and placed a wooden fan on top of each one. I then put a wooden board and counters on a small table ready for Margaret, for she liked to play tric-trac, and I put drinking bowls down for her dogs. When I glanced up, I saw two servants placing archery butts in front of the hedge ready for the prince, for he was due to come out and practise his shooting.

As they moved the straw target a few feet closer, Fleur giggled. 'Last Whit Monday the prince fired his crossbow at such a target, but instead of hitting it he killed a workman. The man was fixing a wall nearby, and the shot landed clean through the back of him. Can you imagine? I should make sure you stand well clear as I assume he is as blind with a simple bow and arrow.'

I looked across at the straw targets. 'But that is quite dreadful!'

'Yes, there was a frightful fuss, but the workman was a known drunk and lecher, and the emperor said it proved a just reward. However, Madame did try to recompense his family as best she could.'

I followed after Fleur, staring at the targets by the hedge and vowed to go nowhere near them.

As the sun rose in the deep-blue, cloudless sky, it became

the most idyllic setting of domestic bliss as the royal wards, with their grooms, rode on their cream palfreys across the grassy terrace. They wore wide wicker hats that gave their faces a dappled appearance, and were chattering to each other. Margaret arrived, followed by Neutken wearing some strange, exotic garb of coloured silk, and we placed the regent's black velvet chair facing the children. I could not help but notice her pensive gaze as she watched them. At her feet, her dogs scampered and played, and we laughed as they tussled over a length of old rope.

'Bonbon, stop,' said Margaret, peering under the legs of her chair at the panting little dog, 'you will make yourself too hot. Come out and be still. Anna, take her away please.'

Eager to be helpful, I picked up the dog and returned to my stool.

I stared intently at Margaret as she looked ahead, lost in thought.

'Those great dark eyes miss nothing, Mistress Boullan,' she remarked, making me start.

'I did not mean to stare, Madame,' I swiftly lowered my eyes, 'it – it is just that you appear very sad.'

Margaret picked up her lacework and turned to me.

'I will tell you a story, Anna. When I was but an infant my mother suffered a tragic riding accident when she was out hawking with my father in the forest of Wynendaele. Her horse refused to go forward, and in a fit of pique, she slapped the horse with her hand. It reared up, throwing her to the ground. Then, the animal fell on top of her, snapping her back against a tree stump like a dry twig. She died slowly some days later, twenty-five years old and carrying a child.' She paused for a moment. 'Do you know, she and my father were blessed, for they enjoyed the happiest of marriages as I did with my Philibert. Both shared a passion for hunting and my father could not deny her anything. At her death, men wept in the streets and the bells at St Rombout's rang for ten days continuously.'

Margaret stared across to the meadows in the distance.

'Then, nine years ago, my beloved Philibert died after catching a chill from hunting in wet clothes and drinking ice-cold water. Well… so they say. I was inconsolable. I spent my days at the castle of Pont d'Ain and absorbed myself in art and literature, refusing to see anyone or be drawn out. I owed my welfare to my dear step-grandmother, Margaret of York, for she brought me here to her palace at Mechelen to care for me.'

The group of ladies fell to silence as they continued their lacework or embroidery, but my curiosity was now fully aroused. 'Madame, I am sorry for your loss, but I do not understand.'

Neutken threw a ball to the dogs, and they scampered after it.

'I am always afraid, Anna, afraid that history will repeat itself with someone else I love. Charles is still a boy, but he is the future of this house and will rule after my father's death. He has inherited Burgundy and Flanders from his father, Spain from his grandfather King Ferdinand, and the Habsburg Empire from his grandfather Maximilian – my own dear father. His empire will be the greatest in the western world and the New World. It is as it should be. Yet it will be a burden and, like the feeble woman I am, I fear demons where none exist. I pray to God to take away my fears and sometimes at night I cannot sleep, for I see death in every shadow.' She paused. 'I know this talk is nonsense. My father insists Charles hunts and shows no fear, for it will prepare him for war and he must appear to the world to be a brave prince. I know the exercise will strengthen his weak constitution and make him fearless in the chase, but I still worry. My father rides with him, of course, to the old *Forêt de Soignes* or the woods at *Heverlee* and we must ride there together sometime. Do you know I still have the little wooden horse my father made for him?'

Her face brightened.

'Charles named it *'Liberatore'* and he would often make the servants push him up and down the gallery as he led his imaginary Christian army against the wicked Turks. He would not stop until he had beaten all the infidels and set to thrashing at a tapestry with his little sword pretending to fight the soldiers depicted in silk. Now, although not strong, he can shoot a bow and arrow, fire a harquebus and use a sword.'

I watched the prince as he threw off his hat, now only too aware of his skill in shooting.

Margaret laughed as Marie trotted around. 'Ah, she has a passion for horses and is already yearning to ride like a man. She shows no fear of racing around on her little jennet. Why, Anna, you have not hunted here yet, have you?'

'No, Madame, but we hunt at home, and I have my own mare called Ciara. Well, strictly speaking, she belongs to my grandmother who loves to hunt, having fine stables in Kilkenny, but I am the only one who can handle the mare. Her name means "little black one", in Gaelic.'

'Ah, I hear Irish horses are very fine,' said Margaret.

'It is true, Madame, for Ciara is sure-footed and swift, and will leap over any brook or stream. On Holy days we visit the fair at Eaton Bridge, and I decorate her mane with green and white ribbons. Afterwards, I race home as fast as possible along the gallop path that winds around the estate. My sister can never catch me.'

'I would love to see England,' said Lady Verneul, picking out a length of yellow, embroidery silk, 'for it sounds a charming place. And how fortunate to have such a handsome young man for your king.'

'Ah, such a glorious king indeed!' exclaimed Lady Reynenebourg. 'Can you imagine? I hear the royal flagship sailed across from Dover to France at the head of forty thousand men, and boasted sails of cloth of gold. How they must have glinted in the sun.'

Neutken jumped up and turned about, her rainbow silks

swirling around her like a ship in full sail.

'Stop, it is too hot,' chided Margaret.

Neutken obediently flopped down.

'Indeed, the king and his forces landed at Calais on the thirtieth day of June and, as a gift, I sent him woollen coats in red, yellow, white and green for every man. Did you know, ladies, he has named his supply ship the *Margaret Bonaventure* in my honour? Let us hope my name brings him good fortune.'

'I hear from my husband, Madame,' said one of the ladies, 'that King Henry has ordered his great guns from the cannon maker here in Mechelen, for they make the finest in Europe.'

'Yes, indeed,' said Margaret, 'for he must have only the best of everything. My ambassador tells me that he appeared magnificently clad with an entourage of three hundred men from his household, followed by six hundred guards. By contrast, my father arrived simply clothed in black, followed by his troops. Well, it is fitting and seemly, for his wife, Bianca Maria, died only last year.'

I glanced up at Margaret's face.

'I am afraid at fifty-four, my dear, he is now an old, spent man.'

'What a sight they must have made!' exclaimed another lady, as she unpicked the lace on an altar cloth.

'Anna,' said Margaret turning to me, 'your father, as Esquire for the Body, will be there on the field with the great nobles and the king's boon companions. No doubt there will be much carousing as men on campaign are wont to do, and your father's skill at making such merriment possible will be put to good use. I hear the king has taken priests, choristers, secretaries, grooms, pages, a vast wardrobe, and a special feather bed. He has even taken a pavilion, made of wood with a chimney of iron, with the royal beasts aloft. It will be more like a glorious summer progress than war!'

She took a glass of wine from the page standing next to

her. 'Well,' she said, sipping the cool drink, 'let the English king have his sails of gold and his velvet pavilions and call himself King of France if he wishes. Let him spend a year's worth of revenue on his venture. He is a beautiful, golden boy and I have a great fondness for him, barely able to deny him whatever he wishes. He frequently sends me gifts and kind letters, and appreciates my female talent for diplomacy.' She laughed as if remembering a private joke. 'I must not mind too much if he is boisterous and, in his enthusiasm, rushes into speaking first and thinking later.'

She then became serious. 'I speak lightly but must always remember my first care is for the safety of my nephew's inheritance, and the keeping of the English king's support for the Netherlands. His protection of the fisheries of Holland, Friesland, and Zeeland is vital. No, I could not have France threaten the future of Charles, for they have ever been the enemy of the Habsburgs.'

She gazed across the terrace to her young nephew as he dismounted from his horse and let it crop the grass. 'All my hopes and dreams rest with him and his forthcoming marriage to King Henry's sister, for then we shall shatter the power of France for good.'

She tossed a ball again to the dogs, and we laughed as they collided, mid-air.

'Such talk, Anna, reminds me that the king has asked for samples of cloth for the Princess Mary's new gowns to be sent over to England, for he wishes them to be in the Burgundian fashion. He has also asked my advice on other provisions she might require, including her attendants. Lady Cerf, make a note, please, and remind me again later.'

The lady bowed her head and turned to me. 'Have you ever seen your king, Anna?'

'No, I have not, but my lady mother tells me he is a giant of a man, the tallest at court except for Charles Brandon.'

Margaret laughed 'Yes, I hear he is tall, and you would barely reach his ribs, little lady. He is a fine king of great heart and generosity, young and strong. If all goes well, you might see him sooner than you think. Now, play something soothing.' She signalled to the musicians to stop, and, resting against the cushions, I picked up the gittern.

As I strummed an English tune, I thought of the king. They said he was young, handsome and generous and all the ladies were in love with him – even, I think, my mother. However, although he loved the company of women, Mother said he was entirely devoted to his Katherine and would kiss her openly and fondly at the slightest opportunity. Good-tempered, slow to anger, he loved his dogs and horses and was ever boisterous and playful. I sighed. In truth, I longed to see this great paragon for myself.

● ●

'You have a letter,' announced Beatrice, entering the chamber and brandishing the beribboned paper. 'Quick, open it and let us share the news.'

I put down the books in my arms and took it from her, recognising my mother's seal.

'Shut the window, for the rain is blowing in,' said Beatrice, leaning across the casement.

I carefully unfolded the paper and started to read out loud: 'My lady mother informs me that Her Grace's pregnancy is proceeding well, and the astrologers and wise women have said that this time it will be a fair boy. It is hoped that the queen's distress when parting from the king has not affected the growing child, and that her fears for his safety while he is on campaign will come to naught. I must remember her in my prayers each morning and night for the plague is yet again in England, and everyone is fearful.'

Beatrice sat down on the bed, removed her shoe, and examined a hole in her stocking. 'Go on.'

'The court is very depleted and quiet, as most of the lords and nobles have escaped to the safety of the country, except for my Grandfather Thomas, who has gone to deal with the Scots. His Howard brothers were disgruntled at being left behind and begged to go to France, but were refused.' My voice began to falter. 'The Scots have taken advantage of the king fighting in France and continue to make mischief along the borders. The marriage of the king's sister, Margaret, to King James has not, it seems, allayed the Scots' hatred for the English.' My voice trailed off.

'And?' pressed Beatrice, peeling off the offending stocking. I looked down again.

'What is it? What does it say?' she asked. 'I cannot read English as well as I speak it. What says the letter?' She grabbed it from me, scanning the beautiful script of my mother's hand.

'I want to read of home,' I sighed, 'not news of the court and war. Everyone talks of the war and it is dull. I want to read about George, Mary and Mrs Orcharde. I want to know what is happening at home.'

Beatrice glanced down at the letter. 'But you complained that nothing ever happens at home, Nan, that it was deathly dull. Look here,' she said. 'This bit says Mary, and here, further down, it says George. What does it say?'

I sniffed. 'Mary is well and last month sang for some visitors at Hever. George has a new cob, since Bramble is now too small for his weight, and a kestrel called Kitty. He writes poems with Tom Wyatt at Allington, and they are most promising.' I began to brighten up. 'Mrs Orcharde is well, but is finding it hard to climb the stairs as her knees pain her, and her cot has been placed in a lower chamber. She wanders around the house mumbling to herself.' We both laughed. 'Sorrel is also stiff and slow and finds it harder to catch the rabbits on the estate. On the whole, everyone is in good health and all praise God for his blessings. Hever has bloomed over the summer, and the new herb garden is now laid. The stables have been enlarged to accommodate more horses, and new outbuildings have been erected for the smithy. Mother trusts that my French is improving and that

I am working hard. Elizabeth Stafford gave birth to a boy at their home in Suffolk, named Henry, after the king.'

I ran my eyes along the page and continued. 'Uncle Edmund has married a woman called Jocasta Culpepper. She is in her thirties, but Edmund could not expect much, being the younger son with no fortune.' I screwed up my nose. 'The Howards will not be pleased with that!' I turned the page over. 'Everyone sends their good wishes, and even the queen has asked if I am happy and well.'

'There,' said Beatrice, 'a lovely letter. Who is Elizabeth Stafford?'

'Elizabeth is an aunt,' I mumbled. 'I attended her wedding. Oh, Beatrice, I miss my home, even though it was sometimes dull. I miss riding Ciara across the estate and through the woods. I even miss grumbling old Margot.'

'Of course you do. At least here our parents often reside at court and so we see them frequently. But think. Madame would not have agreed to you coming to her court if she did not think you were very special.'

I thought of Madame Symonnet's words. 'I will be extraordinary, will I not?' I asked, as I looked out. The rain had stopped.

Beatrice playfully waved the stocking in the air. 'Yes, of course, Anna, you will turn out to be quite the most extraordinary, sophisticated and brilliant young lady ever seen at court, just like your mother. I promise. Now, let us go out into the garden and pick some shower-drenched roses for Madame's chapel.'

*   *

The September rain lashed down, but although our summer stay ended, Margaret did not wish to return to the court at Mechelen until she knew the outcome of the hostilities in France. However, while she waited, she was unexpectedly asked to join her father in entertaining King Henry at the *Palais Rihour* in Lille, to the west of Tournai.

As the light began to break at La Vure and the dawn chorus filled the air, we bustled out of the château on the move once more. Boxes were loaded on to carts, hunting dogs barked and pulled on their leashes, and hawks fluttered on their cane travelling frames.

'Come, ladies,' called Margaret, as she walked to the waiting chariots.

The white mules stood patiently and shook the bells on their red leather harness.

'I trust matters are not proceeding too badly if the king wishes to take time off from the field of glory, and indulge in pastimes of a more, let us say, gentle persuasion.' She stepped into her chariot and plumped up the silk bolsters. Neutken was already seated, carrying Beau, and fidgeted with excitement.

'Is this not wonderful?' asked Beatrice, above the noise of the girls chattering. There was a loud clap of hands.

'*Demoiselles,* please, settle down if you would. Quick, quick!' It was the Countess of Hochstrate, and she did not look too pleased as one of the dogs yapped around her feet. She picked it up impatiently and tucked it under her arm, but when it twisted and nipped her hand, she threw it down onto Veronique's knee in disgust.

We settled ourselves down, and as the great convoy of chariots and horses pulled away, I gave a shiver. To think I missed home! This was far more exciting. Now, I would see our king, the emperor and maybe even my father. I closed my eyes, glad my wits had brought me here instead of my sister.

● ●

The *Palais Rihour* was a strange building for with its church-like turrets it appeared to be a palace made of steeples. As we made our way up an octagonal turreted staircase, to the main gallery, I could hear the church bells ringing outside the windows. Margaret hurried to her father's chamber with one of her ladies-in-waiting, and we retired to ours. No sooner were we settled than the countess entered, and announced that supper, in the presence of the king, was to start at eight of the clock that evening.

'Your finest attire, my sweet maids,' she said, pulling back the velvet curtain of the clothing rail and taking down armfuls of gowns. The girls entered and gathered around, babbling in excitement.

'Tonight,' said the countess, 'we are providing the King's Most Excellent Majesty with an intimate supper. I want you to look enchanting, for he has specifically asked for as many pretty young maids to be present as possible. Now, in the wicker chest, we have circlets and chaplets of silk flowers, and over there girdles, ornaments, and jewels. Over in the large basket, we have sleeves and kirtles. When we have selected your gowns, I will instruct the wardrobe maids to make any alterations required. Now, let us begin.'

Taking the gown that they liked best from amongst the taffeta, damask, and satin, the girls held them up in front of the mirror and twirled about. I browsed the rail, trailing my fingers along the hanging gowns. I wanted to look the loveliest of them all, but nothing took my fancy. Then I saw it: a gown of crimson brocade, with a square neck piped with crimson velvet and pearls. Its fitted crimson sleeves were banded with gold and slashed with bright yellow silk, and the oversleeves of crimson were lined with gold. From the waist, hung a girdle boasting three strands of pearls. It hung wedged between two other gowns, but as I pulled it out, enchanted, it was whisked from my hands.

'Not that one, it is torn,' said the countess, 'and besides it is far too exotic.'

I pulled back the gown. 'But it can be mended, surely, Madame?' I asked, refusing to let it go. 'Please, Madame, oh, please let me try it. I want to look, as you said, enchanting for the king.'

'Well, it is quite lovely,' she conceded, holding out the sleeve of the gown, 'but I am not sure it is suitable for a young girl and, besides, the seamstress would have to alter the bodice and shorten the hem. I think maybe the pale blue would suit your complexion better. Young maids always look lovely in subtle hues.'

My face fell and I forced my eyes to fill with tears of disappointment. 'But – but – Madame,' I pleaded in a choking voice, 'at home my sister, as the eldest, is always given the loveliest gowns to wear and I have to wear her cast-offs. Old gowns that are patched and mended. I have always longed to wear something fit for a lady, such as this, but I am always overlooked. I am told I am too plain, too small to be of any account. It makes me feel so miserable knowing that I am not as lovely as she.' I lowered my eyes, tears falling down a face abject with misery, not in the least ashamed of my gross exaggeration.

The countess stared in alarm. 'Oh, my goodness, Oh, my dear, why how dreadful. Please do not cry so. Oh, very well, but mind, no jewellery, for the pearls on the bodice will suffice, and it is quite decorative enough. Quickly now, before I change my mind.'

My face miraculously brightened as I clutched the gown and brushed past Christa. Her face appeared sullen as I moved towards the mirror and held the vibrant, crimson cloth against my slight figure. It was magnificent, as had been my performance.

'You always get what *you* want,' she hissed, an insipid cream gown draped over her arm. I ignored her. What did I care if she and the other girls looked plain? I was going to stand out from them all.

*   *

That evening, I caught my first glimpse of the emperor, surrounded by his gentlemen, at the top of the grand staircase. Dressed in a gown of murray and gold, over which hung the Order of the Golden Fleece, the long full skirts of his magnificent black gown appeared regal, but not ostentatious.

On his head, he wore a great beaver hat covered with black ostrich plumes, tilted far to one side to show a cap beneath decorated with gold aiguillettes. Broader and more heavily set than those nobles around him, with a high arched nose, his lively, restless eyes darted from left to right, taking in all those present. I could see, thankfully, that Margaret had not inherited his nose, but their fullness of face was similar, as was their ready smile. Although an old man, the emperor's brown hair was barely tinged with grey and he wore it combed down to touch his shoulders in the fashionable style. As he walked forward, limping slightly, he turned, bent down to my height and, touching my cheek, remarked how charming I looked. He then patted my head and winked. His manner was fatherly as he moved towards his daughter, kissing her tenderly on both cheeks and admiring her collar of emeralds.

Having cast off her widow's barb, Margaret's new stylish black hood made her appear young and girlish, as did the dark green of her gown. As she processed with her smiling father down the marble steps, there was a sparkle in her eyes and a coquettish smile. However, by the time we had entered the hall to a fanfare of trumpets the emperor's face had turned sour, and I thought Margaret appeared nervous.

When a second fanfare rang out, accompanied by clapping, the most beautiful vision entered the hall. Was this the plump, petulant boy I had once seen at Rochford Manor? A loud gasp of admiration filled the air as the King of England strode over to the emperor and his daughter.

Never before had I, and no doubt any of the people present, seen such a tall, handsome man. Far younger than the emperor, he was magnificently dressed in white satin, with a huge collar of pearls set in gold and laid upon ermine. I stared at the miniature gold cannons, whistles and balls dangling from his slashed sleeves and was utterly bedazzled. The skirts of his coat were striped with gold, and he wore white boots of the finest kid leather. His black velvet cap, studded with rubies and pearls, sat atop his straight auburn hair which touched his broad shoulders. The young king stood surrounded by his nobles, but my father was not with him. However, I was too overawed to be disappointed, for the king's vital presence filled the entire hall.

He strode forward and kissed the emperor – who now appeared plain in comparison – on both cheeks, and, taking Margaret's arm, escorted her to the throne.

Neutken, dressed in yellow Bruges satin, took her place at the regent's feet, and I took my place with the maids on the steps, watching as each of the nobles and ladies were presented to the king.

Wearing such a beautiful crimson gown, my hair braided and plaited with ribbons around my head, I could not but revel in the glances thrown my way as each gentleman approached. I had ignored the advice of the countess and at the last moment worn heavy ruby-red earrings. They wobbled when I moved my head, and I felt very sophisticated compared to the other girls. In fact, Rosaline, lovely as she looked in a gown of pale sea-green damask, appeared to have made little effort at all, and wore no adornment whatsoever.

With the king on her right, Margaret expressed the high esteem with which she and her father held him, and he thanked her for the splendid supper. He smiled warmly at the emperor sitting on her left side with his lords and nobles dressed in their finest robes and furs.

Brow furrowed, the emperor appeared tense. 'Where's Fox?' He turned abruptly.

'My dear brother,' replied the king, in faultless French. 'You must forgive the absence of Bishop Fox, but he is still indisposed after Thérouanne. My other lords you know,' he added, stretching out his hand as they bowed.

'Not too indisposed I trust?' enquired Margaret.

The king raised an eyebrow and shrugged. 'Well, time, and the physician, will tell. 'Twas a bad kick from his mule in his privy parts and he can neither stand nor sit. But he sends you his warmest wishes.' The king held out his jewelled cup for wine. 'It is a great sadness to me, that men such as Edward Carew are not here to enjoy the triumph. Killed by a French bullet as he sat in one of the pavilions. Talbot lost a leg, other brave knights dead. A terrible loss.'

Margaret lowered her eyes.

'You heard of the plot?' he scanned the chamber with his small, restless eyes.

Margaret nodded. 'Indeed, Your Grace, it was an abomination. Are you not fearful that such a thing could still come to pass?'

The king drained his cup and it was immediately refilled.

'I am not destined to be assassinated by a lunatic,' he said, still gazing ahead. 'We caught the perpetrators and, hopefully, the site of their rotting, caged corpses will put an end to such foolish attempts.'

'But why?' pressed Margaret.

'A myriad of reasons, dear Madame, with no thought or sense behind them. Soldiers' discontent over the sour beer, sickness, England's involvement in the war, the cost – you put a name to it. You heard I hanged eighty thieves for robbing our money chests before we even left Calais? One damned setback after another, and to what end? To have me dead, England thrown back into civil war and France victorious.'

'Sire!' cried Margaret, rising to her feet. 'France will never enjoy victory over England! Let old Louis spit out his venom, let him do his worst. I trust in the skill of your English archers to overcome such dishonoured a nation!'

The king smiled as she sat down, for she was somewhat embarrassed by her outburst.

'Forgive me, Majesty; let us talk no more of war. For your enjoyment, I have the most beautiful young lady with a song of my own composing to entertain you. You recall she sang for you once before?'

The king asked if it was the girl with the golden curls. Margaret nodded.

'Ah, Etiennette la Baume,' he said, turning to her

excitedly. 'You could not have chosen a more fitting enter-tainment, for from the moment I first set my eyes upon her I have been struck with the dart of love. Why, I have never seen such beautiful ladies as you have here. Ravishing. As ravishing as those preserved cherries you sent me – I must cultivate them at Greenwich. Ah, here she comes.'

Applause filled the hall as the drapes parted and a young girl stepped forward. Fair again. Beauty was always fair, I thought, sitting on my marble step. Even the ladies depicted in the magnificent tapestries on the walls of the hall were blessed with golden hair. As they sat surrounded by their suitors, I noticed there was not a dark-haired lady among them. I turned my attention back to the girl before me. She was simply dressed in a white, square-necked gown, her sleeves puffed and banded with blue ribbon. At her neck, she wore a narrow collar of pale blue sapphires. On top of her long golden hair, she wore a matching blue ribbon, and she wore no adornment on her ears.

The musicians bowed to the royal party from the gallery and struck up a haunting tune on their lutes, violas, and recorders. The girl's beautiful, clear voice filled the air as the king gazed dreamily ahead, and raised his goblet with a lustful smile. When she had finished, she backed away through the arras to rapturous applause, capturing the hearts of all present.

After her, a troop of dancers wearing exotic dress and feathers entered, and after them came acrobats, jugglers and a fool with a dancing dog. Dancing for the guests followed, and food was brought to the tables, but after eating only a small portion, the emperor rose abruptly, as did those about him. He then announced that he would retire early for he was not feeling well. Margaret looked alarmed, but he impa-tiently waved her away with his hand.

'Brother, stay,' protested the king, holding his arm fast, 'ladies wait to be danced with, and they will be much offend-ed. I also wish to play the gitteron and cornet for you. Surely, you would not deny me so simple a pleasure?'

A pink flush rose up the emperor's muscular neck, and a vein throbbed at his temple. 'By your leave, Highness, I wish to retire for I am a weary old man. I shall leave such cavorting to the young, and trust you will play for me on another occasion. I bid you goodnight.' He bowed to the king.

'Margot, enjoy the evening's revelries.' He kissed her three times on both cheeks and left, hurriedly followed by his gentlemen.

Margaret stood mortified but checked herself and turned to the king. 'Why, I hear, sir,' she said, 'that you have the reputation of being the finest dancer in Christendom. No man can leap higher than you, or dance through the night without respite. Is this true?'

Her remark was a triumph, for the king threw back his head and guffawed loudly, his chagrin at the emperor's exit forgotten. He was the centre of attention again.

'Tis, true, Madame, tis true, I wear the lot of them out, I'll warrant you,' and quite unexpectedly, he grabbed Margaret's hand and placed it on his thigh. I stared in astonishment as I watched from my place on the step. Margaret gasped.

'Feel that,' he whispered, 'a dancer's leg, firm and strong. Feels good, does it not?' Margaret blushed with embarrassment.

'There is one other man with a leg that good – well, not quite as good, but good enough – and that is Charles Brandon.' He pointed to a tall, good-looking man, who looked remarkably similar to the king. The man rose to his feet and bowed. The king clapped his hands loudly. 'Come, let the dancing begin.'

'But, Your Grace, can he really be as skilful as yourself?'

'Indeed, he is, Madame, watch him. He is a superb dancer, an excellent horseman, and he and I are as brothers. He is a goodly figure of a man and, I have to say, at an age when he is eager to settle down and wed again. I would like to see him well matched. He would make an honest husband, too, beyond reproach, and is very devout. Why, he attends the blessed Mass three times a day, more frequently during the observance of Lent.'

'Three times?' Margaret was amused.

'Oh, indeed Madame, but let me be frank,' said the king, wiping his mouth on his napkin and turning towards her. 'What thoughts of you? Such comeliness should not be wasted in this widowed state. Have you not thought of marriage again?'

Margaret, taken aback, beckoned to me to pass her fan.

I rose, careful not to step on my gown, and passed it to her with a curtsey. As I did, I could not help but look boldly into the king's eyes and give a faint smile. He stared back, eyes narrowed with some curiosity, and I noticed their deep blue irises. He appeared to be appraising me in some way, for his eyes lingered in what could only be admiration.

Margaret took the fan with a nod, and I returned to my place, feeling a thrill inside. The King of England had looked at me – *me!* Beatrice squeezed my hand, but when I looked up, I saw that he was still staring, fascinated.

'Was that not Bullen's child, Mary?' The king helped himself to the marchpane set before him. He nibbled on the sticky, pink treat.

'Yes, Your Grace,' replied Margaret, glad of the change of subject. 'But that is his youngest daughter, Anna, and she is staying at my court for her education. She is the most willing of my maids, vivacious and amusing, with a gift for dance and music.'

The king drained his wine and wiped his lips on his napkin again. 'Youngest daughter you say? It is as well she is amusing for she is not your usual fair maid, is she, Margot? Personally, I like maids with hair the colour of honey, with full duckies like my beautiful mother. Well developed. Ripe.' He gazed over to Rosaline. 'I told my Katherine as much, right from the onset, and ordered her dark Spanish ladies

with their hairy upper lips straight back home. Thomas More
had the measure of them when he described her attendants
as Ethiopian pygmies!' He burst into boyish laughter. 'No,
I must have pretty English maids at my court. My queen is
fair herself with hair the colour of wheat that hangs thick and
heavy as a long mantle. And she has soft, grey eyes. What a
rare beauty. Not as rare as my young sister Mary, though, my
little Princess of Castile. Now she *is* exquisite and delicate.
Your prince will be marrying the greatest jewel in Europe –
excepting your gracious self, of course.'

Margaret, with an amused smile, inclined her head at the
heavy-handed compliment.

The king then gazed languidly at Rosaline as she passed
the sugared almonds to Margaret, for the girls round breasts
were trussed high above her pink rose gown and moved
seductively as she breathed. She smiled at the king.

'Delightful, delightful,' he purred, taking an almond
from her silver tray. 'What a ripe beauty, as beautiful as my
Etiennette.' He glanced back at me. 'Bullen, you say? I can
see the child there has the dark looks of the father, but she is
very thin. Sallow too. Her mother is buxom and fresh-faced.
How old is this – this…'

'Anna. She is called Anna, Your Grace, and she is thirteen. Plenty of time to grow,' said Margaret, taking a pink
almond herself.

The king frowned. 'She looks half her age and is far
too gaudy and overdressed for a maid – although one is
hardly over-gilding the lily. Ha!' His eyes rested sensually on
Rosaline again before glancing back at me, not knowing that
I could understand French.

'Does she have her mother's witch of a temper?' He bit
into the almond with a crack and waved the half-bitten end
towards me.

'Fie, Your Grace,' said Margaret, 'I would not condone
any tantrums from my maids. Anna is a most amusing and
agreeable girl of good manners. She is a talented musician

and is most entertaining. There is no waspishness there. I do not know her mother, but her –'

'I do,' interrupted the king, with a knowing smirk, 'Elizabeth Howard, old Surrey's daughter. What a hellcat she is.' He sniggered like a naughty schoolboy.

'How does a beautiful woman like Elizabeth have such a child? Is she consumptive? I trust the other sister is more buxom, or Bullen will never marry them off.'

He laughed loudly as I sat there feeling utterly humiliated. Was I sallow-faced? Did I look gaudy? The emperor did not think so. And what did he mean calling my mother a hellcat? Now, at this minute, I felt horribly aware of my sallow skin and my childish, brittle form. I looked at the other girls with their hair the colour of spun gold, a bloom in their cheeks, and gently swelling breasts. Compared to them my dark eyes were too large, not pretty and tilting or the colour of cornflowers, and my mouth too wide. Worse still, I should not have begged to wear the crimson gown. It was too obvious, and I felt cheap.

I pulled out my earrings and tucked them inside my sleeve, outraged at the king's ungallant and boorish words. I hated him, and I knew that I would never forget his insult to my mother, for I found it impossible to forget a slight, no matter how small. The emperor would never say anything so ungallant.

The king turned to Margaret with lowered voice and I was quickly forgotten. 'But come, Margot, what was I saying? What of your comfort? What say you to a fine new husband? You cannot moulder away in the single state forever. Such beauty is wasted. What say you? Throw away your mourning clothes and be a woman again.'

'Hush, Your Grace. You know I honour my dead husband with my widow's weeds. It is a state in which I have made up my mind to remain. It would be unseemly to remarry, although I might possibly – and I say possibly – be persuaded if a man as fine as yourself could be found, but alas, there is none to match your worth. Knowing Your Grace, I cannot imagine ever having the slightest wish for any other man. It would be unthinkable, quite unthinkable. I must be content with widowhood for eternity for there is none like yourself, unless of course, he stepped down from Heaven.'

The king beamed and kissed her hand, and as I watched Margaret, I caught a glint of coquettishness in her eyes.

'Ah, but there is, there is such a man,' said the king, excitedly, 'right there in front of you.' He pointed again towards Brandon. 'Who finer than Charles Brandon, marshal of my army? He is a man who can dance and leap and – and I have to say this, Margaret, in strictest confidence – has worshipped you from the first moment he laid eyes on you. He is dazzled by your fair beauty.' He smiled. 'What thought you of his prowess at the dance? Was he not impressive, a fine figure of strength and manliness? What a match! Think on it. You, dearest Madame, would have my royal blessing, and since Brandon is like a brother to me, you would be as a dear sister. What say you? Could you not encourage his suit?'

I watched as Margaret opened her mouth and snapped it shut it again, like a gasping fish. She was genuinely speechless.

'A drink, if you please,' she managed to say, holding forth her empty cup.

The king leant forward and beckoned Brandon to approach the high table. 'Here comes the man now. Let us have discourse with him and learn of his intent.'

Brandon leapt up the steps with great agility and swept a low bow, his face still red from his exertions. The stale smell of sweat wafted forth, and I could see that his doublet was soaked wet beneath the arms. Close up, he really was as handsome as the king.

'Your Grace,' he gasped, catching his breath.

'This will be interesting,' one of the nobles whispered, 'a mongrel sniffing out a pedigree bitch on heat.' His companion covered his mouth with his hand and tittered.

Brandon appeared to falter. 'Madame,' he stammered.

'Je – je suis servant loyal et – et…' His voice trailed off as he stared pleadingly at the king.

Margaret seemed bemused as the King let out a great roar of laughter, and clapped his hands on his thighs. 'Christ's nails, Brandon! What sort of a greeting is that, eh? Ha! A fine wooing this will be when you speak such mangled French! I shall have to be the go-between for you two lovebirds. What a fine state this is!' He looked as if he would choke and the company at the table leant forward to see what was the cause of the merriment.

Margaret, to her ladies' amazement, took the joke in good part and offered her hand for Brandon to kiss. He pressed it to his lips in reverence and, as she stood, bowed low.

'Enough, sir, please rise,' she said, but he would not let go. He kept tight hold of her hand and she was unable to sit back down.

The king threw his hands up as if helpless. 'What can I do, Madame? Mayhap he requires a token of your affection or he will stay prostrate forever.' Margaret laughed, but then, without warning, Brandon slipped the gold initialled ring off her finger, tried it on his little finger, admired it, and placed it inside his gaping doublet.

'Larron!' cried Margaret, grasping the thin air, but Brandon did not understand the word 'thief'. She looked around, startled. *'Dieffe!'* she tried in Flemish, but Brandon swept a bow, walked backwards down the steps and disappeared between the hanging drapes. Margaret sank back into her chair, obviously alarmed at the prank. She beckoned to one of her ladies and asked her to go after Brandon. I watched as the lady scuttled away in pursuit.

'Forgive, him, forgive him, he is love lost,' laughed the king, throwing back his golden head.

'Sir, I am happy to play this game but I must beseech you to return my gold ring. The initial *"M"* set in black diamonds stands for Mary of Burgundy. It is known to be mine, my mother's, and will be recognised if the gentleman flaunts it for all the world to see.'

The king nodded, wiping his tear-filled eyes, and took her hand. 'My dearest lady, I will give you another of far greater value, but it will be as you wish. I will see no embarrassment ensues. None whatsoever. But think on this matter, for I fear my dearest friend will die from a broken heart if you do not return his great affection.'

'Your Grace, I would not have the gentleman's death on my conscience, if, of course, he be a gentleman. To prove he is worthy of the title I would have him return the ring immediately, for none can ever be of higher value. I will gladly give him another if he wishes – I promise,' she added, quickly, looking at the king's peeved face. He was annoyed that she was spoiling his game.

'Come, Sire, I have a mind to dance with you alone. Would Your Grace partner my poor steps?'

I watched as Margaret and the king made their way down from the dais, the courtiers sweeping to one side. The regent loved dancing as much as he did and clapped as he leapt and cavorted around her. After the dance, the king, perspiring heavily, led Margaret back to her seat and she asked Rosaline to fetch more of the delicious almonds. No sooner was she gone than the king begged Margaret's leave for he wished to speak most urgently to one of his gentlemen.

As we sat on the steps listening to the music, my sullen eyes followed him as he mingled with the guests, stopping for a word here, a word there. He was still the spoiled boy I recalled seeing at Rochford, demanding someone find his lost dog, and I liked him not. Oh, he was handsome, and knew it, but he was a bore, and one day I would say as much.

● ●

With the celebrations at Lille over, the emperor sent a message to his daughter to join him at his private château in Antoing, six miles south of Tournai on the River *Scheldt*. Although barely rested, Margaret obediently set out to meet him, and we travelled once more through the flat Hainault countryside. I dozed, tired from the previous night's celebrations, my head on Beatrice's shoulder. Eventually, as our chariots creaked up the long gravelled avenue, I awoke to see the most beautiful castle of romantic legend I could ever have imagined. If I thought the houses and palaces seen thus far were beautiful, they turned out to be nothing compared to this lovely place.

As the sun glinted on the gleaming, pointed turrets and white towers, Margaret climbed down from her chariot, pale and tired. 'The king's energy is boundless,' she said, yawning, 'and I am weary of staying up all night. Why, he danced till dawn in his shirtsleeves and stocking feet with barely a pause to catch his breath.'

Her ladies took her cloak and her gloves, and Margaret stretched her stiff back. 'Forgive me, ladies, if I go and lie down awhile. I have such an aching head. Lady Brederode, a milk posset if you please,' she said as she swept away towards her chambers.

*   *

A day or two later as we were playing tric-trac, the regent, carrying her dog Bianca, walked into the hall. Having slept long, she now felt quite refreshed and was happy to sit and sew shirts for her father, for it gave her great pleasure. The emperor was delighted that she made them herself, and said that only the angels in Paradise wore such beautiful linen. He was truly a devoted father.

Although I was winning my game with Giovanna, Margaret asked if I would read to her instead, and taking her book of French romances, I sat down at her feet while she sewed.

However, as early evening approached we heard the sound of hooves clattering up the tree-lined avenue and Margaret rose to look out of the window. Through the thick mist, she was just able to distinguish the red and green livery of a great cavalcade of soldiers.

'He is here, my father is here!' she cried, putting aside the shirt.

I felt a frisson of excitement as we rose in unison. Outside, horses wheeled into the courtyard with much jangling of harness and barking of dogs. As the guards opened the heavy door, the emperor strode in, mud and dirt on his clothes, and threw his heavy, wet cloak to a waiting boy. His hair hung limply to his shoulders and he was obviously weary from his exertions on the battlefield. This irked him, making him irritable, as did the dogs jumping up in excitement.

'Get down, stop fussing,' he grumbled, as the dogs ran back to Margaret furiously wagging their tails.

'Rain. Nothing but damned pissing rain I tell you. It's been the devil's own job keeping the tents up, and this mist has been a nightmare. One good day, that is all we have had. One blistering hot, dry day in a month,' he continued, as Margaret flew into his open arms.

We sank in deep reverence as he threw his riding stick onto a nearby chair.

'My dearest Margot, young ladies, forgive my crude words,' apologised the emperor, clutching his daughter to his chest. 'The damp has done nothing for my bad leg, but here I am. I have left the king to it,' he whispered, close to her ear. 'Let the boy have his little day.' He pushed Margaret gently away and scrutinised her face. 'Ah, let me look at you, beloved child. You appear pale and tired. I hear he kept you up until dawn at Lille.'

Margaret frowned as she drew back. 'Indeed, Father, but the king was not pleased when you retired early. It fell to me to keep him entertained, and I was most wearied. His energy is boundless.'

The emperor glanced around, his eyes restless. 'He is young, what do you expect? You are more – more fitted to these matters than I,' he said, waving his hand distractedly. 'You did well at Lille, daughter.' He unlaced the neck of his shirt. 'Negotiations continue. This is good. You have a full report on the Scots?'

Margaret's face turned grave. 'But of course, Father. The whole point of the supper at Lille was to celebrate the English victory at Flodden Field. The king is delighted his queen proved herself capable as regent, firmly taking the reins of government. My heart, though, aches for his sister Margaret, for now she is with child again, and a widow at twenty-three. Her brother, under the influence of Katherine, is saddened for her loss and is trying to arrange for the burial of the Scottish king in London.'

'Who cares?' replied her father, his charm evaporating. 'She is a pampered bitch who squandered the money in the treasury on expensive gowns and gee-gaws. It must be quite a novelty having to spend it on the army – what's left of it. I'm with Wolsey on this – he built a celebration bonfire on hearing of the death of her husband. Good riddance. Ten thousand Scots dead and not even near two thousand English. I tell you by God, Old Surrey knows his tactics. Now there is anarchy in Scotland.'

'Oh, Father, so many dead, so many,' said Margaret, kissing the crucifix hanging from her girdle.

'Aye, well it will teach the Scots a lesson for allying themselves to that warmongering, crook-backed French toad desperate to be pope.'

'Do not forget, Father, 'that you yourself wished to combine the Church and Empire under one crown and have a pope emperor – a hereditary papacy – embodied in yourself. You were – are – as ambitious as Louis, are you not?'

'I cannot deny it, Margot,' said the emperor, taking a cup of wine from the page's tray, 'for I know I could do a more competent job myself. The pope is a young man yet he is a voluptuary. He wants a life of ease with not too much religion and kneeling on cold stone. What concerns him is beautiful art, sculpture and magnificent buildings. He is supposed to be the Holy Father – *the pope!* He also bends with the wind, and I trust him not.' He drained the cup and slammed it down on a nearby table.

Listening to his words I was horrified. This was the pope, God's chosen representative, father of the Catholic faith throughout the world, and I could not believe the words I was hearing.

'But, Father,' said Margaret, 'he is also generous and charitable to the sick, the poor, students and widows – a man of great cheerfulness and good nature. I hear he can refuse no man.'

'Exactly,' said the emperor, 'and they know it. His friends and family swarm around filling senior positions, regardless of suitability. They see the papacy as a personal estate from which to wring as much enjoyment as possible. As it makes him happy to make them happy, they use him for their own ends. What sort of an example is he giving? The clergy throughout Europe neglect preaching in their parishes and do not attend to the people, just their concubines. Mechelen – ay, and I make no excuses for it – is itself a city full of their bastards.'

Margaret tried to interrupt, but her father became even more agitated.

'The Church in Rome is like the stews of Antwerp. It has become a harlot. Murder, rape, buggery, theft, all instantly pardoned and the perpetrators assured a place in Paradise for a fixed sum of money to Rome. How can a man buy absolution from his sins with gold? As for the Low Countries, they are farmed to pay for the extravagances of Rome, a city of vice and – and filth.'

Margaret put her hand on her father's arm to calm him as he loosened his collar further.

'The pope,' he continued, 'has run out of gold from the New World and now wishes to raise funds for the building of a new church in Rome, designed by Michelangelo – it has angered many, particularly in Germany. Have a guess at what he proposes?'

His daughter shook her head.

'To obtain money he has proclaimed indulgences for those faithful who wish to buy the spiritual favours granted to him by God. Pay up and shut up.'

'But honest men want an end to these abuses – men such as Erasmus, Colet and More,' said Margaret.

'Aye, but to no effect, daughter.'

Margaret nodded. 'But come now, Father, we digress. I hear Queen Katherine sent the King of Scots' bloodied coat to her husband to use for his battle banners in France.'

'She would have sent his body if the English had allowed it, but they were too lily-livered. I'd have sent his head in a casket of ale except it would have poisoned good ale.' He laughed. 'Let me rest before I talk in confidence with you.' He turned to go and then stopped. 'Ah, the little maid in red. I hope you are taking good care of my daughter?'

I bobbed down and replied that I was.

'Good,' he whispered, close to my ear, 'I shall be relying on you very much. Please see that there is nothing she needs.' He winked to me as he had once before, and left the hall.

When he had gone, Margaret sat quietly alone, gazing out of the window as if lost in thought for the rest of that evening. As we finally fell into our beds, she stayed closeted in talks with her father, and it was obvious from the sound of their voices that she was not enjoying the early night for which she had hoped.

*   *

The following day the emperor sat in the Long Gallery gazing out at the continual rain. He wore a long, loose grey robe and soft slippers, and appeared deep in thought. It was a homely scene as he sat in our company, as any father might, and I felt a thrill inside. Here I was in the presence of the powerful Emperor Maximilian, and I could not wait to write and tell my mother.

As some of the girls and ladies quietly read, Madame

Saillant watched intently as I sewed my pillow lace. I had never seen lace quite like it before, except on the vestments worn by the priest at Mass, and she had shown me how to lay the paper pattern onto the cushion and prick the pattern out with a fishbone before dusting it with fine chalk. At first, I had been very aware of my little finger, but I soon became skilled in hiding it even while doing this most intricate of tasks.

When I looked up, the emperor smiled at me, and I felt myself wish that my father smiled at me the same way.

Margaret glanced across to him as she played her lute. 'You are thinking of my beautiful brother perhaps?' she asked.

Her father rubbed his tired eyes. 'No, Margot, though not a day goes by when I do not think of him and what might have been. I was thinking of the English king. I agreed to serve under that young puppy to avoid the expense of the campaign – nothing more – but the whole thing is accursed.'

'I am as disappointed as you are, Father,' said Margaret, laying aside the lute, 'but as this entire campaign has cost you nothing and your borders have been secured by English effort, it has hardly been accursed. I fear more for the friendship between you and His Grace. You know he is our greatest ally and, while an enemy to France, a friend to our country and prince. We must not forget the coming marriage to his sister and how he has agreed to a magnificent celebration.'

Maximilian stood wearily up, hands clasped behind his back, and walked over to the fireplace. 'I care naught for such things. I put myself and my troops under his command – a flattery he could not refuse – but then what happens?' He turned around, the fire poker in his hand. 'A scurrilous report is mooted abroad that I, Maximillian, Holy Roman Emperor, am in the King of England's pay and naught but his lackey.'

He began furiously poking the dying embers of the fire. 'That boy – *boy* I say – is flushed with military glory and cares not a whit how he damned well earns it. I despise him and wish to God the Yorkist cause had triumphed after all.

Is it any wonder I retired early at Lille?' He returned to his chair, pulling his robe tighter.

'Tell me again what happened, Father,' said Margaret, patiently.

'That – that fool got lost in the fog! Did you hear? He rode from Lille with a small escort, none of whom had any idea of how to get back to the camp. What a farce.'

I lowered my head afraid I might laugh out loud. How typical.

'The king, lost?' Margaret was horrified.

'Well, do not sound so surprised,' replied her father, studying his ragged nails. 'What fool rides with no protection or guides in the type of weather we have been having? He deserves to be assassinated.'

There was a moment's uncomfortable silence.

'Anyway,' he continued, 'the French king knew he would have to fight the English and the Flemish, and I was ordered to rendezvous immediately with King Henry to discuss what action to take. The king set up a magnificent camp across the river and drew up his battle lines. I wore the English livery of St George in the king's honour and arrived with a small company of men. The fools didn't recognise me until they saw the black eagle on my standard. I was conducted to a magnificent tent of gold and blue velvet, emblazoned with the initials 'H' and 'K', quite magnificent, what a show. I will tell you something, though,' he added, 'the Duke of Buckingham outshone every man present, even the ing. He wore a gown of purple satin smothered in antelopes, swans, spangles, gold bullion, and gold lace. Tasteless. He is full of spleen, grumbling how the king seeks to give honours to young men rather than the older nobility. He is probably right.'

He rose from his chair.

'Christ's nails, Margot, what weather we are having! The ordnance became bogged down in mud, barely able to be moved, and our fine Flemish mares struggled as they sank.

Still, the brave men of Bruges advanced on foot carrying anything they could get their hands on – poles, swords, even sharp iron tent pegs. The French called them artisans, weavers and fullers, but the Flemish killed the French knights spearing them with their *boutehastes*. Seeing all was lost, the French threw off their weapons and armour, even cutting it off their horses to make them run away faster. Two thousand took flight, and we pursued them for three miles like wild boar in a hunt. What a sight.'

Margaret arose and offered her father a cherry from a platter. He put one in his mouth.

'Where was I?' he mumbled, spitting out the stone. One of the little dogs padded up and licked it, expecting it to be a titbit. It was disappointed.

'Ah, yes, on the seventeenth day of August the king left his camp and set off with his artillery. He was informed that fifteen thousand French cavalrymen were riding forth to relieve Tournai that very day, so he drew up his battle lines and arranged his battlefield with a sumptuous tent. Even his advisors said it was unwise to have his pavilions out on the front line, but he would not be told. Oh no, he had to do it his way. Inexperienced, and it showed.' He smiled at me, aware of my rapt attention.

'He is young and eager,' excused Margaret, 'and as for experience, this is his first campaign. He yearns to win his spurs.'

Her father frowned. 'Anyway, *I* took Thérouanne – as I had thirty-five years earlier – on the boy's orders, and razed it to the ground. We then met in a splendid ceremony, and I looked magnificent.'

'Oh, tell me,' said Margaret.

Her father's face became more animated, pleased at her interest. 'I faced the king with great plumes streaming from my helm, my robe in black and gold, my great brown mare with black eagles on her saddle cloth. As for Thérouanne, now it is as rubble. The cathedral I left untouched for I would not commit sacrilege against a sacred thing. As we speak, the king presses on to Tournai.'

Quite spontaneously, without thinking, I stood and applauded. The other ladies stared at my sudden outburst and frowned.

The emperor threw his head back and laughed. 'You enjoyed my tale, *demoiselle?*'

My eyes blazed with admiration. 'Indeed, sir, for I think you are magnificent, as a true ruler should be, a seasoned warrior.'

The emperor then beckoned me to him and, to my surprise, kissed me on both cheeks. As he leaned close, his linen shirt gaped open a little, and the aroma of civet rose from the warmth of his skin. Towering above me, he appeared the most powerful of men, strong and vital and I did not want to move away. It was the strangest of feelings.

He straightened up. 'Well, Margot, the end is in sight. At first light, I must leave you again and make my way to Tournai.' He walked over and kissed her tenderly on the cheek, taking another cherry.

Turning to me he smiled. 'You really are the most delightful young lady,' he said, as he padded out of the gallery.

＊　＊

On the twenty-third day of September, Tournai, exhausted by the relentless battering, surrendered. It had no choice, for over eighty thousand now homeless peasants had taken refuge within its walls, and the city capitulated through sheer starvation. On Sunday the twenty-fifth, we heard how at ten in the morning, the king made his triumphal entry into the vanquished town. He handed the keys of the city to Charles Brandon, an act of favour and prominence noted by those present. The emperor said he did not wish to accompany the king in his triumph, for he did not want to detract from his glory. The king, believing him, was overjoyed that his ally had given him the place of honour. In truth, the emperor could not stomach the whole show and was furious that the king had taken, and then kept, Tournai. It was not his original plan to let him occupy the town, for he wanted Tournai for himself since it was on the borders of his own dominions of Burgundy, and he felt misled. The fact that the whole campaign had cost him nothing but his pride seemed to have escaped him. Margaret was disappointed by the whole miserable affair, fearing for the friendship between her father and King Henry, and tension ran high.

Later, the emperor returned to his château, where we had remained. I was glad, for I would see him again. He described how he had secretly watched the magnificent entry made by the king, how the local girls had thrown garlands of flowers, and the thieves begged to be pardoned. The emperor said the king was now bent on three weeks of celebrations with no expense spared. Wolsey assured him that he would see to the details of the occupation, thus ensuring his master would be free to enjoy an endless round of banquets, masques and tournaments. King Henry seemed bent on nothing but pleasure, to the emperor's disgust – and mine.

* *

I was awoken by the sound of raised voices coming from the direction of Margaret's chamber.

'Beatrice, wake up,' I whispered, nudging her. *'Beatrice!'*

She moaned and turned.

'Listen, someone is angry.'

Beatrice raised herself sleepily up on to one elbow to listen. 'Perhaps it's the ghost of Baron d'Antoing,' she murmured, pulling her bolster over her head, and turning her back to me. 'Go back to sleep, it is still dark.'

I lay, alert, listening to the voices as they grew louder. Margaret was arguing with her father, and I had never known her raise her voice before. I squeezed carefully out of bed, trying not to disturb Beatrice or the other girls. Chilly in my nightshift, I tiptoed down the wooden stairs, past the

Great Hall and the guards on duty, and noticed the flickering firelight beneath the door of Margaret's chamber. The voices were now quite clear, and it was obvious an awful disagreement was taking place.

'Father, you surely cannot be questioning my loyalty to you. If I thought I could be of service to you, I would go. Why, have I not time and again pawned my possessions to find you money?'

'Then tell me why? Tell me your objections?' The emperor's voice sounded angry.

'Father, the invitation is for you to accompany me as the emperor. You cannot be absent again.'

I heard the movement of a heavy chair.

'Here, sit down, Margot, you appear to be in a state.' The voice sounded calmer.

'I am not in a state! This will be an official visit involving the king's nobles, and it will be seen as an insult to him if you do not go. Besides,' she added, 'in case it has slipped your mind, there will also be a vast, victorious army of men. It is unchristian for me to be seen trotting around the countryside anyway near them. As for my young *demoiselles* and ladies-in-waiting, is it right to expose them to a town full of rough soldiery?'

I heard the chair scrape the floor.

'What a gross exaggeration! You will not be servicing the army like some common harlot,' came the reply. 'You will be visiting the King of England.'

There was a moment's pause.

'Look – the truth is, Margot, I do not wish to go. I cannot trust myself to bend the knee to that – that pompous boy, and I need your charm and diplomacy to keep this alliance safe – at least for the moment.'

'Meaning?' asked Margaret.

'Nothing – it is nothing. You know that I am blunt speaking and will not be able to hide my spleen.'

I heard a glass clink.

'I shall call him son, Majesty, brother, and friend – whatever it takes – and I shall hide my contempt for him. I tell you, Ferdinand plans to bridle him and put such a vicious bit in his mouth he will never forget the hand that hauls him. I am even of the mind to go with Ferdinand in his plan to return Tournai to the French.'

'Oh, now I see how it lies with you, Father! You will dupe the king. He is our most trusted friend and ally, a man without malice or hypocrisy who calls me *"ma bonne seur et cousine."* He promises, on the word of God's anointed, never to treat with the French, without my seal or permission. No, he does not have the cunning of his dead father, or King Ferdinand, or, indeed, you yourself, and so I shall have no part in it.'

'Do not be naïve, Margot. There is no such thing as a trusted friend in politics, as well you know,' came the reply.

'Father, I beg you, you must not trust the French in any matter, let alone return Tournai to them. They will do you as much mischief as they can, for you know the great and inveterate hatred they bear towards this house. Far better to rely on the goodwill of England,' warned Margaret.

'Well, maybe, but come now,' wheedled the emperor, 'I know I can depend on you to smooth matters over. Tell the king it is not fitting for me, so recently widowed, to be seen celebrating and carousing.'

'I see,' said Margaret. 'But it is quite fitting for me.'

'It is.'

I heard him give a deep sigh.

'I am ordering – no, asking you – as an obedient daughter, to use your tact and skills to keep the goodwill between the king and our two countries.'

'Since that is the case, Father, I must go for, as you say, I am your obedient daughter.'

'Margaret! I can see no other way. I do not have the stomach for it, and there is an end to the matter!'

As I stood listening, the door flew open and the emperor

strode out, giving me such a fright that I fell back into the hanging tapestry.

'You have a visitor,' he growled, as he pushed past.

I turned to flee, but Margaret appeared, peering into the dim light, her little dogs gathering around her feet.

'Who is there? What do you want? Why – Anna, what is it, child?' she asked, standing in a loose velvet robe, her hair hanging down in a long plait.

'Oh, Madame,' I said, attempting to curtsey. 'I – I was trying to find the privy closet and took the wrong passageway.'

She took me by the hand. 'Come in. We do not want to disturb the countess at this late hour, do we? You may use the privy here in my chamber. Come, come along, before you catch a chill.'

When I returned from the privy, I expected to be sent straight back to bed, but Margaret asked me to stay. She beckoned to a sleepy young girl in the corner of the chamber to tend to the dying logs on the fire, and placed a black, velvet robe around my shoulders. I gazed around in curiosity and spied a small altar with a picture of the Virgin Mary and Child above it, and below, three small, carved figures standing on the white lace cloth.

'I am much attached to the Blessed Virgin,' said Margaret, following my gaze. 'St Anne, St Anthony, and my namesake, St Margaret, are my dearest friends whose reassurance I seek in difficult times.' She waved the girl back into the shadows.

'Did you overhear what was being said just now?' She sat down at her table in front of the polished steel of her mirror and stared at me in the reflection. 'I am not angry, Anna, although you should not eavesdrop and you will have to tell the confessor.' Her stern expression softened. 'In truth, my father is not himself, for he is a kind and generous man, beloved of his army and people. He is the most wonderful father anyone could wish for, but I fear these last few weeks have caused him distress. Now, take the hairbrush, if you would, and brush out my hair. It is most soothing.'

I unplaited her hair and began to smooth out the long, golden strands.

'When Philibert died I cut it all off in grief,' she said, 'and my ladies followed suit. Now, tell me, why were you listening?'

I looked back at her reflection. 'Raised voices woke me, Madame, and I felt concern for you.'

'Concern – or curiosity?' she asked.

I hesitated before answering. 'Curiosity, Madame.'

'So you lied and did not want the privy?'

I nodded.

'Lying and eavesdropping constitute grave sins and must be punished,' she said. 'I shall let it pass this once, as it was done with the best intentions. But you must never do this again. A maid of honour must always show discretion and be trustworthy – not listen at doors like a spy.' She closed her eyes and sighed as I continued to brush in silence. After a few moments she spoke. 'You will have heard how my father was much aggrieved with me.'

I said I had.

'It was sinful of me to argue with him for it offends God,' she continued, 'for as women we must obey our fathers, even if we think they err in what they request. It is the sacred duty of a good daughter to be obedient. Is that not true, since men rule over all?'

'But why, Madame?' I asked.

'Because men consider women to be full of cunning and trickery – take Eve, or Delilah, or Salome. We can be strong and respected, but it must come through virtue, courage or learning.'

I stood in silence, and, turning, Margaret took my hand.

'You are very young, Anna, and I fear you do not fully understand this. But one day you will marry, and there is something you must never forget: this is a man's world, but you can still make your mark. Remember this: where men use force and threats to get what they want, we women must use gentleness and intelligence. Where men use aggression, we must use feminine skills to steer matters to suit our course. We must cultivate wit and charm, for defiance over a man will never succeed. Do you understand?'

'But, Madame, what if a man is wrong? I have heard Mother tell Father that he is a fool many times when he has done something simple. Once he left the gate open at home and the donkey wandered off and trampled the herb garden. Mother was cross and berated him soundly. Everyone heard. Father was wrong, was he not?'

'Oh, indeed yes, most careless, but a woman should not argue with or chide a man publicly, for they hate to appear foolish in front of a woman. We must even pretend to agree with them, although in our hearts we might think otherwise.'

'But, Madame, that is not honest. Should we not say what we think?'

Margaret laughed as I wound her hair up into a linen night coif. 'Not with men, my dear, for their pride is fragile. You must never be outspoken or loud in your opinions. You must appear to bend to their wishes. Oh, I shall go to Tournai as my father orders and take you all with me. I have no choice but to fulfil his request, and, as a widow, my status will stand me in good stead for this delicate mission. Everyone knows I have dedicated myself to a life of prayer and, as such, I am not of any political use as a marriage pawn. Kings and princes may speak freely with me, for I come as a peacemaker and naught else, certainly not as a prospective bride. Why, am I not known as *"La tante de l'Europe"*?' she asked.

She climbed into the great oak bed. 'Now, read to me a little before I go to sleep.'

She passed me a small book, and I began reading:

> *'The time is troubled, but the time will clear;*
> *After rain fair weather is awaited;*

After strife and cruel great contention
Peace will arrive, misfortune cease to be.
But anyone who murmurs in complaint
Does ill, for, as I understand,
In this our time, regretting but wastes time,
Silence is best for anyone who thinks:
The time is troubled.'

'You read very naturally,' she murmured, as she closed her eyes.

'I find it is easy, Madame, for the words are skilled.'

'Thank you,' she said, 'I wrote them myself.'

I carried on reading several more of her works until she opened her eyes and, taking the book gently from me, laid it on the coverlet.

'You must return to your own bed now, for you must look fresh and lovely for the king and his nobles. Remember, I rely on my ladies' discretion, for you will hear things of the utmost importance, things never to be repeated. Do you understand? Now, let me bid you goodnight.'

Back in bed, I snuggled up to the warm, sleeping Beatrice and thought of the emperor. He was very old, but he seemed such a loving, vital man. I liked the way he winked and petted me. He was not exactly handsome, but he had a presence, and I found myself thinking about him every waking moment. I wanted to tell my feelings to the other girls, but I knew they would only laugh at me for having fond thoughts of a man old enough to be my grandfather, even Beatrice. She would never understand so I decided to keep my thoughts and my fantasies to myself. As to the court, I knew that I still had a great deal to learn, and that much of what I heard was beyond my understanding, but I would try. I would try and understand how it functioned and how a ruler must govern, whom a queen could trust and of whom she must be wary. Then I would be of use to Queen Katherine, for when I grew older I wanted to be just like the regent – clever, pious and good. Like her, I would spend my days reading and acquiring knowledge. I would write poems and play music. I would never be jealous or have a fit of temper, whatever fortune might bring. I would be sweet and gentle in speech, modest in my opinions and wise. I would grow up to be blessed by those around me. Like the regent I would be wise. Like her, I would be loved by all.

Chapter Five

*'For those who love, time is
not enough.'*

Tournai, Late Summer 1513

A sombre mood pervaded the air as we trotted
through the triumphal arch of the city. A few yards
in front, Margaret sat with her ladies in a litter
decorated with yellow ostrich plumes and, on each side, a
young page carrying a flaming torch, walked on foot.

I rode pillion behind Beatrice, wearing my coat and
gown of blue cloth, lined with grey. The Venetian sleeves of
the coat were trimmed with grey ribbon, and beneath my
jaunty-angled bonnet, I wore my hair in a caul of silver net.

Glancing about, I could see that the litter, rubble, and
stones from the siege had been hastily removed, and that
the tapestries and banners from the previous day's triumphal entry were still in place. But the feeling was not one
of welcome.

As we entered the *St Fontaine* gate, I gazed around at the
hundreds of silent citizens clutching their flickering torches

in the fading light. Although there was cheering from the English soldiers lining the route, the people themselves were sullen. They did not want to be occupied, and since the town had suffered terrible hardship and starvation, its people were in no mood for this gaudy show.

The horses nervously jostled and bunched up as they tried to pass through the arched gate at the same time. Our horse kicked out, and the jolt almost unseated me.

'Get on,' urged Beatrice, forcing the animal to squeeze between the horses in front, and so avoid brushing against the rough walls.

The great banner of St George, which the king insisted be raised at the city gates, flapped noisily above, and the ruffling unsettled our horse, which in turn unsettled the ones behind. Seeing this, the grooms squeezed forward to steady the animals, and our colourful cavalcade lumbered on.

Once through, I peered over Beatrice's shoulder and saw ahead an enormous company of nobles gathered in their finery.

'Is my father there?'

Beatrice tried to curb our unruly horse and gave a hard tug on the reins. Maddened by the bit, the horse laid back its ears and bucked violently. This time I became unseated.

'Oh!' I cried, as my bonnet fell from my head and I slipped further down the side of the exasperated animal.

'Hold on, my lady!' cried a gruff English voice, 'here, slide down and I will take your weight. Whoa, now!' The man grabbed the horse's bridle, and as I slid down into his arms, I saw from his green and white livery that he was an English soldier.

'As light as gossamer,' he murmured, as he set me down onto the cobbles.

Beatrice steadied the horse and manoeuvred it to the side, whilst the other riders squeezed passed.

'Thank you, sir,' I said above the noise and confusion, 'but where is my bonnet?'

Another young man, limping badly, picked it up. 'Here, here it is, my lady,' he said, in a strange English accent, brushing it against his doublet to rub off the dust. He placed it back on my head, somewhat askew, with a smile that showed the whitest teeth I had ever seen. However, his leg, heavily bandaged, appeared to be bleeding.

'Sir!' I pointed in alarm.

'Take no notice of Jamie, my lady,' laughed his companion, 'he uses his wound to gain every girl's sympathy.' He took me to one side as Beatrice dismounted.

'Sir, the blood is flowing afresh, you must apply some pressure to it,' she stared down at the seeping stain.

The injured man sat down on the crumbling wall and unwound the bandage. He smiled up at me. 'Fighting at Thérouanne,' he said, trying not to wince, 'I suffered this for my pains. A cannonball exploded nearby and threw me some distance. The surgeon says I will never dance a jig again in Ireland.'

'Ireland?' asked Beatrice. 'Why would you want to dance in Ireland? They say it is wild and cannot be ruled.'

The bleeding began to stop.

'Here, let me,' she said, 'you hold the pad, and I will wind.' She rewound the dirty cloth as the young man's friend held our fractious horse and stroked its nose to calm it.

I looked at the injured man. His red hair fell tousled and unkempt, but his brown eyes twinkled as he smiled.

'Forgive me, *demoiselles*, but whom am I addressing?'

'Mistress Anne Bullen and Mistress Beatrice van Broekaert,' I said. 'I am English, and my friend here is Flemish. We reside at the Court of Savoy.'

'Bullen, you say – Sir Thomas Bullen's daughter?'

I nodded.

'Why, our families are connected, for your grandfather married into my family. Your grandmother is a Butler? Am I correct?'

'Why, yes sir,' I said.

'My name is Jamie Butler, and my friend here is Edward Knevet. I am the eldest son of the 8th Earl of Ormond, and I was following in my father's footsteps learning how to be a soldier. Now – well, now I am not so sure! I may have to content myself with family affairs and managing our estates. What a strange coincidence, quite extraordinary.' He smiled down at me. 'I hope to make your acquaintance again, in the future no doubt, but for now, you must remount, for if you do not catch up the procession, you will be left behind.'

We remounted the horse, and I straightened my gown.

'He is settled now,' said James Butler, taking the bridle and turning the horse around, 'quiet as a lamb. The press and noise were bothering him, and the bit is hurting his mouth. Let him have his head a little and loosen the rein.'

The horse blinked and turned a deep blue eye towards him. I gazed down as Beatrice gathered up the reins.

'Thank you, sirs, for your help,' she said.

When I looked up, James Butler stared at me. 'Such beautiful eyes,' he murmured. 'Do you not agree, Ned?'

His companion slapped him on the back and laughed. 'Farewell, ladies, one day we may meet again – if you come to Ireland,' and with a smile, they both disappeared back into the line of soldiers.

'Oh, Beatrice,' I whispered, as our horse tucked in behind the moving masse. 'Did you hear? Ireland.' I glanced back but he was gone, and I felt a twinge of disappointment for Jamie Butler had a most appealing face.

As we halted at the square, Beatrice pointed ahead. 'The king is there – look!'

There he was again, a man surrounded by his Yeomen of the Guard, head and shoulders above the other men – except for Charles Brandon who stood close by – and I liked him no better. Dressed magnificently in rich armour, he wore gold satin slashed with cream silk, and a cloak of purple velvet covered in *fleur-de-lys* and leopards. From his jewel-encrusted helm fluttered magnificent white plumes. He ran exuberantly up to Margaret's chariot, and I watched as he helped her step down. She was just about to curtsey when he swept her up into his arms and kissed her lovingly on both cheeks. The company around him roared its approval and clapped wildly, but the citizens of Tournai remained silent for they had no wish to welcome the English king. Neither did I.

'Welcome, sweetest and noblest of ladies. Welcome.' He turned with arms outstretched adding, 'and welcome to the fairest ladies in Christendom. We campaigners have longed for your gentle company again.'

The king and Margaret stood conversing for some moments, and when she whispered something in his ear, he roared in amusement. He presented her to some of his nobles and Margaret sparkled and smiled, gracious as ever.

After the greeting, the king escorted her back to her chariot and, once she was seated, he turned to the rest of the company.

'Come, now, by your gracious leave, I shall escort you to the bishop's palace for entertainment and refreshment.' He mounted his bay horse, its trappings covered in silver tinkling bells, and to the loud sound of trumpets proceeded to trot ahead.

●   ●

When the ladies had settled Margaret into her chamber, I was told that I had a visitor, and must change out of my riding clothes and put on something modest and demure before proceeding to see her.

Beatrice and I chose the tawny brocade gown, with its high, square neck and fitted sleeves, and a young maid plaited and coiled my long hair with a russet-coloured ribbon.

'Suitably sober,' said Beatrice, passing me a girdle from which hung a small prayer book.

'I wonder who your visitor is?' asked one of the ladies-in-waiting, as she accompanied me down the gallery. We stopped outside the door of the royal apartments.

'Enter.'

I stepped into the chamber with as much grace as I could muster and my heart missed a beat.

'Father!' I exclaimed, forgetting to make my reverence. As he moved towards me and put his hand on my head in blessing, forcing me to kneel, I gazed up at the rich, black fur collar on his cloak.

'Well, stand up, Nan, and let me have a look at you. Turn round, turn round.' He waved his hand in a circle. 'Well, well, I can see how you have blossomed under this good lady's care. You have even grown a little, and your mother will be most pleased.'

'She is a joy, Thomas, truly a joy,' said Margaret, placing her hand on my shoulder. 'I am in your debt for sending such a charming creature to me. She is a jewel and shows such diligence in her work, never missing an opportunity to study. She is always the first to her lessons and the last to leave. Come, Anna, show your father how well you read French.' Margaret picked up the book of verse laying on her desk and opened a page, but Father moved forward and stayed her hand.

'Madame, your pardon, please forgive me if I say not at this moment.' She appeared puzzled as he smiled. 'I must return to the king immediately with important papers for him to sign, for I have a hundred impatient men-at-arms waiting to be paid. I can stay to talk for but a moment.'

My own smile faded as he offered a seat to Margaret, before seating himself. I watched her, a little taken aback, as she put the book aside.

'I hear, Nan, from this good lady that you have proved useful and such news pleases me. It pleases me greatly. Never forget the enormous gratitude you owe to her.'

I bit my lip, bursting with questions, then, unable to stop myself, burst forth in a torrent of words. 'Oh, please, sir, what news is there from my lady mother and Mrs Orcharde? How doth Mary and George? Does Sorrel still catch rabbits?

Sir, when might I have a dog of my own? You sa…'

Margaret laughed as my father put up his hand to silence my babble, and my voice trailed off.

'Anne! Remember your manners and at least speak in French. Forgive her, my lady.'

Margaret offered him a piece of marchpane from a silver tray.

'All are well,' he added, popping a piece into his mouth. 'Your mother is at court with Mary – what there is left of it,' he added, turning to Margaret. 'Every available man at court has disappeared to fight in France, young and old.'

'Oh?'

'Except the Howards,' he continued, 'they have stayed.' He took another piece of marchpane for he had a weakness for such sweet treats, although these days they troubled his teeth.

'Oh, and Mountjoy has stayed behind to be the queen's advisor. Did you know?'

Margaret shook her head.

'He has the comeliest daughter you have ever seen – near Anne's age – Elizabeth Blount,' he added, glancing towards me. 'She is quite extraordinary, very talented musically. But I digress, the queen is keeping late hours with His Grace out of the realm, for she means to govern well and make him proud. I fear she takes on too much for a woman in the early months of pregnancy. Let us pray she brings forth a healthy boy in February for, God knows, we must have a prince. The wise women and doctors say she will,' he added brightly.

'She has been more concerned with the king's health,' said Margaret, 'than her own, and even wrote to me begging me to send Dr Picot to her husband's side to ensure his well-being.'

'Indeed,' continued my father, pouring Margaret and himself a cup of wine, 'and next to the king, her greatest fear has been the Scots agreeing to a treaty of alliance with France. Typical that they caused rebellion, backed by the damned French, the minute the king was out of the country. Elizabeth has been most fearful for her father as he faced the barbaric Scots. She feels her father is too old to be fighting, but Howards were born to fight. It is what they do.'

'Well, Thomas, I am told your Wolsey fellow was glad to have Surrey out of the way in Scotland and not in France, for I gather he likes to have His Grace all to himself.'

Father grimaced. 'Aye, and there's the cut of it, for there is no love lost between those two. Wolsey made sure the Howards remained in England, away from the king's ear in France. Do you know the queen actually rode north herself to rally troops, keen to show her husband that she was her mother's daughter – the warrior queen, Isabella? Well, the Scots proved themselves a rabble with no discipline. Now their king is dead, and England is victorious.'

Margaret crossed herself. 'They have indeed done well, Thomas, but now I must be honest with you. Do you recall my concern for your English army in France? I feared, due to lack of action, they would prove inexperienced, fat and lazy. I confess you hotly denied this.'

'Aye, Madame, and rightly, too! Englishmen are ever ready for a brawl. I win the wager, and you owe me a falcon complete with bells and hood. See? What do women know of war?'

Margaret bowed her head graciously.

'Very well, Thomas, would you be content to take your hobby back from our last wager? I did win it fairly. Now, perhaps you would like time alone with your daughter to talk a little of her progress?'

My father put his empty glass down. 'No, I give you thanks, Madame, but I must be away. I can see my daughter is thriving with you and I give my utmost thanks. I shall leave her in your capable hands and have discourse with her later. For now, I must attend to His Grace. I give you good even, dearest lady, for I will not be at tonight's supper and thus must take my leave.' He kissed Margaret's hand again, and she smiled warmly.

'God's blessing on you, Nan,' he said, laying his hand on my head as he passed. He bowed low to Margaret and left the chamber.

There was a moment of silence before Margaret spoke.

'Your expression appears somewhat sullen, my dear.' I stared down at the chequered floor tiles. 'Speak, Anna, and raise your head. What is the matter?'

'Madame, I wished to show my father how much I have learnt.'

'Fie, you have done well, Anna, but I hope I do not hear pride creeping into your voice? Pride is but a poor relation of a spirit borne up by spleen. Do not set store by it but practise humility, for I tell you it will grow like a tangled weed over a rose if it is not cut down at early growth.' Margaret studied my face to see if I had understood her. She was not altogether satisfied.

'Come now, your father has much on his mind, and you must not forget that he has important business with the King. It is why he is here. It is why *you* are here. You would not have this honour without his work and good efforts in gaining my friendship. You have let foolish vanity mar your pleasure at seeing him.'

I was unable to agree with her words, for I felt disappointed.

'I am sure your father will talk with you later when he has finished business. As for now, he sees you are well and happy. Come, cheerily, let me see you smile.'

I proffered a thin smile, but inside I felt the usual pang of disappointment I experienced when seeing my father. It was a feeling I never felt with the emperor.

❋   ❋

Trotting into the courtyard of the bishop's palace, a small bodyguard of men-at-arms riding behind, the emperor swung his horse around to the mounting steps. Margaret, playing bowls with the Milanese ambassador and a host of gentlemen, was taken quite by surprise by this sudden, unannounced visit. I watched her leave the game and hurry inside with her father, while her ladies entertained the ambassador and his entourage.

A short while later, still standing outside with a tray of dates and figs for the guests, I watched as she hurried after the emperor, in obvious agitation.

'Father, stop!' she cried, grasping his horse's bridle. 'The king will be most displeased if you ride away in such haste and secrecy, for he wishes to honour you.'

'I cannot help that, Margot,' came the reply, as the emperor pulled his cloak roughly from underneath his seat. 'I shall return tomorrow with the prince to discuss his forthcoming marriage. As for this place, I wish to be gone immediately. Away from this excessive feasting and show.' His voice trailed off as he turned his fractious horse around, forcing Margaret to let go.

'Enjoy the tennis, daughter,' he muttered over his shoulder, 'I cannot stomach a moment's more insincerity and foolery. I give you good day.' He wheeled his horse around again, his escort following behind, across the courtyard.

I felt disappointed, for he had not seen me, and I had dressed my hair differently today with the utmost care. As he left, I walked over to attend to the ambassador and his gentlemen. Margaret followed, her arms outstretched.

'Forgive me, sirs,' she said, trying to hide her embarrassment, 'we seemed to be in such a whirl of activity and celebration. The king plans a tennis match this afternoon to which we must all attend, and tomorrow the prince arrives for a grand tournament. I do not know whether I am coming or going!' She took the ambassador's arm. 'Gentlemen, please join me inside, for some refreshment.'

* *

Rosaline appeared flushed as the regent reached over to

her in concern. 'Are you sick, child?' she asked.

Rosaline shook her head and twisted the silk of her cream gown. 'It is but a headache, Madame, naught to speak of.'

Margaret smiled sympathetically as she sat on a dais draped with red velvet, her ladies seated behind awaiting the tennis match. She wore her black velvet gown and white coif, and a jewelled crucifix lay at her breast. She turned to the Countess of Hochstrate. 'I think she should lie down somewhere quiet – perhaps she should be taken back to the palace?'

Rosaline smiled, a little too brightly. 'Oh no, if you please, Madame, I wish to watch the match.'

Margaret nodded and turned to the Florentine ambassador, Thomas Spinelly. 'I suppose you heard King Henry was exceedingly annoyed by my father not remaining to greet him?'

'Indeed, Madame,' replied the ambassador. 'I was present. Forced to meet with King Henry, your father churlishly refused to get off his horse. The king insisted he at least drink a toast with him, but the emperor sat on his horse in silence, desperate to ride off. The king, full of embarrassed bonhomie and laughter, raised his goblet and tried to save face. It was a farce of the first degree.'

'Dear God in Heaven,' said Margaret. She nodded in greeting to the Duke of Buckingham and Baron Mountjoy, now governor of Tournai, as they took their seats.

Standing to one side, chatting to the dignitaries, I noticed a florid gentleman whom I had not seen before. He was taller than my father and handsome, apart from a scar beneath his right eye, and appeared well-dressed. Like Father, he wore his hair beneath his ears in the new, fashionable style. He selected a ripe plum and since he caught me staring, beckoned me over with his finger. 'And who might you be, young lady?' he asked in perfect French. 'You do not appear to be Flemish.'

'I am English, sir,' I replied with a bob, trying not to

stare at the wart above his lip, 'and a maid of honour to Madame Regent.'

'English? Why, we shall speak your tongue. What is your name, little maid?'

'Anne Bullen,' I replied, brightly.

'Ah,' he said in recognition, 'you must be one of Thomas's daughters. Would you like a plum, Anne? I'm sure your lady would not mind.'

I politely refused.

'Well, what say you to this?' He fumbled in his pocket and brought something out. 'Careful, he might bite.'

I stared at his large be-ringed hand hiding the object. 'What is it, sir?'

'Open and see,' he said, presenting his closed hand.

I turned it over and, very carefully, opened his fingers. 'Oh! It is a gingerbread mouse!' I cried, in delight.

He obviously thought me much younger than I was, as he held the mouse up by its thread of a tail. 'Indeed it is. This is for you, for you have been very patient sitting there waiting for the game to begin.'

We were interrupted by one of Margaret's ladies. 'Shall I take Mistress Bullen back to her place, sir?'

The man shook his head. 'No, no, she may tarry if she wishes.'

As he spoke, a great roar arose announcing the players as they entered the court. I watched as the king leapt over the tasselled cord, his fair skin visible through his fine holland shirt. He pulled the shirt loose from his short velvet slops and began slamming the white, kid leather balls across the gallery. Showing off. Charles Brandon appeared next, to another great roar, and grabbed the king around the neck in jest. As they mock wrestled together, the crowd cheered its approval. Margaret inclined her head as Brandon smiled up at her. Caught off guard, he was promptly hit by a ball, to everyone's amusement.

'You will find the rules quite simple, mistress,' said the

gentleman, as I strained for a better view. 'Here, stand to this side and you will see clearly. The player has to hit the ball over the net to score a point, but he can also score by hitting the ball into one of the three goals on the walls. Do you see, high up there?'

I nodded.

'A player can also bounce the ball off the wall. Now, watch the king.'

A boy ran out, put the ball in to play, and the king slammed it with such fierceness he made me jump. The two players thrashed out ball after ball, the crowd rising and clapping after each point scored, the noise quite deafening. Both players were soon in a sweat and the king, deciding he was better off without it, threw off his damp shirt. He paraded around the gallery displaying his fine, muscular chest with its downy, golden hair, making the ladies squeal with delight, even Neutken. I yawned as Brandon followed suit and the ladies jumped up from their seats, completely obscuring my view. Through the sea of coloured satin and silk gowns, I spied Margaret lean forward in her chair and Brandon bow to her, keeping his eyes firmly on her face. She flushed pink and raised her plumed fan.

The contest resumed and continued throughout the afternoon, neither of the players tiring, until eventually a winner was declared. It was, of course, the king, but he insisted Brandon must accept the golden rose in his place. Muttering ensued as the king was clearly the victor, but he silenced the crowd with his raised arms.

'It is as I wish and I am in a generous mood!' he cried, as he took a piece of cloth and wiped his sweating face. He tossed the cloth into the stands, and there were more shrieks and sighs, as the ladies tried to catch it. Brandon caught a fresh shirt thrown to him by his page and ascended the dais. His damp, tousled hair fell into his eyes as he accepted the prize from the regent.

'I must go and congratulate His Grace on an excellent

game, young lady,' said my companion. 'Please excuse me, and thank you for the pleasure of your company. I wish you well for your future as a lady at court. God bless and keep you.'

* *

Michaelmas was upon us and the day overcast when Prince Charles arrived to finalise the negotiations for his wedding. The emperor said his farewells to the prince and left him alone with his vast bodyguard and nobles, for he did not intend taking any further part in the prince's day. King Henry met the boy on the outskirts of Tournai, and together they rode in a magnificent triumphal procession, not reaching the town itself until nightfall. The prince and King Henry rode over the bridge, the prince in russet velvet, trimmed with ermine, and the king in cloth of gold. The crowd, I was later told, looked on, still silent and curious as the many nobles, both Burgundian and English, escorted them both to the Abbey of St Martin. There, Margaret waited to greet him.

We pressed around the windows of the abbey, trying to spy their arrival, peering through the thick, green panes of glass. Then, to a great blast of trumpets, the escort carrying the royal standard trotted into the courtyard, and the prince and King Henry rode under the archway.

'Maids, stand to, if you please,' ordered one of the ladies, as the regent descended the stairs with her nobles.

In the courtyard, ablaze with torches, the king and the prince dismounted and Charles, at thirteen years old, seemed very small and thin beside him. There was much kissing, hugging and doffing of caps for the king was much enamoured of the young prince and did not want to let him go. However, after a final bow, he took the boy's hand and presented him to Margaret, who was standing in the doorway.

'Never have I met a fairer prince,' he said, tears in his eyes. 'Dear God, how I yearn for such a boy and I can think of no more priceless gift to give him than my beautiful sister, Mary Rose. I bid you goodnight until the morrow. God keep you both.'

Margaret curtsied deeply to the king and kissed the prince tenderly while we stood watching from the doorway. As the king smiled at the ladies, his eyes lingered on Rosaline. She flushed as he winked, mounted his great horse, and with a half rear, clattered back out of the gates.

●　●

'It is not fair!' shrieked the prince, as soon as he was inside the palace. The nobles lowered their eyes, embarrassed, as Margaret passed him a glass of Flemish ale.

'Drink this, dearest, you have had a long day and must be overwrought.' She removed his large, flat hat and smoothed his hair. 'Shall I fetch Dr Picot?'

'No,' snapped the prince, flinching at her touch, 'and I am not overwrought. I am fuming. Throughout the day the English king showed off, rearing his horse, high stepping and cavorting. It made my blood boil. Everyone should have been looking at me, but he rode on ahead while I plodded along behind. I am a fearless rider and can handle a horse as well as he can. I felt humiliated, for the king should have had the good grace to remain by my side, as an equal. It wasn't fair!'

He pulled a sulky face and downed the ale in one gulp as if showing he was a man. He held his empty glass out, and a servant rushed forward to refill it.

Margaret swiftly took the glass from him and placed it firmly back on the tray. 'I know, my darling, but the king cannot resist an adoring crowd. He cannot help himself, and he means no harm. Is that not true, gentlemen?' She turned around, and the nobles politely murmured in agreement.

'Now, come into my chamber, and one of my maids will play you soothing music, or, if you prefer, one of them will read. Tomorrow we have yet another day of celebration with a grand tournament, and you must get your rest. For my part, I will be glad when I am back home in my own bed and can resume a normal routine. Too much rich food and long hours do not suit me.'

The prince, ignoring her words, stormed off down the passageway leaving Margaret to follow behind.

*   *

At three o'clock the following day, amidst a light drizzle of rain, the prince, with his nobles set out for the tournament. The royal party had been allocated a house close to the cathedral, enlarged to enable the prince, Margaret and her ladies to view the spectacle in comfort. The regent sat with Monsieur Antoing de Lalaing, Signor di Gattinara, the Prince Bishop of Liege, Monsieur de la Marck, and other council members. At her feet, sat Neutken wearing a monstrous red and white striped cap and matching gown. The prince, with his gentlemen and Monsieur de Chiévres, sat on her other side. The boy appeared sullen and complained that the chiming bells of the cathedral were making his headache worse. Margaret turned around and asked Christa to fetch him a glass of elderflower water.

'You were upset yesterday,' said Margaret, 'and drank too much ale on an empty stomach. Now, feeling unwell, you must pay the price. It pains me when you do this to yourself, dearest.' She placed her hand on his knee, but the prince moved it abruptly away. Margaret, ever gracious, smiled and folded her hands on her lap.

I looked below, and saw that next to the Cloth Hall a magnificent area for the tournament itself had been fashioned. It was extraordinary, for at the king's request seventy yards of the town's smooth cobblestones had been dug up and removed, and fresh earth laid to allow the horses to run in safety. This, plus the huge golden pavilion set up for the comfort of the competitors, showed just how much of a fortune the king had spent.

As Beatrice and I stared down at the wonderful scene

sprawling before us, the rain now ceased, it was truly a sight to behold. The doorway of each house below had been turned into a food stall selling everything from ale, to fresh bread, cheese and pies. Great strings of fat sausages swung from hooks, along with cooked rabbit, game and pheasant, and delicious smells from the smoking braziers curled up towards the window. The beer, sold cheaply to celebrate the occasion, and the free Rhenish wine, ensured many soldiers were already in their cups.

Margaret turned. 'Anna, are you there? Come here, child. Your father is here somewhere with the English ambassadors. Would you take him this message? I believe he is in one of the houses at the far end of the street. Rosaline will accompany you.'

Rosaline, busy peering into her small mirror, jumped at Margaret's voice and dropped her mirror onto the rushes.

'As – as you wish, Madame,' she said.

I took the folded parchment.

'Come, Anna, we do not want to miss the start of the tournament,' she said, nimbly picking up the mirror and taking my arm.

'Why are we rushing so, Rosaline?' I raised my voice as we ventured out into the noisy market place. It was crowded with people, and I held onto her sleeve, fearing we might get separated.

'I told you, we do not want to miss the start of the contest!' she cried above the din, as we hurried on, finally stopping at a large door.

'The ambassadors have gathered here. Deliver your message quickly, and let us return.'

Inside, a large crowd of nobles stood by the open window, but I could not see my father. I did see the kind gentleman from the tennis match, standing to one side, alone, with a great bundle of papers underneath his arm. Several fluttered to the floor, and I bent down to pick them up.

'Why, Anne,' he cried in recognition, taking the papers

from me. 'Thank you, my dear, how delightful to see you again. Are you seeking your father?'

'Indeed, sir, I have a message for him from the regent.'

'Well, I'm afraid he is down at the lists with His Grace, but he will return here shortly. Can you wait for him?' he asked, staring at Rosaline. She smiled coyly as each man in the chamber appeared to cease talking and turn around to admire her.

'Sir,' she said, 'I must return to Madame for she will be expecting me, but I am happy to leave Anna here. Who shall I say she is with?'

The gentleman raised a finger to her chin and smiled. It lingered a little too long. 'Tell your lady that Anne is with the Dean of York, and go with my blessing.'

Rosaline nodded, and left the chamber as a fanfare of trumpets rose up into the air.

'What is happening, Your Reverence?' I asked.

The dean steered me to the window. 'See, twenty-eight noble knights in purple and gold advance – it means the imminent appearance of the king. Yes! There! See, he comes forth from the golden pavilion. What a magnificent sight.'

I looked down at the king who was in full armour, his helm held in the crook of his arm. On his other arm, he wore a pale-blue silk scarf, with a small golden arrow tied through the knot.

The dean narrowed his eyes. 'Ah, still enraptured by Mistress la Baume,' he murmured.

Below, the king, assisted by his squires, mounted his great black destrier and sat impatiently as they adjusted the straps on the horse's silver Burgundian bard, which was glinting in the watery sunshine. It was engraved with trailing pomegranates – the emblem of Queen Katherine. I was told it had been a gift from Maximilian to Henry on the occasion of Henry's wedding – a most generous gift indeed. A great roar arose as he entered the lists, turning his stamping horse around and around with impatience. He was laughing, his helm now on and raised to show his fair face. His opponent, his horse caparisoned in black and white, also entered the lists led by two squires. He took his place facing the king, as the sky clouded over.

'Your Reverence, what is happening?' I repeated, for I could not see.

The dean dragged a stool nearer to the window. 'Here, child, stand on this and I will explain.'

The other guests moved their chairs further back as it had started to rain again, much to their dismay, and I squeezed into the space.

'Now,' said the dean, 'we call one team the Challengers, and the other team the Answerers. Three men keep the score, two English and one Flemish. They pass the score to the judges – those people there sitting halfway down the lists getting very wet.'

'Oh, one is the Duke of Buckingham,' I said, pointing. 'He is our neighbour in Kent.'

'Aye,' said the dean, 'and his fine robes will be ruined in the rain. That will sour him. The other Englishman is William Browne, the Lord Mayor of London. Prince Charles has nominated the other two judges to keep matters fair. The judges, as you can see, have score cheques. If they draw a mark on the upper line, it is a blow to the head, on the lower line: a blow to the body. If the stroke cuts across the line, a lance is broken. To break a lance on a man's breast plate and unseat him is to win.'

I waited, expectantly.

'Now watch, we are ready to start.'

The king pranced forward on his horse and gave his salute to Margaret, who tilted her head gracefully in acknowledgment. He then saluted his opponent – the young son of the emperor's high chamberlain – and with his red and gold lance raised, galloped towards him. A great roar arose as one of the lances split into shards, flying in every direction. Then, as the heavens opened, torrential rain poured down, turning the churned up earth to mud. The contestants rode at each other again and again, and yet again the lances broke – but not the king's.

'De Walhain is outstanding,' said my companion, leaning forward. 'I am not surprised this is going badly for the king. He will not be in the best of moods.'

A second contestant, a Spanish captain, rode into the lists to challenge the king, but after only one course the king threw his lance down in a temper and left the field. Something had not pleased him, and as he pushed his visor back, everyone could see that his face was flushed with rage and exertion.

'Let us see who comes out next,' said the dean, crossing his plump hands. 'Ah, it is Lord Lisle – let us see what he makes of the Spaniard.'

Charles Brandon rode out, his grey horse decked in blue cloth with yellow horizontal stripes. Margaret leaned towards her balcony in interest, and as she raised her hand, I saw Brandon lower his lance to her in tribute. On his sleeve, he wore a fluttering blue and yellow scarf. He gave a wry smile, and the dean followed Brandon's gaze to Margaret. She lowered her eyes, simpering like a love-struck young girl and covered her mouth with her hand.

'My God,' murmured the dean, 'he wears the colours of Burgundy.'

I looked round at my companion and noticed that his eyes were no longer twinkling, but clouded over. I turned back and saw that the competitors were ready and, at the judge's sign, they began to thunder towards each other.

Brandon, slowed down by the heavy clods of earth, tried to force some speed as he cantered towards his competitor, but his horse slid wide off the mark, legs splayed, down on its haunches. He managed skilfully to heave the animal back up onto its legs, the crowd roaring with approval, but he had taken a hard hit as the Spaniard's lance splintered against his shoulder. Half out of the saddle he lurched to one side and rode out of the lists, passing the king, who now cantered back in on a different horse. The coloured scarf lay discarded and trampled in the mud.

The dean leant forward. 'This is a *disgrace*,' he muttered.

The king rode better this time, but the incessant rain had turned the lists into a dangerous quagmire.

The Milanese ambassador swivelled round in his chair. 'Will they stop the tournament?' he asked of the company.

The dean, inspecting his impeccable nails, spoke up. 'I doubt it, gentlemen. No expense has been spared for this day's show. Why, it would take a labouring man fifteen years to pay for this afternoon's entertainment alone, and I do not think His Grace, or Sir Edward Guildford, who organised this display, would even consider it.'

As a murmur of agreement arose, we continued to watch the king as he eventually found his form.

Towards the end of the afternoon, the tournament ended, and the judges tried to decide who had scored the most points. They were now soaked to the skin, their feathers and plumes drooping in the rain and, from the long deliberations, it seemed they had a delicate task ahead of them. There could be but one winner – the king – and it was going to take all their skill in bending the rules to give the required result. Since the king had recovered from his sulk and was merry again, cavorting and showing off to the ladies, no one cared to see him in another foul mood, and they continued to study the scorecards.

My father then entered the chamber and shook out his dripping cloak. 'Anne, what is this? Why are you away from the other ladies?' He noticed the dean. 'Your Reverence,' he said, kissing the proffered jewelled hand.

'God's blessing, Thomas,' said the dean. ''Tis a shame we have a foul day of it. I hope you have enjoyed the tournament.'

My father wiped his wet face with his long sleeve. 'I have indeed, although there is some confusion over the point scoring. The judges will tarry some time yet. I trust my daughter has not been a burden to you?'

'Marry, your daughter has been merry company, and I seem to be the one deemed most suitable to explain to her the rules of sport. Thus far, we have had a tennis match, now a tournament. Mayhap next a bear-baiting?'

I screwed up my nose and the dean laughed. 'Now, she has a message for you.'

'Oh, indeed, Father. Madame has asked me to give this to you.' I gave him my note.

My father read the contents with a chuckle. 'It is a wager. Always with my lady it is a wager,' he said, tucking it inside his sleeve.

The dean smiled with his mouth, but not his eyes. His eyes were still and unblinking. 'One should never gamble, Thomas, unless one is very sure of the outcome – but then that, of course, would not be a gamble.' He pulled on his cloak and fastened the clasp.

My father stared back, expressionless, and took my arm. 'Indeed, Your Reverence, but on this occasion, I was, indeed, quite sure of the result. Come, Anne, let me return you to the regent. I give you good day.' He gave a stiff bow.

'God keep you, Anne. Good day, Thomas.'

We walked down the steps of the house. 'Have you enjoyed your day, Anne?' asked my father, unusually interested.

'Oh, yes, sir,' I said. 'I have never seen such great beasts as those ridden today. But – but pray tell me, Father, is everyone in good health at home? How does my lady mother?'

'Well, and asking after you,' he replied, avoiding a peddler selling ribbons from his tray. 'Your mother never ceases telling everyone at court of your good fortune.'

'Oh, Father!' I cried. 'What does she tell? Does she know that I speak with the emperor and the prince? Does she know Madame thinks me studious and bright? What says she? Am I old enough to have a dog yet?' I was full of excited chatter.

'A dog?' My father turned as we entered the next house

and hurried up the steps. 'What is this constant dog nonsense? It would be up to the regent to decide, as you well know. As to your mother, of course she gets to hear. She misses nothing.' He took off his damp bonnet, his eyes scanning the vast company as if searching for someone.

Margaret was still seated at the open window, her ladies and maids gathered around, and I noticed Etiennette, the girl who had sung so beautifully at the banquet at Lille. She stood at the balcony in a simple pink gown, laughing with the other girls, pointing to the courtyard below. She wore no ostentatious jewellery, for her beauty shone without adornment. Margaret chatted to the prince, but it was impossible to tell whether he was riveted or bored, for his face showed no emotion. The king, meanwhile, with his helm under his arm again, rode up and down beneath the windows, saluting Margaret, the prince, and the entire watching crowd. He cavorted his great horse around and around, making it half rear before stopping right under Margaret's place and bowing his head to her. She smiled graciously. He then saluted Etiennette, and she clapped her hands in delight, before leaving the chamber. Brandon cantered out next, but Margaret turned away from the window.

'Why, Thomas, come sit with me, and tell me, did you take my wager?'

'I did indeed, Madame, and I win – as I knew I would. He was unable to resist wearing your colours.'

Margaret pretended to be annoyed, but her excited eyes gave her away. 'I did not think Brandon would go this far, and in public,' she whispered.

'I did, for he is reckless.'

'But, Thomas, what does he think to gain from such a ridiculous show?'

'He still hopes to gain your favour, my dear lady. And I do not mean with a mere ribbon.'

Margaret gave a little snort. 'How preposterous,' she said. 'I am a widow. Such foolery.'

Leaving them to talk in private, I joined the other maids who were staring, adoringly, down at the king.

'He is so handsome,' sighed Rosaline, hands held to her face as she leant over the balcony. 'Have you ever seen such a man?'

The ladies threw flowers down to the king, and he laughed as a rose fell towards him. He caught it, kissed it, held it to his heart, and with a great laugh, threw it back to Rosaline. She grabbed at the rose and placed it in her bodice, smiling in delight. I followed her gaze, and saw it fly like an arrow to its mark, to those small blue eyes, holding her totally entranced. I felt jealous, for although I thought the king unkind, I somehow wished he would look at me in such a way, rather than with scorn. I toyed with my long hair and rested on the balcony, but he only turned his horse about and left the lists.

Beatrice shook my arm. 'Oh, look!' she cried, her eyes wide. 'Charles Brandon has retrieved Madame's scarf and is wearing it again for all the court to see. How bold he is. Everyone will be talking.'

I looked to see him cantering about on his horse, the scarf fluttering from his arm.

'Oh, never mind him,' said Gertrude. 'Let us find the girl in pink. I hear the king is besotted with her.'

As I followed her, Margaret rose abruptly and, reaching out for my hand, drew me close. 'Come, here, Anna, and sit with your father. I have told him how much I enjoy your company. There. My favourite little bird will sit with me.' She patted the empty stool. 'I gather, Anna, that you have impressed – and here I let out a little secret – your soon-to-be Bishop of Lincoln. Am I not correct, Thomas?'

My father's expression clouded over as quickly as the day itself, but he checked himself and bowed his head graciously. 'She has indeed, Madame,' he said, 'and that is no small achievement, for little impresses Thomas Wolsey.'

● ●

'What is the matter, Rosaline?' Angelique unfastened the chain about her neck.

Busy plaiting my hair ready for bed, I glanced up.

'Why have you been crying?' she asked.

As the candles flickered, our shadows danced on the white plaster walls.

'Because life is so unfair,' replied Rosaline, lying curled up on her bed.

'What do you mean?' asked Gabrielle.

Rosaline's eyes filled with tears as we gathered around. She sat up. 'You saw how the king wore that Etiennette girl's favour today, the blue ribbon with the golden arrow?'

We nodded.

'Well, the king is apparently besotted with her. However, Etiennette's father has found her a husband, and the king, heartbroken, has ordered his court to wear black ribbons in mourning until he leaves France. He has even agreed to pay a dowry for her – one hundred thousand crowns! I do not understand. He has played me false.'

We stared at each other, puzzled.

'You?' I asked. 'What do you mean?'

'Because he is love-crazed with me, not her, he said as much. He said I had captivated his heart at Lille and I was the loveliest of creatures, far lovelier than her. Those were his very words to me, I swear.'

'What?' Greta stopped brushing her hair and turned around.

'It is true! He said I am beautiful and were it not for – oh, I hate being here. I hate this place!' She threw herself down on the bed and lay sobbing. We watched in horrified silence as the tearful girl sat up again, and reached inside her night shift. 'Look, he wrote this for me – a lover's verse.'

Fleur grabbed the paper from her hand and started to read it out loud:

'Take thou this rose, oh rose,
Since love's own flower it is
And by that lovely rose
Thy lover captive is.'

Rosaline then fumbled beneath her bolster. 'He gave me this, too – a perfect pink rose, wrapped in gold tissue.' We crowded around and gazed at the limp petals.

'When did he send you this?' Greta was askance.

Rosaline wiped her tear-stained face. 'It does not matter when. The point is I love him, and he loves me. He's the most exquisite man I have ever set eyes on, and I know he wants me. But now he is going home.' She started crying again.

I handed the cup of warm milk I had been drinking to her, and she took it with trembling hands.

'Do you really hate this place?' I asked, watching as she drank.

She shook her head and sniffed. 'No – no, not really, but I want to see him again, and he has sent no word to me. He promised he would. Now I cannot sleep for longing and would do anything to feel his touch aga –'

'What?' interrupted Fleur excitedly, 'what do you mean "again"? What has he done?'

'Do not stare so,' snapped Rosaline, 'he has done nothing. But he did give me a passionate kiss, a lover's kiss with his lips parted – and – and he touched me.'

Edda opened her eyes wide, shocked and excited at the same time. 'Where?'

'I told you,' said Rosaline, pushing her hair back from her hot forehead. 'At Lille.'

'I didn't mean that,' said Edda, impatiently.

'Hush!' we cried in unison. 'Carry on.'

Rosaline sighed. 'Do you recall when I left the hall to fetch more almonds? Well, the king followed me out to the pantry. He watched me reaching up for the almonds on the shelf and must have waved the other kitchen girls away, for we were suddenly alone. When I turned around, he was standing over me. I tried to move, but he trapped me and pressed himself hard against me, his lips brushing my hair.'

'Go on,' we whispered in anticipation, now gathered even closer.

'His lips then moved around to mine and – and he kissed me. I kissed him back with such a hunger and passion. I did not know myself.'

Concetta gave a loud shriek.

'He said I had entranced him; he said how he would make me his lady, and – and he started fondling me. I tried to protest, but when he tugged at my gown and pushed me against the wall, I thought I might die. As he began to unlace his – his –'

'*What?*' squeaked Maria, looking as if she might expire herself at any moment. My own mouth dropped open as we sat mesmerised.

Rosaline hung her head. 'Nothing. One of the stewards came in and –'

'Blessed God be praised.' The voice, low and measured, was none other than that of the Countess of Hochstrate, her face ashen in the light of her fluttering lantern.

'Rosaline, come with me.'

Not one of us moved.

'This minute!' she shrieked, causing Rosaline to scramble off the bed in panic. 'The rest of you, get back to your beds.'

We watched in terrified silence as the countess shooed Rosaline out of the bedchamber.

'Now there will be trouble,' moaned Beatrice, closing the door. 'I have never seen the countess so angry. I wonder what will happen when Madame herself gets to hear?'

'We did not do anything,' said Greta.

'To be caught listening was enough,' said Fleur. 'Such talk is base and lewd, and, unfortunately, it was obvious we all found it quite fascinating. How do we explain that?'

'I tried to stop her talking,' said Concetta.

Beatrice threw her bolster at her. 'Liar, you did no such thing.'

'Well, I have done nothing wrong,' I said, backing away to my bed and climbing in. 'Why on earth should I be in trouble? Angelique started it.'

As Beatrice blew out the candle I lay back worried and unable to sleep. The last thing I wanted was to be in bad odour with the regent and incur the wrath of my father. I wanted no part of this at all.

❋ ❋

The following morning, we were summoned to Margaret's private chamber, each of us with a feeling of dread. She sat, grim-faced, in her chair while her ladies and the Countess of Hochstrate stood behind, their backs to the fireplace. Margaret surveyed each one of us slowly in turn. The silence was agony. Once satisfied we were all present she began.

'Ladies, I gather you have been made fully aware of the decision to send Rosaline home.' She paused while her words took effect.

'Oh, my foolish girls!' she cried, standing up. 'A woman's good name is of value beyond measure. Her womanhood, and by this I mean her virginity, is the finest jewel she can possess. Once lost it can never be regained. Do you understand me?'

We nodded, faces sullen.

'You must keep yourself pure for your future husband's sake. Never, ever, let your good name be mangled. I care nothing for this Etiennette girl for she was not one of my maids, and thus not under my protection – but Rosaline?' Margaret shook her head. 'I am deeply saddened she should have behaved with such impropriety, for the king is a married man. To have forgotten this disappoints me greatly. However, I know how the world wags and, trust me, be he king or commoner, no man will take the blame for such behaviour. The world will always blame the weakness in women rather than the foolishness of men. Rosaline has indulged in this foolishness – fortunately stopped in time – and now she is to return home in disgrace.'

I thought of my sister. This could so easily have been her instead of Rosaline, and I would have been embroiled in this mess by association.

'Never be in doubt that the slightest indiscretion will be dealt with in this manner – instant dismissal. And you will most certainly not discuss the details any further. As it is, you will be confessed and do penance – in fact, when we return to Mechelen, I am sending you all to the *Begijnhof* where you will each spend a day in charitable good works.'

Margaret stared in silence, but I refused to look at my shoes like the other girls, for I had not done anything wrong. Instead, I held my head high.

'Now, please return to your duties. I am most displeased and have much work to do.' She swept out of the chamber, tears in her eyes, her ladies and the countess scurrying behind.

We immediately began talking at once.

'I passed the *Begijnhof*,' I said above the chatter, 'when I first came to Mechelen.'

'What?' asked Fleur, distractedly. 'Oh, for the love of God, Anna, that is hardly important right now. Can you imagine what on earth would have happened if Rosaline had – you know – gone further with the king?'

'Shush,' said Maria, 'we are not supposed to discuss it.'

Beatrice sat down on the chair at Margaret's desk and traced her finger around the exquisite silver inkwell placed there. 'Oh, poor Rosaline,' she said, 'it was not her fault. Perhaps he *is* totally irresistible.'

'No he is not,' I said, quickly. 'Besides, the fault lies with him. I do not see why she is to blame.'

'It is not his fault,' retorted Ariella, sharply. 'He is the King of England and can, therefore, do as he pleases with any girl he desires. He is above other men and beyond reproach, even from Madame.'

I asked what the king's pregnant queen would say if she knew.

'What should she say?' asked Beatrice. 'A romantic dalliance with Etiennette and a meaningless fumble with Rosaline has nothing to do with the king's marriage and the love he bears for Katherine. Besides, until the child is born and she is churched, the queen cannot attend to his needs and – according to the law of men – he is fully entitled to such dalliances.'

There was silence before the girls finally drifted out, leaving me alone with Beatrice.

'I think he is hateful for what he has done,' I said, picking up my French book and flicking distractedly through its pages. I felt angry. 'I do not see why the king can do as he pleases. Rosaline now has to return home in disgrace. Where was her sin in this?'

'She should have discouraged him.'

'But Etiennette is not disgraced,' I countered, 'she is to be rewarded and the whole affair treated with open amusement and bonhomie.'

'The regent is only responsible for her own maid's welfare. She must be seen to take the moral ground. She knows the king was at fault, but will never openly criticise him. She cannot.'

I threw down the book. 'What exactly is this *Begijnhof* place?'

Beatrice yawned. 'A large, walled community comprised entirely of pious women who either do not wish to marry, do not have a dowry enabling them to marry well, or do not wish to take the full vows of convent life. They earn their keep through spinning, teaching, dyeing cloth or such like, and can leave the community at any time.'

'Why in Mechelen?'

'It is not just in Mechelen,' she said, 'but throughout the southern Low Countries. Do you not have them in England?'

I said I was not sure.

Beatrice rose up and picked an apple from a bowl on the table. She tossed it to me and took another for herself. 'Did you know,' she said, 'more women live in the Low Countries than men? Many, when widowed, become cloth merchants, innkeepers, and even farmers.' She walked over to the window, biting on the apple, and gazed down on a hunting party.

Hearing the barking of dogs, I joined her. The party appeared sodden wet from the rain as it clattered across the cobbles.

'Life for a woman is so unfair,' she murmured.

I looked at her wistful face. 'What is wrong, Beatrice? What are you hiding?'

'Nothing, it is nothing. Come let us return to the dining hall.'

* *

We left the chamber and walked through the archways of the old palace, subdued and thoughtful. Leaden grey clouds loomed low, and I wondered if we would ever see dry weather again. I longed to return to Mechelen and resume my lessons, for I missed Madame Symonnet, and the delights of Tournai had turned sour. We parted at the dining hall, for I wished to visit the stables to see the new Arab horses recently arrived by ship. I heard they were magnificent. However, when I turned the wall to the smithy, I saw Rosaline sitting on the stone water trough. She glanced up, misery in her red-rimmed eyes.

'Oh, Anna!' she cried, 'what do I do? How do I live without ever seeing him again?'

I sat down beside her and took her hand. She reminded me of my sister after Mother had beaten her, fragile and broken.

'Stop it, Rosaline, you must forget him. The campaign is over, and soon you will return home to your family. Hush now.'

Rosaline sniffed. 'But why could I not have accompanied

him back to England and stayed at his court, secretly somewhere, or – or in the country where he could visit me? Does
he not have a place where he and his friends entertain ladies
away from his wife?'

I looked aghast. 'But, Rosaline, what are saying? You
would not want to go to England to... to be a ...'

'Yes, I would,' she said, defiantly, 'I would do anything
to be near him. Oh God! How slow the hours of my life will
now seem.'

The watery sun showed its face and a flutter of sparrows
flew past. Falconers with hooded birds on their wrists ambled
around the corner, followed by mud-splattered courtiers
returning from the chase. I watched the steam rising off the
flanks of their horses as they were led away by the grooms.

'Well, I think the king is a lecher,' I said.

Rosaline gave a faint smile. 'You would. Wait until you
give your heart in love. Every moment without your lover
will seem a lifetime.'

'Well, I do not like him,' I said, plucking at the ivy twisting around the trough. 'Oh, I can see that he is handsome
– and knows it – but he is married already. Why would you
want to be mistress to a married man? Why would you put
your soul in fear of eternal damnation?'

She gave a wan smile. 'How can it be sinful when his
will is the will of God? When he holds you in his melting
gaze, you are ensnared, and resisting such a powerful man
is beyond a woman's feeble endurance.' She glanced at my
startled face. 'I think you are still too young to understand
such things, but you will. One day.'

'No,' I said, standing up. 'No, I will not. I shall be like
Madame, and read, and make music and dance. I shall have
dogs and horses and avoid foolish, romantic attachments. No
man will steal my heart or my reputation, and I shall marry
where I wish.'

'Oh, well, good luck, you little fool,' came the reply.
'You know only too well that you will not have a say in your

parents' wishes. They will choose, and you will be become your husband's chattel to use as he sees fit.'

I stared at her, defiantly. 'Well, then I shall go into a *Begijnhof.*'

'You, Nan, planting and digging up vegetables? I think not. Why, the fates have something better in store for you.'

We laughed together, and it was good to see Rosaline smile again, although her lovely face remained ravaged from crying.

Serious once more, she turned to me. 'Anna, do not lose your heart to a man you cannot have. Do not go through this agony. Do as your family bid and marry whomsoever they choose, a man of good stock, who will provide for you and father your sons. Do not let your heart be broken. Promise me on your amber cross.' Her voice sounded pleading and intense.

'I – I promise,' I replied, although her words had unsettled me greatly.

●　●

King Henry, meanwhile, pressed for an urgent and private conference with the regent and the emperor, for he wished to leave a large garrison behind to occupy Tournai at the expense of Maximilian. It was imperative, this time, that the emperor appeared and we returned to the abbey to await him. Foolishly, I hoped he would speak to me again. However, as soon as we reached her suite, Margaret began pacing up and down, her little dogs scampering around her heels.

'He should be here. Why is he not here? He promised me he would discuss the garrison arrangements and wish His Grace God speed.'

We removed our riding coats, and the Countess of Hochstrate clapped her hands loudly. 'Now, to your chambers everyone, except Anna, Concetta, and Maria. Stay, please, and tend to Madame. Come now, quickly. Her ladies are tired after their ride.'

The three of us remained, but Margaret was too distracted to notice.

'Write to him again,' she ordered the secretary sitting at her desk. 'Write the following:

> *"Beloved Father, I expected you here when I arrived and I am concerned some ill has befallen you. By your absence here you will surely jeopardise the marriage of the prince, and lose the love of the king. I have written to the king promising him that you will support him as if you were his own father. Repeatedly I have assured the Milanese ambassador that you will be here shortly, and it is vital you arrive as a matter of urgency. Why do you delay?"*

The secretary raised his head, expectantly.

'Write!' she ordered again, twisting her ring and continuing her dictation.

Unfortunately, Margaret's pleading went unheeded, and the emperor failed to appear a second time, fuming over the fact that the king had refused to give Tournai to Prince Charles. He deliberately stayed away, and Margaret was in such a fury she gave herself a severe headache. I was almost as disappointed as she. As she lay on her bed, I sat beside her, a cool, damp cloth drenched in crushed feverfew, in my hand.

'Such a pleasing child,' she murmured, as I dabbed her hot forehead. 'You see how with privilege comes burden, and I am tired, too tired to even think. Am I alone in seeking this marriage? Alone in aiming straight and true?'

As her eyes closed, a tear ran down her cheek, causing her to wince and place her fingers to her throbbing temple. 'If King Henry will trust me but a little longer, the outcome, I am sure, will be of benefit to all parties concerned.'

Chapter Six

*'Each moment well improved secures
an age in Heaven.'*

Mechelen,
Autumn and Winter 1513

On the seventeenth day of October, we accompanied the king in a magnificent procession back to Lille – except of course for Rosaline who had returned with her mother back home to Breda – where he prepared to depart from his kingdom to Calais. He was bound by the Treaty of Lille to return to France before the following June to continue the war with the emperor, and King Ferdinand.

It was a magnificent sight, the king mounted on his great horse, caparisoned in gold and silver cloth. His honourable French hostage, the Duc de Longueville, sat mounted next to him, and there was much laughing and merriment.

Etiennette, the girl who had captured the king's heart, stood on a balcony with her father. On her right, her betrothed laughed and pointed at the absurd sight of the king and his courtiers sporting clusters of black ribbon on their horses' bridles. All joined in the royal jest, dabbing their eyes with a black silk cloth and doffing their caps in a sad farewell as the king passed by.

The ladies of Lille presented Margaret with two beautiful tapestries, representing '*La Cité des Dames*', along with a priceless jewelled gold chalice for Queen Katherine. Other magnificent gifts for Margaret and the prince were loaded into their chariots, including a golden clock, a suit of engraved armour and a wooden statue of the Blessed Virgin. Behind one chariot, two magnificent Barbary horses stood tethered, their bridles and saddles of black velvet, and their manes plaited with black ribbon. Of all the gifts received, these were the most pleasing. Margaret's ladies were not forgotten either. Each received a diamond, and an enamelled Tudor rose in the form of a brooch, and we maids were each given a tiny enamelled figure of St George fighting a dragon, suspended from a golden chain.

Charles Brandon took Madame's hand and kissed it with great fervour, and this time she allowed his lips to linger. As the king slapped Brandon on the back good-heartedly, as if he had not a care in the world, I knew Rosaline was completely forgotten. Now, he was eager to return home to the arms of his pregnant queen.

Amidst the great press of nobles, my father appeared. I gave him my letter to Mother, and he promised he would give everyone my good wishes. Inside my letter to Mary I had enclosed a pretty necklace of gold with white enamelled roses. It was of no small value, and I hoped it would ease my still pricking conscience.

As my father turned to leave, I gently touched his cloak. 'I *will* make you proud of me, Father.'

He gave a cursory nod and, turning back to his companions, instantly began discussing the merits of the king's new horses. I stood, like Rosaline, forgotten.

* *

I sat listlessly as our chariots pulled into the courtyard and watched as Margaret, helped by her ladies, climbed stiffly down. A barking dog ran out, tail wagging, and she picked it up, laughing.

'It is good to be home,' she said, fussing the little dog as it wriggled and twisted in her arms, 'back to my own bed at last. Ah, dearest Patou, you are well, my old friend?' She walked across to her parrot and smiled as he hopped about on a page's shoulder. 'Has he been eating much? He looks very thin,' she said, kissing the bird. It squawked in delight and rolled its ruffled head.

Beatrice placed a cloak around me as I gave out a sneeze. I felt quite dreadful.

'The dear thing must go instantly to her bed,' said the Countess of Hochstrate, directing the pages to bring in the chest of gifts. 'Do not drop it!' she shrieked, as a boy let go of one of the rope handles. 'Mother of God, what a dolt, it contains precious glass.'

At the word 'dolt', the boy received a cuff on the ear, losing his cap.

One by one, carpets, hangings, and priceless statues were taken inside as the ladies chatted with Margaret, her parrot now on her arm.

'Oh, Beatrice, do I have the plague?' I asked.

'Do not fret,' she said, smoothing my hair, 'one of the nuns from the infirmary will bring you a poppy syrup to help you sleep, and you will soon feel much better.'

Within the week, all the maids were taken ill with the same symptoms of congestion, sneezing, and fever. No doubt the over-rich food was the cause, and the fact that we were tired from the exertion of our travels. The countess tended to each girl herself and was nowhere near as formidable as she pretended, for she fussed around each of us like a mother hen. She ordered cordials and broths, and came to our bedchamber at night with liquorice root to ease our exasperating coughs. She even sat with me until I drifted asleep. Before long, she, too, fell ill and disappeared for the rest of the week, followed by Margaret. Dr Picot announced peace and bed rest with an infusion of hyssop and coltsfoot to ease her throat. No councillor was to bring state papers, business or letters to her, and he alone would be in attendance. There was to be no noise in the passageways, no dogs in the bedchamber and certainly no barking from them in the courtyard. Birds must be removed, including dearest Patou. The fires must be blazing, and the chamber kept dark. It was not long before the palace fell as silent as the grave as yet more people became sick.

Within the week, however, I had recovered and could not bear to remain in the fetid closeness of our bedchamber any longer. With the windows boarded up to block out any draughts, I felt suffocated and longed to be outside. Peeping between the heavy drapes, I glimpsed the watery sun. The courtyard appeared abandoned, as the doctor had ordered, and rooftops and cobbles glistened from the recent rain.

Picking up my woollen cloak and trying not to cough, I slipped out into the cool passageway. I then made my way to the library, for I had heard that a new delivery of books had recently arrived from Louvain. When I approached, I was surprised to find the door slightly ajar, for it was usually locked. As I pushed it slowly open the smell of beeswax drifted out. I walked over to the window and pulled back the tawny velvet drapes to let in the light. As I did, a voice from the direction of a large chair made me start.

'Leave it – I like it dark.'

I swept to the floor in haste and bowed my head. 'Sir, forgive me. I – I did not know you were here. I will leave immediately.'

The lanky boy sat with his leg slung over the arm of a great padded chair. 'No, remain there, I command it, for although I wished to be alone, I will now have company – for a while at least.'

I remained in my low position.

'I was hoping,' he sighed, 'to hide from my tutors for an hour or two until they found me. A prince is never alone.'

I glanced up at the thin face of Prince Charles and noticed for the first time how his teeth were crooked. His eyes, though, were compelling.

He continued. 'I have seen you with the other maids, always merry and smiling. What is your name?'

I could not quite catch his words for he spoke in a strange manner, as if his mouth was full and his nose blocked. Irritated, he repeated his question.

'Anne Bullen, Your Highness,' I said, hastily. 'My father is one of the ambassadors to the Low Countries.'

The boy gave a bored flick of his hand. 'Yes, yes, I know of him. Sir Thomas Bullen, a favourite of my aunt. Rise.' He raised a brow in surprise. 'You appear very small. How old are you? Eight, nine?'

'Thirteen, my Lord, this May just past.'

'Well, I am older. By four months.'

An awkward silence followed as he stared blankly, and I felt compelled to fill the void.

'Do you not remember, my Lord, when I first arrived, Madame brought me to the schoolroom to introduce me to you and your sisters?'

He jumped up. 'Do not presume to speak to me unless I speak to you first,' he said in annoyance. 'That is how things are done at court. Have you not been taught manners?'

I stood feeling annoyed at this insufferable bore.

He sat down again. 'Maids come and go. But, yes, I do remember you – you usually have that freckled-faced girl trotting behind. You were in Tournai, dark among our Flemish girls, and I thought you might be Spanish.'

I waited to see if he had finished speaking. 'Oh, no, indeed, my home is in Kent, in England,' I said, struggling to catch his mumbled words.

'Kent you say? I know of some Flemish farmers who grow carrots in Kent.' There was a pause. I had missed my cue.

'Well?'

'Oh, yes, sir, they say the carrots grown there are the sweetest and largest in England, and they use them as a flavour in stews. I miss English food and do not like your salted herring at all.'

As the prince rose from his chair and walked over to the window, I saw that his black, fur-collared robe covered a doublet of rich, brown velvet. Around his neck hung a golden collar, and I noticed that his lank hair appeared somewhat dull.

He placed his hands behind his back. 'I must soon get accustomed to your English ways myself – and those of my English bride.'

'Why, yes, sir, you are to marry the sister of my king, and I have –'

'I do not like her,' he said, deciding to tug back the heavy drapes after all.

'But sir, I hear she is...' My words petered out as he turned and stared at me.

'What? What have you heard? That she is pretty? Vivacious? Spoiled? Or that she is a bad sport at games?'

'Why, no, sir, I hear she is full of learning, loves singing and dances well. I gather Madame sent Monsieur de Pleine to the English court to see her for himself, and he reported back that she was the most beautiful girl he had ever set eyes on, like her mother...' My voice trailed off for the second time, for I could see that the prince appeared peeved.

'What one man sees as beauty another might see as plain. Who could possibly judge what I myself might find attractive? I have seen her portrait, and I do not trust artists. I do not see how a woman could look so lovely, and must assume they play me false. Anyway, Princess Mary does not want this marriage either.'

I was surprised.

'Oh, I know the truth from my ambassadors,' he continued, 'and I know the polite formula expected of me. I call her wife and sigh with longing, and she calls me husband. I tell her she is a pearl beyond price, she tells me I am the greatest jewel in Christendom. I instruct the high chamberlain to enquire after her health and other such niceties, and she writes prettily back that her jaded appetite will only return when she truly becomes my wife. And so on and so forth. But I know she lies and pretends, for I hear she fawns after Brandon, the great ape. I assume you know of him?'

'Indeed, sir, he is the English king's closest companion, and some even whisper his half-brother. I have watched him jousting, and the ladies swoon when he enters the tiltyard.'

'Indeed, even my aunt is taken with him,' muttered the prince. 'You no doubt saw the recent charade played out?'

I felt I was on dangerous ground. 'Sir, I know nothing, truly. I am learning to serve as a maid at court and do not see –'

'Well, you should see,' came the sharp reply. 'You will serve my aunt best by seeing everything and saying nothing. Watch everyone. Listen. Say nothing unless it is to my aunt's benefit. As for my delightful English princess, who knows?' he said. 'But she is still too old.'

'Sir, she will be but four years older than you, surely no great age difference? Our English queen is six years older than the king, and he looks to her wisdom.'

'Well, a prince such as I looks not to his wife for any known thing.'

I hastily changed the subject. 'My mother, sir, has written to tell me that my sister has become close to the princess. She is so delighted she tells all the world at every opportunity.'

'Does she look like you?' He picked at his chewed nails.

'Oh, no, sir, she is fairer than I, and taller. But she is not as devoted to her books.'

A faint smile flickered across his pale face. 'Anyway, my aunt wants this marriage, as does my grandfather, although one never truly knows his counsel for what he says one day, he gainsays the next. So, everyone wants this marriage except the two people taking the vows. They use me to suit their own ends and secure their own power. I am, as yet, powerless to do otherwise. Tied like jesses on a hawk – under the thumb. Monsieur Chiévres understands how I feel and how tired I am of being pulled with leading strings by my aunt. She smothers me. I long to do as *I* wish, for God has decreed that I shall be ruler of many domains – including Spain's lands in the New World. I shall be emperor, and there will be no limits to my power.'

In the ensuing, awkward silence, I watched as two crimson patches appeared on the boy's cheeks.

'Do you know where the greatest threat to Europe today is coming from?' He browsed the great, leather-bound books on the shelves.

I hesitated for a moment. 'From France, sir?'

'No,' said the prince, 'try again.'

I stood mute, for I could not think.

'Although I must say, like my aunt, I detest the French,' he said, pulling out a red velvet covered book, and flicking through the pages. 'In fact, my grandfather hates them with such venom he keeps a secret red book, like this one, in which he jots down any slight or grievance made by the accursed country. He pores over it like a miser over his money and says he will pay them back in full at his leisure.'

The image of my father poring over his accounts entered my mind.

'No,' said the prince, 'it is not the French, but the Turks. They threaten Christendom and the whole of Syria must be freed from their yoke. Signor di Gattinara, my tutor in foreign affairs, tells me that I am responsible to God to protect Christendom and for that purpose alone, I was born. Did you know that I am descended from a long line of German Christian Emperors, Spanish Catholic kings, archdukes of Austria and dukes of Burgundy? They were faithful to the

Church of Rome, and so will I be.'

I stared at the pride in his face.

'When I was born, the sign of Capricorn began rising in the heavens and this, the astrologers said, foretold that such a child would be either a king or an emperor. I was destined for greatness.'

I sighed, tired of his immense self-importance.

'Have you read this?' He pulled down a plain-covered book and opening it out on the wooden table. 'Come here, come nearer.'

I walked over and looked down.

'No, you will not,' he said, turning the pages. 'This is a secret, unpublished copy. It is entitled *'The Prince'* by an Italian, Niccolo Machiavelli. I doubt it ever will be published, for some men with their great love of the new learning rail against it. It states a strong country is based upon sound laws and strong military forces. It does not say strength comes solely through alliances. Alliances are like a woman – fickle and unreliable. I do not trust them. I do not trust your English king. Neither does my tutor.' He continued turning the pages.

'Tell me,' he said, 'is it better for a prince to be loved or feared? Should he be a fox or a lion? How can he avoid being despised or hated?'

I stared at the book. 'My Lord, I think a ruler should be both, by proving as cunning as a fox *and* as strong as a lion. He must be cunning enough to seek out his enemies and their treason, and strong enough to destroy them, whatever his personal wishes or feelings might be.'

The prince gave a smirk. 'You are bold for a mere girl, for so states Machiavelli.' His heavy-lidded eyes made him appear listless, and he wiped a sliver of drool from his mouth onto his sleeve.

'Well, it states here everything a prince must know to be a great ruler. I do not need a woman's opinion, be she aunt or bride.' He slammed the book shut.

'Or *demoiselle*, sir?'

'You forget yourself.' The prince returned the book to the shelf.

I stood feeling exasperated by this dull boy.

'Did you know, child, that this is the finest library of music books in the whole of Christendom? Monsieur Molinet worked tirelessly to make it thus before he died some five years ago. There are manuscripts here for basse dances, chansons, choir books, and holy Masses. My aunt has a great skill in vocal and instrumental music, as you heard, and I have inherited her talent. My grandfather Maximillian has always had a deep love of music, too, and knows more than the composers themselves. He can tell you the writer of any piece of music asked of him, and can even say who steals notes and ideas from another. I, too, shall have music at my court.' He paused, expectantly.

'Oh, I too, sir, have a love of music,' I said, 'and I admire the work of Monsieur Pierre de la Rue.'

The prince raised his brow.

'I – I am but learning, sir,' I stammered, 'and have no great knowledge as yet.'

'If you know something, you should say it,' he said, and I began to see why he was thought of as contrary and difficult. 'Still, my tutor tells me that as long as women seek not to be proud, they do no harm. It is expected of a prince to know much. I have recently started to learn Flemish.'

'But surely, sir, if –' Before I could finish my words there appeared to be a great commotion outside the door. Then, without announcement, several men rushed in, sweeping deeply to the floor, caps in hand. A tutor wearing thick, black-rimmed spectacles tied around his head immediately followed, robe flapping.

'My gaolers,' said the prince, flatly. 'Well, gentlemen, let us to our studies,' and without a backward glance, he strode out of the library back to his apartments.

● ●

I stopped by the half-open door of the council chamber.

'Well, I say it is an outrage, a disgrace. It is being discussed, even as we speak, in taverns and bawdy houses throughout the land.'

As I listened, the conversation inside continued.

'She will have to know,' murmured a voice.

'But how can we tell her? Will you tell her?'

'Not I. Besides, she is unwell, recovering in her private chambers. Dr Picot has insisted no business is put to her until she is quite recovered. It would not do to have her in a state.'

'The longer we leave it, the harder it becomes, and we are in a delicate position with the prince's marriage arrangements,' said another voice.

'I can assure you, gentlemen *that* arrangement is quite forgotten. We now appear to be a laughing stock throughout Europe. Dam the conceited English.'

There were further mutterings as someone closed the door with a thud.

I was left standing in the shadow of the wall, pondering the words I had just heard, and thought it best to hurry back to Beatrice. Back in the Hall I beckoned urgently to her as she stood in line with the other girls, practising new dance steps. Puzzled, she stared at me, but then, as the dancing master tapped his stick on the tiles and the musicians struck up a tune, she hurried to my side.

'Whatever is the matter?' she asked, as I leant close to her ear.

'I have just this minute overheard Madame's councillors saying that the prince's marriage is not to take place after all – and they dare not tell her.'

'Have you been listening at doors again?'

'No – well, yes – but the door was ajar, and I was passing, and I could not help but hear. Well? What do you think?'

'I do not know,' she said, glancing briefly back at the

girls as they began a stately pavane. 'But we will hear soon enough. Madame plans to rise today and walk in the garden with her ladies.' She stared at me. 'Can you be absolutely sure of this?'

'Of course, I heard it from her councillors themselves not two moments past. I recognised the voice of Monsieur de Pleine, head of her council. He said it was a scandal and the court is now the laughing stock of Europe. It has to be true if he said it.'

'But the English king is set on this marriage,' said Beatrice, puzzled, 'as is the regent. She has attended endless meetings, paid for gowns, provisions, horses, and entertainment. She has spent a huge fortune. I know for a fact that she is in constant contact with King Henry and his almoner, deciding who will be accompanying the prince and which ladies are to be selected. Presents have been bought for those accompanying Mary Tudor at enormous expense – why, your parents will be accompanying her along with a great host of English nobles. Preparations are well in advance. Why would they be halted now?'

'Well, the prince himself does not care for the marriage – he told me himself,' I said.

'What? What are you saying?' she asked. 'Why would he talk to you of state matters? Oh, this is a jest.'

'Shush, I am telling the truth,' I said, putting my finger up to her lips. 'He spoke to me in the library. I disturbed him there, but he bid me stay and began a conversation. I tell you, he does not care for his intended bride. I am telling the truth.' I felt peeved at her disbelief.

'Really, Anna, you listen to things that are not your business to hear.'

I disagreed. It was my business for I wanted to know everything going on around me. How else could I learn the machinations of the court?

'Well,' she said, 'we can only wait and see what happens next and – for the love of our Blessed Lady – say absolutely nothing of this, do you hear? Nothing.'

As we wandered over to join the dancing, none of us were prepared for the storm that was about to sweep through the palace.

●   ●

'How could he?' cried Margaret, bursting into the chamber as we sat at a poetry lesson. 'How could this happen?' It was three days later, and she was obviously distressed.

Signor di Gattinara walked beside her while her ladies followed behind trying to keep up with her furious steps. 'Forgive me, forgive me for interrupting, Monsieur,' she said, raising her hand imperiously, as Monsieur Rénard, our tutor, bowed low and we scrambled to our feet. She swept past, knocking papers off the table with a swish of her gown, and disappeared into her private suite. The door slammed, and we began muttering to each other.

'Ladies, ladies, please concentrate and return to your books,' said our tutor, seating himself again and re-adjusting his glasses. He signalled Ariella to read from her book:

> *'Alas, I thought I knew so much*
> *Of love, and yet I know so little!*
> *For I cannot stop myself loving her*
> *From whom I shall never have joy.*
> *My whole heart, and all of me from myself*
> *She has taken, and her own self, and all the world,*
> *For when she took herself from me, she left me nothing*
> *But desire and a yearning heart.'*

'Good. Good, Mistress Ariella. And what can we deduce from such words? Christa? Veronique? Anybody?'

Christa rose. 'Such love is immoderate and obsessive, sir,' she said, wincing at the sound of a crash coming from Margaret's chamber. Something had been broken.

'Precisely,' came the nervous reply.

I sat fascinated by what might be going on

behind the door.

'Now, in reality, a union is one of respect and companionship, not what we might be led to believe here. What does the word troubadour actually mean? Anna?'

He startled me.

'It means one who creates or composes, sir,' I replied, glancing at the door.

'Indeed it does. And the troubadour is but a humble slave to his unattainable affection, usually a highborn lady. For her, he writes his longing and despair. And from where did these poets originate?'

'From the French courts of the great noble lords, sir,' I said, wishing he would cease talking, for I was straining to listen to what on earth was being said.

'Indeed,' said Monsieur Rénard. 'Now, if you would turn to –'

As he spoke, the door flew open, and we stood a second time as Margaret, still in a fury, her cheeks aflame, stormed in.

'Oh, cease this noise, will you!' she cried, as her dogs barked. 'Hand me the letter again.' Her hand flew out to one of her flustered ladies, while the others stood aside, wringing their hands.

'Blessed Virgin in Heaven,' she said, scanning the letter, 'a stable boy and one who is barely literate. Erasmus has written to his friend in England – where else is this – this thing being bandied about? Erasmus has written, and I quote: *"She is to marry a stable boy turned king's favourite. A man of no breeding, a mere commoner brought up in the royal nursery."* Dear God and his saints, am I to be discussed like some infamous whore? It appears that the English king has given Brandon his full support for an illustrious match and instructed him to press forward his suit. Brandon – and I do not blame him in this – has been swept along by this preposterous notion. He has been actively encouraged in this – this foolhardiness.'

In her distress she started to cough.

'Lady Middlebourg, tell my council to assemble and send Monsieur de Lalaing, Monsieur de Marnix and Monsieur de la Marck to me now. I seek trusted friends' advice.' In agitation, she twisted around the crucifix hanging from her girdle. 'How could the king seriously think that one of Brandon's lineage could possibly ally itself to the royal house of Habsburg? Is he insane?'

She paced up and down and then stopped, as if suddenly aware of our presence. We stood in silence as Monsieur Rénard backed into the hanging tapestry, hoping he might fade into it.

'Oh, *demoiselles*, please dismiss,' she said. 'I was hoping to listen to you read, but I have disrupted your discussion, and now I have urgent and most pressing matters to attend to.'

She swept out of the chamber, her ladies scuttling behind. Our tutor, grabbing his books, could not wait to leave and left in a great flurry. Beatrice and I hurried out into the passageway and stood at the top of the gallery, watching the courtiers gathering in groups below. When a party of ambassadors arrived, we knew something was definitely afoot.

'Well,' said Beatrice. 'I can tell you now, such an outburst has nothing to do with whatever you overheard. It is to do with Madame. Madame is in a plight over our handsome Charles Brandon.'

I shrugged.

'See what happens when you listen at doors?' she added.

'Well, I know what I heard,' I said, defensively. 'It is not my fault if people talk in riddles.'

◉ ◉

A palace has no secrets. By nightfall, everyone from servants to kitchen maids, grooms to stable boys, voiced an opinion on the forthcoming marriage between the regent and Charles Brandon. As the Countess of Hochstrate worriedly paced our chamber, she said we were under strict orders not to discuss such a delicate matter. She herself did not fully know the official line to be taken, but until a statement was issued, there was to be no conjecture or foolish gossip. We were to talk to no one and write nothing down in a letter. She was too late. We had already talked of nothing else.

Matters continued from bad to worse, for we later heard how the king, now in Calais, had executed a complete *volte-face* and denied any such collusion in the matter. But the king – and I was there myself to bear witness – had paraded Brandon before Margaret as a perfect husband. He had encouraged him at the joust, and I heard the king saying what a good match it would be and that he, himself, would facilitate any meetings they wished for. Now, he was heartily annoyed by his favourite's behaviour, and Brandon and the regent were left abandoned to face the scandal alone. What a coward he was.

Unfortunately, it was true that people had, indeed, seen Margaret flush and simper at Brandon, and it was no secret that she found him attractive. Did she fear it could have gone further and could she now be wracked with guilt at the thought? Had she encouraged him? Surely she had not given him any genuine hope of marriage? He knew she was a widow – albeit an attractive one – and wished to dedicate the rest of her life to the welfare of the prince, good works and her charities. Had she not said as much? She must have turned over and over in her mind the words she had said to us, whereby men would always think the worse of the woman, conjuring up her feminine wiles and charms to ensnare the man. Now, she was distraught for she no doubt felt a fool. Flattery had made her walk right into a trap.

To my surprise, there was no sympathy from her father either, and he railed at her in his letters saying she appeared foolish and light, reducing her to tears with his harsh words. Had she not seen the political snare? Of course, King Henry would be delighted to have his sister wed to Prince Charles, and his best friend wed to the archduchess. Why else had Brandon hurried over as ambassador to the Flemish court?

There had to be a scapegoat, and publicly the emperor blamed the king, resulting in matters appearing even colder between the two rulers than before. He wrote that gossip had reached Germany, and even King Ferdinand in Spain, and the insult to his family was unforgivable. He pointed out that the king, by his blatant encouragement of his friend, had insulted his daughter and his noble family. It proved the point that the emperor's vanity was enormous, and such a slight could not be forgiven. Seeing Margaret so utterly bewildered and distressed, I felt my feelings for her father fade in the confusion.

Margaret, after her tears of embarrassment had subsided, spent some days in solitude. However, no sooner had she recovered her composure than a messenger was admitted to her audience chamber. As I stood with Lady Middlebourg and her other ladies, sorting through various documents, Margaret looked up at the man's sombre face and, with some trepidation, reached out for the proffered letter. The seal was Wolsey's. No sooner had she read it than she sank to her knees, her face white, her voice soft as she murmured: *'Tribulationes cordis mei dilatatae sunt.'* We quickly dropped down in unison at her words, and I stared at her desolate face. What on earth could have happened?

'Sweet Jesu,' she said, handing the letter to one of the kneeling women. 'It is from the English court. Queen Katherine has given birth prematurely – to a dead son.'

●   ●

Standing at the long wooden table in the stillroom, Veronique ground the marigold petals to a paste. 'Oh, the wretched queen, she must have dreaded his return.'

I took my sheaves of dried rosemary from the basket and started to separate them out.

'Perhaps it was too much for her with the king abroad,' said Maria, tying up a bunch of lavender with ribbon. 'I gather she toiled night and day to prove how trustworthy and capable she was. When she heard of the threat from the Scots, she rode north on horseback at the head of forty thousand men.'

I wiped my hands on my apron. 'Would it not have been better to have given him the son he craved? To ride so far could not have been safe. This is the fourth child she has lost.'

'Of course, it would, Anna,' said Beatrice, 'but she was stubborn and determined to secure the realm against Scotland. Still, she is young, and there is time yet, but I agree a living son would have meant more to the king than any victory over the King of Scots.'

'Beatrice, do you think the king will get his son soon?' I held the bundle to my nose to enjoy its scent.

She took it from me and placed it high over my head on the hooks to dry. 'Marry, of course he will. Such a lusty man will have a beautiful prince to follow him. A russet-haired boy, just like himself. In fact, I'll wager several boys – you wait and see.'

We carried on working in silence, and as I gathered my bundles of rosemary together, I thought of the queen.

The king, away on campaign in France, had heard nothing of the tragedy. Katherine, terrified and deeply depressed, kept the miscarriage hidden from him for fear of spoiling his celebrations. He did not know – and it had been forbidden to tell him – that the baby prince was dead. He, meantime, had enjoyed carousing in Tournai, jesting with his friends and playing the great victor. When he returned to Richmond to surprise his pregnant queen with gifts, he came home instead to a freshly dug grave. His queen had failed him in the one thing he wanted.

● ●

Some weeks later, Madame sat in her private study and unfurled a scroll. Monsieur de Barangier, her secretary, stood close by ready to hand her a fresh quill. She was merry and quite recovered from her stress. It was a peaceful scene as we sat sewing and chattering among ourselves, the dogs twitching in their sleep by the fire. Outside, brown leaves flurried past the window, and in the blustery wind, the panes of glass rattled in their embrasures.

'*Votre humble cousine – Margaret,*' she said, signing the document with a flourish. She sat back, adding triumphantly 'grumble who may, long live Burgundy.' She held out her hand and admired an enormous ruby ring surrounded by diamonds. 'It is always well to have favours owing – remember that, ladies.' She turned her hand to catch the light as I passed Fleur the golden thread.

'The king has agreed to our demands. My father is to support the garrison of Tournai with men and horses in Flanders over the winter, paid for by the king. This pleases my father immensely, for, at the end of the day, the English king's triumph in France has cost him nothing, and his territorial borders have been secured by English efforts. There will also be an invasion of France – a matter that does not please King Ferdinand of Spain – for he fears the growing power of England. Most importantly, I have the king's full assurance that there will be a strong alliance with England, through the marriage of Prince Charles and Princess Mary in Calais, before the fifteenth of May next year.'

She sanded the document, folded it carefully, sealed it with her seal and handed it to the secretary.

'A triumphant political move, I think, and one that, if I might say, could only have been achieved by a woman's touch.'

'Madame,' I asked, 'why does the English king owe you a favour?'

The regent stretched back in her chair with a smile of satisfaction.

'Oh, let us say I have written to him privately, concerning the regrettable incident with Charles Brandon and the immense distress and embarrassment it caused. I told him

I had to take to my bed, which is no lie. I did have to go to bed, but he is not to know that it was with an inflamed throat and cough. Anyway, he is greatly chastised and humbled. In fact, he is mortified that the world and its wife are discussing this silly nonsense, and is desperate to make amends. He has agreed to any request I might care to make, including a public apology for denying his involvement and thrusting me into such a predicament. The king knows he must retain the friendship and influence of the Low Countries, and cannot afford to lose my goodwill. As for gossip, I must weather the storm. Fire without wind will die and fizzle out like a firework.'

I could not imagine the king humbled or chastised by any woman – not even Margaret – and I watched as she closed her tired eyes.

Unable to hold my tongue, I spoke out on a matter I wished immediately I had not raised. 'Forgive me for asking, Madame, but the king's behaviour to you was most unchivalrous, and I understand it caused you much distress. But was he not equally unchivalrous to Rosaline?'

'Rosaline?' Margaret opened her eyes. 'I am afraid the behaviour of Rosaline was a foolish trifle and nothing more. She should have remembered it is one thing to play the game of chivalry and accept tokens, but quite another to play lewd games in pantry cupboards. Her behaviour put me in a very bad light indeed.'

I was taken aback and wondered how much of a 'trifle' it had been to Rosaline. However, the glaring stares I received from the other girls made me realise I had reminded Margaret of something they all hoped had been forgotten.

'But of course, I must make arrangements for you to visit the *Begijnhof.* These past few weeks I have been so distracted, but now, as the colder days draw on, your charitable works will be much appreciated. I shall write immediately.'

I swiftly plied my needle, not daring to look at the faces of the other girls.

'Incidentally, Anna, you will be pleased to know, as a gesture of goodwill, that I have honoured my agreement to Mr Charles Brandon whereby his daughter, Anne, and his adopted daughter, Magdalen Rochester, will come here to my court. I made a promise before this unfortunate matter arose, and I do not break my promises. I have written to Lord Mountjoy to say I am happy to take Anne, and he has secured a place for his pretty cousin, Elizabeth Blount, at Queen Katherine's court, in her stead. I am delighted, for I shall have two *demoiselles* called Anna to serve me.'

She removed Patou from Neutken's arm and allowed him to nibble her lips gentñy with his beak. Christa narrowed her eyes and jabbed the tapestry on her wooden frame hard with her needle as if it had been my arm. Unperturbed, I cared not. English girls were coming to court!

●　●

The November air felt as damp as a dog's nose, and the pale sun lay low in the grey sky as we briskly walked across the cobblestones to the *Groot Begijnhof* of St Catherine. Young boys, busy clearing up the fallen leaves outside the palace walls, snatched off their caps as we passed and then continued sweeping with their birch brooms, nudging each other with appreciative smiles. We walked silently, our eyes lowered and our hoods over our heads, as the countess strode ahead with two servants behind.

Splashing through the muddy puddles, I thought it fascinating to see the housewives in their mouse-grey kirtles, bodices, and mufflers, inspecting the cattle tied up in the busy market. Prospective buyers with sticks prodded the beasts, as some of the cows patiently suckled their calves. At each prod, they gave a low moan and glanced back towards their tormentor. Carts rattled across the cobbles, milkmaids carried their heavy pails, and knife grinders stood occupied beneath the arches of a house.

At the *Grôte Markt,* a tradeswoman, sleeves rolled up,

stood selling large, red-skinned cheeses, sausages and pies to the gathering crowds. I loved market day, for everything and anything was to be bargained for. Rolls of cloth, tapestries, carpets, cushions and such like were paraded before the housewives and merchants alike. A wealthy merchant haggled with a stall keeper over the price of a bear fur, while his wife draped it over her shoulders and preened herself in the dull mirror. Baskets of hunting birds, imported from Prussia, hung from poles and beneath them stood a great wicker crate containing plump pigeons. They fluttered nervously as a greasy cat sniffed at them through the metal bars. Anything could be bought here, from fresh fish to wooden skates and I found it fascinating. As we continued, noisy geese and ducks waddled across our path, and young girls, in crisp white caps and aprons, shooed them out of our way with long sticks.

'Why, Anna, the walk in the crisp air has brought a little colour to your cheeks,' noted the countess, turning to me. 'It is good to walk, for when walking one can pray. True or not, Veronique?' She turned, and caught the girl smirking at a young man as he rode by on his heavily laden donkey.

'Oh yes, indeed, Madame,' she replied, quickly.

'Madame herself visits the *Béguinage,* often walking barefoot, and wearing their brown habit,' said the countess. 'She seeks peace from the bustle of court life with its distractions and worldly cares. It is good to lead by example.'

Winding through the streets, it was not long before we approached the outskirts of the city, with its crumbling stone walls and rolling meadows. When we arrived at the iron gates, a mist hung over the flat fields and, in the distance, the many church spires glinted above in the sun.

'This particular *Béguinage*, Anna,' said the countess, as I stood beside her, 'has well over one thousand ladies living here. It is a city within a city, and is called a court.' She smiled as she acknowledged the gatekeeper.

'Is it true, Madame, women still join their numbers?' Edda gazed at the ducks and ducklings bobbing on the water beneath an ancient stone bridge.

'Yes, indeed,' said the countess. 'I gather thirty have joined in the last two years. Of course, the women grow old, infirm and die, and so new ones take their place. Now, we must make our way to the church to offer our prayers and then proceed to the infirmary.'

We continued past rows of neat little houses, each with a delightful garden, and great piles of golden leaves piled high, leaving the pathways clear. In each garden stood a wooden henhouse, and the hens, feathers full and ruffled, sat huddled against the chill. Young women dressed in full white wimples, brown habits, and long white aprons busied themselves digging the earth. They glanced up and waved as I took Beatrice aside, perplexed.

'Why would they want to come here and be secluded like holy nuns?'

'I told you,' she said. 'They come and go as they wish and retain complete independence. They do not seek charity, for they have their own houses and gardens and answer to no man. They sew, make lace, sell their produce, teach, take in laundry and serve the outside community.'

'But can they do anything? Go anywhere?' I asked.

'Yes, except get married,' said Beatrice. 'It is not a prison, but they must act within the laws of Holy Mother Church. The woman in charge of this great community is called an anchoress, rather than an abbess. For a time, they were viewed with some suspicion, but not anymore. These good women do not wish for the distractions of society, but they do not wish to take full vows.'

'So, no men live here at all?'

'None,' she said, as we walked past a group of women beating rush mats hanging from a rope line. I watched as the dust flew in grey clouds and the women coughed and laughed. Some were very pretty indeed. Some were decidedly not.

A stout woman smelling heavily of sweat and wood

smoke puffed towards us. 'Good day, my lady, good day, *demoiselles*, I understand you have offered to assist in the infirmary?'

We had hardly 'offered,' I thought.

'Excellent,' she said, 'We have old people here unable to work for the chill has affected their bones. We have one with a case of stomach trouble, and a few old dames who cannot eat easily for lack of teeth. It has made them weak. Some, sadly, will never leave the infirmary again, for they will not survive another winter.'

I stood not knowing what to expect.

'Well, come now and follow me. You will see that here we live in complete self-sufficiency. We have a bakehouse, stillroom, slaughterhouse, laundry, much as you would in any large house,' she added, as we trotted behind. 'We even brew our own beer, but we always suffer a shortage of young, strong hands to help.' She led the way down a narrow, muddy alley and I threw Beatrice a look of foreboding as my boots squelched in the puddles.

The infirmary appeared to be a large building with an open gallery at the front at ground level. A large dog feebly wagged its tail as we passed, and a cat, covered in bald patches, sat cleaning its paws on the crumbling, moss-covered wall. To one side of the infirmary stood a farm with cows and goats tethered, and to the other side a large medicinal herb garden. As we entered the building, I saw how the infirmary's high, arched windows let in the light, and as we walked further into the hall, I smelt wintergreen, herbs – and something unpleasant. Something pungent.

Women in brown habits lay either in bed or seated in chairs, some dozing fitfully, some awake. Some moaned in distress, and some were talking gibberish. All looked pale as death. The head of the infirmary handed each of us a long, grey apron, and I noticed mine had holes in as if nibbled by a mouse. I gazed around at the sight before me, fearful I might have to deal with a dead person. To my relief, I was told to approach the old woman sitting by the window.

'She is blind, child,' explained an elderly woman, 'and you must be patient with her. Her name is Madame Juliana van Hattam, and she speaks English and French. Talk to her, or read, and help her to drink the broth put before her. As you sit with her ponder on infirmity. It is a terrible burden that you, yourself, will one day bear. Now, go to.'

I bobbed to the woman and made my way to where the old lady sat. She stared blankly into space, but turned as I approached.

'Who is there?' A golden linnet chirped forlornly in a cage on her table and hopped nearer to the bars, hoping for food. It tilted its head as if listening.

'My name is Anne Bullen, my lady,' I announced loudly in English, close to her ear, 'and I have come from the regent's court.'

The old lady winced and pulled back, telling me she was blind not deaf.

I continued, undeterred. 'Her maids are visiting today to do good works. I am staying at her court to learn French and the ways of a noblewoman.'

The old woman gave a wheezy laugh and shifted in her chair, causing the woollen cover to fall to the floor.

I picked it up and tucked it around her bony form. The pungent smell wafted to my nose, and I saw that it came from stale piss lying in a puddle on the dull, red, brick tiled floor. 'Why do you laugh, my lady?'

'Ah, I am thinking of the court and the ways, as you say, of a noblewoman. Now, what do you look like? Let me trace your face with my fingers.' She reached out to me with her long, brown nails and ice-cold fingers, and as I leant nearer, they rested on my cheeks.

'Ah, you have an oval-shaped face, a pointed chin, and huge eyes. Your brows are fine, and your mouth is wide and generous. Do you have sound teeth?'

I said my front tooth was a little crooked.

'How delightful,' she said, feeling across my lips, 'a face full of character. No matter if it is not perfect – it makes you special. But you seem very slight and fine boned. What is your age, child?'

'I am thirteen years old, my lady,' I replied, as her fingers continued their probing.

'Why, a young lady,' she said. 'I cannot remember being thirteen.' Her face clouded as she withdrew her hands, and I sat down on the stool by her side.

'My lady, have you been here a very long time?'

The woman smiled a dry, toothless smile. 'Why, I have been here since I was twenty years old, and now, now I am – I am – what year is it?'

'It is 1513, my lady.'

'Why, I must be seventy years old, perhaps even older, for I too, was once at court a long time ago, and remember Margaret of York when she was a young girl. Where do you come from?'

'England, my lady.'

'Then no doubt you will have heard of her, sister to your great King Edward and sister to King Richard of York.'

I nodded, then remembered she could not see.

I spoke up. 'My uncle was once married to Anne Plantagenet, daughter of King Edward. As to the Lady Margaret, she was married to Charles the Bold, Duke of Burgundy, and lived in Bruges. But she was a traitor to the Tudor king, for she supported any impostors who rose against him, such as Perkin Warbeck.'

The old woman turned her head towards me. 'He was no traitor,' she said. 'He was a boy of great beauty and charm – marred only by a cast in one eye – and Margaret loved him well. I can still see her sitting with him, their heads close together as she whispered her endearments and encouragement. She knew, Margaret knew, he was Edward's lost boy escaped from the Tower where his poor brother lay murdered. I recall that he had the most exquisite manners that ever coursed through royal veins.'

I frowned. Why did everyone here think Perkin Warbeck really was Prince Richard? Even Mother had said he was a posturing puppet, trained to be the lost prince by the Yorkist supporters.

I changed the subject. 'My lady, Madame Regent says Margaret of York was very kind to her and took her into her care at her palace at Mechelen.'

'It is true, for the lady Margaret was a good soul who gave her charity in secret. Everyone sought her favour. As for me, I cared nothing for courts and court intrigue. I was a seamstress to the duchess, but I came from a poor family, and no husband could be found for me. I had no dowry and, being a somewhat unruly chit, was not thought suitable for a convent.'

'Why were you unruly?' I asked.

The old woman sighed. 'Because – because once I was a winsome thing with flame-red hair, reaching down to my waist, and a fiery temper to match. Men loved me, and I loved them, but I misbehaved and was sent away. I had a child, but she died at three years old. Her name was Alice, and her father, serving under the fourth Edward, was an English archer, broad and strong. Once, yes once, I loved and was beloved. It is hard to imagine, is it not?' she asked, turning her opaque green eyes towards me. I felt repulsed as I stared at her transparent, yellowing skin, mottled with brown spots and her wispy, white hair. I could not imagine her ever being loved by any man.

'Was she pretty?' I was referring to Margaret of York.

She turned slightly. 'Oh, yes, child. She had a round, full face, with a high smooth brow – as was the fashion – and pouting lips which she tinted red from a little pot that she always carried with her. Her cheeks were pale and her eyes clear grey. There was a cough. A nervous cough when vexed – yes, I recall it. She wore magnificent high headdresses covered with layers of scented gauze, and I can still remember the smell – sweet as violets. It lingered in any chamber or hall that she walked through, like holy incense.' As she spoke, a young girl approached with a steaming bowl. She placed a napkin roughly around the old woman's neck and handed me the bowl and spoon.

'What colour is it?' growled the old woman, sniffing the air like a hind catching the scent of the dogs.

'Your pardon, my lady?'

'In the bowl – I can smell it. What colour?'

'It is light brown, my lady, with, I think, mutton.' I stirred the liquid. I could not be sure what the floating lumps of fatty meat were.

The woman grumbled. 'Green. It always smells of something green, like pond water,' she said, sipping noisily as I put the wooden spoon to her mouth. The mixture dribbled down her hairy chin, and I dabbed it with the cloth. She pulled a face. 'Dah! Too much salt, tastes more like seawater.'

I looked over to Beatrice as she helped to change the bedding on one of the beds, for from the strong smell it seemed that the woman in the bed had also pissed herself through, and worse. She had also vomited. Over on the other side, Edda sat mixing comfrey into a paste ready to apply as a plaster to a woman with a broken arm. Maria tried to offer a mixture of rue to another woman, who, from the moaning, appeared to have a griping in her stomach. I sighed as I held the spoon to the old woman's cracked lips and she opened her cadaverous mouth again.

I did not like this place. It smelt of sickness, decay, and death. Even the violas drooped in their bowl. The half-bald cat wandered in with a bloody, dead mouse and sloped away across the tiles. It revolted me. The people revolted me, all dying along with the light, and I did not want to stay. I was young and belonged with the court where there were feasting and music, laughter and beautiful gowns to wear. I did not belong in this place of contagion. I would never be old like this, I vowed, dribbling into a bowl and pissing myself. I continued to feed the woman until she spluttered and waved the spoon impatiently away. She started to doze, but as I rose to leave she stretched her bony, claw-like hand out to me and held me fast. 'Read to me, child. I miss reading for it was always my great joy to listen.'

I felt trapped but sat back down again, and took the small book from my bag. I opened a page and began:

> 'Always loyal, whatever comes,
> In all and everywhere man must be,
> Whether secular or priest;
> Right bids one to keep loyalty.
> God wills, for sure, that we remain,
> In fortune good or sinister,
> Always loyal.
> Suppose the case for misadventure
> Where all does not come right, I know
> Nothing better in the world
> For man to maintain himself
> Always loyal.'

I closed the book, not sure whether to continue or not, for the old lady's eyes were shut. I waited until she spoke.

'You have a pretty voice, child, light and musical.'

'I love to read verse, my lady, and this piece was written by the regent herself.'

The old lady nodded her hairy chin and turned to me. 'That poor lady has suffered a great deal, I know, but that is what court life brings you to: suffering. You will see if you stay. My advice is to live simply without worldly distractions, but I am old and nearer to the judgement of God than you.' She gave a chuckle. 'Enjoy your fine gowns, music, and dancing while you can, for I tell you the vanities of this world will count as nothing when you reach my great age. I require nothing now,' she added, 'but sustenance, water, a little company – and a good priest. But come, let me hold your face again.' She put her shaky hands up to the side of my head, and I felt myself stiffen with distaste.

'Why, what soft hair you have, thick and strong. Is it black?'

'No, my lady, it is the colour of the horse chestnut.' Her fingers trembled.

'And your eyes?' she asked, tracing my brow.

'Almost black, my lady, like a blackbird's.' She nodded slowly.

'Let me tell you what my mind sees, for once I was a wise woman.' Her fingers tightened before I could protest or move. 'No, no, it is true. I developed the gift of keen sight once my physical sight was taken from me, and I saw many things. Let me tell you what now I see.'

She breathed in and, with a sigh, spoke. 'I sense a special child, for you will have a future like no other. I see you surrounded by many people – a great crowd – and yet, you sit alone beneath a canopy. It is a warm day, and pink dog roses entwine around wooden arches. It is a holiday, yet no holy day, for no one is carousing or rejoicing. I can hear the jangling of many horses' bits, the wheels of chariots on cobbles, the marching of many feet. There is a clanking noise of metal, like armour, a tramping sound. Yet this great crowd is mute, sullen, silently watching, curious. The occasion is not one of sadness, but joy. How can it be? Now I see red, red, brightly spilling and gushing forth. Why, it is wine spouting forth from fountains, but no one is drinking. No man is celebrating.'

I attempted to move.

'No, wait, there is something else – you do not sit alone. Another is with you, someone very, very precious – very close – but I cannot see them. I can only sense that they are a part of you.' She took a trembling breath.

'What can you see now?' I whispered. She opened one distant eye.

'Tell me, what month were you born?'

'May, Madame,' I replied.

'Under the sign of the twins or the bull?'

'The twins, Madame.'

She sighed. 'Ah, such a woman shall come to honour and be aggrieved of a false crime.' She pulled me to her and closed her eyes as if in a reverie, rocking to and fro. I smelt decay as I felt her stale, shallow breath on my face. Then she opened her blank eyes wide and turned to face me, her expression full of terror. 'Fly the court. Speak little. Care less. Desire nothing. Pray daily. Live better. Die well.' There was a pause.

'Anything else?' I whispered, desperate to leave.

'Yes,' she cackled, 'you are too small. Get bigger, my little shrimp, get bigger!' She laid her head back and closed her eyes.

I felt disappointed and did not think her much of a seer. In fact, I thought her feeble-minded and foolish. Without saying farewell, I picked up her fallen coif, placed it on her bony lap and hurried back to the countess.

* *

That evening we returned to the palace by torchlight.

'Now, ladies, what have you learnt from your visit to the infirmary?' asked the countess, walking briskly against the chill. As usual, I was the first of the girls to speak.

'I think old age and infirmity are quite disagreeable, but I suppose we must be charitable to those who cannot help themselves.'

'Quite correct, Anna,' said the countess, over her shoulder. 'Faith, hope, love, and charity burn like fire in the heart of a good Christian, and from charity – loving thy neighbour as thyself – will come a greater closeness to God. Remember you, yourself, God willing, will be old one day. You will lose your youth and vigour and walk bent over a stick. Will you bear your infirmities stoically, or curse God for abandoning you to your weakness? It is of no value to be a Christian and praise God only when he or she is in the strength of youth and health. One must praise Him for whatever ill He chooses to send you.'

'The church teaches that suffering on earth means less time spent in purgatory, Madame.'

'Indeed, Isabel, those who suffer will see the face of God sooner.'

'But, Madame,' said Concetta, 'the priest says a man can buy his way to Heaven if he is rich enough. If he can pay for thousands of Masses to be said, or contribute to the building of a church, he does not have to suffer in purgatory at all.'

'Yes,' said Ariella, 'it is the same if a man goes to prison and his friends pay to have him released, even if he has committed a crime.'

The countess stopped abruptly and turned around. 'But is that justice?' she asked. 'Why should the rich man, or the man with influential friends, be allowed to go unpunished. Why should the man with money see the face of God sooner than the poor man? Is that a just law? Is that a just God? No, it is corruption and not the way of the new learning sweeping through Europe.'

Beatrice leant close to my ear. 'The holy priests would not be happy with her views. She should have a care.'

'But surely, Madame,' said Greta, kicking through the dead leaves, 'the poor man is poor from choice, for he shirks work. He is a vagabond, and it is his fault if he cannot pay to have Holy Mass said for his soul.'

'I think, young ladies, we are getting somewhat confused here,' continued the countess. 'Indeed, many people bring on their ills and shame through idleness, but to get back to my original point, I am saying that you must show forbearance and fortitude to whatever ill might befall you, and show charity in your heart. What you think and what God thinks will not be the same thing. In your health and youth, you must support those who are old and infirm and hope that – when you are infirm and cannot raise a spoon to your dry lips – some kind soul will do it for you.'

I was about to speak again, but Beatrice put her finger to

her lips and stopped me. With my head full of questions we continued our walk back to the palace. What was this new learning she spoke of?

* *

Smallpox. The word struck terror into the heart. In England, as soon as the king reached Richmond Palace and discovered the devastating outcome of his wife's pregnancy, people in London began to fall sick. In panic, they whispered the dreaded word 'pox' and blamed it on the huge influx of English soldiers returning from France as they filled the taverns, alehouses and bear-baiting pits. London became quite overwhelmed by their numbers as thousands stopped en route before making their way back to the shires.

The king himself did not escape the epidemic and lay sick with a high fever. Wrapped in wool and flannel blankets, alternating between icy cold and dripping sweat, his skin eventually erupted in blistering spots. It spread panic throughout the court. Mother wrote how the queen had tried to send her ladies away and tend to the king herself, but yet again her closest friends insisted on staying with her. My mother, however, hurriedly took the opportunity with my sister to return to Hever, to the fresher air of the country, while my Uncle Howard fled back to Tendring Hall in Suffolk.

The king was slow to recover, and it made those around him ever more anxious for a male heir. It was a topic of serious discussion at the regent's court, for suppose the king had died? He had poured scorn on his councillors' fears, but Mother wrote saying how it had shaken him greatly. He was also concerned for his queen, for she showed signs of a black depression with constant weeping. Nothing the king did could raise her spirits for it had struck her that if the king died without an heir, she would have no place, no home, no child or husband, and would end her days in a convent. She would be as she was before her marriage, without position or importance, ready to be cast aside. In this sad state, she spent hours with her Spanish confessor, Fray Diego Fernandez, confiding her fears late into the night. Surprisingly, she did not fall ill, although she remained listless and red-eyed, and lay on her bed day after day, barely eating.

When she returned to court, Mother observed how this behaviour depressed the king himself, and he spent his days and nights closeted with his friends playing cards, refusing to attend to any state business and sleeping alone. She also told of the great unrest during that cold autumn, for the common fields around London had been enclosed, and young men had no longer been allowed to shoot their bows, or the older ones walk for pleasure. Arrows were snapped in two and arrests made, and eventually, in anger and despair, a great assembly gathered to cut down the hedges and fill in the ditches. Even the sight of a priest standing high on a wall holding up the Blessed Host outside St Martin's church could not pacify the crowds. The king, furious at their treatment by his own officials, and ever anxious to secure his popularity, rode to Charing Cross with a great retinue to address the crowd himself. Although not fully recovered in health, he sat astride his horse and declared how the finest English bill and bowmen had accompanied him to France and, through their skill and allegiance, had regained a land that once was ours. He would not forsake them now on their return home, and henceforth his council would declare no more fields would be hedged. Each able man must, by order of the king, continue to practise his aim ready for the following year when he would call them again to arms. They were the king's men, loyal and true, and their sovereign would not desert them after their wondrous service to his crown and person. Full recompense would be given to any man whose bow had been broken or taken, and anyone taken prisoner would be released. Those officers of the crown responsible for the enclosure would be punished. The result of his speech was a great, thunderous cheer, followed by a day of celebration.

As the bells rang out throughout England to celebrate his recovery, it was obvious the king was entirely beloved by his people. He was free from all blame whilst his bewildered advisors sat in the prison stews, fuming.

●　●

The morning of Christmas Eve dawned bright as we sorted out our costumes for the celebrations. In the Great Hall, tables were cleared and a clean-shaven young man who I had not seen before entered. Stocky of build and well dressed, he bowed politely to the Countess of Hochstrate and the surrounding ladies.

'Ah, let me see what you have brought,' she said as, with the help of the seamstress, he cast great rolls of silks, satins, gauzes, and tissue across the long, wooden table.

The countess picked up the silk and held it up to the light of the window. 'It is good – very good,' she said, squinting her eyes, appreciatively.

The young man stepped forward, the cut of his burgundy red suit fashionable and expensive, and it was obvious that he was a walking advertisement for his wares. However, his awkward stance, as if not used to such fine garb, spoiled the effect.

'Madame, it is the best in Flanders, brought to you directly from Middelburg. My masters would not have me bring anything to you unless exquisite.'

'By exquisite you mean extortionate?' enquired the countess, turning to the youth.

His face and bull neck reddened.

'Oh, come now,' she said, 'have we not already agreed to buy the stuff? We will take it, and your masters will be well pleased.'

The young man bowed, and as I caught his eye I saw him stare as if appraising me in some way. How impertinent of him, a merchant's boy!

As the Countess of Hochstrate walked him to the door

she turned to him. 'Thank you, Master…?'

'Cromwell, my lady, Master Thomas Cromwell.'

⁕ ⁕

Wiping my fingers on my apron, I quickly threw it off and wondered why I had been summoned so urgently to Margaret's chambers. I felt excited, for today the decorating of the palace would begin, and as I walked through the Festive Hall, I stopped briefly to watch as two strong men began winching an enormous iron candelabra, heavy with beeswax candles, towards the rafters.

When I reached Margaret's private dining hall, she and her ladies were standing around the blazing logs in the fireplace. As the ladies parted, a tall girl in a white, coney fur bonnet and long, blue cloak and a smaller girl in a red cloak turned around.

'Anna,' said Margaret, 'Mistress Anne Brandon and Mistress Magdalen Rochester have joined us. Come, I am sure you will wish to welcome two English girls to my court.'

I greeted them both. 'Welcome to the court, Mistress Brandon and Mistress Rochester.'

Margaret brushed away the dusting of snow from the taller girl's shoulders, and then handed her cloak to the waiting maid.

'So much like your dear father, I see,' she said, gently touching her cheek. 'Losing your mother must have been greatly distressing for you, but I can assure you that while you are here at my court, I shall be as a mother to you myself.'

She turned to the smaller girl. 'Likewise, I say to you. I have promised to take care of you both. Now, go with Anna and tell her all the news of what has been happening in England and Calais.'

With a deep curtsey, I left the chamber holding Anne's cold hand, while Magdalen followed behind. We made our way to the Festive Hall, now a bustle of activity, for musicians were tuning up their instruments ready to practice, and two boys were bent over their brooms, busily sweeping out the fireplace in preparation for the great Yule log. This year it had been kindly donated by the Mayor of Mechelen.

'I am delighted to see you both,' I said, leading both girls to a bench in the corner of the hall.

'Did you understand what Madame Regent said when she spoke to you?' I asked.

'Oh, yes indeed,' said Anne, nodding enthusiastically. Magdalen nodded, but then Anne appeared bashful and hesitant. 'Well, no – not exactly. My French is not good – not like Magdalen's, but,' she added, 'I do hope to improve.'

I smiled encouragingly at the girl.

'My father,' she continued, 'was supposed to have come here with us, but there has been a great deal of strange talk concerning him, which I do not understand. I gather the king will not let him return here for a while, but I know not why. My father was quite put out as he wished to join in the Christmas revels, but the king made him stay at Richmond. Master Wingfield has come in his stead. Do you know why?' she asked.

'Oh – oh, something and nothing,' I said, trying to sound merry. However, I knew, sooner or later, she would hear the gossip surrounding her embarrassing father.

'And you, Magdalen?' I turned to the small, silent girl.

'Tell of your adventure!' said Anne, eagerly.

The girl appeared nervous as she spoke. 'My father is English and lives on his own in Calais, for my mother died of the plague. One day I had a terrible accident.'

'Go on,' I said, as she removed her fur cap and let her pretty brown curls tumble down.

'Well, as I sat on the wall in the harbour watching the boats, a boy grabbed the purse attached to my coat. I turned to push him away but lost my balance and fell off the wall into the water below. I screamed and screamed for I could not swim and my coat became heavy with water, weeds, and filth.'

'And?'

'Well, Mr Brandon – who was standing by the quay – leapt into the water and, with his great arm around my waist, pulled me to the side where there were metal rings and steps. Then another gentleman heaved me out of the water onto dry land.'

'Mr Brandon did that?' I asked.

'Yes, and he took me to my father and gave him money from his own purse to replace that stolen from me. My father said he was deeply in his debt, but Mr Brandon said he would like to take him out fishing, which he did, and over the weeks he and father became good friends. In the evening I would sing for Mr Brandon, and after some months he offered to adopt me as his daughter. Of course, my father said that was not possible, but Mr Brandon said that with my father's permission he would supervise my education and ask the regent to agree to place me here at her court.'

There was silence. Well, well, I thought, there is a heart beating inside that great ape after all.

'That is my story,' she said, with a shrug.

'Tell me of your family,' I said, turning to Anne Brandon and taking her cold hands in mine.

'My mother was from the Neville family,' she began, 'and she and my father – Charles Brandon – were betrothed to be married, but I was born before –' She stopped and bit her lip.

'Well, instead of marrying my mother, Father married a wealthy aunt. My poor mother was left with a babe, but no husband. Her relatives were horrified, and my father was forced to put aside his marriage. He married my mother, and they had another girl, my sister Mary, who is now three. Of course, such – such things were kept hidden from me, but people tell you things. You know – spiteful things.' She looked sad.

'Mother died last year,' she continued, 'shortly before Lady Day, from a fever, and my father betrothed a girl my own age. I like her very much. However, she does not like my father and says that when she is older, she will not have him for no earthly thing. He has been told to put this betrothal aside for the sake of his honour, but what will become of me?'

I looked at her sad face and thought a man of twenty-nine and a girl of eight was a sorry match indeed.

'It must be dreadful losing your mother,' I said, placing my hand on Anne's sleeve, 'but one day you will have another good woman to care for you.'

She brightened up.

'But where is your family?' she asked.

'My home is in Kent, but Mother is at home with my older sister, Mary. Father, as you know, is one of the king's ambassadors. This Christmas, he is taking my brother George to court for the first time to take part in the Christmas masque.'

'Why is your sister not here then?' asked Anne.

'Do you know,' I said, cheerfully ignoring her awkward question, 'you have both come at the most exciting time of the year, for tonight we shall celebrate Christ's birth with a wonderful ceremony. Our Advent fast will be over, and we shall eat again of sticky sweets and other confections. Now, come with me.'

The girls rose up together.

'It is time for us to dine and afterwards you must help me make the kissing bush, which will hang in this hall. Everyone who passes beneath it must take a kiss from those closest to them, so beware! The girls collected the mistletoe this morning – you know it cannot be collected before today – but we must find a large quantity of nuts, oranges, apples and ribbons to decorate it with. Concetta and Maria think we should use gold ribbon, but I have a mind to try something different. We have the large wooden frame made already and must collect it from the smithy. Come, let us go there now before we eat.'

Both girls smiled broadly and I was delighted to have new friends about me.

I will never forget that first snow-covered Christmas Eve at Mechelen. The entire court assembled outside the palace in the snow, while the children of the Chapel Royal sang out the good news of Christ's coming birth. Margaret, the emperor, the prince and princesses stood on the stone balcony facing the old palace and gazed down on the richly dressed ambassadors, city dignitaries, churchmen and nobles. We maids, muffled in our warm, fur-trimmed coats and fur caps, stood with the Countess of Hochstrate clutching our lanterns and watching as our warm breath curled up into the crisp, night air.

After the carolling, we made our way to the *Grôte Markt* and on to St Rombouts. I had visited the church before, but its very size, with its arches and pillars painted with scenes from the Old Testament, never ceased to amaze me. The numerous torches flickered across the wooden statues of the Twelve Apostles adorning the stone pillars, and the light danced on the stained glass windows, illuminating the family tree of the House of Burgundy. As I closed my eyes and listened to the choir sing the *'Gloria in Excelsis Deo'* I squeezed Anne Brandon's hand and smiled at Beatrice sitting a little further away.

When the service was over, Margaret walked back up the long aisle with her father, her ladies following behind.

'You know, I have high hopes for this coming year,' she said, taking his arm and kissing him on the cheek. 'King Ferdinand has signed the Treaty of Lille, and has written to the English king that it is his fervent hope to live and die in your friendship.'

'A pretty speech,' said her father, waving at the crowds of townspeople gathered outside the church doors. 'He hopes, if victorious, we will bind ourselves in a joint attack against the Turk. Holy war or not, wars cost money I do not have.'

A great cheer, followed by a carillon of bells, filled the

night air. Christ was born! As we wound our way back to the palace, through the crisp, still falling snow, the chapel choirboys rang their hand bells in celebration.

• •

The festivities continued for several days, and I finally found the chance to talk to Beatrice alone. Although the hall was crowded with dancers, I spied her kneeling with one of Madame's dogs, trying to untangle its leash from the leg of a table. As the servants hurried to clear away the dishes, the dog was obviously in the way.

'I am sorry. I did not think,' I said, looking at her downcast eyes. 'I was befriending someone new to the court, as you did with me. That is all.'

'Sometimes, Anna, you are so selfish the way you seek attention. And the moment something, or someone, bores you, you rush off to find the new and novel. I thought *I* was your best friend.'

I stood lost for words for she was right. I did find new people and new things exciting, and Beatrice had proved dull of late. She seemed distracted, uninterested, and content to fade away into the background. I was not. I wanted to make my way, to be seen, to be part of everything, to know everything. Yes, I was distracted by fresh gossip and intrigue – and there was plenty from Anne Brandon.

'I only want *you* for my friend,' I lied. 'Anne is a child, and I wanted to ensure she was not left alone.'

'Is that true?'

'Of course! You and I will be friends forever.'

'Will we?' She returned the dog to one of the ladies-in-waiting.

More at ease, I continued to watch the merriment and Margaret dancing with her father. She appeared young and happy, rubies sparkling about her neck, as she moved on to her next partner, Signor di Gattinara. She laughed at the kissing bough swaying above them, but the elderly statesman seemed thoroughly embarrassed and moved quickly on to the next lady. It was while Margaret was thus dancing that a messenger strode through the hall, shaking the snow from his cloak. He walked up to the emperor, removed his cap with a flourish, and with a curt bow, whispered to him. As Margaret spotted them, she stopped and walked over to join them. After a few moments, she, the emperor and Signor di Gattinara returned to the dais, deep in conversation. It was apparent they were discussing something serious, as Margaret arose from her chair, her minister at her side. As she passed the maids' table, I heard her speak.

'Tell me again, Signor, what do we know of the situation? Will she die?'

* *

I sat by the crackling fire, sorting out Margaret's precious jewels ready for her to wear that day.

'Check each piece is secure in its setting, Anna,' said Lady Brederode, handing me a gold cross studded with coral. 'You know Madame has a great love of coral, for it contains medicinal properties. Now, where did you put the matching eardrops?' I rummaged through the open casket.

We were busy with our task when Margaret walked into the chamber with her ladies. As we stood, she aimlessly picked up one of the pearl necklaces on the table and tossed it carelessly down again. She seemed distracted until her advisor, Monsieur de Marnix, appeared, and they hurriedly disappeared into the adjoining chamber. The door stayed open, but although I kept my head down with my task, my ears, as usual, were wide open.

'Monsieur,' began Margaret, 'this is grave news indeed. I gather from de Burgo, my ambassador at the French court, that the queen lies at her château in Blois and passes water and blood with great difficulty. What can this mean?'

As I glanced up I could see Monsieur de Marnix standing

with his back to the fire, warming his hands.

'Madame, the fever has worsened, and we have concerns it is the stone. The French doctors do what they can, but rumours abound she will not see the week out.'

'I see,' said Margaret, nodding. 'Anne of Brittany is a woman I admire for her artistic tastes, her refinement, her piety – she and I have long been friends. Thirty-six is middle-aged, but still, a good woman wasted on France, eh?'

'Indeed, and in her time betrothed to both your father and the young Prince Charles,' replied her minister.

'Ah, my dear friend, a lifetime of wasted childbearing and miscarriages has given her nothing but grief. She lost her son only last year. Thank God her daughters Renée and Claude survive.'

'As yet, they do, Madame. Renée is a sturdy three-year-old, but Claude is a weak little thing, fourteen now, and betrothed to that big, boisterous François, Comte d'Angoulême. Such a coupling will rend her in two. The French king is without male issue and should Queen Anne die…' His voice trailed off.

'Simple,' said Margaret. 'François, as the king's cousin, becomes king through Salic law and the claim to Brittany comes to him. You are aware, my dear friend, that a female cannot take the crown of France.'

'Indeed, but if François claims the throne, a woman *will* take the power.'

'You mean my sister-in-law, the Comtesse d'Angoulême?'

'Who else? You know she is a woman of immense ambition, for her little "Caesar" and is loathed for her dishonesty and nefarious activities. She could prove formidable. Yet the French have high hopes for this golden boy of eighteen becoming king. However, although Louis might be decrepit at fifty-two, a broken man living like a pauper, he will not put aside the obsession that he can still father a son and keep the royal line.'

'Ah, but has he put aside the obsession that he can still

have Milan?'

'Madame,' came the reply, 'he is as tenacious as the sign of the crab he was born under, scuttling back and forth with his acquisitive claws. Why, a crab would have been a more fitting device than the porcupine he chose.'

'On the contrary,' said Margaret, 'I think a porcupine is quite apt, for he who meddles with him will certainly suffer the consequences.'

'Perhaps, but as for marriage I wonder what princess he will trap next in his great claws?'

Margaret raised her eyes. 'Fie, Monsieur, his wife is not yet in her grave. I will pray for her recovery, but you must keep me informed of any developments from de Burgo. Meanwhile, we must await the turn of events.'

Her minister bowed.

'Now, if you would excuse me, I must prepare for the entertainments with my ladies.'

Chapter Seven

'Life is fleeting death is sure.'

Mechelen and Brussels,
Winter and Spring, 1514

After Mass on that first day of January, Margaret commanded we attend her in her private chambers. We had already spent hours assisting her and her ladies in choosing suitable New Year gifts for her family, guests, and the court, and she had made certain that we were aware of the taste of each person of note who would receive a present. A great array of gifts had been brought in by merchants from Antwerp and Bruges and laid out on the sideboard for Margaret to peruse. A silver spoon, a goblet, a turkey carpet, a portable altar, a filigree pomander that opened up to show the tiny Christ child in a manger – many such things were passed between us. The ladies from the *Béguinage* also came to the palace with a variety of goods such as lace cushion covers, cakes, pies, and small woodcuts depicting holy images known in Mechelen as 'The Good Lord's Playing Cards'. The ladies hoped to sell these items to the court, and I watched as Margaret admired a lace veil. Now we were to receive our own gifts from her.

'What gifts did you send home, Anna?' asked Greta, as we walked swiftly along.

'Well, to my dear nurse, Mrs Orcharde, I sent a pair of warm gloves that I had embroidered myself. She feels the cold badly in her hands. To my mother I sent a lace kerchief and to father I sent one of Madame's poems, copied out in Latin – although our tutor helped me. To my sister Mary, I sent a lace collar, and to my brother George, a book of French fables. Master Wingfield kindly took the gifts over to the English court before the holiday.'

We hurried on, all chattering about the presents our families had sent as we made our way to Madame's private chamber. When we arrived we sat around her on the floor cushions, the ladies standing behind.

'Come, Giovanna,' Margaret took the first item from Lady Saillant. 'I think this will become you right well. My blessings upon you.' Giovanna kissed her hand and took her gift – a beautiful set of pearl drop earrings set in gold.

One by one the girls sighed in raptures over a silver pomander, an ivory and garnet studded comb, a bracelet set with amethyst stones, and a new pair of sleeves. Beatrice received a brooch in the form of a leaping deer with rubies for its eyes, and appeared ecstatic as I helped pin it to her gown. However, I began to feel uneasy, for the cupboard soon began to empty.

'Now, what do we have for you, Anna?' asked Margaret of one her ladies. 'Let me see. Ah, yes, I have this. Step forward, child.' One of the ladies reached into the cupboard and passed her a tiny, jewel-encrusted collar. Made of pale blue buckram, studded with blue sapphire stones, it appeared very small.

'Come, come and take your gift,' encouraged Margaret.

'Why, it is beautiful, Madame,' I held it up to my neck.

Margaret laughed. 'No, no, my dearest girl, this is not

for *you* to wear. It is not a necklace. Bring her in!' She clapped her hands loudly, and a maid instantly appeared holding a tiny, white-haired puppy. She placed it on my lap.

'Oh!' I cried in astonishment.

'I know, my dear, but do not thank me, thank your mother, who pleaded continually with your father until he could bear no more. You know I do not allow my young maids to own dogs – such a privilege is normally only reserved for my ladies – but I am inclined to make an exception.'

The little ball of fur whined.

'Your father is such a dear friend that I can refuse him nothing, and desperate for some peace, he asked – no, begged – my master of the kennels to find a suitable pup for you. She is a Barbichon, and since she has no name, you may decide what to call her. However, in honour of my mother and Burgundy, I request all dogs in my household have names beginning with the letter "*B*".'

I stared down in awe as the girls crowded around. She was the prettiest creature I had ever seen, and I felt over-whelmed with joy.

'Madame, is she really mine?'

Margaret nodded. 'Indeed, and the collar is my gift to you. Let us see if it fits.' As she tried to fastened the collar around the puppy, it gnawed playfully at her fingers with its needle-sharp teeth.

'Now, Mistress Brandon, I have not forgotten you.'

Anne Brandon reached for her gift of a gold necklace, interlaced with pearls, and by the look on her face, she was delighted.

'Now, young ladies, since my personal gifts have been given, duty states we must go down to the hall and see what kind gifts I have been given by members of my own and foreign courts. Lady Cerf, please take the puppy away.'

● ●

We spent the next agonisingly slow hours standing in the

Festive Hall, as Margaret and the emperor graciously received some of the most precious gifts from the representatives of King Ferdinand of Aragon, King Henry of England, King Manuel of Portugal, King Christian of Denmark and Norway, and even His Holiness, the pope. Sir Robert Wingfield, on behalf of the King of England, gave a magnificent solid gold inkwell within a leather holder, embossed with flowers, a fine set of quills, and a beautiful Italianate desk carefully carried in by two gentlemen. I watched as the emperor moved his hands across the smooth, cherry wood, appreciating the fine grain and workmanship. In return, the ambassador received forty yards of damask and silk for his own use. My father sent a magnificent ivory chess set, my mother sent Margaret a pair of exquisite white leather gloves fringed with silver tinsel, and countless other English nobles gave similar gifts. After the nobles and diplomats came the Companies, such as the crossbow makers, the brewers, the weavers, the dyers, the painters and the numerous other guilds in Mechelen. I counted forty-two. It was past midnight when we retired, and on reaching our chambers, there, whimpering and trembling on the rushes, quite alone, sat my little puppy.

'Oh, let me hold her!' cried Maria.

'No, let me,' argued Veronique, grabbing the ball of fur.

Ariella frowned. 'Stop frightening the poor little thing. Here, Anna, she is yours. You take her.' She picked up the whining pup and placed it in my arms.

'What will you call her?' asked Beatrice.

'Well, I have thought and thought all day, and as she is quite beautiful, I shall call her Bonny.'

'Ah, it suits her,' said Edda, over her shoulder, as Greta helped her to unlace her sleeve.

'No one else is allowed to have a dog,' muttered Maria, stepping out of her kirtle and kicking it out of the way. 'Why can you have one?' Fleur picked it up off the floor and laid it over the chair, for she could not abide untidiness.

I shrugged, not caring if she was jealous, and walked back

to my bed carrying Bonny. On the coverlet, I noticed a letter.

'It is from my mother,' I said, unfolding the paper. 'Oh!' I cried reading down.

'What is it?' asked Edda, 'is it good news?'

'Oh, my goodness. My sister is coming here to Mechelen! Mother writes that Mary is to be one of the Princess Mary Rose's attendants when she marries the prince, since she has charmed the princess to such an extent that the girl has insisted she accompanies her to her new country.' I looked up from the familiar script. I was not sure if I wanted my sister's pretty face stealing all the attention away from me. I continued reading. 'Why, my father and mother are to accompany my sister when the princess sails to Calais.'

'So you will see your family sooner than you thought,' said Beatrice, 'for we shall be in Margaret's retinue, accompanying the prince when he meets her.'

I nodded.

'Oh, listen, apparently the king has spent a vast fortune on preparations for the wedding with solid gold salt cellars, plates, and cups. Even the bridal bed has been made of cloth of gold and the princess will have over one hundred officers, servants, and ladies. She says not a soul is allowed to know anything of the wedding gown, except the king's councillor, Dr Knight, and Margaret herself. It is a great secret, but it is sure to be the most beautiful gown we have ever seen. The lodgings in Calais have finally been chosen, and prepared with costly hangings. Can you imagine?' I asked.

'Yes,' said Christa, 'and next week we have fittings for our own gowns. I spied rolls and rolls of white tissue delivered here to the seamstress just the other day. Do you suppose that it is the stuff?'

We laughed amidst the speculation, and as I picked little Bonny up, I buried my face in her warm fur. She smelt of wood smoke and, as we settled into bed, I drifted into a blissful, contented sleep, thrilled at the thought of seeing my family and now owning my very own dog.

❀ ❀

That night I dreamt of Hever. Standing in the meadow, my apron full of flowers, I swirled around and around, until I felt caught by someone I could not see. As their arms enfolded me, a great love and warmth filled my heart. The figure leant close to my ear and whispered with a sweet voice: 'I am here, little one, I am here. My spirit will never leave you, for I shall always watch over you.'

As my flowers turned into larks and flew away, I tried to catch them, but I only awoke with a start. Bonny wriggled around, whined and licked my face, making me smile, and Beatrice gave a moan as she turned over. I lay in the half-light of dawn musing on my strange dream but soon drifted back to sleep again, warm and content. It had been the most wonderful Christmas season, and now, with the year 1514 upon us, it was a time full of hope and promise. I slept, blissfully unaware of the heartache that the next letter from home would bring.

❀ ❀

Great tears splashed down my cheeks as Anne Brandon took my hand. We were alone in the schoolroom, and although I tried to read further, I could barely see the words before my eyes.

'Do not cry so,' murmured Anne, closing her history book. I looked up at her concerned face, older than its years. 'Madame Symonnet will be back before long, you do not want her to see you thus.'

I said I cared not and besides, I knew my dear tutor would understand. I rose and gazed out onto the snowy courtyard. The frozen fountains no longer tinkled with water, and the crows perched silently on the bare branches of the trees. I hated winter. And now she was dead – my own, my beloved. A year to the day of my brother Hal's dying, she too, had succumbed to the harsh winter cold and released her hold on life. Oh, my sweet, sweet nurse, if I had known I would never see you again, I would not have crossed the narrow sea. My heart was breaking.

Mrs Orcharde had died quietly at Hever, with Hannah and the servants present, clutching a corn dolly that she had bought me long ago at a fair. The letter from my mother stated that my nurse would be buried at Hever, and I would, therefore, be able to visit her grave on my return. It was small comfort, and I wondered how my father felt, for old Mary had nursed him so long ago and, yet again, he had not been at home. It seemed court duties must come before everything.

'There is a parcel with the letter,' said Anne.

I fingered the small, cream package by my side. I had carried it around with me, unopened, all morning.

'Do you not wish to see what is inside?'

I wiped my hand across my dripping nose and tugged at the blue ribbon. The paper fell away, and inside I saw a small book of hours, its pages worn and the ribbon marker faded. On the first page, I read the words: *'For Nan: Remember me when thus you gaze, upon the writing on this page.'*

Anne laid her hand on my shoulder. 'Please stop. You will make me cry too. At least you still have your mother.'

'But you do not understand, Mrs Orcharde *was* a mother to me. She would play hood man blind, and comfort me in thunderstorms when I hid under the stairs. She would take me to the fair and help me to make flower garlands. In winter her hands were always red and worn and – oh! – she – she will not have worn the gloves I sent her for her New Year's gift.'

'Wait,' said Anne, 'there is something else in the parcel, something shiny. What is it?'

I fumbled in the paper and found a golden letter *"B"* with a bail, as if it had once hung from a ribbon. I gazed at it nestling in the palm of my hand. *"B"* for Bullen, I thought, wistfully. I read the attached note to myself: *'To my dearest Nan, wishing you a healthy and happy New Year, from your loving nurse, Mary Orcharde.'* I shut my eyes tight. I shall treasure this always, I thought, curling my fingers around the smooth gold.

'Let me see,' said Anne. 'Oh, it is beautiful. Perhaps you could wear it around your neck on a ribbon?'

I looked down miserably. 'Perhaps, one day.'

The door slowly opened, and Beatrice peeped around.

'I forgot my book. Anna, you will make yourself ill crying,' she said gently, sitting by my side. 'What can we do to help?'

Anne Brandon gave a little shrug as I showed Beatrice the book and golden letter.

'"*B*" for Beatrice,' she said, taking it and holding it up. I grabbed it back. It was mine, and it was precious. No one must touch it.

'Come,' she said, 'let us return to the palace. There is something I know will give you much comfort.'

We left Anne and returned across the cobbles, through the main gate, and up the great staircase. To my surprise, the chambers were quiet. In fact, they were deserted. Beatrice explained to the gentleman-at-arms that we had been asked to fetch Madame's writing materials. He opened the door without hesitation, and we found ourselves inside her intimate private chamber, full of treasures.

'Where is everyone? Where is Neutken?' I asked quietly, gazing around. Patou squawked on his perch and bobbed his head up and down in curiosity.

'All out,' said Beatrice, clicking the door shut. 'Margaret, the prince and her ladies are out hunting and the other girls are all at their lessons.' I must have looked unconvinced, for she sighed. 'It is true, I saw everyone clatter out of the courtyard with my own eyes and they will not return until the light fades.'

'Should we be here alone?' I asked, feeling like an intruder.

'I have to show you something,' said Beatrice, glancing

back over her shoulder and walking towards an ornate desk. She took a large key from the drawer and bent over a golden casket standing in a stone recess.

'What on earth are you doing?' I asked, looking around. We were forbidden to open any private boxes, let alone take keys from drawers. We could be dismissed.

She opened the creaking lid of the casket and gently lifted out a large piece of cloth. Then she carried it carefully over to the bed and started unfolding it, bit by bit. It was long and fell to the floor. She stood back. 'Well – what do you think?'

'What is it?'

'Look again,' said Beatrice.

I moved closer and stared at the dull cloth. 'It is a drawing – an outline of two men.'

'No, Anna, look closely. It is one man, but not any man.'

I stared again at the cloth and, no, I definitely saw the faint outline of two men.

'Look at the face,' she whispered.

I leaned closer. Was it the emperor?

'The face before you, Anna,' Beatrice crossed herself, 'is that of the Son of God himself.'

'What?' I said. 'That? But who drew it? And why is it drawn on a piece of old cloth?'

'No, no, this has not been drawn by an artist. This is an imprint.'

I stared at the cloth with its brown marks and stains.

'This cloth is a funeral shroud, the shroud that Christ's body was laid in when he was brought down from the cross and laid in the tomb. See, there are a back and front which, when folded, make the shape of the Holy Christ's body. There is the spear mark on his side, and there – see the brown marks around the head – that is where the bloody crown of thorns was placed.'

I gasped as I stared at the face of the old, bearded man before me. He looked nothing like the paintings I had seen.

'But he looks so very, very old,' I whispered, afraid my outspoken words might be blasphemous. 'How did it get here?'

'Through her marriage to Philibert, Madame inherited this along with many Savoy tapestries. It is their holiest and finest treasure, and used to be kept in the chapel at Chambery, the capital of Savoy. It was in June, twelve years ago now, when Madame and Philibert placed it there with great ceremony. They put it on display the following year, and many thousands of people came to view it, for it has miraculous powers. It will go back on display soon.'

'But Beatrice,' I said, staring at the face on the cloth in amazement. 'Is this really the Christ? The same image that St Veronica had printed on her veil when she wiped His face on the way to Calvary?'

She nodded. 'That veil is among the Pope's treasures, Anna.'

'But this – this – is surely the most important relic in Christendom, more important than a piece of the true Cross or drops of the Virgin Mary's milk. Does not the Holy Father wish to have it?'

Beatrice giggled. 'Of course he does, but this is the one treasure he cannot have. He covets it because they say if you touch the shroud, sorrow will vanish and you will gain great indulgences and many graces. It promises a long and happy life, full of favours on this earth, and in Heaven an eternity of bliss.'

'Who promises?'

She placed her hand on the cloth and closed her eyes tight in concentration. 'The pope, of course, he said he was spoken to in a dream. Now, close your eyes, make your wish, and your sorrow will vanish.'

As we both knelt, I put my hand out to the cloth, feeling the linen in my fingers. It did not feel very special, but I closed my eyes and prayed. Prayed for solace in my grief.

'Beatrice,' I opened one eye. 'Do people who have died

appear to you in dreams? People you have loved?'

She opened her eyes as she crossed herself. 'Of course. Sometimes my grandfather does, although I do not always see his face. I know it is him because I always awake feeling comforted. Why do you ask?'

I shrugged as I helped her fold the shroud and return it to its casket. As we left the chamber, Beatrice carrying the quills and inkpot, I realised my tears had stopped – for the moment at least. However, as night fell, and for nights to come, I cried myself to sleep. The Holy Shroud had not worked its magic.

• •

'Dead?' she asked, putting her hand up to stop the musicians playing. As the sound of the lutes faded away, we looked up from our books. Margaret sat staring at the swarthy man in front of her, his heavy fur robes covered in a sprinkling of snow. 'Is this true?'

'Indeed, it is true, Madame, some ten days ago on the ninth day of January. With your permission we wish to call a council meeting immediately to discuss this – this development.'

'I see,' said Margaret, rising from her desk, and crossing herself. 'May eternal rest be granted unto her.' The sound of 'amen' rippled through the chamber as we looked at each other.

'Dear God, this is a cruel winter,' she said, turning to her ladies. 'Death's hand seems to be with us at every turn. It touches queen and commoner alike.' She sank back down to her chair. Although Margaret hated the French, she did not extend this feeling to Anne of Brittany and was truly grieved.

'You could not have known sooner, Madame,' said Monsieur Chiévres, 'none of us could. News arrived as quickly as it could, but Blois is a great distance to ride in such foul weather.'

'Well, as you say, as you say. I shall, of course, order

mourning and Holy Masses for her soul,' said Margaret.

'The only people rejoicing at her death,' said Chiévres, 'are the Comtesse d'Angoulême, her precious son François, and his sister Marguerite. They remain at Cognac, delighted no son will now be born to old Louis. The French throne comes ever nearer to François, and the fickle court – once sycophantic to Anne of Brittany – now stumbles over itself in the rush to honour his mother. I gather King Louis is scandalised at François' behaviour, for he already acts as if he is king, squandering money and ordering everything to be made out of silver and gold for his personal use. It is disgraceful at a time such as this.'

'Was the end quick? Tell me plainly,' said Margaret.

'The duchess, Madame, had a very high fever, which worsened over the last five days. They say she writhed in agony with the blockage, but before she became delirious, she made her peace with God.'

'We must be grateful, then, for God's mercy,' said Margaret. 'Now come, let us proceed to this most urgent of councils.'

Once they had both gone, the chattering began.

'Well, well,' said Veronique, running to the door to check no one was outside listening. 'Anne of Brittany is dead, and King Louis is without a wife. No doubt he has locked himself away at Blois, weeping and wailing like a demented lunatic, for they say he truly loved her.' She threw herself onto a chair in a dramatic pose of grief.

'Maybe,' said Ariella, 'but I gather from my brother that King Louis said that should his wife die he would take another as soon as is decently possible. With just two girls as heirs, he is desperate for a son.'

'But he is old and decrepit,' said Christa, 'with foul breath, sagging jowls and yellow skin. Who would want him for a husband?'

'Ugh, how awful,' Fleur screwed up her nose, 'I would hate to be a queen or a duchess and marry such a hideous old man. To have him drool and pant over me, licking my face. As to having a child by him, I cannot imagine.'

Beatrice slammed her book shut. 'Can we please discuss something else?'

'How awful to have to produce a prince,' said Greta, ignoring her. 'Imagine being permanently *enceinte* until a son is born, to have to suffer much and then die like the duchess. For what?'

'I think an ugly man could be tolerated if it meant living in a palace, having a grand title and anything you wished for,' I said.

The girls stared at me, astonished.

'Anna,' said Beatrice, her voice low and tense, 'you would not say such a thing if you were really the wife of some wizened old man. You like beautiful things, not ugly things that smell of death and decay. As for childbirth – wait till you suffer its pangs, hour after hour in agony, crying to St Anne as you bring forth a useless, mewling girl when your husband demanded a son. Then, when you have barely recovered, to have to do it again and again and again, and hate it!'

Bonny jumped off my knee, alarmed by her outburst, and scratched at the door, eager to be let out.

'Beatrice, I am just making a point. Besides, girls grow up into women. Why should they be useless? Look at Margaret. She rules as well as any man – better – why do we have to have male rulers?'

'Because that is how it is,' said Edda. 'Royal girls and girls with ambitious families will be used for marriage alliances only. To increase the wealth of their families and to provide sons, if they can.'

'If they can?' I said, loftily. 'Why, that would be of no concern to me. Boys run rife in my family, and my Bullen and Howard lineage is full of them. My Howard mother brought my father a child almost every year. When I marry, I will have a house full of lusty sons.'

'Anna,' said Greta, 'you have not even begun your

courses. How can you even talk of having sons?'

'I will start them,' I replied, my dark eyes glaring. 'Soon.'
I looked across to Beatrice and watched as she suddenly left
the chamber in tears. Now what was the matter with the
tiresome girl?

*   *

The wonderful Feast of the Purification of our Blessed
Lady fell on a crisp February day. We heard from Margaret's
ambassadors in England that the king had rewarded many of
those who had fought for him in France with new honours.
During the magnificent ceremony held at Lambeth Palace,
he also honoured the victors over Scotland. My grandfather,
the old Earl of Surrey, had done marvellously well at Flodden
and the dukedom was at last restored – a cause of great celebration for my mother and family. The new duke now owned
two castles, and eighteen manors. The Howards were back
in favour and there was much to celebrate at their manor
in Lambeth.

A cause for not celebrating was the creation of Charles
Brandon as Duke of Suffolk. We were not surprised to hear
how many at court, my father included, were furious to hear
of Brandon's new title, but the Duke of Buckingham was
near apoplectic. How could the king make a commoner a
duke for no other reason than he always let the King either
win at tennis or a wager? Everyone knew that when Brandon
jousted he made sure his horse stayed close to the barrier,
rather than run wide, thus allowing the king to show off
with a hit every time. It was preposterous! However, since the
king had executed Edmund de la Pole, Earl of Suffolk and
Yorkist pretender, the year before, the title remained vacant
and he now bestowed it on this even bigger fraud. It was
insufferable! Brandon proved he had no skill in politics – his
only talent was in sport and violating women. Now, as his
wealth increased to huge proportions, he found himself the
chief nobleman of England. Buckingham, utterly disgusted,

deliberately stayed away from the ceremony and took himself off hunting.

With a noble title, the old rumour of a marriage between Charles Brandon and Margaret began circulating yet again, and the king wrote to her to ask her plainly if this rumour was true. What were her true intentions? He knew what she said in public, but what were her private thoughts? She wrote bluntly stating the new duke must look elsewhere for a wife, and she had no desire of ever marrying again. It was her final word.

Buckingham flew into a further fury when Thomas Wolsey – as predicted – was made Bishop of Lincoln. His wealth had increased considerably and, on the advice of his physician, he had rented from the Knights Hospitallers, a large site of two thousand acres on the River Thames. No one thought it was for his health, certainly not Buckingham. Why, Wolsey was even considering his chances of accepting a cardinal's hat from Rome, and his name was heard more and more throughout the courts of Europe. A proud man such as Buckingham could suffer no more. No, Wolsey and Suffolk were cut from the same coarse cloth, and he hated them both. The only difference between the odious pair was that Wolsey was ambitious for power and glory, and Suffolk ambitious for a life of ease. However, both required wealth and the king's ear to achieve what they desired.

On a merrier note, the preparations for the war against France were well under way, with King Ferdinand, the emperor, and Margaret promising their full support to England. The king continued to build more ships, each bigger and better than the last, for the French were already seeking a quarrel and had raided the Sussex coast. Infuriated by their activities, King Henry bragged that it would not be long before the power of France would be crushed like a slug beneath his shoe forever.

Privately, he was well content, for he had taken to his bed a mistress – the lovely Elizabeth Blount. Just fourteen years old, the daughter of Lord Mountjoy, I heard this news from my sister, who said Elizabeth – or Little Bessie as she was known – was very talented at music and had captured the king's heart. Whenever he wished to visit her privately at Jericho Priory in Essex, his courtiers joked that he 'was going to Jericho.' Before long, the phrase 'oh, go to Jericho,' had become something of a curse, since the gentlemen who accompanied the king on these secret visits had to wait, day and night, with nothing to do while he took his pleasure. Apparently, Queen Katherine knew of this place, but it was never discussed. She knew of Jericho and the tower in Greenwich Park where her husband kept his wine and 'delicacies'. I thought of poor Rosaline, but however hurt Katherine felt, she would not hear a single criticism of the man she adored.

❧   ❧

'Beatrice, they have returned,' I said, rubbing the window-pane and gazing down on the fresh snow covering the palace courtyard. I watched as the prince and his companions cantered noisily through the gate and churned the snow up into a fine spray. The flared nostrils of their sweating horses blew warm air like dragon's breath, as grooms ran out and threw rugs over the horses steaming flanks. Great hunting dogs barked and strained at their leashes as a large sack, tossed down onto the snow, spilled forth the bodies of various dead fowl. The huntsmen, sliding on the icy ground, pulled the snarling dogs back.

'Look at Jean de Saxe,' said Edda, over my shoulder, 'he might only be twelve, but he is already so handsome.'

'The Duc Sforza is far more appealing,' said Maria, pushing her aside, 'and no mere boy. How I wish he might skate with me.'

The prince took a cup of warming wine, and the surrounding company toasted him with a raucous cheer: 'Our prince!'

He smiled in amusement. It was St Oswald's day, his fourteenth birthday, and he was considered a man at last.

'Quickly,' said Beatrice, 'let us go down.'

I put on my blue coat and picked up my red squirrel bonnet.

In the main reception hall, on the opposite side of the building, we took our places with the Countess of Hochstrate and all the ladies-in-waiting.

The gentleman usher banged the floor with his heavy stick. 'Silence for Her Imperial and Royal Highness, the Dowager Duchess of Savoy and their most Serene Princesses!'

Margaret appeared in a long, black velvet coat, an ermine Flemish hood and matching ermine gloves. Behind her walked the three princesses dressed in dark blue, ermine-trimmed coats, accompanied by Lady Beaumont wrapped warmly in a woollen cloak.

'Rise, ladies,' said Margaret, fastening her glove, 'we have a cold day of it, but the mist is lifting, and the sun is trying to break through. The prince and his companions have returned and will join us shortly.'

'Anne,' said Anne Brandon, 'you will not let me fall, will you?'

I agreed we would hold hands together. I did not tell her that I had not skated much before either, since we had been forbidden to walk on the frozen moat at Hever.

When the prince appeared with his band of companions, we swept low in reverence. I caught his eye, and he proffered a slight smile before sweeping aside his great beaver hat and kissing his aunt on both cheeks. 'Madame, I thank you for organising this celebration. Last year you provided a boar hunt in the *Grôte Markt,* and this year a skating party. My companions and I will accompany you, by your gracious leave.'

I sidled up to Maria as she tucked her hair into her black fur cap. 'A boar hunt?'

'Yes, special viewing stands were built in the *Grôte Markt* to enable the crowds to watch. However, a stand collapsed, and several people were injured. Then, the prince's horse, slipping and sliding on the snow and sand, unseated him, and he fell. He did spear the boar in the end, but poor Margaret was beside herself. The emperor, who was present, said it would make a man of him, but this year Margaret has organised something a little less perilous.'

Outside the palace, the most beautifully decorated sleighs waited to transport our party down to the canal. One was shaped like a ship with masts and sails, one like a dragon, and yet another sported a castle turret. Each was upholstered with sumptuous velvet and fur, and I stood, enchanted, as the grey horses wearing yellow and blue plumes, stamped their hooves in the snow. As we took our seats the trumpets blasted, and the horses, led by their grooms, moved silently off.

Church bells chimed in celebration as we progressed to the *Veetmarkt* and the *Grôte Markt*, the Belfry and the Cloth Hall. Past St Rombouts, we continued to the hall of the Great Council of Mechelen, where many flags and banners fluttered in the chilly breeze. On this special day, the area along the route had been closed, and all markets ceased to trade. However, it still did not stop people wishing to see the spectacle, and they cheered and waved from the bridges.

We were to skate at the *Vismarkt*, and it had been specially cleaned and scrubbed, for Margaret had ordered that no trace of smell must pervade the air. In fact, the fish market had been cancelled since the previous week while the cleaning took place.

When we arrived at the banks of the canal, the flags and pennants in the prince's colours of white, yellow and red flapped in the breeze, and in a grand pavilion, maids served hot food and drink. The prince and his companions were quick to have their skates tied on and soon pushed off to the centre of the frozen canal. Margaret and her ladies, meanwhile, took their seats in one of the larger booths and were served goblets of warm hypocras.

The Countess of Hochstrate announced we could sit or skate as we wished, but she, herself, would not be skating today.

'That,' said Beatrice, 'is because last year her skate became unlaced and she tumbled onto the ice. She lay sprawled out like a great, wet fish.'

'I cannot wait to try skating on a canal,' I said, tying the ribbons of my bonnet beneath my chin. 'Is it hard?'

She shrugged. 'I do not know. I have skated since I was a child of three and have no recollection of ever learning. Everyone in the Low Countries skates for recreation or necessity. Since the River *Dijle* flows around the city, the people use these waterways, when frozen, as roads, gliding along on their skates as they go about their business. Now, let me show you how to put these on.' She took the skates from the servant girl who stood shivering with cold.

'You can see how the metal blades – sometimes made of bone – lie close to the ground and the wooden platform is attached to your boots with these criss-cross straps, like so. Now, make sure you secure them tightly. You do not want to fall on the ice!'

I did as she said and saw that Greta had already taken Anne Brandon's arm, and that they were standing on the edge of the icy canal. Anne did not look at all happy and stood clinging on to the wooden barrier, her warm breath rapid in the cold air.

'Now,' continued Beatrice, 'remember to keep your blades upright, push off with one skate – like this – and make a smooth glide.' She slid off onto the frozen water. 'Come on,' she laughed, turning in a circle.

I boldly moved on to the ice.

'Stand straight, Anna.'

I moved towards her, and she took my gloved hand. It was good to see Beatrice laugh for once.

'Push and glide, push and glide,' she said, as I stared down in concentration.

'No, look up,' she waved as Ariella swept smoothly past, followed by the ladies and gentlemen of the court.

'Now, remember,' said Beatrice, 'it is important that the nobility appear elegant when skating. There must be poise and grace. Look at the ladies there.' A group glided effortlessly past.

Before long, with the aid of her hand, I had discovered the rhythm of gliding. I began to laugh. George would love this! I glanced up to see Anne Brandon, with Greta and Veronique on either side, now enjoying herself immensely. Her cheeks were flushed red, and she had already discarded her fur cap.

'Let me try alone,' I urged, dropping Beatrice's hand. I pushed off and found I could skate unaided. I held my chin high, straightened my shoulders and was away.

Beatrice pulled up beside me. 'Put your arms behind your back, like this.' She did an elegant turn, straight as a post, and skated off to join the other girls.

I pushed off again and soon found that I had a natural balance and grace. Up and down I skated, boldly striking out and avoiding the others as best I could. However, I could not avoid the prince's companions as they rowdily skated up and down, dipping under each other's legs and trying to play leapfrog. No dignified elegance there, I thought, as one of them brushed past, causing me to wobble. The prince laughed and cried out to them in great merriment, for they had now formed a chain, with him at the front. Margaret waved, clearly indulging this horseplay, but as the young men gathered speed, I, unfortunately, skated across their path. There was a violent crash as we collided, and I landed on the ice with a hard thump, more shocked than hurt. The prince skated over and stopped abruptly, his blades making a fine spray of ice.

'Forgive them, *demoiselle*, that was most unworthy behaviour,' he apologised, holding out his fur-gloved hand.

I tried to take it but slipped down again with a bump.

'Sir – forgive me – I cannot rise,' I said.

The prince stared down, his long, thin, face pale despite the exertion. His companions skated back, and he flicked his head impatiently for one of them to haul me to my feet. I scrambled up, and as the young man held me, I brushed down my ice-spattered coat.

'Leave us,' commanded the prince. His friends left with a bow and skated back towards the pavilion.

'Up until that moment you skated very elegantly,' he said. 'Would you accompany me?'

I was taken by surprise. 'Oh, yes indeed, sir, I would be most honoured, but I am not very skilled.'

'But you were skating with some speed and confidence. They do say a person skates and rides a horse in much the same manner as they might walk or dance, either with grace or not. Everyone has noticed how gracefully you move.'

I smiled up at the prince and took his proffered arm. We glided along in silence until he spoke. 'Do you think me dull and slow?'

I hardly knew how to answer such a peculiar question, but before I could speak, he continued.

'I am not. I hear everything and forget nothing – like my grandfather. Not a letter or dispatch comes to the palace without me knowing its content. I have a passion for trivial details, and sometimes I lie awake at night, waiting to see what dispatches have arrived. I have this great hunger to know everything that happens within the court. It is like some devil within me, a fixation, and I cannot rest.'

'But I do, too, sir! I have a great longing and thirst for knowledge, and new things.'

His mouth twitched in a faint smile. 'I find daily minutiae fascinating, and one day, when I am ruler of the Netherlands, this will prove most useful. Now, tell me, what talk is there from the English court? Tell me something I have not heard from my ambassadors.'

I thought hard for a moment.

'Well, sir, Mother tells me many at court are shocked at the elevation of Charles Brandon to the Dukedom of Suffolk, and my Lord Duke of Buckingham is in a fit of pique.'

'Everyone knows that,' scoffed the prince. 'Try again.'

'The new Bishop of Lincoln, Thomas Wolsey, has bought an enormous plot of land to build a great house on. Father has seen the plans and says it is more like a palace and will outrival the king's court.'

'Not of interest,' he said. 'Is there nothing else?'

'The king has another mistress.'

'Oh?' He turned to face me.

'Why, yes, sir, they say she is a lady-in-waiting to the queen, and goes by the name of Jane Popincourt.' I smiled broadly, feeling pleased with my worldly talk.

'So, the king presumes to insult my aunt again with one of her own household.'

I quickly realised my mistake. 'Oh, no, no, sir, it is a great secret. Nobody else knows.'

'So how do you know?'

'From my sister, Mary, sir, for she wrote to me saying that she had heard the king's companions jest —'

The Prince stared ahead. I had said the wrong thing entirely.

'You did not heed what I said to you in the library, *demoiselle*,' he said. 'You should see and hear everything, but repeat nothing, particularly gossip.'

I felt chastised and trapped. 'Sir, I was hoping to amuse you. I am sorry,' I said, remembering what an obnoxious boy he was.

'You must learn to think before you speak and to be aware of the consequences of what you say,' he said, doffing his cap as a group of giggling young ladies skated passed.

'Well, it is of no matter. I know of this Mistress Popincourt.' I felt my cheeks glow warm and fell silent. We continued to skate, and although aware that people were staring, I continued to hold on to the prince's arm.

'My Lord,' I said, desperate to change the subject, 'my mother, father, and sister will be attending the Princess Mary at Calais, and I cannot wait to see them again. It has been so long and I have much I wish to tell them.' I hoped that speaking of family matters might place me on safer ground.

The prince sighed. He was not interested in my family. 'Ah, my wife. One day, when King Ferdinand dies – probably of his asthma – I shall become the King of Castile. My wife and I shall visit Spain on a glorious progress.'

'Oh, sir, I would love to see Spain, myself. Queen Katherine tells my mother that it is a beautiful country, with warm, balmy nights and gardens heavy with the scent of orange groves. The skies are deep blue and cloudless, and although it is hot outside, the houses are cool. She describes how the Alhambra Palace boasts magnificent galleries, all painted in ochre, orange and rose gold, with rose covered walkways to avoid the sun. In the morning, when the sunlight seeps through the white wooden screens, it leaves a dappled light on the cool, marble floors.' I fell silent, conscious that I had talked too much.

The prince's dry lips twitched. 'Very prettily said. You make me long to be in Spain myself, although here is my home and here I wish to remain – for now. I hear from Signor de Vaca that your Spanish is coming along quite well. He has singled you out as one of his more talented pupils. I cannot pronounce words correctly in French let alone Spanish, but I do have an ear for languages. I do hear the words and continue to study hard. My grandfather Maximilian had the same problem with speech and was practically dumb until he was five years old. I would always prefer to listen rather than talk.'

I smiled. 'Sir, I am afraid I talk too much.'

We came to a jolting halt by the wooden barrier, and a page leant over with two goblets of warm, spiced ale and a tray of wafers. The prince offered a goblet to me, and I took it, watching the steam rise.

'Sir, I do not speak Spanish; in truth, I do not. French is

the language I excel in.'

He bit into a wafer, the crumbs flaking down his tunic and cloak. I then watched as he frantically ate one after the other, rapidly cramming them into his mouth, and I could see why he had the reputation of guzzling down anything put in front of him.

'And what plans do your family have for you?' he said, spraying crumbs and then wiping his full mouth.

'I am not privy to their plans, sir, and I go where they bid me.'

'But suppose, since it is within my gift, you remain here and join my new wife's household instead of remaining at my aunt's court? I am sure the princess would like an English companion, and I intend to have young blood at my new court myself. I am tired of old, meddling women and decrepit councillors.'

I did not know what to say, but I had heard how the princess was most extravagant and liked to have her ladies attired in the latest, daring fashions. And although Margaret had proved kind, it would be far more exciting to serve a young princess, free from the troublesome cares of state and not forever dressed in widow's weeds.

'Of course,' said the prince, 'I would have to discuss it with my aunt for she is in charge of her ladies and maids, and she would not thank me for meddling with her household. But as this would concern my future wife and her happiness, I cannot see how she could refuse me.'

I stared at his emerald and gold earrings as they glinted in the winter sunlight. His face had softened, and behind the boasting, there was really just a fragile boy.

'Why, indeed, sir, it would be the greatest honour to be in your wife's service, if Madame agreed. My family would be delighted beyond measure. But – why do you take this trouble, sir? Why do you deign to talk to me when other, more worthy ladies seek your attention?'

He shrugged. 'Because of all the simpering ladies and

maids around my aunt, only you appear to be willing to speak your mind and tell the truth. Of course, you talk too much – it is a female weakness, and it is irritating – and you have not yet learnt discretion and diplomacy. But it is to be expected of one so young,' he added, pompously. 'I also find you amusing, running about chasing that little dog you have. I have watched you from the window, shouting at it to come to you and then becoming quite cross when it runs off, stamping your foot in irritation. Oh, yes, I have seen you, and you have made me laugh. You have quite a hot temper when you think no one is watching. But you do not fool me. I think you are quite shrewd inside that dark little head of yours, playing the willing maid to get what you want.'

He handed his empty goblet back to the servant and sig-nalled for his companions to join him. They skated over and bowed low. As the prince skated away he turned and doffed his great hat to me. 'Well, Mademoiselle Bullen – enjoy your dreams of Spain…'

●　●

Shrovetide was the last day of court feasting before the court was shriven in readiness for Lent. On Ash Wednesday, before Mass began, we knelt before the altar as Madame, the prince and the royal children took the holy ashes from the dean of the chapel. I thought of Mrs Orcharde, for I held the prayer book she had given me in my hands, and turned the well-worn pages.

I looked at Beatrice with the grey mark from the ashes on her forehead, and saw that her eyes were squeezed tight.

'What are you praying for?' I whispered, close to her ear.

She opened one eye. 'I am praying that something will not come to pass.'

'What?' I asked surprised, but she put her head down on her hands, as the Countess of Hochstrate turned round with a frown.

'Naught,' said Beatrice under her breath.

I nudged her arm and smiled, not knowing what she was talking about, and then shut my eyes piously in prayer.

*   *

Throughout the holy season of Lent, we were kept busy at the court at Mechelen with almsgiving to the poor, visits to the sick at the infirmary and other such acts of mercy. The regent had repaired to the court at Brussels with some of her ladies to attend to the wedding details of Princess Isabeau, and thus ensure matters would be ready by Trinity Sunday, the twelfth of June. We, meanwhile, attended Mass twice a day, with no dancing or gaiety, but instead the reading of religious books. Several times we visited the *Béguinage*, but this time the gardens were full of snowdrops and the evening light lingered a little longer. Silently, we crept about performing our Lenten duties, moaning that we would much rather be dancing and having fun. However, none of us realised just how much pain Margaret was suffering. I did not find out until later, on her return, when I watched in horror as a lady carefully lifted a tabard of rough sacking from Margaret's back. When she told me that the sores were causing Madame to bleed, she sent me off to the infirmary to fetch a rose petal paste to soothe the skin. On my return, as one of her ladies took the tabard away, the soothing paste was applied. Margaret, somewhat embarrassed, explained that she offered up the pain as penance for the soul of her dear, dead husband and brother, and I was to tell no one. She told me Queen Katherine, in England, also wore such a garment in the hope that her suffering would please God and he would send her a son. It did not.

*   *

Late March brought blustery winds that blew the petals off the narcissus, and swirled our gowns and veils around as we strolled in the palace garden. Margaret walked in front with her ladies and I, with some of the other maids, followed behind. As we continued down the gravel path and into the long arbour, I could hear Margaret discussing the coming wedding of Princess Isabeau.

'But such a solemn occasion takes months and months of arranging,' she said to Lady Saillant, holding a hand to her veil as it fluttered in the breeze. I noticed her usually neat nails were ragged at the sides.

'Why such sudden haste? I would have preferred at least six months to arrange things in their proper place. We have been a year preparing for the prince's marriage, and I fear that Isabeau's wedding will not do sufficient honour to our house. Well, I suppose at least her wedding gown is magnificent, and two hundred and fifty thousand gulden have been raised for her dowry. What of the maids' gowns?'

Lady Saillant passed the fabric samples in her hand to Margaret. 'Everything is accomplished. They will look quite beautiful. Fresh flowers will be sent to Brussels on the day, to arrive no later than nine in the morning. Parties will be arriving between ten and eleven of the clock.'

Margaret took the samples, glanced at them distractedly and handed them back.

I smiled at Beatrice as we walked behind. 'Did you see?' I asked, linking my arm through hers. 'Such beautiful silk! I cannot wait, can you?'

Beatrice put a hand up to her hair and swept it from her face. 'If you say so,' she said. 'God, I hate windy weather.'

We walked along in silence and it was obvious that, yet again, she was in an ill-temper. She was always out of sorts these days.

'I have asked,' said Margaret, 'for the princess to stay here for another year, for thirteen is too young for a bride. Am I foolish, Lady Saillant?'

The lady shook her head. 'It is never foolish to want our children close.'

'I have some private concerns, too,' confided Margaret, 'regarding King Christian's behaviour, which I have expressed to my father. Do you not think he is too old at thirty-three? My father says that it matters not, for this way he shall have Hapsburg dominance in the Baltic, something he has been labouring towards for some time.'

I walked close behind her, keeping an eye on Bonny for she was apt to run off into the shrubbery after squirrels.

'Indeed, Madame,' said Lady Saillant, 'but do not worry, for I hear he is a good-looking man, full-bearded, gifted and educated. I think the princess will do well from this match.'

'But,' continued Margaret, avoiding Bonny as she scampered across her path, 'this Christian is a man much concerned with the common people – which, of course, is a good thing – but he does not share the same concern for his own nobles. It is unwise to alienate them, and I worry that he is not popular with those in power around him.' As she was speaking she stopped abruptly, for at the end of the arbour there hovered a deputation of men. They swept low in greeting.

'Ah, Signor de Lanuza, my greetings to you, and you, Signor Gilaberte! We are engaged in wedding talk.'

Both men clutched their hats in their hands and stepped forward to kneel and kiss Margaret's outstretched hand.

'Now, ambassadors, to what do I owe this pleasure? I trust your King Ferdinand is well?'

I quickly picked Bonny up, for she was sniffing at one of the gentlemen's boots.

The smaller, stooped gentleman moved forward, appearing rather uncomfortable, and gave a nervous cough. 'Madame, we have been sent to find you immediately, since there is a matter of extreme urgency and delicacy that cannot wait.'

'Well, gentlemen,' Margaret opened her arms wide, 'you have found me.' Her ladies laughed. The gentlemen hesitated.

'Come now, you may speak freely in front of my ladies,' she said, turning. 'What is it you have to say, gentlemen?'

The larger man cleared his throat. 'My lady, I must inform you that your father and King Ferdinand of Spain have made a secret truce with France.'

Margaret stared blankly at the gentleman, who kept his nervous eyes fixed firmly on the ground.

'They – they have done what?'

'A truce, Madame,' came the stiff reply. 'England now stands alone against France – although she does not yet know it. King Louis has made his peace with the pope and is no longer under threat of excommunication. It is –'

'What exactly are you telling me?' asked Margaret. 'A treaty was signed here at Mechelen last April – a binding treaty – between the emperor, King Ferdinand, Pope Leo and King Henry, against the power of France. Is that not so?'

'Madame,' said the gentleman, 'the alliance has broken up and England stands alone and unaided. And there is worse: the emperor has agreed that should King Henry's sister Margaret not wish to marry King Louis – and Scotland seems to be reluctant here – your niece Princess Eleanora will marry him. Your father did offer you yourself, but...' He glanced nervously at his companion, desperate for support. 'By your leave, Madame, may – may I tell you this in private, as it is somewhat delicate?'

'Speak!' commanded Margaret.

We stood in tense silence.

The gentleman straightened up. 'King Louis has refused you on the grounds that you' – and here he cleared his throat again – 'that you are too old and might not bear him the heir he crav...' His voice petered out like a snuffed candle as Margaret turned white with anger.

'Too old? Too old, by God!' she cried. 'How many times must I say we will have *no* dealings with France?'

'But, Madame,' added the gentleman hastily, 'if Princess Eleanora marries Louis, any son she has will be the heir to the throne of France. With Prince Charles married to England, and Eleanora married to France, the prince would rule over a united empire under one ruler – himself.'

'And where, might I ask, is honour in this? Since when do we break our word and rend our treaty in two? I gave my word to King Henry that we would wage war on France.'

'Madame, with respect, it was your father who gave his word, and his word has now changed,' replied his companion.

'You imply that my father is a double-dealer and a twister?'

There was silence. That was precisely their meaning.

'I see,' said Margaret. 'And is this *treaty* signed?'

'Signed and sealed by your father.'

'But surely, gentlemen,' she pointed out, 'such agreements can be broken on a whim, can they not?'

Silence again.

'Then tell me of the war. Are we not sworn to attack France this summer? Sir Robert Wingfield informs me that King Henry has gone far with his preparations for the campaign. Who will now inform him of this betrayal? Will you Signor Gilaberte? Or you, Signor de Lanuza?'

Both men stood embarrassed.

Margaret, losing her composure, put both hands up to her face in despair. 'This news cannot be true,' she sobbed, 'we have made a promise, a bond. To be forsworn, thus, is more than I can bear. And my children, my young wards: Eleanora, Charles, Isabeau, and Marie – I shall lose them in one fell swoop, my little ones. My greatest care.' She slumped into the arms of Lady Saillant, as we looked on, aghast.

'Ladies,' said one of the gentlemen, 'take the regent away where she can be private, and tend to her. She has suffered a grave shock.' He was obviously relieved that this nightmare of an audience had ended.

• •

Back in her own chambers Margaret would not cease crying.

'Ferdinand! My father said that snake would do

something like this – put a bridle on King Henry. Now he has dragged my father to Hell as well. Where is the English ambassador, Thomas Spinelly? He must know nothing of this. Word cannot get back to England with news of this – this treachery.'

Her chief ladies of the privy chamber bustled to and fro, fetching warm milk as she sat distraught at her desk. I entered with a small terracotta jug containing spring flowers, hoping to cheer her, and placed them on her desk, in silence.

Margaret gave a wistful smile. 'Thank you, Anna, but it will take more than these flowers to mend a broken word sworn in good faith. Tell me, what age are you now?'

I told her.

'My little Eleanora is not much older than you. I cannot bear the thought of her wedded to King Louis. I would rather have sacrificed myself. It is shameful. How can I tell her?' She began weeping again. After some moments, she looked up, her eyes blazing, and banged the desktop with her fist. 'God's blood, this is Monsieur Chiévres' doing, for he ever undermines me and seeks to influence the prince to all things French. I am not such a fool as to be unaware of how many courtiers in the prince's household would prevent his marriage, and cause mischief with England. By God, I wish I could deal them a blow they would not forget.'

I picked up the music book that I had left on a chair. This, indeed, was treachery. Was no man to be trusted?

'I do not understand my father,' continued Margaret, wringing her hands. 'He has undermined my political efforts when I thought we were as one mind and heart, that of friendship with England. France is making peace only to tear the other powers apart. Can my father not see this? England is the greater threat to France, not Spain, or even Austria, and it is to England's mast we have bound ourselves, come fair or foul weather. I will not make a shipwreck of my conscience. No, no, this cannot be. I must write to King Ferdinand and my father.' She sent for her secretary and sat back at her desk.

The dispatches to Margaret from King Ferdinand of Spain explained that there must have been some gross misunderstanding. He agreed that it was well-known that Margaret and her father were of one mind, and he was shocked how she now complained of this peace with France. Was it not what she and the emperor had both agreed? If not, it was too late and on no account must she try and dissuade him. Surely she must see that it would bring peace instead of war, and great rewards to the young prince? It soon became a painful realisation to her that the emperor had acted on his own account, without any regard to her wishes, and she felt utterly duped. To add to her horror, she also discovered that King Ferdinand had had the audacity to secretly approach her confessor and urge him to sway her mind, in the confessional, towards France. She was deeply offended by this breach of trust and had the confessor dismissed from court. Little by little, she knew her authority was ebbing away. It would not be long now before Prince Charles's minority came to an end. She would be subject to him, and his advisors would use him to their advantage.

Letters from the emperor himself were equally unsettling, and he told her that he had now suggested to King Henry that he thought it might be wiser if the marriage between Prince Charles and the king's sister be postponed for a little while. He was not sure that Calais was the most suitable place for the wedding and now preferred Antwerp or Mechelen itself. As to the coming war, he informed Margaret that there would no longer be one. King Henry, of course, was not to know this, for although the emperor had taken thousands of pounds off him already to pay for his extra forces in the forthcoming campaign, he hoped, by delaying, to gain even more gold. With luck, he would continue to be paid, although he had no intention now of fighting. Margaret was bound by oath to say nothing of the matter to King Henry, for as yet he knew nothing of her father's duplicity. Pope Leo also refused to say anything, and was happy to allow King

Henry to keep thinking that the campaign was going to plan. The king was well and truly tricked and the emperor and King Ferdinand were highly pleased with themselves. It was triumph of deceit and Margaret was appalled. In fact, I had never seen her look so desolate.

*   *

We were glad when Lent was over and the court able to dress, at last, in its finest clothes and celebrate the great feast of Easter. Laughter filled the galleries as casement windows were flung open to air the chambers and fresh meadowsweet and lavender were strewn upon the floors. Five days earlier, we had heard that King Henry's sister, Margaret of Scotland, had given birth to a bonny boy named Alexander, Duke of Ross. She retired to Stirling Castle with her new baby and her young boy, James, refusing the marriage proposals of both King Louis and the emperor. Now that his sister had two fine sons, King Henry felt sure that his turn was, by the grace of God, next. Desperate to please her husband, Queen Katherine travelled yet again to pray at the shrine of Walsingham, in Norfolk, certain that this time she would succeed. Meanwhile, the regent sent a beautiful gold cup as a christening present to the Scottish queen, and a letter of congratulations to King Henry, and raised her own spirits by busying herself with the preparations for Princess Isabeau's wedding.

Chapter Eight

'Light and shadows by turn.'

Mechelen and Brussels
Spring and Summer, 1514

A heart-rending cry filled the air. We stopped our dancing, stared at each other, and scurried to the door of Margaret's outer chamber.

'What on earth is the matter?' asked Christa, as we crowded around.

'Shush,' whispered Fleur, 'I am trying to listen.'

Anne Brandon stared up at me, and I put my finger to my lips.

We heard Beatrice's voice. 'I cannot, Madame,' she wailed, 'do not make me do this, I beg of you.'

Margaret's voice, in contrast, sounded low and soothing. 'Come, come now. There is nothing I can do, or would even wish to do. You will go from here with a goodly sum of gold and my grateful thanks for the service you have done me.'

Our hands flew to our mouths.

Veronique gasped. 'Did you hear that?'

'Gold,' said Anne Brandon, her eyes wide, 'she said gold and service. Is Beatrice a spy? Is she?'

Before I could answer, the door flew open and we jumped back as Beatrice, distraught, ran from the chamber. One of Margaret's ladies appeared. 'Would you come in please?' I wondered if I had forgotten to do some task and quickly followed her. Margaret was seated at her desk holding a letter as I curtsied low to her.

'Ah, Anna, please, sit here on this stool.' She turned, and I saw her ladies sitting in the corner, eyes cast down. 'There is something you should know. Beatrice will be leaving my service and returning home to be married. Is this not wonderful news?'

Married? Why had she said nothing to me?

'Unfortunately, as you saw, she is deeply distressed by the decision to go forward with the match, although she knew her family had arranged this matter a year ago. The gentleman in question is a count – a wealthy and influential gentleman with a large property in Antwerp, where Beatrice's family live, and a grand château in Leuven. She is most fortunate indeed.'

'But, Madame, when is she to leave?' I asked, shocked.

'Her family wants her to return to Antwerp immediately, for the wedding is to take place within the month. I shall, of course, be giving her a substantial gift, for I will be sorry to see her leave. However, it is her parents' wish and I have no intention of interfering, for this is a family matter. Besides, she is at an age when she must start her own household and family.'

I did not know what to say.

'Do not look so dull, Anna, this is supposed to be happy news,' said Margaret, trying to sound cheerful. 'Come, I know you will be sorry to lose your friend, but this will come to you one day. You must all leave me and return to your families – or new husbands.'

'Madame, forgive me for asking, but why is she so upset?

Does she not like this match?'

Neutken, shuffling a pack of playing cards, shook her head, as Margaret rose from her chair and turned her back to me.

'Fie, liking and not liking are but a nonsense. I am sure she will "like" him in time, for this is a magnificent match worthy of her family, for it brings great honour.' She moved towards her parrot proffering a piece of dried fruit. He squawked with delight and stepped onto her outstretched arm. 'Marriage is rarely a matter of personal happiness, as you well know, but a chance to bring wealth, comfort and security to one's family and kin. She must not be so ungracious.' She stroked the parrot's plumage and placed him carefully back on his perch. 'We must do that which we are born to do,' she continued, her voice trembling with emotion. 'Soon, as you are aware, my dear Isabeau will be married to the King of Denmark, and Princess Marie will return again to the court at Hungary. Eleanora must go to King Louis. Charles will go one day to Spain. Thus, we lose those we love. Remember. Now, please go to Beatrice and comfort her.' Without turning around, she raised her hand and signalled for me to leave.

Back in the maid's chamber, I picked up Bonny and immediately set about searching the palace, gallery and gardens until I eventually found Beatrice by the garden house. At the sound of my steps, she turned around with a jump.

'Beatrice, Margaret has just told me. Why did you not say? Why did you keep this from me, your dearest friend?'

She clutched me tightly. 'Oh, Anna, I could not bear to imagine this might actually happen one day. I tried to shut the horror out of my mind and pretend it was not there.'

'But, Beatrice,' I said, as we sat down on the bench, 'how wonderful to marry a count and be mistress of your own household.' I tried to sound cheerful, but did not feel it.

'Did Madame tell you of this count?' she asked.

I shook my head and put my hand down to stroke Bonny. 'No, I do not suppose she did. He is forty years old, with a face scarred by smallpox. He drinks, has had two wives previously and beats his dogs. I did not expect to love my husband, but I did hope I might find someone to like and respect.'

I felt shocked. 'Forty? But that is old,' I replied, forgetting how I had thought the emperor, in his middle fifties, charismatic and attractive. 'Surely your family would not betroth you to such a man? They would not want you to be unhappy in this way.'

She gave a small laugh. 'Well, they have. My father is an ambitious man, more interested in a man's wealth than my feelings. When I dared to show my horror, he was furious. He said marriage is of such immense family importance that it cannot be left to the vagaries of my personal likes or dislikes. He raged at me, saying houses could be made or broken depending on whom they were affiliated to, and that this was a match of great benefit. He refused to be forsworn.'

I stared at her, aghast, as she continued.

'I was sent here to learn how to be such a man's wife and chattel, and now my father feels that I am at an age when I should honour this match. He said that as seventeen is considered the ideal age to have children, I will have time to get accustomed to my new state. I should rejoice. Rejoice? I prayed and prayed that this match might never happen, but I gather my betrothed is anxious to have this matter settled. My God, he is old enough to be my father!'

'He is very, very old,' I agreed, picking up Bonny and sitting her on my knee. 'I have often wondered what you were praying so hard for in church,' I said.

'Yes,' she said, in a small voice, 'and I prayed on the Holy Shroud, God forgive me, that some ill might befall the count. Now, I am mired in sin and must go to confession. Here at court, I see so many attractive young men – particularly among the prince's companions – and I hoped, beyond hope, that I would be matched to someone at least nearer my own age.'

'But Beatrice,' I said, 'fondness is possible, surely? Look at how Margaret's mother adored her Maximilian. That marriage was arranged, yet they were inseparable.'

'Yes, but at least Anne of Brittany had twelve suitors to choose from and chose the one she favoured the most. She had the faint hope of marrying a man she found attractive. I had no such choice.'

I remembered something. 'Do you recall me telling you of Uncle Howard's wedding at Thornbury?'

She nodded.

'Well, my sister writes of how young Mary Stafford, after the weeping and upset on her wedding day, is now quite used to her husband. He is much older, but they have reached an understanding.'

'I care naught for her,' came the reply. 'You know, this will come to you, one day,' she warned, staring ahead. 'You must be deluded if you think you are placed here out of the goodness of your father's heart. Being thus groomed, tutored and fashioned is for one reason only – to attract someone who will bring financial reward and influence to your family. It is the way for children of ambitious parents.'

'But you said women in the Low Countries could do whatever they like. They have far more freedom than women elsewhere in Europe. You could remain single and run a business such as, well, a brewery or something?'

Beatrice turned her head and stared at me. 'A brewery – and with what money?'

'With your gift from Madame.'

She raised her eyes. 'What gift if I was not getting married?'

'Well, could you not be a cloth merchant?'

'Anna, those women are housewives first. They marry, their husbands die, and to support their children they take over the business. For most, it is a necessity.'

'I know this,' I said, peeved. 'And I shall never find myself in your position, for my parents would not match me to a man I cared naught for.'

'Really? Well, you wait and see,' continued Beatrice, sullenly. 'Then, when you are abed with child, your husband will take a mistress. He might even take one before if he chooses and, grumble as you might, there will be nothing you can do.'

'I would *never* allow such a thing,' I replied. 'Never. He will be true to me alone.'

Beatrice gave a wan smile. 'Did you know that the King of Denmark has a mistress? She is Norwegian, a pretty commoner whose mother is a genius at administration and has become his first councillor. Both mother and daughter have bewitched the king.'

'But he is marrying Princess Isabeau.'

'Indeed he is but, as you see, the business of marrying Isabeau has nothing to do with love. The king and the emperor seek to unite houses not hearts. Margaret is unhappy, as is the emperor. He insists the king gives up his "little pigeon", but he refuses, for he has no intention of giving up a sexually experienced woman for a green girl.'

'But Beatrice, what shall I do without you? You have been my friend since the very first day I arrived here.'

'You will have Anne Brandon,' she said, stroking Bonny.

'That is unfair. Anne is sweet, but she is not you.'

'Well, whatever happens,' she continued, 'for the moment you shall stay here at Mechelen and, who knows, maybe one day you will go to Spain and end up marrying some rich Spanish grandee.' She put her hands to her face. 'Oh, I shall miss the celebrations of the prince's wedding. I shall miss everything!'

'But Beatrice, you will have your own wedding,' I said, putting Bonny down and watching as she set to chewing merrily on a twig held between her paws. She had not a care in the world.

'I wish I had chosen someone myself,' said Beatrice, 'contracted myself secretly, and then there would be nothing my parents could do. Oh, Anna, take your future into your own hands before, like me, it is too late.'

'Do you know what I would hate most?' I said, swinging my feet as I sat. 'I would hate to be married to a man who did not amuse me, a dullard. To be unable to converse, or share poetry and music would be purgatory for me. And he has to be rich and influential. I could never marry a man of humble means, for I want to live in a grand house. Is such a thought a sin?'

Beatrice sighed. 'Probably. Everything is sinful. As to amusing and clever, well, maybe you will get both, but it is an unlikely wager. No, better to take a lover.'

As I sat I remembered Rosaline's words: 'Marry whom your parents choose. They would know best.' Surely she was right? Yet when it actually came to it, marriage seemed to cause such misery. Princess Eleanora would be forced to wed the hideous King Louis, Prince Charles would wed a girl he cared nothing for, Isabeau would suffer a man with a mistress in tow – and now Beatrice. From what I had seen thus far, marriage did not seem a desirable state, and yet I knew that I would have to marry if I wanted my own family. Would I be able to choose? As we sat in silence, a deep anxiety disturbed my peace of mind. A week later my friend departed the court.

❀ ❀

King Henry paced the court, apoplectic with rage. He had discovered that Ferdinand of Spain had made peace with France, and his wrath knew no bounds. Support for England was now totally withdrawn. The king raged through his palace at Greenwich and was in such a foul humour that even his best friend, Charles Brandon, avoided him. Mother wrote that she had never seen such anger in a man, for the king was like a demon possessed, throwing chairs, stools and anything else in his way aside, as he strode through the gallery. Standing hidden behind a pillar in the hall, she watched him as he kicked open the door to the council chamber,

'What man can I trust!' she heard him bellow, as the

door flew open and he gave full vent to his anger. 'Do you know, Edward? You, Charles? Tell me. I see no faith in all the world save in me alone!'

His terrified councillors sat quaking around the table.

'I have been used, cuckolded and taken for a green fool!' he brought his fist down heavily on the table. 'Twice before Ferdinand has tricked me and twice, in the generosity of my heart, I blamed the incompetence of his ambassador, Caroz.'

The silent faces stared down at their papers.

'Well, now I see clearly how promises from Ferdinand to invade France with his support are as empty as a wind-blown bladder. I spit on him!'

'Sire – Majesty.' It was the calm voice of the Archbishop of Canterbury, as he rose to his feet. 'There is talk that the Emperor will also renege on his promise. As you will be aware, there have been disturbing rumours from our ambassador, Thomas Spinelly, in the Low Countries. As yet, we must take them as, well, rumours.'

'Well, what do you advise? Wolsey? Howard?'

Thomas Wolsey stood next. 'Your Grace,' he said, pushing back his heavy chair, 'my advice to you has never wavered, but ever been constant. King Ferdinand has played you false, and the emperor vacillates. You yourself have said it is time that the Most Christian King in Europe – Your Grace himself – showed the world whom God truly favours in defence of his elect on earth, the pope. I, each of us, can concur with what Your Grace's conscience dictates. My labours of these last few weeks have been only to this end. We must support the Holy Father and look to an honourable peace.'

'Aye,' agreed the archbishop, 'and did not the pope support Your Grace in his illustrious marriage to Queen Katherine, thus ensuring his eternal friendship?'

He could not have made a more unfortunate remark, for Mother said she heard something heavy hurtle across the chamber and hit its mark with a crash.

As the councillors were thrown out of the chamber, my

father – who had been waiting outside – bravely entered, and succeeded in calming His Grace down. However, the king cast around for a scapegoat, someone he could bully and reduce to tears, and his wrath fell upon his wife, daughter of King Ferdinand, and now his great enemy. He accused her of being a spy and said that she had been aware of her father plotting all along. Illustrious marriage? How could he have allowed himself to be tied to her in such a fruitless alliance? He would lock up those responsible in a dank, dripping cell and have the key thrown away. Prudently, my father did not remind him how, quite miraculously, he had forgotten that it was his will and longing to marry Katherine and, at the time, had fought against the advice of his wiser councillors.

My mother hurried as quickly as she could to the queen's chambers. When the king arrived, she described how Katherine wept and begged her husband to acknowledge the fact that she, too, felt nothing but disgust towards her father. But he would have none of it. Mother watched as the terrible argument stormed and when the king tried to leave the queen's chamber, Katherine fell onto her knees, her hair loose and tangled, crying in the most pitiable way.

'Sweet Jesu, you cannot leave me thus,' she wept. 'I am naught without you, my love. I swear by the blood of Christ I knew nothing of this. Nothing of my father's treachery.'

'Leave me, Madame!' the king raged, pushing her down, helpless, onto the rushes. 'And someone get rid of these damned barking dogs before I have them destroyed! I want an annulment. This marriage was never meant to be, by God. I want you and Spain out of my life forever, cut down like the dead, rotten branches you are. Wolsey is right. He has ever been against Spain. Let us do it quickly. Get my secretary. Draw up the papers.' He rushed over to the desk and, with one great swoop of his fist, cleared it of documents and books. Finding a clean sheet of paper, he started frantically scribbling, dipping his quill furiously into the golden inkpot. 'You sicken me,' he muttered, under his breath, 'with your fawning and scraping and your treacherous activities behind my back. My wife – my own wife betraying me thus.'

'Henry!' cried the queen, in anguish, 'you cannot cast away the mother of your prince.'

'Taunt me no more with boys, Madame, for where are the boys you promised me? I see none, do you? I even have a mind to adopt my sister Margaret's child, James, as my heir. No, I am writing to your father,' he said, head down.

The queen continued to weep as the king scribbled furiously. A moment later, in despair, he swept the paper onto the rushes, sending the inkpot and quill flying. He then leapt up and rudely pushed past my mother and Lady Gordon, his fair face and neck puce, the veins at his temple throbbing in anger. Maria de Salinas, one of the queen's few Spanish ladies, hid behind the cupboard, quaking.

'By Christ, get her from my sight,' he said, hand covering his eyes, 'before I do her harm. Get her out! I refuse to look upon her for a month.'

The frightened ladies froze, unable to move.

'Henry,' sobbed the queen, lying helpless on the rushes. 'I am carrying your child. Your *child*.'

The ladies in the chamber remained still, including my mother, who stood grasping the trembling hand of young Elizabeth Howard. The king halted in his tracks. He turned slowly to peer at his wife through narrowed eyes, and she nodded through her tears.

'What trickery is this? What game now, Madame?'

'No game, my Lord, it is true. The doctor has confirmed it. I wanted to wait until – until I was fully sure and through these dangerous first months. Praise be to God, Hal, I am carrying your son.'

The king appeared incredulous for a moment and then flew to the stricken queen, joining her on the rushes, kissing and stroking her hair, shame in his flushed face.

'Oh, my love, my sweet Katherine, is it true?' he muttered, crossing himself, 'have the doctors confirmed it? Forgive me, Christ, forgive me. Look at me. By God, I hardly know myself when I am in a rage. Blessed Lady in Heaven, grant no harm has been done to the child, sweet Jesu, no harm.'

Crying, he rocked his wife gently in his arms, her golden hair spilling across his great thighs. 'Get out!' he bellowed, making the ladies scramble to the door. 'Lady Salinas, fetch *aqua vitae* for the queen. Lady Scrope, fetch a shawl and leave us be.'

My mother had witnessed the whole sorry scene and was deeply shocked and disturbed by the king's rage. She had never seen him so angry one minute and so utterly tender sweet the next. It quite alarmed her. Did anyone really know this volatile young man, whose mood changed like the wind? How dangerous would this unpredictability prove?

＊　＊

The king soon recovered his optimism and good humour and held a great joust, in honour of his yet unborn prince, at his new tiltyard in Greenwich. The queen and her ladies, including my mother, sat in the royal box all newly decked with green and gold velvet and clapped wildly as the contestants entered the lists. To their surprise, two men rode out, dressed as humble pilgrims in cloaks of leather and hessian. The ladies busily tried to guess who the two disguised strangers on horseback might be, but it was all for show for the king and Brandon were the two tallest men at court and so known to all. When they did throw off their cloaks, there was the expected gasp of surprise and admiration from all.

The king was, as usual, the hero of the day, although my father had ridden skilfully, too. It had been a spectacular show, and so many lances were splintered or shattered, the pages had to run and fetch more from the armoury.

＊　＊

In London, the Spaniards flew into hiding for fear of

attack, and on the streets, the people rioted against them. Always a nation suspicious of foreigners, and only too willing to blame them for every mishap, Londoners threw them out of their lodgings, their bags following them from the top windows. As the Spanish ambassador departed, he grumbled that wherever he ventured, he was like a bull with darts thrown at him, and he wondered if he would ever leave the country alive. Katherine, however, beloved by all, held her head high in public. She spent hours on her knees, praying desperately to Our Lady and St Catherine, desperate in case her baby had suffered in the storm. She knew that now she was pregnant the king would relieve himself again in Bessie's bed, but still she prayed. Prayed the sumptuous scarlet cradle her husband had ordered made would soon contain a prince.

●   ◉

On the second day of May, Princess Marie departed the court at Mechelen to meet her bridegroom, Louis of Hungary. She was nine years old and he eight, and it was accepted that a marriage would only take place in some years' time. However, although this was a short visit, it was still a tender parting. Out in the courtyard, the prince and his sister Isabeau made their farewells. Isabeau appeared quite merry, for she knew that after her own wedding in a few short weeks she would be allowed to return to Margaret's care until the following August.

The regent fussed over Princess Marie as the girl sat in her litter, tucking a satin wrap around her knees. 'You must be a credit to your grandfather,' she said, plumping up the bolster, 'do you agree, Countess?'

The woman nodded and patted the Princess's hand.

'And keep up your singing lessons. I shall want a report of everything you do and shall await your letters. Promise me you will write. Yes?'

'I shall try to be the best of princesses, Madame.'

Seeing her anxious face, Margaret broke down and,

reaching forward, held the girl close to her. 'Oh, my dear child, my little one, God grant you a safe journey. I shall have no peace until I hear you have safely arrived. I want to hear from Florent d'Egmond the moment you reach Maastricht. Now, you have your young ladies to accompany you and Countess Verhoeven. God be with you.'

She stepped back, straightened her shoulders and gave the signal to depart. The princess leaned over the door, tears on her cheeks. Margaret, in tears too, shook her head and waved away the concerned Lady Brederode with a flick of her hand. 'No, no, 'tis naught,' she said, blowing her nose into her kerchief, 'I shall always find partings painful, even when temporary. But it has always been my father's deepest desire to obtain Hungary and I have no sway in this matter. Now, I wish to walk in the garden. Anna, would you attend me, please? I am in need of your merry company.'

* *

The day fixed for Prince Charles's marriage to Princess Mary came and went, for it was now reported that the plague had broken out in Calais, and Maximilian feared for the prince's life. It was deeply frustrating. First, there had been a change of venue, then concerns over costs, then fear of French hostilities, and now this. It was true the French had already attacked England, but it was reported that the English had retaliated with such fierceness that old Louis was on the brink of suing for peace. However, there seemed to be endless setbacks, and a palpable feeling of expectation hung over the court. Margaret expressed her concern to her father over the fact that no new date was forthcoming, but he told her to be at peace for Wolsey, on behalf of his king, had assured him matters were proceeding as planned. Soothed, Margaret continued to check guest lists, lodgings, and other domestic arrangements. The cost had continually risen, spiralling out of control, and now amounted to an almost incalculable fortune. There had been much to do, and she had signed and approved the list of those English persons who would make up the prince and princess's retinue. Princess Mary had even sent eighteen milk-white palfreys from the royal stables at Holborn as a gift for Margaret's ladies to use, all trapped in Tudor green leather. As the grooms trotted these beautiful creatures out into the courtyard for inspection by the Master of the Horse, I gazed out of one of the top windows and thought how magnificent they looked. They must have cost a great fortune!

• •

As I sat dealing the playing cards to the gathered company, laughter echoed from Margaret's chamber. When the door swung open, she appeared, waving a document in her hand.

'It was too big even for his great royal head,' she laughed to her ladies, pointing to the script. 'The cap was only meant as a token!'

'A hat of purple satin and ermine,' read one of the ladies, peering over her shoulder, 'sent by His Eminence himself in Rome. Why, the Venetian ambassador says at least thirty thousand people watched in the streets around St Paul's church. What a wonderful spectacle it must have been.'

'Anna, I gather your father was there,' said Margaret.

I glanced up from the cards in my hand. 'Indeed, Madame, Mother said they both attended in their newest garb, and the king appeared immensely proud. Hundreds of nobles and ladies attended him, for it was an important affair. I am told the gift of the cap and sword were consecrated by the Holy Father himself.'

'Well, you will see your father again soon, for he is coming to Brussels.'

The Spanish ambassador, still at Margaret's court having survived the storm, threw in his card. 'Madame, the pope wishes Europe to see he is a friend to England. Is that not so?'

'Indeed,' Margaret turned, 'and we wish to be seen as a friend to England. We *are* a friend to England.'

The ambassador gave a sly, sycophantic smile, and picked another card. From the expression on his face, his luck was running out. 'As you say, Madame, as you say,' he said. 'But might I be so bold as to add that your father seems to be of a different opinion?'

Margaret handed the document to one of her ladies, her playful mood quite evaporated. 'Oh?' she asked. 'What are you implying?'

'With respect, Madame, he seems to be forever making excuses,' came the reply.

'The plague is hardly an excuse,' said Margaret.

'Forgive me, Madame, but I have heard no such report of ill humours in Calais, although we know malaria is the scourge of the town, rather than the plague, surrounded as it is by damp marshland and stagnant channels. My sister is there visiting relatives and says at present there is warm, fair weather with no oppressive hot wind that brings disease. This infernal delay is —'

'Oh, get out!' cried Margaret. 'Must I stand here and suffer a lesson on the climate of Calais? Leave my presence this instance — and leave my father's opinions where they belong — with him alone. Now, go from my sight.'

The ambassador rose and threw his cards onto the table. It was a poor hand. He bowed stiffly, fastidiously sniffing his silver pomander, and left the chamber.

⁂

The silken ropes on the great canvas awning tugged in the breeze as the sun beat down. It was Trinity Sunday, the day that Princess Isabeau must marry, by proxy, King Christian of Denmark in front of the Great Hall in Brussels. My father and several other English ambassadors stood together, having arrived in Brussels the day before, and I hoped he would have time to speak with me. The Danish ambassadors had delivered their king's good wishes and, with great pomp, Monsieur de Cambray, standing in place for his king, repeated the words of espousal to the little princess. She made her own promises in a clear, firm voice, her cheeks flushed beneath her long, fair hair and jewelled crown. We maids stood behind, holding the train of her russet brown gown, dressed in cream damask, edged with gold, and matching caps. I caught my father's eye, and he nodded approvingly. After the vows, the sweating assembly moved to the Great Hall. Margaret sat next to the nobles, lords, and ambassadors, with her ladies at the side. The emperor was absent but the prince, cooled in the heat by a young boy with a large fan, sat next to the ambassador from Spain. I sat close to my father and smiled at him, but he was deep in conversation with Margaret and the other gentlemen.

After a grand supper, a night tourney took place in the newly decorated tiltyard. Under the full moon, flaming torches lit up the lists, and banners and streamers hung limply in the now breathless air. After the tourney, exotic dancers from the New World, fire-eaters, acrobats and even dancing dogs performed. As the tables were moved back and the musicians tuned their instruments, my father asked if he might have the honour of dancing with me. I proudly took his outstretched hand.

'You appear to be growing up into a very elegant young lady, Nan,' he said, as we placed our palms together and began our steps, 'but you are still slight. Are you eating enough?'

'Indeed, Father, more than enough.' We turned around with a hop.

'And your conversation? Your spoken French is good I hear?'

'Father, I frequently assist Madame as a translator for those guests whose French is poor.'

'Quite an honour,' he said, over his shoulder. We turned again and clapped our opposite palms together, then moved on to other partners. When we reached each other again my father continued.

'Your grandmother has been unwell again and refuses

to move from her bed. It would be much easier if she came to court, but she will have none of it. Your own mother is with the queen, busy stitching coverlets for the coming prince. Again.'

'Is Mary forgiven?' I asked.

Father's lip curled. 'She is as far as my mother is concerned. Anyway, your sister seems to amuse Princess Mary, which could prove useful. She misses you,' he added, 'and hears of your progress. It has done her good to remain under your mother's watchful eye.'

'It must be quiet at Hever,' I said, with a swirl of my gown.

'It is as Mother likes, without children to disturb the peace. Mrs Geddynge visits once a week to bring books for George, but he needs to be with boys his own age, away from the influence of women.'

'Is Sorrel still chasing rabbits around the estate?' I asked, sinking to a deep reverence as the dance ended.

'Oh, did your mother forget to tell you?' he replied, nonchalantly. 'I had him destroyed last month. Too old.'

I gazed sadly after him as he walked away and then proceeded to engage one of the ambassadors in conversation. Dear, dear Sorrel. My old dog had been such a comfort to me, helping me with my first steps as a child. He had not growled when I pulled his tail or poked at him, but whined in gentle resignation. I loved him, and I would miss him. True, I now had Bonny, but Sorrel would always have a special place in my heart.

I slipped through the boisterous crowd, for I wished to be alone in the palace garden, and as I walked aimlessly along the rose-bordered path, I thought sadly of my old dog. I could still hear the music drifting through the open windows, but the laughter and sound of voices only made my eyes fill with tears. Through the blur, I saw the trees and bushes twinkle with lantern light, and bent down to one of the fountains to splash cold water onto my wrists. It felt refreshing after the oppressive heat

of the hall. I closed my eyes, but on hearing the crunch of feet
on gravel turned round to see the prince and his sister, followed
by attendants. My quiet moment was about to be spoiled.

'Ah, Mistress Bullen!' cried the prince, a little unsteady
on his feet, 'does not my sister appear to be the most elegant
creature you have ever seen?' He carried a crimson and gold
doublet slung over one shoulder, and his open shirt, drenched
in sweat, revealed his puny chest.

'Indeed she does, sir,' I swept low, 'my congratulations
and felicitations to you and your family.'

The prince scrutinised my face. 'Why are you upset?
This is a joyous day.' He threw back his head and turned in
a circle, gazing up at the starry sky. 'Such a night as this is
blessed by Heaven.'

I rapidly blinked away my tears. 'Tears of joy, sir,' I
replied, smiling.

He leant forward to the fountain and splashed the cold
water onto his flushed face. The drops clung to his lashes
and, laughing, he shook his wet head, just as Sorrel used to
when he had come in from the rain. The prince then started
splashing the water towards his attendants, who shrieked
with laughter. I had never seen him behave so playfully.

'Come, come,' he said, turning to Isabeau, 'shall we
return to the dancing?'

The girl took his proffered arm, but as her brother
turned his back to me, he swayed. 'My hands – my hands
feel so strange – tingling – and I – I feel so light h–' Before
he could finish the sentence he fell with a crash, face down
onto the gravel path, his eyes rolling.

'Charles!' shrieked Isabeau. 'Quick, get him to his feet.
Do something!'

I rushed forward, but his attendants pushed me aside.
They turned him over, one of them frantically shaking his
clenched jaw, and slapping his cheek.

'My Lord, can you hear me? Come to, sir.'

Isabeau began to cry as she stood staring down at

her brother.

One of the men turned. 'You, maid! Find the physician immediately. Go to! The prince is unconscious.'

∗ ∗

I slept badly, and it was barely dawn when I arose. Covering my shift with a cloak, I called quietly to Bonny and the other dogs still half asleep in the passageway, and tripped down the staircase into the still air.

'The prince has the plague,' whispered a page to another, as I let the dogs run onto the dewy grass. 'The plague is here in Brussels.'

'Stop your nonsense!' I cried, turning to the boys as they hurriedly put on their liveried doublets, and tucked in their loose shirts. They must have fallen asleep by the garden wall after the festivities. 'Go to your business.'

They ran off, and as I walked towards the rose garden, I thought of the night before. Poor Isabeau had cried constantly, and it was a fine end to her wedding day. I picked a handful of fresh roses and when the dogs had done their soiling, returned to the palace. The Hall seemed unusually quiet as I made my way to Margaret's chamber with the flowers. I expected her to be at the prince's side, but, to my surprise, she was already sitting at her desk in her blue velvet night robe, her hair pinned up.

'Anna, thank you for last night,' she said, her face tired and pale.

'Oh, I did naught, Madame, other than fetch the physician.'

'My dear girl, I heard you were as swift as a hare, found the physician, fetched oil of cloves, cleared the prince's chamber of his dogs and brought in his dropped doublet. I thank you.'

'And the prince, Madame?'

'Much recovered,' she replied, brightly. 'The physicians say the waning of the moon affected the boy, although I am more inclined to think eating too little and drinking too much at the wedding caused him to faint. I am writing to my father to tell him of the news.'

As she picked up her quill, something in her face perturbed me, for she would not meet my eyes. I waited in silence and then watched as she sat back with a sigh, a defeated expression on her face. She threw down the quill. 'He has the falling sickness.'

I stared at her, horrified.

'You are to say nothing to anyone, do you understand? This cannot be made public. The physician, sworn to secrecy, has treated him with castoreum, and the prince is now sleeping.'

I nodded, shocked by her words, as she put her face in her hands. 'Dear God, if anything happened to such a precious child I would never recover from the grief. Never. All my hopes rest with him.'

⚫ ⚫

The following week we were still in Brussels for the prince could not be moved. The word spread that he had collapsed with a fever, but had recovered, and the church bells tolled in thanksgiving. He was eventually allowed out into the garden where he sat in a wicker chair, his musicians playing nearby, and his dogs asleep on the terrace steps. On his head, he wore a straw hat, and it cast a shadow on the large bloody graze on his nose. He must have hit the gravel hard when he fell.

'He does look frail,' said Ariella, opening the chamber window and looking down. The sky had begun to cloud over, and there was not the slightest breeze.

'Stupid, stupid boy,' said Gabrielle. 'Had he not fallen ill I would be out of this ghastly heat and enjoying the cool woods at La Vure.'

'Do not say such things,' chided Fleur, fanning herself. 'Anyway, I like this palace for the gardens are so pretty. The emperor has done a wonderful job planting so many rare and beautiful flowers. The Countess of Hochstrate says he always asks his envoys to bring some rare plant back from their travels.'

Gabrielle rolled her eyes in boredom as I turned around, a self-satisfied smile upon my face. '*I* overheard one of Madame's ladies say that King Henry thinks this business about the prince falling ill is just another excuse for more delays, but I know it is not true. I know a very special secret.'

'What do you mean, Anna?' asked Christa.

The girls gathered round as I became the centre of attention.

Veronique walked into the chamber, brushing her hair. 'What is not true? Ugh, this heat is unbearable,' she said, flopping down onto one of the beds. 'I hate being in the city when it is this stifling. It is so disagreeable.'

'What is not true?' pressed Christa.

The girls moved closer as I slowly poured cold water into a bowl for Bonny and put it down for her. She raised her head but was too listless to move and flopped back down again with a yawn. I began to fiddle with my long hair, enjoying the suspense.

'You are to tell no one do you hear?' The girls all stared at me. 'I have it on very good authority that the Prince has the falling sickness,' I announced. 'He could easily die at any moment.' The mouths before me gaped open as I climbed onto my bed and picked up my book. I looked up. 'What? What have I said now?' I asked, nonchalantly.

Before anyone could reply there was a loud clap of thunder, and drops of rain began to fall very slowly against the windowpane. *Plop – plop – plop.* As they fell faster, an immense downpour followed, and outside on the terrace, we heard a frantic scrambling as the musicians gathered up their instruments and scurried with the prince back indoors. A great storm was about to break.

Chapter Nine

*'Hours fly, flowers die, new ways pass
by – love stays.'*

La Vure and Mechelen
Summer and Autumn 1514

It felt good to be back at La Vure, away from the city with its noise and bustle, and Margaret retired to deal with her correspondence.

The following day I watched as the girls played Hoodman's Blind on the terrace.

'Come, Anna, come and play,' said Greta, glancing across to me. The other girls joined in her plea.

'No, I would rather sit awhile and read,' I said.

There was a collective moan, but as Maria tied the silk scarf around her head, the game began again. Calling Bonny, I skipped down the steps of the stone terrace, along the mossy path and down towards the lake. I could still hear the girls laughing, but they could no longer see me, for I had chosen to sit with my back against a large, shady tree. I smiled as Bonny snapped at the shimmering blue dragonflies by the water's edge, and laughed as she gingerly paddled among the lilies and reeds. I then opened the letter from my father. He asked of my health and general polite niceties, saying that I must be a woman of good reputation and virtue, now and until such a time when a place was found for me with the queen. She would only wish to talk with me if I were a good and pious woman, for she would accept nothing less. I must continue my French as he had instructed, for he knew how useful this would be at court, knowing it was my duty to obey him in all things. Most importantly I must do nothing that might dishonour the name of Bullen. He wrote that if he heard anything but praise for me, I would be fetched home immediately.

'Anna?'

I jumped, quite startled, and looked up to see Concetta. 'Why do you sit here on your own?'

'It is naught. I wish to read a letter from my father, that is all.'

She stood, chewing a long blade of grass.

'All is well,' I said, with a smile, folding the paper. She wandered off with a shrug, leaving me to ponder my father's words and the vexed question of how I might reply.

The following afternoon, I decided I must find Madame Symonnet. I was fortunate, for this year Margaret had allowed my tutor to accompany her to La Vure, since my tutor's sister had died back in February and she was no longer able to stay with her. I wandered through the cool glade of trees, my pale blue gown billowing out behind, and my hair free. Here we could relax, and as I walked, a long twig in my hand, I pondered on what I should write. I found Madame Symonnet in the summer house, dozing in a large wicker chair, a contented white cat curled up on her lap. As I put my hands over her eyes, she gave a start, and the cat sprang down.

'Ah, such cool fingers can only belong to a certain young lady.'

I giggled, giving the game away, and showed her the letter

from my father. 'What do you think?' I asked as she read it.

'Well, Anna, to impress your father you must respond to this immediately. You must write back and say that you understand what is required of you – basically that he has nothing to fear – and what great joy it will give you if Queen Katherine speaks with you when you serve her at her court. You must tell your father you will work hard for him, for he is your guide. How when he –'

'Oh, dear Simone, would you write it for me? My written French is poorer than my conversation. I could copy it down, and Father would be most impressed.'

My tutor frowned. 'Fie, I will do no such thing. But I will help you. Go in and bring my little writing desk, quill, paper, and ink, and we will see what we can do – and mind the ink does not spill.'

When I returned we sat in the cool summer house, I with the little wooden desk on my knees, writing, and my tutor sitting beside me. I twirled the fine swan quill in my fingers and thought.

'*Sir,*' I said as I wrote, *I understand by your letter that you desire me to be a woman of virtuous repute*… How do you spell virtuous in French?'

Madame Symonnet scribbled the spelling down. 'It is no matter, *cherie*, if you make a mistake. You can correct the words neatly above if you have to.'

'But I want to get this right,' I sighed, staring at the messy inkblot on the paper. 'Let me begin again.'

I began writing in my plain, unembellished hand, correcting mistakes and asking my father to excuse my spelling, and humbly commending myself to his good grace. As the sun began to sink in a golden haze, I signed my name at the bottom.

'There, 'tis done. What think you? Will it do?' I blew away the loose grains of sand.

Madame Symonnet took the paper from me. 'It will do nicely, Anna. A very sober letter and one to please your father greatly. Now, you must go and see if Madame requires anything and I will give your letter to the messenger. Come, Bonny.'

We left the summerhouse and walked across the clipped grass back to the lodge. As we walked, I smiled smugly to myself. I would show Father that I was far more sensible than my sister, even if she had made friends with the princess. She might be older than I, and share the princess's French tutor, but I was sure her French would still be poor. My parents were right to send me to the regent's court instead of her. I would show them how I had grown into a sober young lady, and how accomplished I had become in the year since leaving home. I would be the one to be noticed, not Mary. No one would ever know or care who she was a court, no matter how prettily she sang. I linked my arm in my tutor's, and we laughed together as we plucked a bunch of pink-tipped daisies. Then, as we stepped onto the path, I saw Anne Brandon running along the gravel, her hair dishevelled and her cheeks aflame in the heat.

'Anna, come quickly!' she cried, in alarm. 'It is Madame, come quick, come quick. She is dying!'

*   *

'But why do I have to go home?' I asked, as Greta hurriedly pulled me aside, out of the way of the white-faced, scurrying women.

'Because you have no choice, you goose – or that Brandon girl. You cannot stay at a court that is no longer a friend to England.'

'What do you mean?'

'The English ambassador had an audience with Madame and –'

'But she receives no one here, except her father.'

'Will you *listen*,' she said, pinching me. 'He insisted on seeing her there and then and she had to receive him in her retiring robe.'

I stood in silence, rubbing my sore arm.

'He informed her that a week ago, at Wanstead, Princess Mary solemnly renounced the promise made to marry Prince Charles –'

'I told you that the marriage was over, but no one believed me,' I interrupted.

'Anna, the ambassadors in London have signed a new contract binding her to King Louis of France.'

'*What?* But –'

'But nothing, it is over,' she said. 'There will be no bride for our prince and no celebrations at Calais. Madame collapsed on hearing the news and Dr Picot had to revive her from a dead faint.'

'I do not understand,' I said, confused, watching the commotion unfold as we stood.

'Come,' said Greta, 'let us go to Madame's chamber and see what we can do to help.'

As we approached, I heard the most frightful crying, and a man, carrying a basin of blood, rushed out of the door. I then saw Margaret sitting at her desk, sobbing uncontrollably. Neutken stood on a chair gently rubbing her mistress's back, while her secretary hovered to the side. I moved quietly into the chamber and stood against the wall, unseen.

'I accept none of this,' wailed Margaret, slamming the desktop hard, making Neutken jump. 'Monsieur Thienne – write to King Henry to say I cannot understand the report I am hearing.'

'If I might speak, Madame?'

Margaret rose and waved her hand impatiently.

'Madame, with respect, we have been truly duped, for King Henry has made peace with France. He has even gone so far as to ask King Louis to be godfather to his coming child.'

The regent blanched. 'But he asked me to be Godmother! Dear God, the prince. The poor boy must be told nothing of this misunderstanding.'

'Madame, I beg of you, it is too late, he has already

been informed in Brussels,' stated the secretary. 'As for King Henry, there is no point in writing to him. There is no "misunderstanding," as you say.'

Margaret stared at him as if a terrible truth were dawning and sank back down in her chair. 'My Charles knows?'

There was silence.

'Well – now I see how it lies,' she said, her voice trembling. 'I am alone. We already knew that King Ferdinand had backed out of his promise to assist King Henry, but as to the marriage of the prince to Mary of York, the agreement has run these past seven years until both were old enough to marry. Why let me proceed with the marriage arrangements? Why has the king made such a fool out of me?' She stared around helplessly, as her secretary stepped forward.

'Madame, the king, seeing how the land lay, has acted decisively and ruthlessly, and, rather than fight France alone with Swiss mercenaries has switched his allegiance to King Louis. It is what the pope wanted, hence his sending King Henry the Cap of Maintenance. It was a bribe, nothing less, and there was much pressure from His Holiness, Wolsey, and Fox on the king's council, to make this peace. It was politic.'

'And since when is breaking an oath politic!' roared Margaret.

The secretary clicked his fingers, and a lady passed him a silver pomander containing aromatic leaves. He offered it to Margaret.

'It is as if scales have been lifted from my eyes,' she murmured, waving the pomander away, 'for now I see things clearly. The council must have deliberately detained the prince in Brussels, without my support and presence, to tell him the news they were so relieved to hear. Charlatans! A poor, helpless boy, standing alone against the most powerful men in the land, each one of them in their hearts pro-French. With what delight they must have informed him of the news.' She rubbed her tired eyes.

'Madame, if I might say, the prince bravely held his

own against the council,' replied the secretary. 'Flushed with anger, he asked them if he was to marry the princess or not. One of the council proceeded to tell him that because he was inferior to King Louis and –'

'He did what? Which of them dared to say such a thing?' Margaret rose to her feet, her red-rimmed eyes now flaming.

The poor man continued. '…that Louis, as the most important king in Christendom, should have the wife of his choice. They reminded the prince that, secretly, he had shown no desire to marry the girl anyway. The prince then gazed out of the window onto the terrace, and pointing, asked one of the gentlemen present to fetch him the hawk held there. Confused, the gentleman asked why, since that particular bird was far too young and inexperienced to be of any use for hunting. He would find him a better one. Besides, why, at that very moment, was a bird of such importance? The prince turned angrily round and demanded that the bird be brought up to him.'

'And?'

'After a few moments, it was presented to him, and he slowly began to pluck the young bird of all its feathers. The councillors stood stunned and silent, until one asked why he had done such a thing. The prince replied that just because the bird was young, it was held of small account and, being young, it had neither squawked nor complained. The council had plucked him in a similar manner because he was still a boy, but the time would come when *he* would pluck *them*.'

'Bravo!' cried Margaret, 'would to God I could pluck out the eyes of Chiévres and the whole lot of them myself.' She snapped her fingers in defiance at the secretary, but then her eyes dulled. 'I am no fool. I see that my influence over the boy is finished,' she said. 'The council push for his minority to end so that he can rule without my guidance. Well, it is no surprise to me. For a long time, I have felt my father has lost confidence in me, excluding me, leaving me confused as to what his thoughts might be. I fear that Charles has too, for he listens more and more to the men about him. But be warned. King Henry promised in writing to marry his sister to the prince. He has broken a contract drawn up by Wolsey and signed by himself at Lille, and I am shocked to the depths of my being. I shall tell the world of his perfidy and publish the document of the signed treaty. He promised me that he would never treat with France. *Never.* He has broken faith with me, and I can never look fondly upon him again.'

'Madame, with respect, we must face the fact that King Henry was not the first to break his word. King Ferdinand took the first step in treachery followed –'

'By my father,' interrupted Margaret. 'See, there is no need to mince words with me, Monsieur, but the King of England has betrayed me more, together with Wolsey.'

'Madame, it is said that the king can do nothing without this Wolsey by his side. He showers him with gratitude for bringing peace with the French, while Wolsey devotes his time to realising his own vaulting ambitions. Of course, being a churchman, he wants no scandal, and so has put his own, secret wife, Joan Larke, aside, and had his daughter adopted. They have been abandoned.'

'Then she and I are one,' said Margaret.

◦　◦

'Sweet Jesu, it is like a tomb in there,' moaned Isabelle, as we sat by the river. She batted away a lazy bumble bee. 'Everywhere I go someone is weeping and wailing, Margaret the most. I swear Lady Waldich is making her worse, with her fussing and flapping – and you hardly help,' she continued, with a frown.

I stared ahead at the dogs lying beneath the shade of the tree. In the distance, swans occasionally dipped their sleek necks beneath the water as they glided aimlessly upon the river.

'Well, what do you expect?' I replied. 'Now, because you say we no longer have an ally in England, I shall have to go straight home back to Hever, or Norfolk or some other Godforsaken hole. Elizabeth Blount has taken the only vacant place left at Queen Katherine's court, and so there is no room for me. It is so unfair!'

'I told you Madame would have no place for you anymore – or Anne and Magdalen, for that matter,' said Angelique, taking an apple from her basket.

I flopped back down and turned my face away, plucking the blades of grass beneath my cheek in frustration. 'I have rehearsed all my steps and lines for the wedding pageants,' I grumbled. 'Hours of preparation, hours of dreaming of what gown I will wear, hours of dreaming of Spain, all for nothing. Now there will be no wedding.'

'Anna,' said Edda, 'every one of us has worked hard for months and we feel just as miserable as you.'

Anika fastened a daisy chain around her neck. 'I hear the emperor is trying to wheedle compensation from King Henry for the cost of the preparations made by Margaret. How dare he! Once King Ferdinand was out of the game the emperor was too, and he knew it. Now he has the effrontery to haggle for money.'

'Well,' said Greta, 'now it is England, France, and the Pope against Spain.'

'Oh, politics, it is all too tedious,' sighed Maria, yawning.

'Well,' continued Greta, 'I've heard it said that Wolsey is behind this, for he wants to keep in favour with the pope. The pope supports France and Wolsey, and has urged the king to make peace too.'

'Stop it. Stop it all of you!' I cried, sitting up. 'I am sick of hearing the name Wolsey. What of *me*? What will become of me now?'

'What of you?' asked Angelique.

'What of poor Mary Rose?' asked Veronique. 'She will have to marry the oldest, pock-riddled hunchback in Europe. Ugh, he's an old man and she barely nineteen. How revolting.'

'He might be ugly,' said Edda, 'but they say that he is kind and soft-hearted. The people love him, hence his name 'Le Père du Peuple'. Perhaps he will be kind to the princess.'

'A kindness would be to leave her alone,' said Maria, making the girls laugh.

'I hear his nephew, François, is the one she will have to watch out for. Eighteen, handsome, tall – and he adores women,' added Ariella. 'He says a court without women is like a garden without flowers. He even gives a New Year's gift each year to the whores at his palace gates.'

'Well,' said Christa, 'as Louis has no male heir, François, as senior prince of the Blood Royal, is heir presumptive. If your English princess is as pretty as they say, Anna, she will have her hands full fighting off the attentions of both Louis and François!'

'François is already married,' said Veronique, 'to that fat Claude girl.'

'Well, King Henry has spoiled everything,' I moaned. 'Now, there will be no palfreys and no procession, no dancing or celebrations. And I was going to sing a solo. I have spent hours with the choirmaster.'

'Oh, for the love of God,' said Maria. 'We all know, as Madame's favourite, you are chosen to shine at every opportunity, but the politics of Europe do not revolve around you and your silly wishes.'

'Strange to think that the king had sworn friendship to Margaret,' said Veronique, twirling a blade of grass between her teeth. 'How could he do such a thing?'

'He is a king first,' explained Greta, 'and a friend second. He has to be. What did the emperor once say? Rulers have no friends, just allies. Anyway, let us talk of lighter things and not spoil this beautiful day. Later, we can feed the swans, but keep control of Bonny, Anna, you know how she likes to chase them.'

Ignoring the girls, I picked up my book and flounced off with a face like thunder, back to the palace.

* *

The following day, as we played bowls in the park, we heard from Margaret's ambassador that Princess Mary had been, predictably, horrified at the match with Louis. She had screamed and cursed and worked herself up into such a state that she had threatened to jump off the roof at Greenwich Palace. Queen Katherine managed to calm her and fetch her down from the balcony and, when she was safely in her arms, tried to cheer her by pointing out how jealous her sister Margaret was of her good fortune. She would be Queen of France, while her sister froze to death in Scotland. But it was useless. The Princess, kneeling on the floor, wept before the council and no man could bear to raise his eyes to her, particularly Wolsey who had brought the whole thing to pass. She begged, pleaded and wept at her brother's knees until he, too, was reduced to tears. In the end, he had to lock himself away at the far end of the palace to avoid hearing the constant wailing. He was terrified that if he saw her misery, he would give in to her, and so refused to look upon her distraught face. She knew this and constantly banged and hammered on the door to his chamber, saying she would die there alone on the cold stone if he did not help her. Eventually, my mother and her ladies managed to drag her away, limp and exhausted, back to her bedchamber where she cried herself to sleep.

By the eleventh of August, a formal marriage treaty had been signed, and when the news reached the ears of the people of London they were as upset as the princess herself. France was England's natural enemy, and the English were still smarting over the hostilities at Sussex. They were horrified that their beautiful Mary Rose should have to marry the most odious king in Europe. Women throughout London said it was a disgrace and refused to attend the celebrations and bonfires held in the city. The Spaniards and the Netherlanders were equally outraged because their prince had been passed over, and they felt concern and humiliation in equal measure.

Three days later, at Greenwich, the Duc de Longueville stood as proxy for his French master, and the marriage was celebrated before the court with great pomp and magnificence. A great many ambassadors – except the Spanish, to Queen Katherine's dismay – were present, as were many lords and nobles, my parents included. At the palace, the king wore cloth of gold, but as he took Queen Katherine's hand, my mother told me how she appeared tired and drawn in her pregnancy, compared to the surprising vivacity of Princess Mary. The girl had obviously dried her tears, put on a magnificent gown of silver-grey, purple and gold, and played the princess. She shimmered with jewels, wore a magnificent diamond in her hair sent by King Louis as a wedding gift, and smiled throughout the day. In fact, her apparent joy rather baffled everyone, considering all the tears and drama. The girl, like her brother, seemed as unpredictable as an April day.

※ ※

To my delight, Margaret informed me that she had no intention of sending me, Anne or Magdalen back home. In fact, she said that she had become so entirely dependent on my cheerful company and willingness to help, that she could hardly imagine her circle of maids without me. She held no grudge against my father or the Duke of Suffolk and although she was uncertain as to when, and if, my father intended coming to her court again, she trusted their friendship would survive the storm. She refused to have her household upset by politics and, besides, she had promised my family that she would continue to further my education. Here I was to remain, and I could not have been more delighted. For the present, at least.

※ ※

The sun beat down on the terrace as we cut the stems of

pink roses, our broad-brimmed straw hats shading us from the sun's glare. To our surprise, Margaret joined our company. She had remained inside for a week and appeared pale and subdued. Now, pulling on her canvas gloves, she smiled, and silently clipped off the blooms. Behind her, one of her ladies held a large, flat basket, and in it, she laid the roses.

'I hear Princess Mary was greatly distressed at losing my nephew as a husband,' said Margaret, carefully fingering a thorny stem, 'and everyone in Europe is shocked, none more than I. The girl has gone from having a young groom to an old man in one swift stroke. One moment she is Queen of Castile, the next Queen of France. Thus, are we women used to satisfy the whims and ambitions of men.'

Her lady-in-waiting took the rose from her, and smelt its sweet perfume.

'Prince Charles is unhappy,' continued Margaret, 'for he has quite changed his opinion of the princess, having been assured by one of his closest friends, who has actually seen her, that the portrait sent to him was indeed a true likeness. She really is that lovely.'

'Well *I* hear, Madame,' said the lady, 'that the princess has only calmed down because she has exacted a promise from her brother saying that if she marries Louis this time, her next choice will be her own. It is an abomination, he an old, sick man and she so young and full of life. Can you blame her?'

'More fool her if she relies on a king's promise,' countered Margaret. 'Anything would have been promised to entice her to do his bidding.'

'Possibly,' said the lady, moving closer to the shade of the wall. 'But rumour has it that the contrary Princess is madly in love with another, and he with her, and she intends to marry him as soon as she is free. She utterly denies it, of course.'

'What utter nonsense.'

'Indeed, Madame, King Louis might live for years, and

she might die in childbirth, but if she does survive him, she swears nothing will deter her next time, neither king nor council.'

'And,' said Margaret, turning around with a smile, 'who does rumour say this great prince she loves might be?'

'Why, Madame, rumour has it that her heart is set on Mr Brandon.'

* *

The regent walked briskly along the gallery to her suite, and I could see from Signor di Gattinara's face that matters had gone badly. The prince had been present, silent and sullen, but before the end of the meeting he had apparently stormed out with his councillors and companions. Margaret's influence on him was truly at an end.

I curtsied as she passed, but then she stopped abruptly and turned about, causing Gattinara to almost bump into her. 'Anna, should you not be at your lessons?'

'By your leave, Madame, since Madame Symonnet is unwell today, I have returned to continue with my poetry, unless there is something else you wish of me?'

She stood thinking for a moment. 'Come and play for me, for I have a new book of chansons.'

Back in Margaret's chamber, Arabella sat grooming the balding Patou, Magdalen combed Beau, and Neutken had set to cleaning the curios in a small cabinet. She had laid them out on a platter and gave each object a careful polish as she hummed to herself. Gaudily dressed as ever, today she wore a pink and yellow gown far too big for her small frame.

Margaret sighed as she sat down. 'Peace at last,' she murmured, as Gattinara placed his papers down on the table. 'I will peruse those later,' she added, glancing at them.

There was a moment's silence, and her minister appeared to have something on his mind. Hesitantly, he looked at Margaret. 'Madame, forgive me,' he said, 'but should King Louis die – and we know this is a possibility – do you agree

Princess Mary might still wed Prince Charles? Oh, I know what you said lately, rash words cried out in bitterness and disappointment, but I disliked what I heard in council.'

Margaret bristled. 'And I dislike the rest of Europe viewing my nephew as second best, Monsieur, as well you know. It is an insult to our house. England has made peace with France for one year, and so keeps Tournai, but that peace might fail if Louis dies, which as you say, is a possibility. I agree we must keep on good terms with England – although my father refuses to see this – for we remain in a vulnerable position and require safe passage for our trading ships.'

Gattinara nodded and tapped his fingertips together.

'But would King Henry consider it?' asked Margaret. 'I felt deeply angered and humiliated on first hearing that Charles had been thrown over, but having composed myself and reflected, I cannot allow the Netherlands to stand alone. Perhaps we should be party to this peace between England and France after all?'

'I see a faint possibility, Madame, if the emperor could mend the alliance, but frankly, I see no such thing happening. The King of England feels betrayed by him and who is to say that your father will keep his word in future?'

Margaret glanced over. 'Anna, the music book is on the virginals. Please play something soothing.'

I lifted the cream velvet cover off the instrument and started playing. I had chosen one of Margaret's own compositions for I knew it would please her.

'Did you hear of the gifts sent by Louis to Mary?' asked Margaret. 'There were so many outrageous, showy baubles they had to be piled into coffers and carried into the Presence Chamber by mules. Forty-six diamond and ruby ornaments, bracelets of pearls, girdles and necklaces in the shapes of Tudor roses and fleur-de-lys. I gather she wore the most vulgar trifle at her betrothal.'

Gattinara raised his eyes. 'Madame, with respect, the "Mirror of Naples" is a piece of such immense size everyone present gasped. The pearl hanging down from the diamond alone is as big as a pigeon's egg, and hardly – if I might make so bold – a mere trifle.'

'Yes, well, I can imagine King Henry's covetous eyes lighting up at such a gift,' said Margaret.

'Madame, you know his greed well. He had the thing valued immediately by the court jewellers.'

'And?'

'Sixty thousand crowns.'

Margaret sighed. 'We could easily have produced something far more tasteful.'

'With respect, Madame, the jewels would have had to come out of your own coffers, for your father has sold many of his treasures due to a shortage of money,' replied the minister. 'However,' he continued, 'he must be chagrined by the fact that King Henry is able to pay four hundred thousand crowns as a dowry for the princess, and Louis is paying for her wardrobe and expenses to the sum of thousands of francs. Dozens of gowns, hats, and stockings. You ladies are quite beyond my comprehension.'

Margaret smiled as I played. 'We have wasted an enormous amount of money on preparations ourselves. To think I was allowed to continue with futile plans when the money could have gone to the infirmary.'

Gattinara then mentioned that the Earl of Worcester, among others, had now reached Abbeville in France to finalise the marriage and the peace treaty. King Louis, meanwhile, waited in Paris, desperate to see his new bride, sad because although he repeatedly sent her love letters, none were forthcoming from her. Eventually, the Duc de Longueville insisted she wrote some kind words which, with great effort, she did.

'Well,' said Margaret, 'the princess will be leaving Greenwich for France soon, and her chosen ladies and maids will be ready to depart. The thing is done.'

'Chosen yes, Madame, agreed no. King Louis was appalled to discover that one of the maids of honour turned out to be that Popincourt woman, mistress to the Duc de Longueville and, it is said by some, of King Henry himself. The duc had managed to obtain a place for her, but Worcester let Louis know of her lewd behaviour, and Louis had her struck off the list.'

I glanced over to Margaret, remembering my conversation with the prince, while skating, about this woman, and saw she now had Patou on her arm, aimlessly stroking what few feathers he had left.

'Well, well, how they swarm like bees to a honeypot, all desperate for a place.' She stood in silence before speaking. 'Tell me, do the arrangements for Zeeland progress well?'

'Everything is in order, Madame, and ready for whenever you wish to depart.'

She nodded.

As her minister bowed to take his leave, I slipped down from my stool and curtsied. He smiled. 'You play delightfully, little mistress. Pray, continue for your lady requires your soothing company. Now with your permission, Madame, shall I send in your women?'

⁂

I stared incredulously at the writing before me. 'My sister is going to France,' I said.

Greta glanced up from her needlework.

'She is officially on the list.' I felt a familiar pang of jealousy.

'Oh? What says she?' she snipped off the thread with her tiny silver scissors.

I unfolded the letter. 'She says that the princess has asked her to accompany her to the French court, along with the other young ladies, headed by the Countess of Oxford as their chaperone.' I paused and looked up. 'But Mary's French is hopeless. What on earth is the use in her going?'

'Does it matter when you say she is such a pretty thing,' replied Greta, folding the cloth.

'But *France?* Trust her to wheedle her way back into favour.'

'There, 'tis done, you can hardly see the repair.'

I ignored Greta, lost in my thoughts. Although I was happy with the regent, I would much rather go to the French court, for I had heard talk of the outrageous, extravagant fashions worn by the ladies in Paris, regardless of propriety. They even wore rouge and lip stain, and it sounded the most exciting place to be in all the world.

'Oh, come now, Anna, are you sulking? What more is to be said?'

'Nothing, I suppose.'

'Oh, I see, you think it would be more fun to serve a young queen at a new, exciting court,' teased Greta. 'You are afraid you might miss something.'

She was right. I returned to my letter and read that the princess had started taking extra French lessons with her tutor, Mr Palsgrave, and that Mary was allowed to join in their conversation. Apparently, they spent most of the time tittering together and acting the silly goose. How typical. Greta smiled at me as I rolled my eyes, and continued to read. Our grandfather and Uncle Howard had been placed in charge of the princess's voyage to France, and the whole court, including our parents, were to accompany her as far as Dover. It was going to be Wolsey, but the king decided to appoint Grandfather Howard instead. Mary said that was because Wolsey is soft-hearted with the princess and the king is afraid that she will wrap him around her little finger and lead him a merry dance. However, as we knew only too well, Grandfather Howard is deaf, bad-tempered and an old soldier, and would take no nonsense from the girl.

'Well, I am glad you will be staying,' said Greta, unfolding another shirt. 'I like you here.'

As I read the rest of the letter to myself, my smile soon faded. Far from being pleased that my sister was on the list for France, our parents, according to Mary, had flown into a state of acute anxiety that she found highly amusing. Terrified that Mary would behave lightly, they had tried to persuade the princess that my sister would be far better staying behind in England. The princess flew into high dudgeon and said she would go to her brother and demand Mary be kept on the list. If my sister were not allowed to go, then neither would my mother or father or anyone else in my family. Mother, in a state of panic, knew the king would grant his sister anything she desired to avoid any more scenes, and quickly dropped the matter. She did not want to be the one upsetting him again, for she was becoming more and more wary of his moods.

'Greta, does the *mère de filles* keep good order?'

'No, not particularly, for I gather from Countess of Hochstrate that the Countess of Oxford is – forgive me – rather slack and a poor choice. She is surprised at the appointment. Why do you ask?'

● ●

The weather had proved fine and pleasant, although a little cool, and as we sat in the walled garden at Mechelen, Margaret perused the latest dispatches from England. As her secretary handed them to her, one at a time, I helped Magdalen wind up a ball of wool and watched as some of the other girls repaired linen for the infirmary. Margaret told us that the princess had departed on the twenty-third day of September. She read that the king and the court had made a magnificent progress from Greenwich to Dover, banners flying and trumpets sounding. The king had ridden proudly at the head of the party, and the Dukes of Suffolk and Buckingham, along with Archbishop Warham, followed behind with all the nobles and knights, including my grand-father, uncle, and father. Queen Katherine, meanwhile, sat with Princess Mary in her litter, although the princess insist-ed on riding for most of the journey so that she could show off her beautiful new gown and jaunty cap to the crowds. At least two thousand people had made their way to Dover, and many ran out from their villages to watch the cavalcade pass. They threw flowers at the princess and cried out for shame that their "Queen of the May" must leave English soil.

'She would have been more than just "Queen of the May" married to the next emperor,' said Margaret wistfully, stroking Bella, asleep on her knee. 'She would have been queen of a vast, new empire.' She looked down. 'Anna, it says here that the Duchess of Norfolk, having twisted her foot and unable to ride, sat in her litter and poked her head out of the flap throughout the entire journey, grumbling to anyone who would listen. Apparently, she continually complained because Mrs Joan Vaux, Lady Guildford, had at the last minute supplanted the Countess of Oxford, and felt it was a family slight. Lady Guildford – or Mother Guildford as the princess has called her since childhood – rode triumphantly, nose in the air past the duchess, while her ladies and maids of honour trotted behind.'

I smiled, imagining the duchess's disgruntled face.

'Anyway,' Margaret continued, 'Old Lady Guildford, is a far soberer choice, and she speaks fluent French. I read, Anna, that your mother and sister, along with all the other ladies, rode on horses bedecked with Tudor green and white ribbons. How picturesque.'

I finished winding the wool and returned it to the basket as Margaret continued reading from the next sheet. We heard that by the time the cavalcade had reached Dover, the clouds had gathered and the weather turned foul. A great wind had blown forth, followed by driving rain, and it ruined the beautiful plumes and ribbons on the horses. The banners and garlands in the streets lay bedraggled, and the townsfolk had to run inside for cover. Instead of a stately procession, a mad scramble ensued as everyone rode as fast as they could towards the castle before their beautiful clothes and hats were ruined in the squall. Then, without warning, Margaret gasped, and her hand flew to her throat.

'Oh, Holy Mother of God!' We stopped our tasks, and all eyes turned towards her. 'It – it says the ships bobbing in the harbour were buffeted to pieces, and one of them, the *Great Elizabeth*, far out on the water, grounded at Sandgate. Hundreds were left for dead, or injured!' We crossed ourselves. 'Everyone had to wait for calmer weather which took fifteen days, but on the second day of October, at four o'clock in the morning, the princess took her leave of the queen, and her brother led her weeping down to the water's edge. It was a pitiful sight, but the king, who hates tearful scenes, slipped quietly away and made the Duke of Suffolk stay and lift her down into the waiting boat. Thus, the princess left Dover for Boulogne. Dear God above.'

She stared ahead as we sat in silence. 'Those poor, poor souls,' she said quietly, shaking her head. 'As to my Lord of Suffolk, I read he did not sail away with her. A wise decision I would say, in the circumstances.'

'Madame,' said Lady Constance, closing her book, 'nothing associated with that man is ever wise. I hear the duke is travelling later to attend the coronation.'

Margaret rose from her chair and gazed up at a great flock of starlings. They clouded the sky as they rose and dipped in dark formation. 'Well,' she mused, 'I must go to my chapel, and pray for those lost in this tragedy. Ladies, please attend me.'

However, as she bent down to pick up Bella, we heard frantic steps crunching across the gravel.

'Gentlemen, such unseemly haste,' chided Margaret, as Gattinara and three members of the Council flew, wheezing and panting, into the arbour.

'Madame, my – my lady,' gasped Gattinara, 'forgive – forgive this intrusion but this moment we have heard of a terrible storm. Terrible.' He stood holding his side, his face red as brick as he tried to catch his breath.

'But we know of it, gentlemen,' came the calm reply, 'I am repairing to pray in my private chapel as we speak.'

'No, no, Madame, there is far worse,' said Gattinara. 'The Princess Mary, all her ships were lost in the storm. Fourteen great galleys remain unaccounted for. It would seem from incoming reports that no man or woman has survived. Not one. All are lost!'

* *

The Countess of Hochstrate touched my white face with her hand as the girls stood, dumbstruck, in a huddle by the window.

'But my mother,' I said, utterly bewildered. 'My father, my sister, my uncle...'

'Come now, lie down, and we will fetch something to ease you.' The countess flicked her head sharply towards Christa, who flew out of the chamber. 'Now, child, try and remain calm. Listen to me. No ships have been found as yet. No wreckage. That is good. That is good.' I stared at her, my tearful eyes wide with terror. 'We must wait for more news.'

'But they said no man survives, they said it!' I cried, sitting back up, my thin shoulders shaking as I sobbed. As I sat, my mind raced with the most terrifying thoughts. How could I lose my entire family at sea? I had already lost my dear nurse and now this. What would become of me?

'Yes, dear, but, well – the ships might just be lost off course,' said the countess, glancing about in exasperation. 'Where *is* that foolish girl?'

In fear and despair, I threw back the coverlet and tried to climb off the bed. 'I want my mother!'

The countess pushed me back down and stroked my hair, just as Christa returned and handed her a cup. 'Come now, dearest, drink this,' she said, holding the cup to my lips. Between the sobs, the contents dribbled down my chin and mixed with my tears. 'Poor girl, now lie back and sleep, come. Lift your legs.' She pulled up the cover. 'Drink, Anna, the poppy is soothing.' She then glanced around. 'All of you out of here, except Greta, and draw the drapes to. The girl must have a dark chamber and rest. She has suffered the most dreadful shock.'

Everyone, including the countess, marched briskly out, closing the door, except for Greta who sat on the side of the bed. She took my hand. 'Do not be afraid, Anna,' she said, stroking my fingers.

My eyes heavy, I looked at her through a numbing haze. 'I want to see Mary, I want my sister,' I whimpered.

Greta nodded. 'I know, I know. And you will. We must wait for more news. Reports are coming in that nothing has been found. We must trust to God's mercy. Are you still feeling light of head?' she put her hand up to my brow. I nodded. She peered nearer. 'Well, you are not feverish.'

I pulled back the coverlet and pointed to my stomach. 'I have an ache here, and my head hurts, too.'

As I spoke, the door opened, and Margaret rushed in with one of her ladies. 'Anna, my poor, poor girl,' she said, as Greta rose and curtsied.

I gazed drowsily up as Margaret sat beside me. 'Madame,' I said, trying to sit up.

'Come now, you must be a brave girl and wait with me for news of your family. In the meantime, we will pray the rosary together and trust to our Blessed Lady, the "Ocean's Star", to intercede for us all.' Her lady-in-waiting passed her the gold filigree rosary beads, and we made the sign of the cross together.

'Madame?' I asked. 'Please would your lady draw back the drapes. I would rather see the light and hear the birds singing outside.' I saw her nod, heard a rustle of a gown, and felt my eyes grow heavy. I think I was asleep before the first paternoster.

• •

The court lay in confusion, for some reports said the ships had been sighted and some that they had been blown back to the English coast. Others told of a battered wreck foundered off the French coast, said to be the princess's own ship. At Greenwich, Queen Katherine had taken to her bed in distress, and tried to remain calm for the sake of her unborn child. The king, on his knees in his chapel, prayed for his sister's safety, as days passed by with no news. I cared not a jot for Princess Mary, only for my family, and lay on my bed, my face turned to the wall. My stomach ached, and I felt light of head as my mind raced in panic. I wanted to be sick. What would become of George and me without my mother, father, uncle and my sister? I could hardly bear the thought of returning to Dame Margot. Yet what if she died from grief and shock? We would have to go to live with our Howard relatives. I felt terrified, for without my family I was as nothing, a mere rock hurled into space, and I vowed silently to myself that if God spared them, I would obey them in all things, please them in all things, and do whatever they asked of me.

I thought of my sister and longed to feel her arms about me. To hear her laugh and sing again. How could I ever have been jealous of her, or hurt her so? As my tears fell, I clutched my psalter and felt desperately alone, for it was a truly terrible time of uncertainty. When Margaret eventually summoned me to her chamber, I entered in trepidation.

'God be praised, child,' she said smiling, 'our prayers have been answered. You have your family still.'

Forgetting to curtsey, forgetting all decorum, I ran into her arms and began sobbing with relief.

'Come now, what is this?' Margaret searched my face. 'This is good news.' She patted a nearby stool. 'Come, sit with me and I will tell you what happened.'

I sat trembling with emotion, wiping my nose and tears, as she began. It was true the weather in the narrow seas had turned foul again, and for four days and nights, the ships had been tossed off course with such force that the princess's ship became separated from the rest. My Uncle Thomas, panic-stricken lest her ship was lost forever, for he had no sight of it, was ready to cast himself into the sea like poor Uncle Ned. Ten ships were blown to oblivion and were thus reported lost. This was the news we had heard. However, the princess's ship had battled on until Boulogne was sighted. The vessel then grounded on a sandbank in the French harbour and Princess Mary had to be lowered into a rowing boat and rowed towards the beach. Sir Christopher Garnish, a knight in her party, carried her in his arms, wading through the water to the safety of land. Fortunately, at over seven feet tall, the water barely reached his knees. The princess and her ladies, including my poor mother, sister, and Howard grandmother, were in a terrible state and collapsed on the sand, their fine gowns ruined with salt water, seaweed, and vomit. Weak from lack of food they could barely sit for retching until the men carried them further up the beach, exhausted, but safe.

Four ships had made the journey, and, thank God, my family were on two of them. They were saved. In fact, very little of value was lost – neither gowns, jewels or gifts – for they were with the princess. Her brother had made quite sure that if she failed to arrive safely, then neither would her fortune. On no account would it fall into the acquisitive hands of the French. Now, fully recovered, the princess and her great train were travelling in magnificence to Paris, via Abbeville, where she would wed King Louis.

I kissed Margaret's hand fervently and held it tight to my wet cheek. She gently put her hand on my head.

'Go to the chapel and give thanks to God,' she said.

As I rose to leave and closed the door, I overheard her murmur. 'Lady Constance, if the worst had happened I could not have stood by and left such a lovely girl without a mother. I would have taken her for my own.'

As I rested with my back to the door, eyes shut in silent prayer and relief, I wondered would it have come to that? Was I destined to live my life out here in the Low Countries? When I opened them, I felt unsteady and had the most dreadful headache. Was it the shock of hearing the news? No – there was something else, for I felt quite peculiar. I waited a moment as the two gentlemen-at-arms stared impassively ahead and, when I felt steadier, walked as quickly as I could through the palace. A large, hot press of courtiers stood beneath the main staircase clutching petitions, waiting for Margaret to appear. In fact, there was such a large crowd of people I could barely move forward. As I tried to push my way ahead, I heard a familiar voice above the noise.

'Nan! Nan!' Madame Symonnet squeezed through the crowd. 'Such wonderful news of your kin,' she said, finally reaching me. I felt myself sway. 'My God, child, what is wrong? You are as white as a church candle.'

'Make haste,' I said, tugging her sleeve, 'I must go to my chamber for I feel quite faint.'

'Are you ailing?' she asked, her hand beneath my arm.

'I do not know,' I said weakly, 'my stomach is griping. I think I have been poisoned.'

* *

I lay on my bed staring at the countess. She stared back from her chair, hands folded serenely on her dark blue gown.

'Drink it,' she ordered.

'Do I have to?'

'Yes, you *do* have to.'

I narrowed my eyes. 'How did Madame Symonnet know?'

She smiled. 'Experience. You had a terrible shock and it brought on your courses. You have grown into a young woman and high time too. I was being to be concerned that something was amiss for this has been very tardy in coming.'

I wrinkled up my nose.

'And if you pull a face like that, Nan, it will stick. Now, you had better get used to this for, apart from when you carry a child, this will be your lot for the next twenty years. Come now, sit up.'

I stared down at the cup with its brown, steaming brew.

'Lady's mantle, raspberry, marigold, and mugwort,' explained the countess, as I took a sip. I shuddered. It tasted as disgusting as it appeared.

'Does it always hurt so?' I asked.

'It is life,' she replied, 'although as welcome as a frost at harvest. Now, I assume your mother has prepared you? You must take care, and remain indoors. No exertion such as horse riding, tennis, or bowls. A little light walking is acceptable, but you may wish to keep to your chamber. You must not become chilled or walk in damp grass in your soft slippers. I advise that you abstain from eating red meat, but instead partake of cooling custards and drink milk. Oh, and write to your mother, for she will want to know that matters proceed as they should. Now, I will go and fetch fresh wool and cloths.' She leaned down and kissed me on the forehead, picked up her cloak, and left the chamber.

I curled up clutching the bolster tightly, and felt warm and drowsy. I thought of my beautiful mother, how near I had come to losing her, and how my life would have been turned upside down. I longed to see her now and smell her scent of sweet violets. Dear, dear Mother. As to Mary, how could I ever forgive myself for treating her so badly? She was my sister, and I would never, ever be cruel to her again, or think unchristian thoughts. Even the thought of losing my grandmother, Agnes, filled me with horror. I felt very alone and uncertain, no longer a confident girl, but frightened, vulnerable and insecure.

When I eventually heard the sound of laughter and voices on the stairs, I knew that the girls were returning from their lessons. Arabella flew through the door first, followed by the others, and from the expression on their faces they already knew my situation.

'You should be pleased,' said Maria, bouncing on the bed beside me. 'Your parents will now be haggling for a rich husband to provide them with lots of bonny grandchildren.'

'Three boys should be sufficient to start with, followed

by girls,' teased Fleur.

As they returned to their tasks, I knew my peace had ended. As had my childhood.

* *

The regent was not pleased. As her ladies silently arranged the flowers and picked up her books, no word passed between them. Even Neutken sat subdued, braiding her hair with a red ribbon, although once or twice one of the ladies gave me an encouraging smile. Lady Constance picked up Margaret's guinea pig and, with the other ladies, quietly left the chamber. The suspense made my heart race faster, for I had no idea why Margaret had asked to see me, or why she appeared so annoyed. I stood there as she tried to fasten the clasp of the diamond bracelet glittering on her wrist. It appeared to be broken.

'Well, this is most inconvenient, Anna,' she said, obviously irritated. She flung the bracelet down onto the desk.

'They have been packed off home – the lot of them.' She stared at my puzzled face.

'That letter there,' she pointed, 'is from your father at the French court. He tells me that there has been a dreadful argument resulting in an outburst from King Louis and tearful scenes from his new bride.'

'Why, Madame,' I asked, 'is the king displeased with her?'

'Displeased? He is delighted. No, he vented his spleen over the ridiculous number of people who had accompanied her from England and who now wish to remain. It would appear that anyone at the English court who could utter a single syllable of French, no matter how mangled, attached themselves like leeches to those who could get their names put on the lists for France. I, for once, can hardly blame Louis, except he has inconvenienced me greatly.' She turned away.

'I read, Anna, that he took a particular dislike to Lady Guildford and packed her off to Boulogne. The distraught princess wrote to her brother saying she refused to stay in a strange land without the counsel of the good lady. Her pleas were to no avail, although Wolsey did try to have Lady Guildford reinstated. He was unsuccessful, for the position of la mère des filles has now been given to a woman of the French court, a Madame d'Aumont.'

I stood, still none the wiser as to why I had been summoned.

'Apparently, there was a great commotion as the king shooed all the ladies out in a fury.' Her face began to soften.

'Will all her ladies be returning to England?' I thought of my sister Mary.

'No,' she said, 'and that is what has inconvenienced me. Louis has relented now his painful gout has eased, and has allowed his wife to keep just six ladies of her choice – and you and your sister will be among them.'

'*I*, Madame?' I was taken aback.

'Indeed. Your grandfather, Old Surrey, has persuaded King Louis to let his granddaughter Mary stay, being a friend and a similar age to the princess, and his second granddaughter – you – are to join her. He says since you speak fluent French, you will be able to help the princess with her conversation. The princess, appeased by this suggestion, has ordered that you join your sister at the French court as soon as possible.' Margaret appeared deeply disgruntled. 'I am sorry,' she continued, 'but this really is quite unacceptable. I have lost Rosaline and Beatrice, and now I am to lose you, too. Anne Brandon and Magdalen Rochester will stay, but this is most tiresome. Quite frankly, I have a mind to keep you here until I have time to find a replacement. It could take months if I wish to be awkward.' She waved her hand airily at the letter, as if dismissing it.

'The other person who is furious with this situation is the Duke of Suffolk, since he feels that your grandfather is trying to feather his own nest by ousting Wolsey's choice of attendants, and so sabotage Anglo-French relations. It would appear that the dismissing of the ladies-in-waiting was solely an attempt by Surrey to upset Wolsey and please King Louis in one stroke. Wolsey had hand-picked the ladies himself and was deeply offended by your grandfather placing his own Howard kin in the royal household. The whole matter has degenerated into a common mud-slinging match.'

'I – I am uncertain what to say, Madame,' I said, my face clouding at this attack on my grandfather.

She paced around distractedly, biting her lip. 'Well, I shall be damned if one of my loveliest *demoiselles* is snatched away in this manner to serve my enemy at his court. The king might be virtuous, but I shudder at the thought of you in the same vicinity as that lascivious boy, François.' She looked at my shocked face.

'Forgive me, I am not ill-tempered with you, and have no wish to slight your family. I know you have no choice in this matter and must do as your father wishes. It is of small comfort to read that he is very embarrassed, as well he might be. First, he begs me to have you here and now he begs me to let you go. Of course, he says none of this is in his hands and that he is helpless against a royal command from the princess.'

'Madame,' I ventured, trying to hide the fact that I was bursting with excitement at this wonderful news. 'I would be honoured to stay if you would have me.'

She smiled and placed both her hands on my shoulders. I now felt terrified that she might change her mind.

'My dear girl, I would keep you here forever if I could, but I fear I cannot. We must do as your family wishes, much the same as Beatrice's.' She reached out and touched my hair. 'You have learnt much since coming to my court, and I am bursting with pride. You came here as a young girl and will be leaving now as a young lady. You have worked hard with Madame Symonnet, and the countess has only fine words to describe you. You have progressed with your music, dance, and poetry, and have ever been the most helpful of my maids.

In short, you have proved a joy and a comfort, and I hate to think of losing you. However, what I want is of no matter. Your grandfather wants you back, and so I cannot hold you a hostage, can I?'

I lowered my eyes afraid that she might read my thoughts, for I could not wait to go to France and see my sister!

'In a moment I shall reply to your father. He wishes you to return to the court at Paris with the escort he has sent to Mechelen, ideally in time for the coronation. Now, would you please send in the Countess of Hochstrate? I must discuss this matter further with her. She will be listening outside the door.'

•   ❋

Two days later, in the library, the regent snapped shut the book in her hands and laid it down on the polished table. She smiled as I stood before her in my rose-coloured gown. It had been altered twice already and was looking somewhat worn.

'Anna, time is short, and when sorting through my writings I came across something I would like to give to you. Among it is a piece of advice that I think might be useful.'

I watched as she turned and ran her fingers along the shelves until she came to a small book, bound in red velvet. She took it out and opened it at the yellow silk marker. 'Would you read it aloud for me?' she handed me the volume.

Solemnly, I began:

> 'Watch for your servants,
> Find out beforehand all about them, my demoiselles,
> And you will discover which ones
> Are the deceivers.
> When they speak, their language
> Is sweeter than the talk of young girls
> Be careful.
> In their hearts they are
> Aiming to fool you,
> For they have their methods

Now as it has always been, watch out.'

I looked up to see Margaret staring wistfully at me.

'I could give you anything I wish as a leaving gift, but I wanted to give you a treasure that cannot be stolen or lost. I want to give you advice.'

'Madame, did you write this?'

She nodded. 'I wrote it from bitter experience, and now I pass my words on to you. Be careful. You will be placed at a new court, and while King Louis lives, a noble court – in as much as the French can be noble.' She gave a wry smile. 'He may yet have a son, but if his new queen fails, his second cousin and nearest heir, François, will take the throne. That makes me very uneasy.'

I listened carefully, as she continued.

'We live in a time when physical prowess is more important than morals at court, where beauty and a handsome face count for much. The old, chivalrous days of my father are fading like the summer sun, and a new dawn is beginning. We live in momentous times! Three young rulers will take centre-stage in Europe and the world will change.'

I watched her as she browsed along the shelves again before turning to face me. 'Be wise with those in whom you confide. Keep your own counsel and your own values, regardless of those around you. Whatever care is met at court, it is a still a dangerous place, full of canker and vice, no matter how vigilant you are. You must choose your companions wisely, and if anything should occur troubling to your conscience inform your elders forthwith, for you will be entrusted to their care and good sense. Speak your truth plainly and clearly, and it will keep you out of harm's way.'

Her sombre words disturbed me.

'Be loyal to your princess – no other – and never be deceived by sweet talk that flatters, makes you proud or feel of more worth than God intended. Remember your station. Beware of those who might use you to seek their own gain with honeyed words and foolish praises. I was once there myself, as Queen of France at the Château d'Amboise until I was thirteen years old, and I know the temptations you will encounter.' She smiled. 'But come, do not look perturbed. No doubt you will find good people, and they will find you, and I shall always be interested in your progress.'

I closed the book in my hand.

'Now, repeat my motto.'

'Fortune, Infortune, Fort une,' I replied.

'That is correct. Fortune, misfortune – and a heart strong enough to meet either, for fortune is fickle. Never put your trust in the things of this life such as position or wealth. Put your trust in God only, for all worldly matters prove fleeting.' She looked at me with great seriousness and pressed her hands over mine. 'Keep this book and remember me when you read it. It contains other writings, too, which I trust you will find enlightening.'

'Oh, Madame,' I gasped, quite overcome. I realised I would miss this wise, kind woman for she had truly proved as dear as my own mother.

'Remember me,' whispered Margaret earnestly. 'I ask nothing more.'

As she took me into her arms, I could smell her sweet perfume. 'Ah, what a winsome creature I have come to love, with those dark, knowing eyes. Now, I do have another gift.' She walked over to the table and handed me a large object covered in a linen cloth.

I unfolded it carefully, and my eyes widened in delight. 'Oh!' I cried, my fingers tracing the inlay of mother-of-pearl. 'Oh, it is *beautiful!*' Blue and yellow ribbons decorated the neck of an exquisite lute.

'You must promise me that you will keep up your music and use it to accompany your pretty singing voice. Despite all I have said, it is such an exciting time to be young, and you have much to look forward to. France is a very beautiful country indeed.'

I turned the pegs to tune the strings. 'Is this really for me, Madame?'

She nodded and smiled broadly as I strummed. 'But wait – I have just one more small thing to give you. I only give them to my ladies, but I wanted you to have this.'

I put the lute down as she took out a black velvet purse from the drawer of her desk and handed it to me. Pulling open the drawstring, I found inside a familiar silver badge. The marguerite, a symbol of patience and simplicity, could not have been more fitting for so gracious a lady. What device would I choose if I ever became as great a lady as she? I began to pin the brooch to my gown, but Marguerite lowered my hand and closed her fingers over mine.

'No, my dear. This badge is the past. You must now look to the future to the *fleur-de-lys* of France, to your new French Queen. Your devotion must be to that device and to that device only, until you return to your homeland of England.'

I glanced up at her pensive face.

'Now, no more of this nonsense,' she added, turning away, 'for tomorrow you must depart. All is ready, and you will leave at first light. A Monsieur Bruay will take you to Paris, along with two other gentlemen and a chaperone, Madame Dupont. There, in Paris, you will be reunited with your sister. Now, I may not see you again as I leave shortly on my postponed trip to Zeeland, so I shall say my farewell here. You must also go and say goodbye to the countess, ladies, and girls. God bless you, Anna, and remember my words. Serve no one but your mistress, the French Queen. Be loyal and true.'

'I shall never forget you, dearest lady, never.' And I meant it.

●   ●

On a chilly, October dawn I descended the palace staircase, my fur muffler snug around my neck, and in the cold, grey light waited for the horses. The night torches still burnt bright, although the sky was beginning to lighten with a thin yellow streak. The Countess of Hochstrate kissed me on both cheeks and shivered in the cold. She watched as I was lifted onto the chestnut mare, while Monsieur Bruay and his companions – one leading a spare horse loaded with belongings – trotted over.

Madame Dupont adjusted her travelling gown as she sat on her horse, and when I looked up, I spied the girls standing on the little balcony overlooking the courtyard. We had had a tearful farewell, but most were envious of my new life at the French court, especially my dear Madame Symonnet. How I would miss those enchanting hours spent in the schoolroom with her by my side. 'I hear it is far more exciting than Mechelen,' she had whispered, holding me close.

The girls had crowded around as I pulled on the soft, cony gloves they had given me as a present, and I held the fur to my cheeks in delight. 'Oh, I shall miss you all so much!'

Now they stood huddled on the balcony, their woollen cloaks drawn close against the chill.

'Take care, Anna. Write to us!' called Ariella.

'I will, I will, I promise!' My horse turned about, and as we trotted away across the familiar cobbles, under the great archway, I twisted around to glimpse once more the red-brick palace that had been my home. I wanted to remember the picture of the morning guards taking up their duties, the dogs barking, messengers arriving with dispatches and the palace awakening. I looked across to one of the mounted escorts and saw my little Bonny safely tucked inside a leather bag on the saddle. I thought how amusing she appeared with her head peeping out. In the other great bags were the wonderful gowns and shoes that Margaret had allowed me to keep. The ones I had first arrived in now barely fitted.

As we continued down the street, passing the houses with their pretty shutters, I pondered on what lay ahead. Now, I would be moving on to new people and new customs, to a new palace and a new princess. No wise matron like

Margaret, but an impetuous, volatile young girl. What would she be like to serve? Would she be kind to me? What if she was cruel? I had heard that she could be difficult and wilful, and threw a rage if she was refused anything she wanted. What if I displeased her? As to my sister, although there had always been a rivalry and jealousy between us, I was horrified that I might have lost her forever in the shipwreck. Now, I was glad that she would be waiting there to meet me. Despite her faults, she was still my lovely, foolish, winsome Mary. I longed to feel her close again for I desperately needed to hold someone from my family in my arms.

At the *Grôte Markt*, the tower of St Rombout's church loomed dark against the sky, and I prayed silently to the saint to protect me on my journey. As we turned down the empty, cobbled street towards the *Brusslepoort* gate, I gazed at the roofs of the houses. How I would miss the sights and sounds of this fascinating place.

'Ready and with me?' asked my escort, turning his head to our guide.

'Aye, sir,' came the reply.

'Then let us take the great road south.'

I shortened the reins and kicked on my horse. With a thrill of excitement, I threw back my head and laughed. Wait for me, Mary, wait for me. I am coming to France!

SOURCES

I have not listed every book and source used for this novel, but for those who might wish to read more about these early years, I hope the following will be of interest:

Belloc Hilaire; Lingard, John, *The History of England Vol. 4* (Colorado, University Libraries, reprinted by BiblioLife)

Bruce, Marie Louise, *The Making of Henry VIII* (London, Collins, 1977)

Calendar of State Papers, Domestic and Foreign.

Carso, Patricia, *The Fair Face of Flanders* (Ghent, Scientific Publications 1969)

Clark, Dr Michael B.Sc., Ph.D (Cantab), M.P. *Rochford Hall, A History of a Tudor House* (Stroud, Alan Sutton Publishing 1990)

La Clavière, R. de Maulde, *Women of the Renaissance. A Study in Feminism* translated by George Herbert Ely (G P Putnam's Sons, 1900)

Correspondance de L'empereur Maximilien ler et Marguerite d'Autriche 1507-1519. (New York, reprinted from a copy in the New York Public Library) de Longh, Jane, *Margaret of Austria, Regent of the Netherlands* (New York, W.W. Norton & Company, 1953)

Dixon, William Hepworth, *History of Two Queens: Catherine of Aragon and Anne Boleyn* (1874, reprinted by BiblioBazaar, 2009)

Eichberger, Dagmar, *Women of Distinction, Margaret of York and Margaret of Austria* (Davidsfonds/Leuven, Brepols Publishers, 2005)

Gwyn, Peter, *The Rise and Fall of Thomas Wolsey,* (London, Barrie & Jenkins 1990.)

Hall, Edward, *Chronicle: containing the history of England, during the reign of Henry the Fourth, and the succeeding monarchs, to the end of the reign of Henry the Eighth, in which are particularly described the manners and customs of those periods.*

Hare, Christopher, *The High and Puissant Princes Marguerite of Austria* (London, Harpers and Brothers, 1907)

Harris, Barbara J, *English Aristocratic Women 1450-1550. Marriage and Family, Property and Careers* (Oxford, Oxford University Press, 2002)

Harris, Barbara J *Edward Stafford, Third Duke of Buckingham* (Stanford, California, Stanford University Press, 1986)

Head, David M, *The Ebbs and Flows of Fortune. The Life of Thomas Howard, Third Duke of Norfolk* (Athens and London, The University of Georgia Press, 1995)

Hutchinson, Robert, *House of Treason* (London, Weidenfeld & Nicolson 2009)

Kleinschmidt, Harald, *Charles V, The World Emperor* (Stroud, Gloucestershire, Sutton Publishing, 2004)

Mee, Arthur, *The King's England, Kent* (London, Hodder and Stoughton Ltd, 1936)

Morris, Sarah, & Grueninger, Natalie, *In the footsteps of Anne Boleyn* (Stroud, Amberley Publishing, 2013)

Norris, Herbert, *Tudor Costume and Fashion* (New York, Dover Publications, 1997)

Norton, Elizabeth, *The Boleyn Women* (Stroud, Amberley Publishing, 2013)

O'Day, Rosemary, *The Longman Companion to the Tudor Age* (London and New York, Longman, 1995)

Robin, Diana; Larsen, Anne R; Levin, Carole, *Women in the Renaissance, Italy France and England* (Oxford, England, ABC CLIO 2007)

Robinson, John Martin, *The Dukes of Norfolk: Quincentennial History* (Oxford, England Oxford University Press, 1982)

Round, J.H, *The Early Life of Anne Boleyn, A Critical Essay, 1886.*

Sim, Alison, *Food and Feast in Tudor England (*Stroud, Gloucestershire, Sutton Publishing 1997)

Simons, Walter, *Cities of Ladies Beguine Communities in the Medieval Low Countries 1200-1565* (Philadelphia, University of Pennsylvania Press, 2003)

Sipple, Mavis, *Rochford, A History* (West Sussex, England, Phillimore & Co Ltd, 2004)

Starkey, David, *Henry Virtuous Prince* (London, Harper Press, 2008)

Strickland, Agnes, *Lives of the Queens of England* (Continuum, 2011)

Tremayne, Eleanor E, *The First Governess of the Netherlands, Margaret of Austria.* (London, Methuen & Co, 1908)

Tyler, Royall, *The Emperor Charles the Fifth,* (London, George Allen and Unwin Ltd, 1956)

Weir, Alison, *Henry VIII, King and Court,* (London, Jonathan Cape, 2001)

Wheatcroft, Andrew, *The Habsburgs,* (London, Viking, Penguin Group, 1995)

Wilkinson, Josephine, *The Early Loves of Anne Boleyn* (Stroud, Amberley Publishing, 2009)

Wilson, Derek, *In the Lion's Court* (London Hutchinson, 2001)

Vehse, Dr.E Demmler, Franz, *Memoirs of the Court Aristocracy and Diplomacy of Austria Part One* (Reprinted by Kessinger Publishing)

Verhulst, Van Adriaan, *Historishe Stedenatlas van Belgie Mechelen,* (Gemeentekrediet Group 1997)

Acknowledgements

Dr David Starkey for being so kind in replying to me and offering his advice.

Lesley Headdon, the Rev Thomas Holme and Mr John E Vigar for information about the Thomas Boleyn memorial at Penshurst.

Mr John Kirwan, Ms Melosina Lenox-Conyngham, and Izabel Pennec-Murphy from Kilkenny Castle, for information on the Butler family.

Gill Cannell, Parker Library, Corpus Christi College, Cambridge.

Mr Ken Ward for information on the Julian and Gregorian calendar.

In Rochford, Mr Maurice Drage for help in explaining the town's history and that of Rochford Manor.

Professor Michael G Brennan, MA, Professor of Renaissance Studies at the University of Leeds, for information on the Duke of Stafford.

At Hever, Jane Apps, the Head Steward, who kindly assisted me with documents.

In London, the very helpful staff at the London Library.

In Mechelen, my excellent city guides Mr Rudi van Poele and Mr Ivo Verpoorten. In the Department of Archives, Mr Dieter Viaene and Mr Willy van de Vijver. The warmth and hospitality I received was overwhelming, and I could not have written this book without their knowledge, assistance and guidance.

In Lille, France, Michael Vangheluwe, for information on the documents of Margaret of Austria in the Archives départementales du Nord.

Claire Ridgway from The Anne Boleyn Files, and Tim Ridgway from MadeGlobal Publishing for helping this book to grow.

To Sarah Westcott of Addendum Publishing for her advice and encouragement.

Peter Harvey for his invaluable help in editing my manuscript.

Finally, to my partner, Mike, for buying me a laptop and insisting that I now had no excuse not to begin Anne's story. Thank you for getting me started!

Author's Notes

My interest in Anne Boleyn began many years ago. Back then, while a great deal was known about her later life as Queen of England, very little had been written about her childhood and youth. I wanted to understand more about those early years, and so I began to collect as much information as I could.

The date of her birth was a complex problem, but having consulted every available source, I decided to go with 1500, rather than the later date of 1507. I also chose the month of May as I felt a May birthdate suited her witty, lively personality and complex character.

The more I delved, the more I realised that Anne had been born into momentous times, with three young princes waiting in the wings to occupy the thrones of England, France and Spain. The old medieval order of life was disappearing, and the seeds of new religious ideas were beginning to take root. As Anne grew up in this exciting world, she was set on a course that shaped her mind, her ideas, and her personality. A course that resulted in her winning a crown and becoming instrumental in changing the face of English history. She paid a great price for fame, rather than obscurity. Could she have changed her destiny? Would she have wanted to?

I have spent many hours and days at Hever, Blickling,

Rochford and Thornbury and so was able to get a good feel for the places that Anne herself would have known and recognised. My time at Mechelen, in Belgium, was invaluable, as at the palace of Margaret of Austria (also known as Margaret of Savoy) I was allowed, with my city guides, to go into rooms not normally open to the public. It is a truly lovely place, worth a visit by anyone interested in Anne's story.

I have kept to the facts as much as possible in this book. All names, places and events are accurate, but as this is a novel, I have had to put forward some imagined scenarios and names for lesser characters, to aid the story. I hope my thoughts are still believable.

Finally, in my book Queen Katherine is spelt with a 'K' rather than a 'C'. Since a contemporary print shows the initial 'K' appearing on the trappings of her husband's horse at a joust, I have decided to use this spelling. It is a small point but one I wanted to explain.

About the Author

Originally from Derbyshire, Natalia trained as a graphic designer and illustrator, before deciding to become a museum curator and fulfil a passion for all things historical. Working with collections ranging from toys and military objects, to Royal Crown Derby China, she is now retired and divides her time between London and Derbyshire.

In her spare time, Natalia likes to walk in the Derbyshire countryside, research the Tudors, and travel abroad.

This is her first novel. Her second book, *The Falcon's Flight*, covers Anne's time at the French court.

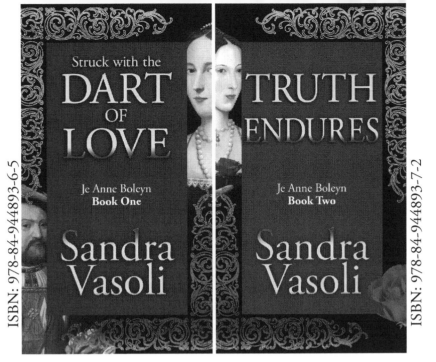

In a love letter to Anne Boleyn, Henry VIII wrote: *"It is absolutely necessary for me to obtain this answer, having been for above a whole year stricken with the dart of love, and not yet sure whether I shall fail of finding a place in your heart and affection…"*

Sandra Vasoli's Je Anne Boleyn series is a compelling memoir, narrated in a richly detailed, authentic voice, which depicts one of the most exceptional women in the history of England: Anne Boleyn. It is at once romantic, eloquent, and insightful. Through the series, the reader will come to know Anne as an intimate friend.

"This is a beautifully written, first-person account of Henry VIII's courtship of Anne Boleyn. The first book begins at their first real exchange, and ends at their marriage." – **Janet Wertman**

"I love that Sandra Vasoli's Je Anne Boleyn novels have the feel of a memoire. It's as if I've sat down with Anne herself to hear the tale of how she came to be the king's love and executed queen. Vasoli fills her tale with rich detail, yet it is extremely readable. Without giving away too much, I can say that I really enjoyed the way Vasoli ended her heart-rending saga." – **Adrienne Dillard**

THE RAVEN'S WIDOW

A Novel of

Jane Boleyn

ADRIENNE DILLARD

ISBN: 978-84-946498-3-7

Jane Parker never dreamed that her marriage into the Boleyn family would raise her star to such dizzying heights. Before long, she finds herself as trusted servant and confidante to her sister-in-law, Anne Boleyn; King Henry VIII's second queen. On a gorgeous spring day, that golden era is cut short by the swing of a sword. Jane is unmoored by the tragic death of her husband, George, and her loss sets her on a reckless path that leads to her own imprisonment in the Tower of London. Surrounded by the remnants of her former life, Jane must come to terms with her actions. In the Tower, she will face up to who she really is and how everything went so wrong.

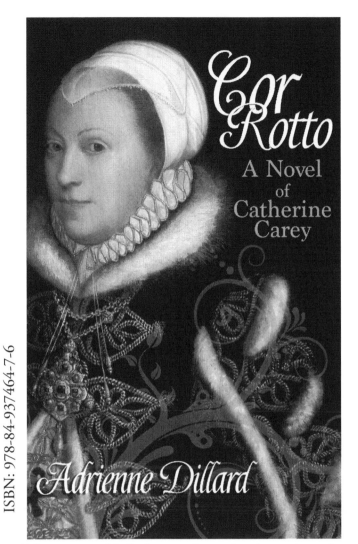

Cor Rotto
A Novel
of
Catherine
Carey

Adrienne Dillard

Fifteen year-old Catherine Carey has been dreaming the same dream for three years, since the bloody execution of her aunt Queen Anne Boleyn. Her only comfort is that she and her family are safe in Calais, away from the intrigues of Henry VIII's court. But now Catherine has been chosen to serve Henry VIII's new wife, Queen Anne of Cleves.

Just before she sets off for England, she learns the family secret: the true identity of her father, a man she considers to be a monster and a man she will shortly meet.

This compelling novel tells the life story of a woman who survived being close to the crown and who became one of Elizabeth I's closest confidantes.

Historical Fiction

The Sebastian Foxley Series – **Toni Mount**
The Death Collector – **Toni Mount**
Falling Pomegranate Seeds – **Wendy J. Dunn**
Struck With the Dart of Love – **Sandra Vasoli**
Truth Endures – **Sandra Vasoli**
Cor Rotto – **Adrienne Dillard**
The Raven's Widow – **Adrienne Dillard**
The Claimant – **Simon Anderson**

Historical Colouring Books

The Mary, Queen of Scots Colouring Book – **Roland Hui**
The Life of Anne Boleyn Colouring Book – **Claire Ridgway**
The Wars of the Roses Colouring Book – **Debra Bayani**
The Tudor Colouring Book – **Ainhoa Modenes**

Non Fiction History

The Turbulent Crown – **Roland Hui**
Anne Boleyn's Letter from the Tower – **Sandra Vasoli**
Jasper Tudor – **Debra Bayani**
Tudor Places of Great Britain – **Claire Ridgway**
Illustrated Kings and Queens of England – **Claire Ridgway**
A History of the English Monarchy – **Gareth Russell**
The Fall of Anne Boleyn – **Claire Ridgway**
George Boleyn: Tudor Poet, Courtier & Diplomat – **Ridgway & Cherry**
The Anne Boleyn Collection I, II & III – **Claire Ridgway**
Two Gentleman Poets at the Court of Henry VIII – **Edmond Bapst**

Children's Books

All about Richard III – **Amy Licence**
All about Henry VII – **Amy Licence**
All about Henry VIII – **Amy Licence**
Tudor Tales William at Hampton Court – **Alan Wybrow**

PLEASE LEAVE A REVIEW

If you enjoyed this book, *please*
leave a review at the book seller
where you purchased it. There is
no better way to thank the author
and it really does make a huge
difference! *Thank you in advance.*

Printed in Poland
by Amazon Fulfillment
Poland Sp. z o.o., Wrocław

58387646R00226